Cads' Choice

Book #3 of the Cad's Trilogy

CHERYL HOLT

Praise for *New York Times* Bestselling Author
CHERYL HOLT

"Best storyteller of the year . . ."
Romantic Times Magazine

"Cheryl Holt is magnificent . . ."
Reader to Reader Reviews

"Cheryl Holt is on my 'favorite authors' list. I can't wait to see what she'll write next."
The Reading Café

"A master writer . . ."
Fresh Fiction

Here's what readers are saying . . .

"OMG! I just started reading this series yesterday. It was hard for me to close my Kindle and go to bed. So, so good!"
Artemis

"Cheryl Holt has packed in so much action that the reader is constantly spellbound. So many characters, so vividly portrayed! Rogues, unfaithfulness, loyalty, and delightful dialogue. You will love this book!"
Gladys

"It was fabulous! I laughed, I cried, I got angry, and I smiled. I read the whole book without stopping."
Robin

"Action, drama, and intrigue. I read it in one afternoon. I couldn't put it down!"
Gina

"You just can't wait to turn the page to see what happens next. Outstanding!"
Margaret

"This book is such an emotional roller-coaster. I cried and laughed and cheered. It was so good!"
Colleen

CHERYL HOLT BOOKLIST

LINKED HISTORICAL ROMANCE SERIES

CADS
CAD'S WISH
CAD'S PICK
CAD'S CHOICE

LOST GIRLS
SOMEONE TO LOVE
SOMEONE TO CHERISH
SOMEONE TO WED

ALWAYS
ALWAYS
ALWAYS YOURS
ALWAYS MINE

JILTED BRIDES
JILTED BY A CAD
JILTED BY A SCOUNDREL
JILTED BY A ROGUE

FOREVER
FOREVER YOURS
FOREVER MINE
FOREVER AFTER
FOREVER

BABY CALEB DUET
ONLY YOU
ONLY MINE

LOST LORDS OF RADCLIFFE
HEART'S DELIGHT
HEART'S DESIRE
HEART'S DEMAND
SCOUNDREL
HEART'S DEBT

RELUCTANT BRIDES
WICKED
WANTON
WONDERFUL

LORD TRENT
LOVE'S PROMISE
LOVE'S PRICE
LOVE'S PERIL

SPINSTER'S CURE
PROMISE OF PLEASURE
TASTE OF TEMPTATION
DREAMS OF DESIRE

EROTIC HISTORICAL ROMANCES
LOVE LESSONS
TOTAL SURRENDER
ABSOLUTE PLEASURE
COMPLETE ABANDON
MORE THAN SEDUCTION
DEEPER THAN DESIRE
FURTHER THAN PASSION
TOO HOT TO HANDLE
TOO TEMPTING TO TOUCH
TOO WICKED TO WED
SECRET FANTASY
FORBIDDEN FANTASY
DOUBLE FANTASY

HISTORICAL ROMANCES
SWEET SURRENDER
NICHOLAS
(republished as MY SCOUNDREL)
MY ONLY LOVE
MY TRUE LOVE
THE WAY OF THE HEART

CONTEMPORARY ROMANCES
MOUNTAIN DREAMS
SEDUCE ME
KISS ME
LOVE ME

NOVELLAS
MEG'S SECRET ADMIRER
KNIGHT OF SEDUCTION
SEDUCING THE GROOM

OTHER NOVELS
A SUMMER WEDDING AT CROSS CREEK INN
MUD CREEK
THE WEDDING
SLEEPING WITH THE DEVIL

NONFICTION
LITTLE MIRACLES

Cad's Choice

Cover Design Angela Waters

Paperback and Digital format: Dayna Linton • Day Agency • www.dayagency.com

ISBN: 978-1-63732-816-3 (Paperback)

ISBN: 978-1-63732-817-0 (Digital Book)

Library of Congress Pending

First Edition: 2021

10 9 8 7 6 5 4 3 2 1

Printed in the USA

Cads' Choice

Chapter One

"Are you in or out, Captain? Will you bet?"

Sheridan Stone sighed with resignation, feigning little interest in his cards, as if he held a losing hand. He threw a few coins in the center of the table and said, "I think you're bluffing, so I'm in."

He was an excellent gambler, and he had a heightened ability to track the cards, so when he gambled for real stakes, he usually won. It was hard to best him at any endeavor, especially a wager, but when he was sitting in a seedy tavern in a port town, he pretended he wasn't versed on the rules.

Mainly, he was present to listen, gossip, and hear what he wasn't meant to discover. He told others he was simply waiting for supplies to be purchased, for his ship to be loaded.

His crew affected the same attitude. They gambled, made friends, and visited the whores. When Sheridan hoisted his sails, and they departed, he'd have accumulated many interesting details that would be sent to England in coded dispatches.

He wasn't a spy precisely. He was a gatherer of information that could be used by government officials to evaluate the intentions of the kingdom's enemies. With war spreading in Europe, every tidbit was important.

He obtained news about ships and shipments, about freight and secret payloads—such as armaments—that shouldn't be delivered, and he ensured they didn't arrive. It was dangerous, exciting work for which he was thoroughly suited.

He'd spent years in the British navy, trying to obey orders, but he'd been too arrogant to meekly comply with commands, so he'd constantly been in trouble for insubordination. He was a skilled mariner and brawler though, and his superiors had decided he could be put to other tasks, carrying out mischief the government denied.

He was much better on his own, pursuing subterfuge. His activities protected his prior navy compatriots, as well as British merchants, and his reckless daring-do brought him enormous satisfaction. But it was draining, and he was tired.

The previous summer, he'd been wounded, boarding a pirate vessel that had been smuggling guns, and he wasn't fully healed. He'd been slashed in the leg, so he limped, and his balance wasn't steady. He also grew fatigued more easily, and he wondered if he shouldn't step aside for younger men, but he was only twenty-eight. He refused to view himself as *old*.

It was a chilly October night, a Saturday, and the tavern was packed with an array of sailors, villains, hangers-on, and petty criminals. He was in France, at the harbor in Boulogne, so the chief language being spoken was French. He understood it sufficiently to converse, but there were a dozen others drifting by: Portuguese, Spanish, Italian, even some Arabic.

The evidence of far-flung locales always made him happy.

He loved to travel, to explore exotic places and rub elbows with intriguing characters. His current career offered that to him, and he had to figure out a way to continue. He couldn't let a paltry injury force him to walk in a different direction.

"What's it to be, Captain?"

At hearing the question, he realized how avidly he'd been woolgathering. He either had to bet again or fold. There was a pile of money on the table, but he never drew attention to himself by winning a large pot.

He tossed down his cards. "I thought you were bluffing, but you weren't. I'm out."

The other players laughed, and the winner scooped up the coins. No one pondered his comment, except for a young man standing across from him. His brows rose, as if he knew Sheridan was lying. Had the petite oaf been peeking over Sheridan's shoulder without his noticing?

The prospect was unnerving. His position depended on stealth and blending in, so he never liked anyone watching him too closely. He particularly didn't like anyone peering over his shoulder, and he was irked that he hadn't sensed the prying snoop. In such a risky establishment, where a fight could break out with scant provocation, it was never wise to be lazy or careless.

The dolt saw Sheridan studying him, and he lurched away and was swallowed up by the crowd. Good thing. Sheridan always had schemes percolating, so he couldn't have a busybody interfering. Yet if a person was stupid enough to butt his nose into Sheridan's business, he was adept at fabrication and could instantly invent any believable story.

The dealer shuffled the deck to start another game, so Sheridan pushed back his chair and slid away. He went to the bar and called for a shot of whiskey, downing it in a quick swallow, then he set down the glass and turned to leave.

For just a second, he noted the same short sneak scrutinizing him again—much too curiously for Sheridan's liking. The fellow was twenty or so, and he had such pretty features that he could have been a girl. His hair was inky black and curly, barely restrained by a ribbon. He had big green eyes, rosy cheeks complete with dimples, and lips that—on a female—would simply have been made for kissing.

It was perilous for such a fetching boy to strut about in the dissolute spot. There were plenty of corrupt lechers who would be delighted to abscond with him, and he looked very naïve. Would he detect the hazards that were lurking?

"Not my problem," Sheridan muttered to himself.

There were too many gullible men in the world. They were eager to journey to foreign areas, but as he'd learned the hard way, calamity sprang up when you least expected it. *He* had caused a ton of calamity for the unwary. If the little ass got himself into a jam, it wouldn't be a surprise.

What game was the annoying prick playing? He was probably a pickpocket, and Sheridan patted his coat to ensure his purse was hidden, then he headed for the door. He was finished for the night and would stroll around the harbor to his rented lodging. He'd commissioned a minor repair on his ship, and it gave him an excuse to tarry for two weeks. He would spend the interval eavesdropping on sailors.

He was very rich; his entire family was wealthy, so when he came ashore, he could afford opulent quarters. He had a taste for the finer things in life, and since he was almost always at sea and living in rough conditions, when he pulled into port, he indulged his whims.

His bodyguard and valet, George Barnes, was waiting for him outside. They didn't speak or acknowledge one another, and George would follow at a slow pace. He was a tidy, fastidious man who never stood out, who dawdled in the shadows. He had many odd talents that shouldn't have coalesced, namely that he handled Sheridan's clothes and guarded Sheridan's back.

At age forty, he was shorter than Sheridan's height of six feet, and he was thin and wiry, not possessed of Sheridan's bulk or brawn, so he didn't appear imposing, and people always underestimated him. His hair was grey, his eyes too, so when a witness was asked to describe him, they never could.

He didn't drink, gamble, or chase loose women, so he had none of Sheridan's vices, but he was tough and strong, and he could be incredibly violent when violence was required.

The street was busy, packed with carriages, horses, carts, and pedestrians. He was meandering through the traffic, when suddenly, the petite oaf from the tavern popped up next to him. Again, the fiend had sidled too near without his noticing, and he stiffened with alarm.

"Pardon me, sir," the boy said, "but are you English?" Sheridan didn't reply, and the boy thought he didn't understand. He tried French. "*Pardonez moi, monsieur . . .*"

"Yes, I'm English." Sheridan responded more curtly than was necessary. "What is it you need?"

"You're a ship's captain, aren't you?"

"Why would you know that about me?"

"You seem quite a bit above an ordinary sailor."

Sheridan snorted. "You're keen at assessing details."

"I was wondering . . ."

The boy halted, so Sheridan halted too, although he couldn't have explained why. He was fatigued, his leg wound aching, so he was too grouchy to be polite. He glared down, braced for any query. It was a port town. Any sort of dubious, illegal, or immoral request might be tendered.

Up close, the fellow was even prettier: smooth skin, long lashes, a smattering of freckles across his nose. He was dressed appropriately, in a blue coat, short pants, and buckled shoes, but he was too shapely to be a male. Sheridan was a connoisseur of women, and he recognized a bosom when he saw one.

Was he staring at . . . at . . . a girl? If he was, he wouldn't be surprised. During his travels, he'd stumbled on every peculiar sight. If she'd been attired like a female, there was no predicting what trouble she'd encounter. As a boy, she'd be safer. Not a lot safer, but a tad.

"Wondering what?" he asked.

"Might you be headed to England?"

He was, but he lied. "No."

"Oh. Well . . . ah . . . are you acquainted with any captains who might be sailing in that direction?"

"No."

He—or maybe she?—nibbled on a bottom lip, and the coy gesture left Sheridan certain *he* was a she. The discovery tugged at his conscience. She probably needed assistance, but he wasn't about to insert himself in a stranger's dilemma.

In his world of criminals and villains, there was rarely a benefit to compassionate conduct.

Without warning, a small boy dashed out of the crowd and bumped into him, as if by accident. Sly, quick fingers reached for his purse, but it was tucked away where it couldn't be found. The child was there and gone in a flash, and Sheridan might have assumed it was a random attempt, but it dawned on him that she had to be in league with the furtive pickpocket.

It had been a typical assault, one that usually succeeded. She'd distracted him, then her partner had struck. If he hadn't been so wary, his money would have been stolen, which was exasperating. If he didn't start paying better attention to his surroundings, who could guess what might happen?

He grabbed the miscreant and pushed her against the wall of a nearby building, a knife at her throat. Behind him, George raced by, having observed the incident and being intent on catching the child.

Sheridan kept his focus where it belonged. He leaned in, his large, masculine body crushed to hers, and his curiosity about her gender was assuaged. She was definitely a female. Two very curvaceous breasts adorned her chest, and he had a thigh between her legs. There was no cock dangling there.

"Call to your accomplice," he said. "Tell him to come back. At once. He and I have to have a chat."

"I have no idea who you mean."

"Liar. Call to him or I'll summon the law."

She scoffed. "There's no law in this place, so it's an idle threat."

"If you've deduced that there's no law, it's because you investigated the matter. It's easier for you to commit your crimes when you've figured out in advance that no constable will stop you."

She inhaled a deep breath and shouted, "Help! Help! I'm being kidnapped!"

It was a port town, so people never interfered in a squabble. It was a swift way to get killed. Nary a person glanced over at them.

"Nice try." He clapped a palm over her mouth to silence her. "No one cares that you're being kidnapped, so no one will rush to your aid."

She gazed up at him, appearing impish and even a tad dangerous, then she went limp, her weight dropping in an instant. He lost his grip on her, and she collapsed to the ground and skittered away.

He captured her rapidly, seizing her by her coat and lifting her to her feet. She kicked at his shins, but he simply wrapped an arm around her waist and balanced her on his hip. She was a tiny sprite, so it took no effort to restrain her.

George was approaching, but he was empty-handed. The town was a maze of alleys and shadows, and George's prey had vanished like a rat down a sewer.

Sheridan marched off, George by his side, as his prisoner spat curses he couldn't believe a female would have learned. He ignored her and continued on to his rented lodging. It was a cozy apartment, with windows that looked out over the harbor. When he stood in the front parlor, he could stare out at his ship, and the sight brought him comfort.

George unlocked the door, and Sheridan hauled her up the stairs to his rooms on the second floor. He tossed her onto a chair and said, "Stay there and don't move."

Of course she didn't listen. She leapt up to run out, but George was behind her. He slapped his palms on her shoulders and pinned her to her seat.

"What is your name?" Sheridan demanded.

She hemmed and hawed, then said, "Miss Sophia Cantwell. What's yours?"

He didn't bother answering. "You're British?"

"Yes."

"I presume there is a good reason you are dressed like a man and prowling in a foreign tavern?"

"Yes, there is."

He waited for her to expound, but she was mulishly defiant, and he asked, "And that reason is . . . ?"

"None of your business."

"I'm making it my business. Who was your little friend?"

"Are you referring to the boy who jostled you?"

"Yes. Who was he? If you were hoping to rob an unsuspecting drunkard, you should have picked a better mark."

"I wasn't trying to rob you. I asked you for help." She nervously studied his parlor. "What will you do to me?"

"I haven't decided. Whip your back bloody? Cut off your hand to brand you as a thief? Hang you on the wharf as a warning to others?"

"You wouldn't punish me like that," she huffed.

"Why are you so sure?"

"Your clothes and accent indicate you're a gentleman."

"If that's what you imagine, then you have completely misconstrued the sort of tyrant I can be."

She slid to her knees, her hands folded as if in prayer. She was a fascinating, infuriating pest, and he'd never met a female quite like her.

"I throw myself on your mercy," she said, "and I beg your kind assistance."

"I decline to provide it."

Her jaw dropped. "You can't . . . can't . . . decline!"

"I can and I have."

"You're a gentleman. I just know you are."

"You're wrong. Now state your situation and be quick about it."

Suddenly, the door from the stairs was flung open, and her pickpocketing ally burst in. He was ten or so, a street urchin with snarled blond hair and cunning blue eyes. He was agile and lithe, and so slender a stiff wind could blow him over, but he was holding a very large knife.

"You will pardon me," he said, his French accent very thick, "but you will be letting her go, and she will be leaving with me."

"For pity's sake," Sheridan grumbled.

George was fast as a snake. He stepped over, clouted the boy on the side of the head, and plucked the knife away. The boy lunged at George, and he was a fierce fighter, but George swiftly subdued him.

He plopped the child onto the chair next to Miss Cantwell, and he bent down and muttered in his ear, "Behave yourself, you little knacker, or I'll whack you even harder. What will happen to your Miss Cantwell then?"

"You hit him!" Miss Cantwell complained.

George didn't reply, but Sheridan said to her, "Yes, and he'll inflict even more damage if you don't start talking. I'm prepared to listen, but I'm not very patient. What mischief are you pursuing in Boulogne?"

She was still on her knees, and she peered up at him, her mind whirring, as she sifted through various plausible excuses, but he was never easily swayed. Especially not by a woman, and he was positive, whatever narrative she voiced, it would be a whopper of a lie.

"Well, Miss Cantwell?" he said. "Entertain me with your tale of woe. I'm curious to discover if I'll be moved."

"Oh, you will be, sir! I'm certain of it."

"I can't abide your theatrics. Get off the floor and sit down."

She hesitated, then complied, which was a surprise. She was so disagreeable, and it was no mystery why she was still a Miss. What man would dare to marry her? Her impudent inclinations were clear, and any fellow who shackled himself would be sorry forever.

"Why are you in France?" he said. "War is brewing, and it's obvious you're alone and on your own. What transpired to place you in this predicament?"

"I came two years ago. With my cousin."

"Male or female?"

"Female."

"Where is this supposed cousin now?"

"She wasn't a *supposed* cousin. She was a *real* cousin, and she died. She had a baby, and she never regained her health."

He nodded to the boy. "Who is this? How is he connected to you?"

"He's my servant, Pierre Gascón, and he's very protective of me. I apologize if he offended you."

"He didn't offend me. He tried to rob me."

"I'm sure you're mistaken. He's just a child. He never would have."

"He's just a child who's a petty criminal. Are you short on funds? Is that it?"

"Yes, that's it. My cousin had her baby in a village east of Boulogne."

Sheridan frowned. "Why would she have?"

"Can I not say?"

"No. Why are you here? Tell me the truth. I won't release you unless you do."

Pierre spoke up. "But you will let her go? *Oui*?"

George pinched his ear. "Shut up, you irksome fiend."

The boy bit his tongue, as Miss Cantwell gnawed on her bottom lip, and Sheridan had to look away. She was very pretty, and he didn't like to recall that she was.

"Miss Cantwell!" he snapped. "You're exhausting me. Please continue!"

"My cousin was seduced by a scoundrel in London, so her father sent her away to hide her shame."

George mumbled, "Now we're getting somewhere."

"We had to stay in France until she named the cad who'd ruined her, but she refused to reveal his identity, so her father wouldn't permit us to come home."

"Why wouldn't she name him?" Sheridan asked. "She could have married him and had the child legitimized."

"The rogue . . . ah . . . was already married."

It was a common occurrence, and since Sheridan led a very dissolute life, one that was filled with doxies who'd fallen off the moral path, he tried to never judge. But . . .

He didn't believe a word that had tumbled out of her delectable mouth.

"If she's dead, why are you still in France?" he asked.

"Her father died too. In England, and our money stopped, so I don't have the funds to book passage. I'm positive I know who stopped them too, and once I'm back, I'll shoot him right between the eyes."

She was ferocious, and he suspected she probably would shoot some obnoxious dolt right between the eyes.

"So you're attempting to get home," Sheridan said.

"Yes. Will you take me?"

"No. Is this why you're robbing people in taverns? Are you stealing in order to obtain the amount necessary to purchase a ticket?"

Pierre couldn't remain silent. "The *bébé* is hungry, and we have no food. She will not starve when I can pick the pocket of a rich brute like you."

Sheridan didn't like to hear that remark, and he winced. "Where is this baby, Miss Cantwell?"

"At our rented room. The proprietor's wife is watching her, but we are down to our last farthing, and I am desperate."

"What is the baby's name?"

Miss Cantwell scowled. "Emily. Why?"

"She is your cousin's child? Not yours?"

Miss Cantwell stiffened with affront. "Yes, she's my cousin's child. Do I look like the sort of female who would have maternal tendencies?"

He laughed. "No, you definitely don't."

"Won't you take me to England, sir?" she said again.

"Quit asking me."

"Shall I beg more intensely?"

"No. It's annoying."

He glanced at George, visually seeking his opinion about them, but George shrugged, telling Sheridan it was his choice. Unfortunately for Miss Cantwell, he never involved himself in another person's problems. The world was a hard place, and he couldn't save every lost soul. Plus, he was certain her problems were self-induced.

"Why are you dressed like a man?" he asked her.

"Why would you suppose? It's a terrible town, overrun by ne'er-do-wells and criminals. I'm safer like this."

Pierre flashed an angry glower. "You would not be believing the things that have happened to her. I have been the one to make her change these clothes—so the scoundrels will not harm her."

George pinched his ear again. "I told you to be quiet."

"I will not obey," Pierre said. "She is a woman. Is there no man who will aid her? I am just a boy. I cannot give her what she needs."

It was an impassioned speech, but Sheridan assumed it was false outrage. The wily pair couldn't be trusted. Who could predict what nonsense they'd perpetrated? They'd likely bribed and blackmailed their way across Europe.

"I will not help you sail anywhere," he said to her, "but I will do this."

He reached into his coat and withdrew his purse. From her avaricious expression, it was clear she'd been hoping he would, but he wasn't about to be too generous.

He slipped her a few coins, and when she counted them, she scoffed with disgust. "How will this help?"

"Buy some supper. Buy some milk for your baby."

"It's not my baby," she insisted. "It's my cousin's baby!"

"Don't let me catch you out on the streets again tonight."

"Or what?" she defiantly sneered.

"Or . . . you'll find out."

Short of turning her over to the law, he didn't have many options, and he wouldn't want her jailed anyway. It was scary to imagine how the guards or other prisoners would react if they learned her true gender. Besides, she was correct that no authorities patrolled the harbor, so no official justice could be imposed.

She'd noted his hesitation and said, "I'll be shaking in my boots, waiting to discover how you will penalize me."

"You have a very smart mouth. You should be more circumspect or it will get you into trouble."

"In case you haven't noticed, I am already in trouble. How could a sharp tongue worsen my situation?"

She stood and marched for the door, her accomplice tagging along behind. Her back was ramrod straight, and she appeared very regal, as if she had drops of noble blood in her veins. On observing her imperious demeanor, he felt guilty that he hadn't been more gracious, but the instant he realized he was second-guessing, he shoved the notion away.

Mischief practically oozed out of her, and he was busy, protecting the British Empire. He wouldn't allow her to distract him.

"That was interesting," George said once their footsteps had faded down the stairs.

"You are a master of understatement, Mr. Barnes."

"Was any part of their story true?"

"I figure *she* is the one who has a bastard daughter. Other than that, anything is possible. She claimed her cousin's father sent her to France, but I expect her own father was the culprit. He'd have been anxious to be rid of her. What man could tolerate such a disrespectful, insolent harpy?"

"She doesn't make very good choices."

"It's the least of her issues."

"She's pretty though," George said. "Didn't you think so?"

"Yes, she's very pretty, and I'm sure she uses her attributes to great effect on idiots like me."

"Be careful or you'll be sucked into the whirlwind that swirls around her."

"There is absolutely no chance of me being sucked into it."

George barked out a laugh. "Famous last words."

Sheridan would behave like a dunce over any beautiful female. The men in his family were renowned cads who regularly scandalized the citizenry with their mistresses and affairs. They were scorned and lauded for their antics, depending on who was being asked for an opinion.

"I could never be enticed by her," Sheridan said. "She'd drive me mad before the first day was out."

"What would you wager? Will we cross paths with her again?"

"We'll be in port for two weeks, so I have no doubt we will. She'll be sneaking through the taverns, searching for her next mark."

"What if she's really stuck here," George said, "and needs to travel home? That little blighter, Pierre, was genuinely incensed on her behalf."

"I'm convinced it was an act."

"What if it wasn't? Maybe I should investigate to see if anyone knows her."

Sheridan blanched. "Don't you dare. We're not getting involved with her."

George smirked. "Shall we bet on it?"

"We don't have to bet. We should call ourselves lucky that I escaped with all the coins in my purse."

"Not all of them," George pointed out. "You handed over a few to her, and it's probably what she wanted in the end."

"She *wanted* the whole pouch, so she went away thwarted."

"How will she occupy her time for the rest of the evening? Will she eat or will she rob some other bloke?"

"I have no idea, and we're not speculating."

"What if there's a baby? What if she was candid about that portion of her tale?"

"George!" Sheridan testily said. "Let it go."

"You opened your purse—once—so she'll be back, and she'll have invented a new sob story to lure you into being even more generous."

"She hasn't the gall to approach me again, and if she tries, I'll take a switch to her."

"You will not. You were charmed by her."

"You are deranged to think so." George gave a mock salute and started out, and Sheridan asked, "Where are you off to?"

"I thought I'd wander for a bit to guarantee they've vanished."

"Didn't I just tell you to let it go?"

"Yes, but you're not my nanny. I'll see you in the morning."

He slipped out, and Sheridan listened as he tromped down the stairs and exited the building. Then he walked over to the window. It was dark, the sky cloudy, rain likely. Ships bobbed in the water, their lanterns swinging with the retreating tide. It was a sight that always soothed him.

With the excitement concluded, it was terribly quiet, and he felt like the loneliest man in the world. He was missing home, missing his brothers, missing England, with its familiar people and routines.

Gad, he was even missing his father, and he never missed his father. Why was he loafing in France, chasing street urchins and liars, when he could be sitting in London with his brothers? Why stay? Why keep on?

Yes, his work was important, but hadn't he surrendered enough to King and Country? Wasn't he allowed to quit?

The wound on his leg pounded, reminding him he wasn't completely healed. It seemed like an omen, like a grim message, so he'd remember that he could have a different life. Did he want a different life? Could he bear a different life?

It would be easy and ordinary, with no sword fights, no ships to board, no pirates to subdue, no enemies to slay.

Could he stand it? Dare he proceed? It was a question that had no answer.

He stared outside forever, and when it occurred to him that he was pondering Miss Cantwell and wondering where she was, he staggered off to bed.

He wasn't a man who obsessed. He was a man of action and duty, of courage and commitment. Miss Cantwell was an annoying piece of baggage who'd bothered him when she shouldn't have, so he wouldn't contemplate her again.

The very idea was stupid, and he tried to never be stupid.

Chapter Two

SHERIDAN WAS WALKING DOWN the wharf, winding past wagons and crates. The signs of healthy commerce always pleased him and made him remember why he relished being a sailor.

He'd spent a few hours on his ship, checking the minor repairs that he'd commissioned. It was mid-afternoon and the temperature brisk. Autumn was passing, and winter would arrive too soon. Would he return to England to mope in the wet and cold? Or would he weigh anchor and head south? Why not spend the winter months in the Mediterranean?

He could ply his trade on the Portuguese or Spanish coasts. There were plenty of reasons to spy in those locations. Why not journey to a warmer climate?

The problem was that, for reasons he couldn't clarify, he was homesick. England was calling to him in a manner it rarely did, and he supposed it was due to the recent alteration in his circumstances. His father, Neville, had become Earl of Swindon. It was so shocking that Sheridan was amazed the Earth hadn't spun off its axis.

Neville had never believed he'd inherit the earldom. He'd had three older brothers, and a slew of nephews who'd been in line before him, but they'd proved themselves an unlucky and frail lot. His brothers had gradually passed away, then his nephews had begun to vanish too, from accidents and disease. The last one had died the prior year, and *voila!* Neville was the earl.

Because his father had viewed himself as safe from any elevation that would saddle him with responsibilities, he'd lived a life of dissipation and vice. He gambled, chased loose women, and regularly scandalized the kingdom with his immoral antics. He was fifty, but he hadn't slowed down. He was as corrupt and lustful as ever.

His low spot on a tiny branch of the family tree had allowed Sheridan and his two brothers to revel and misbehave too. Nothing much had ever been expected of any of them, and as they'd grown up, they'd adopted their father's bad habits. They caroused and chased loose women too, and they'd developed reputations as dedicated bachelors and cads.

All of that would have to end. His brother, Hunter, was now Viscount Marston and would be the next earl. Warwick, his other brother, was in line after him, and Sheridan was staggering behind them. They'd never imagined themselves as husbands, mostly because they'd never envisioned matrimony as a state they'd like to embrace, but with their father's rise to prominence, their reckless philandering had to be tossed out the window.

Hunter had to pick a bride and start siring some heirs. Warwick and Sheridan would probably have to get going too. As their uncles and cousins had demonstrated, they couldn't loaf and hope the title was protected. They had to vigorously work at it.

Sheridan tried to picture himself settled down as a husband and father, but he simply couldn't fathom it. His own father had been wed twice and widowed twice, and both experiences had been horrid mismatches. Sheridan hadn't witnessed a single example of a *good* marriage, and he had no idea how a union could be structured to anyone's satisfaction, but . . .

His father was an earl and his brother a viscount. Changes had occurred, and more changes were coming. How would he weather them? When he peered down the road, five or ten years in the future, where would he like to be?

Sailing was hard. It was a task for young men. So were sea battles and ship assaults. Would he keep on? Should he keep on? How long could his battered body tolerate the difficult life he was leading?

Suddenly, a kerfuffle erupted down a side alley. There was shouting and some very colorful curses were hurled. He glanced over, and three people were fighting. An old hag had pitched some luggage out onto the cobbles.

"You witch! I'll kill you for this!" One of the brawlers spoke the threat in precise French, and Sheridan blanched. Apparently, he'd recognize that voice anywhere.

He focused in and realized it was Miss Cantwell and Pierre, and he wasn't surprised in the least to find her at the center of a fracas. She was a magnet that sucked in trouble, and he'd like to meet her relatives and have a caustic discussion with them.

Why hadn't they reined in her excesses? Why hadn't they made her conduct herself properly? They'd left her free to roam the streets and land herself in ridiculous jams. Didn't they care what happened to her?

She was still wearing trousers, and before Sheridan could move, she'd pulled a knife out of a pocket. She grabbed the other woman and stuck the tip of the blade under her chin.

"Whoa! Whoa! Whoa!" Sheridan yelled as he dashed over to intervene.

He yanked Miss Cantwell away, but she hadn't heard him approaching, and she was so enraged that she swung around with the knife. He plucked it away and threw it over his shoulder with no injury inflicted.

"Miss Cantwell!" he snapped. "What are you thinking?"

"I owe this . . . this . . . *putain* some rent, and she wants Emily as payment."

He was startled by her use of the French word for *whore*, but he was also confused by the name Emily. Who was that? The prior night, she'd blathered on about her predicament, but he'd scarcely listened to her tale of woe.

"Emily is your baby?" he asked.

"She's my cousin's baby, Captain! Not mine. This annoying shrew"—she gestured offensively—"has evicted us because I'm out of money, and she claims Emily will be her compensation. In this terrible town, can you imagine what such a foul harpy would do with a pretty, blond baby? How much could she sell her for?"

The woman tried to slink away, and Pierre seized her so she couldn't escape. She wrestled with him, but he was a tough little nut, and he wouldn't release her.

"Pierre!" Sheridan barked. "Stop it!"

"She will not be having Emily, *monsieur*," Pierre replied. "Not while I draw breath."

"I'll handle this," Sheridan grumbled.

He pried Pierre away, then loomed over the woman. At six feet in height, with wide shoulders and long legs, he could be very intimidating. Add in the fact that he was heavily armed, and he was extremely imposing.

He had a knife dangling on one hip, a pistol on the other, and a sword strapped to his back. Various other weapons were tucked out of sight: a knife in each boot, a smaller pistol in his coat, and a metal rod shoved up his sleeve that could be utilized as a bludgeon if he needed to club someone's thick head.

He chatted curtly with the woman and learned she ran a decrepit boarding house and probably let rooms by the hour to sailors and prostitutes. Miss Cantwell owed for five days lodging, and to cover the bill, she had decided to keep the baby.

Sheridan had to agree with Miss Cantwell. In a town of villains and criminals, what sins might be committed against a baby girl? If she was fetching and sweet, she would be auctioned off to the highest bidder.

He asked the amount of Miss Cantwell's charges, and the termagant stated a preposterous sum. In the end, he gave her half of what she'd requested, then he marched through the door, saw a housemaid holding a tiny blond girl, and he jerked her away.

She was a toddler, age two or so; he wasn't a good judge. If she'd understood any of what had transpired, she didn't show any alarm. She simply snuggled herself to Sheridan's broad chest as if she'd always belonged there.

He walked out into the sunshine with her, and she was pretty as a porcelain doll, like a cherub that might have been painted on a church ceiling. She had curly blond hair, a Cupid's mouth, rosy cheeks, and the most glorious blue eyes. The Stone family members were renowned for their attractive features—golden blond hair and big blue eyes—and she looked a lot like *him*.

She could have been a Stone cousin, and to his great disgust, he sensed an instant kinship, which was unnerving. He delivered her to

Miss Cantwell, and the baby took it all in stride, patting Miss Cantwell's cheeks with her chubby hands, as if they'd been playing a game.

The hag was glaring, obviously feeling cheated, and he ordered her away. For a moment, she refused to budge, so he stepped menacingly toward her, and she scurried inside and slammed her door.

He turned to Miss Cantwell, pointing to the three bags the old cow had tossed on the ground. "Are these your belongings? Is there more inside?"

"No, that's all I have left."

There was a mournful tone in her voice, and tears flooded into her expressive green eyes, so they were even more striking and luminous. A fellow could get lost in those eyes.

"Are you crying, Cantwell?" he asked, horrified.

"Yes."

"Why would you cry? The incident has concluded."

"I'm distressed, you vain oaf, and I can't help but be relieved."

"You're bawling because you're relieved?"

"Yes, and because I'm still very, very angry."

"Well, cease your blubbering. I can't believe I've been forced to deal with you again, and I can't have you weeping."

He whipped away and picked up her knife and the two heaviest bags, then he motioned to Pierre to pick up the third.

"Come with me!" His command provided no opening for an argument.

She argued anyway. "Where are we going?"

"To my lodging."

"Don't be absurd. I can't accompany you there."

"I'm not giving you a choice. You can't be allowed to gad about on your own. You have no ability to take care of yourself, let alone the children who are depending on you. I am saving the town from your incompetent influence."

"I don't like you," she ludicrously said.

"What has that to do with anything?"

He gestured to Pierre who was a male and thus would behave more logically. The boy recognized that Sheridan should be in charge. When he started off, Pierre followed him, but Sheridan quickly realized she hadn't moved. He halted and glanced over his shoulder, and the sight she presented was tremendously disconcerting.

With her holding the baby in her arms, she could have been a Madonna. She was beautiful and tormented, and clearly, she'd been battered by life. On witnessing her exhaustion and despondency, he was awash with an unusual burst of compassion.

It was hard to be a female, and he was glad he'd been born a man. If a woman encountered difficulties, she had so few options in how to respond to them. A single female was especially vulnerable to the whims of fate. Miss Cantwell claimed she was trapped in France, and he'd scoffed at her story, but perhaps it was true.

Could he leave her to her own devices? He didn't think so. Normally, he was detached and self-centered, but he liked to assume he could be a kind person when kindness was required.

"It will be all right, Cantwell." His manner was gentle and coaxing, as if she were a skittish mare. "I promise."

"I just want to return to England. I just want this to stop."

"I'll get you to England." He hadn't intended to extend the offer, so he'd surprised himself. "I swear I will. Your troubles are over now."

Emily settled the matter for her. The baby waved at Sheridan and said, "Go, go?"

Miss Cantwell stared at him forever, then her shoulders slumped, as if with defeat. "Yes, we'll go."

Sheridan nodded imperiously, then he spun and stomped off. He didn't peek back again. He could sense her there, watching him, tagging along. It produced an intriguing, curious feeling inside him, and he liked it.

Sophia stood at the window of the Captain's apartment, and she gazed out at the harbor, at the boats bobbing in the water. The autumn days were short, so evening had arrived, the sun dipping below the horizon already. The sky was a lavender color that was swiftly fading to indigo. Stars were beginning to twinkle.

She was incredibly morose, and she warned herself to buck up, to adjust her attitude. Her situation might have finally changed for the better—if the Captain could be trusted.

His rented quarters were on the waterfront, as if he couldn't bear to be away from the sea. The place wasn't fancy, but was functional, clean, and warm. It had a parlor, dining room, and two bedchambers, and he'd given her one of them. She was terrified he hadn't meant it though, that he'd have her put the children in one and share the other one with him as a reward for his being so generous.

If that turned out to be the case, what would she do?

Well, she wasn't completely at his mercy. He'd taken her knife, but she had a small pistol in her pocket. She knew how to use it too, and if he attempted any tomfoolery, she'd shoot him without hesitating. Her recent foibles had left her that jaded and dangerous.

She hated to be such a pessimist, but after the tragedies she'd suffered since her cousin Caroline's death, she'd had to accept that there were very few men who were honorable. They looked at a young, pretty female and presumed she could be exploited for nefarious purposes.

When she'd initially been stranded in France, with no funds and no answers from home, she'd figured she could find help in the port town. British ships constantly docked, and she'd believed her plight would spur a captain to transport her to England.

Instead, she'd been propositioned and insulted. She'd been locked in rooms by aggressive fiends who'd intended to ravage her. She'd been robbed and tricked, dismissed and conned, and her dire experiences had ruined her faith in humanity.

It was why she'd started dressing in coat and trousers. Pierre, who was smart and cunning, who saw the world as it truly was, had convinced her to hide her gender. At first, she'd scoffed at the notion as being too improper, but after she'd tried it, she'd found it rendered a safety she'd needed.

Men were much more obliging when they thought she was one too. None of them had assisted her, but the ruse had protected her from unwanted advances, so it had been worth it.

Emily and Pierre were napping in the bedroom. The poor boy was a nervous wreck and rarely slept. He was too worried about what might befall them when his eyes were closed.

His mother had worked as a housemaid for Caroline and Sophia, but she'd died from the same influenza that had ultimately claimed Caroline. After they'd passed away, he'd remained with Sophia. While he was an extra mouth to feed, he was a gift too. He was a tough, loyal fighter who defended and advised her. He noticed hazards approaching and enemies blocking her road, so she could duck for cover.

Footsteps sounded on the stairs, as someone climbed up from the street, and she expected it would be the Captain. He'd departed hours earlier, shortly after conveying them to his residence. He hadn't clarified his mission, but had simply delivered the admonishment to not leave and to not engage in any mischief while he was away. He'd promised to have supper with him when he arrived.

As the door opened, she braced, prepared for any eventuality. He blustered in, and she relaxed slightly, but not completely. He was incredibly handsome—tall, blond, brawny, strong. His blue eyes were fierce, and they missed no detail, but she didn't like handsome men. They always turned out to be rats.

The more attractive a fellow was, the more important and entitled he assumed himself to be, and that sort of confidence could be extremely perilous to a young female on her own.

Three servants followed him in, two maids and a footman. They were carrying packages, and she smelled food and was reminded that she was starving.

"I've brought reinforcements," he said.

"Good. I've been standing here thinking I could use some reinforcing."

"That's my feeling exactly."

It was chilly outside, so his color was high, his cheeks flushed, his glorious hair windblown and messy. He looked amazing. His shoulders were wide, the type a woman could lean on when she was alone and in trouble, and she yearned to run over and wrap her arms around him like a drowning person.

The footman left again to retrieve more packages, and the Captain said to her, "I've hired two maids for you. One can help you with your private needs, and the other can serve as a nanny until we get you on a ship to England. Will that be enough?"

"Well, yes, two will be fine. I'm just . . . just . . ." She cut off, not able to explain what she *was*. "Thank you."

"You're welcome. Now then, might you have a gown in your portmanteau?"

"Yes, why?"

"We're having supper together, and it's been ages since I dined with a female. I refuse to proceed when you're attired like a man. I want you fetching, charming, and interesting. Can you manage it?"

"I shall give it my all, just for you, but will you please keep your voice down? Pierre and Emily are napping, and I wouldn't like to wake them. I'd like them to sleep until morning."

He winced. "I forgot that you came with human baggage. I would rather have them sleeping too, so I will be quiet as a mouse."

She motioned to one of the maids, and they tiptoed into the bedchamber. There was a closet at the rear, and they snuck into it and spent a half hour making her more presentable. She studied herself in a mirror, deciding she didn't look too bad.

Her black hair was curly and unruly, and it was difficult to restrain it, so for the Captain, she tied it with a ribbon and let it hang down her back. It wasn't very stylish, but they were tucked away in an unremarkable house along the harbor. It wasn't as if she was at the palace.

She was too pale though, and she'd lost weight, so she was a tad gaunt. Her mouth was pinched from so much fretting, and she practiced smiling a few times, forcing her lips to curve up instead of down. If it killed her, she intended to maintain a cheery façade throughout the meal.

Despite his acting like an ogre the prior evening, he was being quite gallant. So far, he was the only male she'd encountered in France who'd exhibited the slightest concern for her welfare. He hadn't tried to grope, disrobe, or ravage her once, so she would adopt an optimistic attitude.

If he grew amorous or dangerous, she had her pistol hidden in the pocket of her skirt. She never went anywhere without it.

She crept out, relieved that she hadn't disturbed either child. She emerged into the parlor and continued on to the dining room behind it. He was there, seated at the table and drinking a glass of wine. He'd washed, shaved, and had put on a clean shirt. His hair was damp, and she could smell soap and . . . *man.* The realization tickled her innards in a feminine manner that was exasperating.

Apparently, there was a tiny, deeply-buried part of her that was enchanted by him, but then, he was irresistible.

He toasted her with his goblet and said, "I've started without you. I had a long day, and I couldn't wait."

"You were allowed to begin without me. You're being very kind, and we've already become a bother."

"You're correct. You have become a great bother, but I imagine I'll survive."

"I shall keep the children out of your way, and *I* shall behave myself."

He snorted with amusement. "I'm certain, Cantwell, that it's impossible for you to behave. I haven't been acquainted with you for a full twenty-four hours, and I have yet to witness any conduct I would describe as rational or modest."

She shrugged. "I've had several hard months. I admit it, and I won't apologize for my actions. I'm not a big, strapping fellow like you. When problems arise, I can't exactly pound a miscreant into the ground to settle our differences."

"I understand that."

He stood and pulled out a chair for her. She went over and sat down. It was a small table, so she was right next to him, their feet and calves touching. Her initial instinct was to shift away, but he'd notice and gloat, so she stayed where she was.

The footman poured her some wine, then refilled the Captain's too as he gestured to a sideboard.

"I had our meal delivered from an ale house down the street. I didn't know what you'd like, so I hope you're not fussy."

"I'm never fussy," she claimed, and he laughed.

"Liar. I predict you fuss constantly."

She smirked. "Maybe, but I'm trying to be less persnickety."

"Shall I let our new footman serve us? Or would you like to serve yourself? Are you afraid I'll poison you if you don't check the food first?"

"I'm not worried about being poisoned. I'm worried about other things." He was aware of what she meant, so she didn't have to clarify. "Promise me you'll mind your manners, and we'll get on fine."

"I have no manners," he said. "I was raised like an abandoned wolf pup who roamed with no supervision or direction. I never learned how to carry on like a human being."

"I don't agree with that statement. You're living in an apartment with a roof, floor, and furniture. You even have servants. You're not camping in a ditch. It appears you've accumulated some social graces."

"We'll see if I can muddle through our meal. As I mentioned previously, it's been an eternity since I dined with a female."

"You won't eat with your fingers and lick your plate, will you?"

"I can't guarantee what you'll observe, so you should brace yourself for any distressing sight."

He grinned a grin that was so seductive and so mesmerizing that she was thoroughly rattled by it. He was tall and blond, muscular and brawny, like an ancient Viking warrior who would steal away with all the trembling maidens in the village. Who could have sired such a magnificent male specimen?

It wasn't fair for him to be so handsome and intriguing. In his company, she felt little, pathetic, and beaten down by life, but then, she'd been searching for a champion, and he seemed like an excellent candidate to assume that role. If he didn't annoy her by acting outrageously, she suspected she'd finally receive the conclusion she sought.

He waved to the footman, and the man filled two plates and brought them over. She saw roast beef, steamed vegetables, and fresh, buttered bread. None of it was fancy, but the aroma was heavenly, and her stomach growled so loudly that the Captain snickered.

"How long has it been since you ate?" he asked. "I gave you some money last night. You were supposed to purchase food with it."

"I fed Emily and Pierre instead."

"You have to take care of yourself before you take care of them. What if you expired because you were neglectful of your condition? Who would watch over them then?"

"Thank you for your marvelous parenting advice. I'm sure you—as a dedicated bachelor—know all about it."

She stopped and frowned. He wasn't wearing a wedding ring, so she'd presumed he was single, but when men were traveling, they often concealed their true circumstance.

"Are you a bachelor?" she asked.

"Yes, definitely."

"You don't have a sweetheart waiting for you at home?"

"Gad, no."

"Why has no lucky girl latched onto you yet?"

"What sane father would give his daughter to me?"

She chortled with merriment. "I completely concur. What sane father would?"

He picked up his fork and motioned to her plate. "Get moving. I can't have you faint from hunger."

She'd never dined in such an intimate way with a man before. Especially not with one who was so virile and masculine. The moment should have been awkward, but she was starving, and she couldn't fret about the proper mode of interacting.

In a prior period, when she'd been an ordinary young lady living an ordinary life, she wouldn't have been caught dead in a bachelor's apartment, but she'd been in a downward spiral for several years, and she'd had to lower her standards.

She picked up her own fork and dug in with glee, as if she were a beggar at a banquet. The footman stood at attention in the corner, trying not to gape, and once she'd gobbled every bite, she glanced over at the Captain.

"If I have a second helping of everything," she asked, "will there be enough left for the children to have some when they awaken?"

"I am very rich," the Captain said, "and while you are staying with me, there will be no shortage of food. Have as much as you like. If you finish what was supplied, I'll have the servants run out to fetch more."

He'd been sated with just one serving, and he dawdled, staring as she shoveled it in like a stevedore, gulping down more and more until she was stuffed. Then she eased back in her chair, blew out a heavy breath, and muttered, "I needed that."

He chuckled. "Is your appetite always this robust? If you're a regular glutton, how are you so slender?"

"I'm not a glutton, but recently, food has been hard to come by. When I have some presented to me, I never pass up the chance to over-indulge."

"You're playing on my sympathies," he said.

"Yes. Is it working?"

"You're in my lodging and under my protection, so it appears to be."

"Are you a kind man, Captain?"

"Not usually. You're bringing out a whole new side to my personality."

"Will you expect favors as a reward for your generosity?"

"No, but I will expect rectitude and moral conduct. Can you manage it for the few days it will take to find a ship to convey you to England?"

"Will you really send me home?"

"Yes, I'll send you, and all of France will thank me."

She snorted at that. "What is your name, Captain? I should probably know it."

"It's Sheridan Stone."

At hearing that it was Stone, she wondered if he was related to the despicable cad, Neville Stone, but she didn't inquire. It was a common surname, and there were thousands of people with it scattered around the kingdom, so it wasn't likely.

She also didn't inquire because, if she found out he and Neville Stone were kin, even if it was a distant connection, it would be difficult to remain civil, and he was being very sweet. She wouldn't start a quarrel.

"Are you from London?" she asked.

"No. I grew up in the country."

"Like an abandoned wolf pup?"

"Yes."

"Didn't you have a parent to rein in your excesses? Wasn't there anyone to worry that you weren't learning to act appropriately?"

"My mother died shortly after I was born, and my father was never home. He liked to revel in London, so we were raised by lazy, incompetent servants."

"Who is *we*?" she asked.

"I have two brothers, and we were wild and incorrigible. It was impossible to control us, so our servants didn't try."

"I pity them."

"So do I."

He extended his glass, and they clinked the rims together, sharing a smile that was overly fond, so it was quite disturbing. It seemed as if they were flirting, which she would never attempt. They were alone, so she could quickly land herself in a perilous situation.

He realized they were flirting too, and he was as bothered by it as she was. He shifted away from her, and as he moved in his seat, he winced.

"What's wrong?" she asked.

"It's nothing," he claimed.

"It's not *nothing*. I can see that you're uncomfortable. What is it?"

"I was injured a few months ago. In the leg. It pains me occasionally."

"You were injured? And here I thought you were a demigod. How could you have been laid low?"

"I was in a skirmish; slashed with a saber before I could prevent it." He frowned. "It was my own fault. I'm a terror when I'm in a fight, so I was careless."

He offered the comment nonchalantly, as if being slashed by a saber was an incident of no account, and she suffered a huge wave of sympathy for him. Men led such hard, often violent lives, and she speculated over his employment.

She'd envisioned him blithely sailing the seas, barking orders as he glided across smooth waters. Evidently, his endeavors were a tad more treacherous than that. Was he a pirate? Was he a smuggler?

"You were stabbed?" she asked, her tone aghast.

"Not stabbed precisely. It was more of a bad cut on my thigh. I'm better now, and I scarcely notice it."

Was he convincing himself or her?

His cheeks reddened, as if he was embarrassed to have mentioned his wound. She didn't suppose he was prone to private confessions.

"Will you have dessert?" he asked, anxious to change the subject. "I think there's pie."

"I would love a piece of pie. Maybe even two pieces."

He jumped up and retrieved it himself, not waiting for the footman to pitch in. It gave him an excuse to avoid her gaze. With a dramatic flourish, he set it down, then returned to his chair.

"Aren't you having any?" she asked him.

"As opposed to you, I'm stuffed, and I couldn't eat another bite."

"If I gobble this down, will I shock you?"

"You've been shocking me from the moment we met. I immediately recognized that you were a woman. In the tavern? You were too pretty to be a man."

"I congratulate you on your perceptive skills. You have to be the first fellow who figured out my ruse."

"Most people don't really look at what's directly in front of them."

"Too true, Captain Stone. Are you a pirate?"

He smirked. "If I admit that I am, will you quail with alarm?"

"I'm not much of a one for quailing."

"Praise be. I can't abide a trembling ninny."

"Then you and I will get on famously. I'm tough as nails."

"I've realized that about you."

He started talking, explaining that he wanted to hear every detail about why she'd departed England, about how she'd been stranded. The prior night, she'd told him some of it, but obviously, he hadn't believed her, and he needed to have her repeat her story, probably to check for inconsistencies.

His voice was a soothing baritone that lulled her into a sense of security she shouldn't have embraced. Her tummy was full, the room warm, the company pleasant, and without her being able to stop her weary slide, she dozed off. She was being extremely rude, but she couldn't stay awake.

She began to dream, and she was on a tropical beach, the sun shining down, the water a brilliant turquoise, which was odd. She'd never been to the tropics, but she had a vivid imagination. Her cousin, Caroline, was off in the distance, walking with Pierre's mother. They halted, and Caroline called to Sophia, but she was speaking in a language Sophia didn't understand.

In a vague way, she noted that Captain Stone had ceased his monologue. He chuckled kindly, as he said, "I declare, Cantwell, you are a horrid guest. You might have warned me I had bored you to tears."

She struggled to rouse herself enough to reply, but she couldn't. She was eager to return to Caroline, to deduce what she was saying.

"Let's put her to bed," he said to someone. "Is there space on the mattress with the children?"

"Yes," a maid whispered.

Sophia was lifted off her chair and snuggled to Captain Stone's broad chest. It occurred to her that she'd like to remain there forever.

"You were correct about one fact, Cantwell," he murmured. "You are a great bother."

He carried her into the bedchamber and laid her on the bed next to Pierre. The housemaid covered her with a blanket, then they tiptoed out. She didn't stir, but smiled groggily and tried to find Caroline again, but her cousin and the beach were gone.

Instead, she fell into a deep, deep slumber, and as she drifted off, she caught herself thinking that Captain Stone just might be a gentleman after all, so apparently, there was one of them left in the world.

Fancy that.

Chapter Three

"WHAT WILL HAPPEN TO us?"

"Captain Stone swears he's sending us to England."

Sophia stared down at Pierre, and he frowned and asked, "Can he mean it? Will you trust him?"

"For the moment," Sophia said, "I'm telling myself I should. I don't have any other option."

"If he tricks you, I will kill him in his sleep."

He could be such a vehement sprite of a fellow, and she sighed with dismay. "You are much too young to harbor such dangerous ideas."

"I may be young, but I will not permit you to be deceived or cheated ever again. I will always protect you."

It was afternoon, and they were ambling along the wharf, studying the ships, watching as cargo was loaded and unloaded. It was a loud, busy spot, crammed with sailors, merchants, passengers, and vendors, all of them intent on their business.

With the Captain having assumed custody of them, their trek was leisurely, rather than terror-filled, and she'd forced herself to relinquish the anxiety that usually plagued her. She could sightsee like a lazy tourist.

Emily was behind them, being carried by the new nanny. The nanny was good with her, and she'd quickly gotten her into a stellar condition. She was wearing her blue dress, with a white pinafore. Her blond hair was tied with a blue bow that matched the color of her dress and eyes. Her bloomers had been washed and pressed, her shoes polished. She appeared to be the daughter of a rich, important man—which she was.

When people passed by her, they stopped and smiled, delighted to have such a fetching cherub brighten the dreary place.

Emily saw the Captain approaching before Sophia did, and apparently, they'd become friends.

"Cap! Cap!" Emily cooed, and when Sophia glanced around, the child was practically oozing flirtation.

Heaven help the person who was in charge of her when she was sixteen. Would it be Sophia? She couldn't imagine that being Emily's ending. Besides the fact that Sophia had no money to support her, she had no maternal tendencies. They came naturally to other women, but not to her.

If Emily was left in her care, who could predict what sort of tart she might grow up to be? Her parents had both been recklessly immoral, and she appeared to have inherited their wicked proclivities. She would definitely need a firm hand, but Sophia couldn't provide one. She could hardly manage herself, let alone a little girl.

Captain Stone marched up, and Emily reached out to him so he'd lift her away from the nanny and hold her himself. He was the type who'd be tantalized by a pretty face, and without hesitating, he obliged her.

"Hello, Miss Emily," he said. "You're looking very smart today."

At the male compliment, Emily preened and patted his cheeks, babbling a string of toddler nonsense that was a mix of French and English that only Pierre could decipher.

Sophia observed them, and they had many of the same features, the same golden-blond hair, the same big blue eyes. If Sophia hadn't learned who Emily's father was, she might have speculated whether it wasn't Captain Stone. They were that similar.

He was quite comfortable with a baby on his hip, and she wondered if he realized how easily Emily had slid into his arms. No doubt he viewed himself as a dedicated bachelor, but Sophia suspected he possessed the parental inclinations she lacked and, in the future, once he was wed, he'd be an excellent father.

"Where are you headed?" he asked Sophia after Emily paused to take a breath.

"We're just walking. We have no destination in mind."

He turned to Pierre and said, "May I borrow Miss Cantwell for a bit?"

Pierre was aghast. "It will be just the two of you? I can't be thinking this is proper."

"We will constantly be surrounded by other people," the Captain insisted.

Sophia elbowed Pierre and said, "I'm the adult in this relationship and you're the child. Please don't fret over me so much. It's not healthy."

"My health is fine," Pierre huffed, "but we barely know this Captain. How can we be certain he will not abuse you?"

Sophia raised a brow at Captain Stone. "Well, Captain? What is your plan? Will you abuse me?"

He snorted with disgust. "I will be a perfect gentleman."

They said goodbye to the children, and the Captain gave the nanny some coins so she could buy them a candy. Pierre was distraught at the notion of Sophia traipsing off, but underneath his bluster, he was still a boy, so the offer of a sly bribe of candy would keep him from complaining too much.

Once they'd departed, she and the Captain went in the other direction. She couldn't guess what he wanted, but it was a lovely afternoon, the sun shining, the winds calm, and she was strolling with a handsome rogue. When had that ever happened?

She had a vague recollection of dozing off at supper the prior night. It seemed as if he'd tucked her into bed. She was fairly sure she hadn't staggered there on her own. She'd slept deeply and hadn't awakened until it was full morning. He'd been gone by then, but his cadre of servants had been lurking and eager to tend her. She'd been bathed, fed, and coddled, which had been a marvelous treat.

He peered down at her and grinned. "May I confess that you are the worst guest in the world? At supper, right in the middle of one of my best stories, you began to snore."

Her cheeks heated. "I thought that might have occurred, but I was so exhausted I couldn't remember."

"I had to carry you to bed as if you were a toddler yourself."

"I'm embarrassed to the marrow of my bones."

"No, you're not. You're so annoyingly brazen that I'm positive you've never been embarrassed a minute in your life, but is there a *thank you* in there somewhere? I'm being strangely considerate, and I demand you fawn over me."

"I refuse to thank you repeatedly. You're so vain that your head will swell, and you won't be able to fit through any doors."

They stopped at a ship, the gangplank lowered, a sailor guarding it. She read the name of the vessel that was painted on the side: *Stone Maiden*.

"This is yours?" she said.

"Yes. Will you come aboard?"

She clucked her tongue. "Before I agree, I should warn you that I'm armed."

"With what? I took your knife."

"I have a pistol in my skirt, and I'm not afraid to use it."

"No, you're not afraid of anything, are you?"

"I'm afraid of *you*. I'm afraid you might turn out to be a despicable fiend."

He said to his sailor, "Can you assure her for me? Am I a despicable fiend?"

The boy blushed, then stammered, "Ah . . . yes?"

Sophia laughed heartily, and it felt so grand to be merry, even if it might not last. "Yes, Captain Stone, I will come aboard, but why have you invited me? Are you hoping I'll be impressed? If so, I can state that there's no need. I'm already impressed."

"I've impressed you? My goodness! I didn't even have to try."

She studied him, studied the ship, studied him again. She wasn't scared of him, but if she'd had a chaperone, the woman would have had a fit of the vapors over the mere suggestion of her accompanying him. But she didn't have a chaperone, parent, or anyone who cared about her really. And she was twenty.

She could make her own choices.

"Why are you asking me on board? What's your reason?"

"We have to discuss your predicament, and I didn't think we should do it in my lodging. The place is small, and Pierre curious, and I figured there might be issues we have to address that you wouldn't want to mention in front of him."

"All right. Lead the way."

"Ladies first."

He gestured flamboyantly, and she started up. He climbed after her, a firm hand on her back to balance her as the plank swayed to-and-fro. A sailor at the top helped her onto the deck, then the Captain guided her to a hatch and down a set of stairs into the bowels of the ship.

The stairs were a relief. She'd expected there would be a ladder, and she'd have had to clamber down it, with the Captain at the bottom, peeking up her skirt.

"We can chat in my cabin," he said.

"You haven't forgotten about my pistol, have you?"

"Believe me, I will ponder it every second."

He opened a door and stepped in. She followed. It was a tiny room, but it was tidy, with every item stowed away, as was typical on a sailing ship.

There was a desk in the center, strewn with maps and navigational tools. A bunk was tucked along one wall, and there were chests and cabinets that contained books, charts, and knick-knacks, providing evidence that he was probably learned and literate.

It was sumptuously luxurious. The rug on the floor, the furniture, the blankets on the bed, were constructed of the finest materials. He'd previously bragged that he was wealthy, and obviously, he hadn't been lying.

He sat down at the desk, as she snooped, pulling books off shelves, fingering trinkets, assessing his cache of weapons. He watched silently, as if he were an indulgent parent.

Finally, she plopped onto a chair across from him. He'd retrieved a liquor decanter from a drawer, and he pointed to it.

"May I pour you a brandy?" he said.

She wrinkled up her nose. "I don't drink hard spirits."

"I don't have any wine."

"It's the middle of the afternoon. I don't need any."

"Will you mind if I have a glass?"

"Have at it. You shouldn't deny yourself simply because I'm present. I promised I wouldn't be a bother, remember?"

He scoffed. "We've already established that you are nothing *but* a bother."

She wouldn't argue about it. Instead, she nodded to the horde of swords, sabers, knives, and pistols. "Why do you have so many weapons? I asked you once if you were a pirate, and you never answered."

He smirked. "What can I say? I'm a violent fellow, and I engage in many violent activities."

"But *are* you a pirate? I ought to have some idea of the sort of man I've begged for assistance."

He stared for an eternity, and just when she thought he'd explain, he said, "We're not here to talk about me. We're here to talk about you. Why are you in France? I recall what you told me the night we met, but tell me again. Let's see if you can keep your stories straight."

"I'm honest as the day is long."

"That, Cantwell, is a bald-faced lie. You are a conniver and schemer, and I'm stunned that I've allowed myself to be lured into your web. I'm convinced you have ulterior motives."

"I admit it. I'm trying to coerce you into liking me so you'll be kind."

"Don't make me regret it."

"Haven't you started to regret it? After all, you suddenly have me, a boy, and a baby to care for. It has to seem a heavy burden to an unattached bachelor."

"The three of you haven't been around long enough for me to grow exasperated. Now quit stalling. You're in France, and your family has cut you loose, so what mischief were you perpetrating that would spur them to penalize you?"

"Why would you automatically assume *I* was the culprit? Couldn't it be that my kin are the villains?"

"I'll decide how to respond to that question after I hear your entire tale of woe."

She sighed dramatically, as if he was being a great pest, but she had no qualms about apprising him as to the full extent of her dilemma. When her cousin, Caroline, had still been alive, her scandal had been painted as shameful. Her father, Oscar, had certainly viewed it as being reprehensible, but Caroline was dead. Her father too, and Sophia had custody of Emily.

Sophia had been left on her own to muddle forward. Caroline's secrets weren't Sophia's. She could blab them to the world without concern or consequence.

"I am a poor relative," she said.

"How poor?"

"Pathetically poor. Ridiculously poor. Hideously poor."

"Who was your father?"

"Benjamin Cantwell. He was a dreamer and schemer—and a poet."

Captain Stone winced. "There's not much money in poetry."

"No, there's not. He had grandiose plans and wild notions, but none of them ever came to fruition."

"Is that why you have such insane attitudes? You inherited them?"

"I have no insane attitudes. I am simply a lonely, bewildered female who's surviving in desperate circumstances."

"There's nothing lonely or despairing about you. In my opinion, you're an annoying nuisance."

She grinned. "I'm that too."

"Your father is deceased?"

"Yes. My mother too, since I was a baby. Father tried to raise me appropriately, but it was a lost cause, then he died when I was ten. I was sent to live with his cousin, Oscar. Father named him to be my guardian in his Last Will."

"You still haven't clarified how you wound up in France."

"My cousin, Caroline, spent the summer in London with some acquaintances. She wasn't chaperoned very well, and she was seduced by a scoundrel."

He shrugged. "It happens."

"When her condition was revealed, her father, Oscar—"

"The same Oscar who is your guardian?"

"Yes, the very same. He insisted she identify the rogue who had ruined her. He intended to arrange a quick marriage, but she repeatedly refused."

"Wasn't he already married? Isn't that what you told me?"

"Yes, and I think that was why she remained silent, but so long as she was recalcitrant, her father was determined to punish her. He wouldn't let us return home, so we were stuck."

Caroline had finally confided the man's name to Sophia, but not until she'd been about to draw her last breath. She'd begged Sophia not to permit Caroline's family to ever have control of Emily. After her father, Oscar, had been so horrid to her, she couldn't bear the idea.

Instead, she'd pleaded with Sophia to deliver Emily to her father. She'd wanted to guarantee Emily was reared in the style she deserved. It had been a deranged request, whispered by a dying woman, so Sophia had sworn she would do it, even though she couldn't imagine how it would be accomplished.

The exalted man wasn't even aware he was a father. Caroline had never contacted him about it. She'd been terribly foolish, assuming he would miss her and come for her, that she'd inform him when he arrived and he'd love her for it, which had only proved how unhinged she'd been about him.

Sophia could have chastised Caroline for being so gullible, but then, she'd been seventeen when he'd seduced her. What did a girl know about amour at seventeen? What did she know about anything?

Nevertheless, Sophia had promised her cousin that she would convey Emily to her father, that she would demand he claim paternity and support her in a toplofty manner. When Sophia had tendered the vow, she'd deemed it frivolous and expedient, spoken in the urgency of the moment.

Caroline had been failing fast, and Sophia's agreement had calmed her. In the same situation, who wouldn't have offered the same vow?

She'd figured she could shuck it off afterward, but she hadn't understood the gravity of a deathbed promise. It weighed on her. There was a solemn, almost religious feel to it, as if God was watching to see if she'd follow through.

"Were you close to your cousin?" the Captain asked.

"We were like sisters."

"I'm sorry for your loss then, but is Emily really your cousin's child? She's not yours? If she is, you can admit it. I won't judge you."

Sophia tsked with exasperation. "Shall we travel to the country and visit Caroline's grave? Shall we fetch Pierre so you can interrogate him? What will it take to convince you?"

He scrutinized her forever, then he nodded. "I guess I'll quit harassing you about it, but this seems very dubious to me. What became of your money after she passed away? Why are you broke and alone?"

"Her father paid the rent on our cottage and provided us with a stipend, but he died too. I received a letter from home just as I was writing to tell everyone she was deceased. Then our allowance stopped."

"Who stopped it and why? Can you give me a credible explanation? Did you anger your relatives? Why would they abandon you?"

"I think it was one of my cousins. He never liked me, and once Oscar was gone, he'd have been in charge of the finances. I would have been the first expense that he cut from the estate accounts."

She was sure that's what had occurred, and the brute wasn't a cousin, but it was too convoluted to clarify, so she didn't expound.

Her guardian, Oscar, had had two daughters: Caroline and her older sister, Aurora. He'd never had a son, but he'd had another ward, Miles, who'd been raised with them. Oscar had doted on him and had arranged for him to marry Caroline or Aurora. Miles was to have been Oscar's heir and, after the wedding, would have inherited the family's property of Riverglen.

Caroline had scuttled her part of the plan when she'd ruined herself, so Miles was left to woo Aurora, but he hadn't persuaded her to proceed to the altar.

Sophia had never been close to Aurora, as she'd been with Caroline. Aurora was spoiled, snooty, and pretentious, and Sophia suspected she was holding out for a better candidate than Miles. If she never found one, she'd wed Miles, but in the meantime, Miles had been hung out to dry as he anxiously waited for Aurora to implement the conclusion Oscar had envisioned.

Aurora simply wasn't cooperating as had been expected of her.

Miles was spoiled, snooty, and pretentious too, and Sophia loathed him. They were both Oscar's wards, but Sophia was kin and Miles wasn't. Yet he pictured himself—because he was a male—as being far above her in every way. He was a dunce and charlatan who'd ingratiated himself for greedy purposes, and she'd never been circumspect about her allegations.

She wasn't surprised that he'd stranded her in France, but she wondered if Aurora or her mother, Millicent, realized what he'd done. Millicent especially. Sophia couldn't believe Millicent would be so cruel and petty. Then again, when Caroline's predicament had been revealed to her parents, Millicent had insisted she be sent away.

If Sophia never came back, Emily would never be brought back either, so they could all act as if the girl had never been born. Perhaps that was the true situation. Perhaps Millicent was hoping Sophia would vanish and Emily would vanish with her.

"Why doesn't this cousin like you?" the Captain asked, interrupting her morose reverie.

"I have no idea. I'm such a *likable* person. Can you imagine me generating venom from anyone?"

He snorted with amusement. "What happened after your allowance ended? It appears you've encountered numerous difficulties since then."

"I buried Caroline, then I started packing to sail for home, but despite how often I wrote about my intentions, I couldn't get a reply. My rent was due, so I lost our cottage, and I'm a foreigner, so it was hard to obtain help in the village where we lived. Everyone was French and I wasn't."

"You didn't reside in Boulogne?"

"No. I rushed to the coast, thinking I could find a ship to transport us across the Channel, but I never had any luck." She paused and frowned. "Actually, I had plenty of luck, but it was all bad. I've been robbed and lied to, tricked and deceived. I bought fares for us on three different vessels, but the men stole my money and sailed away without me."

"Well, that's dastardly."

"I certainly thought so. I've approached dozens of British so-called gentlemen, but they wanted *favors* in order to furnish any assistance."

"It's a port town. They probably figured you weren't really an innocent maiden."

"Or maybe they assumed I *was* an innocent maiden, and it would be hilarious to force themselves on me. I've been locked in rooms and trapped in carriages. I've been groped, fondled, and propositioned in ways that would make you blush." She shrugged and sighed. "So I dress in trousers and carry a pistol in my pocket. I know how to use it too."

"If I convey you to England, do you have a place to go? Do you have family there?" He leaned forward on his elbows and studied her eyes. "Tell me the truth."

"You are so ridiculous. Haven't you been listening to me? Yes, I have family there. Yes, I have somewhere to go."

She couldn't guess if she'd be welcome at Riverglen though. She'd have Emily with her, so any foul reaction was possible, but she would demand they let her stay. After Oscar had died, her guardianship had passed to Millicent, so she was Millicent's ward.

Millicent had to aid her. Didn't she?

The prior few weeks, if she'd learned one fact about herself, it was that she was a fighter. She didn't take *no* for an answer, and she didn't tolerate fools. When she saw Miles again, she would ask him if he'd cut off her money. If he snickered and bragged that he had, she would shoot him and suffer no regrets. The world would be better off without him, and when she climbed to the gallows, she'd be smiling.

"I've only inquired," the Captain said, "because I won't inflict you on the good citizens of England if there's no reason for it. I won't deliver you, merely to have you plying your mischief over there instead of here."

"I'm a moral, decent person!" she fumed. "I've simply had to deal with some problems. If you'd experienced a catastrophe that was even remotely similar to what I've endured, I'd like to discover how *you* would have muddled through."

"I'm a man, so I wouldn't have had to worry about the behavior of other men."

"Precisely."

He stared at her, his intense gaze digging deep. She felt as if he was delving down to the bottom of her black heart, where her petty vanity and fury were concealed. She didn't care for the sensation at all, and she yearned to fidget, but she held herself very still, refusing to let him see that he unnerved her.

Eventually, he sat back. "I suppose I believe you. About most of it anyway. I'm fairly sure you're an adept liar, so I will swallow it with a grain of salt."

"I am an adept liar. You're correct about that, but I haven't been lying to you."

"How am I to assess that comment? You're a liar, but you're not lying *now*? Every other word that falls out of your mouth is debatable."

She chuckled. "Well, how honest are you? Will you send me home?"

"I will send you. There may be a bit of a delay until there's a ship headed in that direction *and* a captain who will agree to have the three of you as passengers."

"Why won't you take us?"

"I'm not headed to England, but even if I was, I'm superstitious. Women are bad luck on ships."

"What a perfectly ludicrous attitude. If that's so, why have I been viewing you as a rather modern fellow?"

"I'm modern in some areas, but not in others. I don't sail with female passengers, and I figure I'm pushing my chances simply by having you strut about in my cabin."

"Ha! You brought me here so you could show off. You wanted to flaunt your private quarters so I would recognize how important you are. You expect me to be awed."

He frowned, as if the notion hadn't occurred to him. "That can't be right, Cantwell. I don't even like you, so there is absolutely no benefit for me to show off."

"You don't *like* me? That can't be right either. I'm wonderfully likable. People have always said that about me."

He chuckled too, and for a moment, his expression was warm and fond. It rattled them both, but he was most disturbed by it. He stood abruptly, indicating the meeting was over, so she had to stand too. To her great surprise, she was wishing the conversation wasn't finished. He was fascinating and interesting, and she would have liked to tarry with him for the rest of the afternoon.

He rounded the desk to walk her to the door. She turned too, and it was such a small space. She bumped into him, and suddenly, they were crushed together from chests to toes. Their proximity produced sparks, and though it was very strange, Time seemed to stop. The noise outside on the busy wharf ground to a halt.

It appeared as if the universe was marking the encounter, ensuring they paid attention. It was peculiar and thrilling, and she'd never felt anything like it. He was a tad startled too, but he hid it better than she did.

He glared down at her, his confusion evident, and bizarre as it was to imagine, she thought he might dip down and kiss her. She'd been kissed in the past on a few lovely occasions: at the harvest fair, after a community dance. So she knew the amorous signs a man displayed when he was considering it.

Was he attracted to her? She was very fetching, but he'd just mentioned that he didn't like her. Men were such odd creatures! How could he dislike her, but be eager to kiss her?

She stepped away, and the sparks settled, the passionate air dissipating. He went to the door and gestured for her to depart. She strolled by him, her skirt brushing his legs, and the slight contact ignited a fire in him. He astonished her by reaching out and grabbing her wrist.

His hot gaze roamed down her torso and lingered on several feminine spots he had no business evaluating. She would have scolded him, but he wasn't appraising her in a lascivious manner. No, he was bewildered by what had transpired and trying to make sense of it, but she suspected there was no explanation.

Her cousin, Caroline, had insisted some couples were destined to be together. She'd claimed that was why she'd ruined herself, that she hadn't been able to fight it. She hadn't wanted to fight it. Sophia had deemed Caroline's musings to be silly, but maybe there were some rare couples whose relationships were meant to be. Maybe Sophia and Sheridan Stone were one of them.

It didn't matter though. She was leaving for England very soon, and *he* didn't like her. She'd never see him again, so it was absurd to ponder issues like attraction and bonds.

He released her and motioned for her to continue on, and she climbed up to the deck. He ordered a sailor to escort her to his lodging.

Merely to needle him a bit, she asked, "Why won't you escort me yourself, Captain?"

"I'm busy, Cantwell, and I've wasted too much time on you today."

"Will you join us for supper?"

"I haven't decided."

"I hope you will."

He didn't reply, but urged the sailor to get moving. She was hurried down the gangplank, then guided down the wharf toward his apartment. The entire way, she could feel him watching her. She told herself she was being ridiculous, that he was much too vain to be focused on her.

Finally, when his ship would have disappeared from view, she couldn't bear it another second. She glanced back and . . .

There he was! At the rail and staring at her as if he couldn't look away.

"Well, well, what do you know?" she murmured.

She waved, but he was too snooty to smile or wave in response. She grinned with delight, whipped away, and kept on.

"Will you miss me?"

Miss Cantwell's question was sassy and impertinent, and Sheridan said, "No. You're trouble and mischief, rolled into a pretty package. I'll be glad to see you go and all of France will celebrate."

"Don't be grouchy and don't hurt my feelings. Here at the end, we should pretend we've been sweethearts for ages. You have to lie and tell me you'll be bereft forever."

"As you wish, Cantwell. I shall be bereft forever."

He glowered so sternly that she laughed, and he caught himself grinning like a fool. He never spent much time around gently-bred females. His life had constantly been filled with men—and very few women.

He'd been raised by lazy, incompetent footmen, then he'd attended school and had been taught by grumpy, strict male professors. He'd enlisted in the navy at sixteen and had been bossed by severe, rule-oriented male commanders. For the past several years, he'd captained his own ship of tough, brave sailors.

They frequently interacted with women, but they were whores in port towns, so the respectable, moralistic variety was a rarity. Yet he was familiar enough with the species to recognize that she was completely unusual.

He was very typically British, and if he'd had to state an opinion, he'd have insisted he preferred women who were modest and a bit shy, who went to church on Sunday, and who deferred to the men the Good Lord had placed over them.

Had he been wrong about that?

She was funny and impudent, and he was fascinated by her and even a tad charmed. Apparently, he was physically attracted to her too. The prior afternoon in his cabin, there had been an odd moment when she'd bumped into him and sparks had ignited.

Gad, he'd nearly kissed her! It had been an insane impulse, but she simply stirred emotions in him that he didn't like. The sooner she sailed away, the better off he'd be.

They were standing on the wharf, and she was about to board the ship he'd booked for her. The previous night in a tavern, he'd stumbled on a captain who was heading to London. He hadn't been opposed to taking Miss Cantwell and the children. It was a short trip, and Sheridan had spurred him to agree by doubling the price he'd quoted.

Briefly, Sheridan had flirted with the notion of *not* paying her fare, of having her loaf in France for another week or two so she could continue to entertain him, but that was deranged thinking. Once he'd realized he was considering the absurd idea, he'd pulled out his purse and handed over the money.

The housemaid who'd been serving as a nanny was holding Emily, and she said to Miss Cantwell, "Would you like me to carry the baby up the gangplank for you?"

"Yes, please. It's very kind of you to offer."

He'd tried to convince the girl to journey to England with Miss Cantwell, but she was French and wouldn't leave. Miss Cantwell had struck down the suggestion too, by mentioning that she had no money for wages.

The comment had him wondering what conditions she'd face when she reached her home. He'd almost asked her where it was located. If he knew where she was, he could stop by in the future to check on her, but his yearning to do just that was bizarre.

He didn't inquire about her family or destination. He wasn't interested in her and wouldn't obsess.

If she suffered difficulties later on, it wasn't his problem. He'd already been more generous than was necessary, and she wasn't his responsibility. He had no authority over her and didn't want to have any authority. In fact, he pitied any man who ever attempted to constrain her. It would be a losing proposition.

"I'll walk behind you," Pierre said to the nanny, "to keep Emily steady. She's so heavy these days."

"*Merci*," the girl replied.

Emily peered at Sheridan with those gorgeous blue eyes of hers. She frowned dramatically and said, "Boat . . . ?"

Evidently, she'd assumed he would be traveling with them.

"I'm not going with you," he told her.

Tears bubbled up, and she appeared as if she was about to weep, and Miss Cantwell bustled forward, her tone scolding. "Don't you dare bother him, Miss Emily. You get yourself up on the ship, and I'll join you in a minute."

The nanny started off, Pierre climbing with them, but Emily stared over the nanny's shoulder. Her scrutiny made him feel guilty, as if he'd failed her. Though it was peculiar, her woeful expression left him eager to rush after her, to claim he'd been lying and would travel with them after all.

He said to Miss Cantwell, "She'll be a handful when she's older."

"She's a handful now."

"You'll have to chase off the boys with a very big stick."

"By then, I hope I'll have her settled in a situation where I won't have to fret over her. There are many people in the world who would be much better at being a mother to her than I am."

"You still deny your maternal instincts?"

"I can barely dress myself in the morning. I'm totally inept, and I'd worry about anyone who had to rely on me."

She was being much too hard on herself. She'd been pitched into chaos by her relatives, and she'd fought like a tiger to protect Emily and Pierre. She was quite remarkable, but he wouldn't tell her so. There was no point in gushing.

"Have I thanked you sufficiently?" she asked.

"I haven't been counting, but I'm certain you could be even more grateful."

"You've nearly restored my faith in humanity."

"I'm not a complete ogre."

"No, you're not, which I am very happy to have learned."

She grinned up at him, looking pretty and impish, and his heart flip-flopped in his chest. Obviously, he was smitten, and the discovery was hilarious. He liked lithe, slender women, the kind who floated across a ballroom floor as if their feet barely touched it. He liked grace, beauty, and exquisite manners.

He *didn't* like impertinence, sass, or quirkiness. Or did he?

He yanked his gaze away and withdrew a small pouch from his coat. It was filled with coins, and he slipped it to her furtively so no bystanders would see him giving her money. It would provide miscreants with reasons to befriend, then rob her.

"This is for you," he said. "You'll need food and lodging in London, then coach fare for the ride home. I won't have you wandering the streets there as you were wandering them here."

"You just might be the best man I've ever met."

"Once you arrive," he said, "do you really have somewhere to go?"

"Yes, I really do."

"You'll be welcome and safe?"

"Yes. I'm not sure what happened with my allowance, but I'm family. My cousin is still my guardian."

"How old are you?"

"Twenty." She was so young that she hadn't yet come of age.

"You're not fibbing, are you? You have a guardian? Someone is watching over you?"

"Yes, and I'll be fine. *We* will be fine."

It was the worst moment for him. He was so anxious to ask where she was headed, so he'd know where she'd be. He was concerned about Emily too, with an intensity that was astounding.

He almost told her how to contact him if she was ever in a jam, but that was a ridiculous idea. Hadn't he warned himself—over and over—not to get involved in her life? Besides, he was rarely in England anyway. Why furnish her with contact information? If she sent for him, he might not receive any message for months or even years.

She wasn't his problem, and he wouldn't put her in a position where she'd assume she could depend on him. Though he'd lied to her about it, he was returning to England himself. It might be a short visit, but then, it might become lengthy. Considering his low health and grim mood, he might retire. He might settle down.

He would be busy pondering big issues and big changes, and he couldn't be distracted by a flighty ninny like Miss Cantwell.

A whistle blew up on the ship, and suddenly, sailors were running, orders being called.

He nodded to the gangplank. "You should climb aboard. They won't wait for you."

"I'm going home! Thank you, thank you, thank you!"

Surprising him, she leapt forward and hugged him with all her might. Her curvaceous body was crushed to his in a way that was sweet and riveting, and he hugged her back for as long as he dared. She was the one to pull away.

"I will miss you so much," she said.

"Think of me occasionally, would you? I'd like it if you would."

"I will think of you constantly. Forever!"

He dipped down and kissed her on the cheek. It was stupid and brazen, but he couldn't resist. He was being pelted by the absurd perception that it was wrong to part from her. The sensation was so powerful that he shook it away.

"Goodbye, Cantwell." His tone was warm and fond. "Try to stay out of trouble, will you? Don't make me regret delivering you to England."

"You won't regret it. I swear!"

A second whistle blew, and without another word, she whipped away and dashed up to the deck. A sailor helped her steady herself, and Sheridan observed as the nanny handed her Emily. Then the same sailor guided the nanny down to the wharf. Miss Cantwell stood at the railing, holding Emily, with Pierre by her side. Pierre frowned down at Sheridan, as if he was glad to have wrenched Miss Cantwell away from him.

Miss Cantwell smiled, but Emily plaintively wailed to him, "Cap? Cap?"

She reached out, begging him to accompany them, and Miss Cantwell scolded her again. "Stop flirting, you little monster. Captain Stone is a rogue, and he likes it too much." She waved down at him. "Goodbye! I miss you already!"

He chuckled and waved back, then the baby started to fuss, and Miss Cantwell vanished from view. He dawdled, expecting her to pop up again, but she never reappeared, and he was stunned by how irked he was.

As the ship was dragged out into the current, George Barnes walked up and asked, "Are they on board?"

"Safe and sound."

"And . . . gone! Praise be."

If George had any opinion about how morosely Sheridan was staring out to sea, he didn't mention it.

"I'll be at the tavern," George said, "having a glass of ale. Will you join me?"

"In a few minutes."

George smirked with disgust, then left him to his misery.

Sheridan remained where he was—an aloof, solitary man—who felt as if his heart was breaking. A tugboat drew the vessel past the jetty, then cast off so the ship could catch the wind. A sail was hoisted, then another and another. Very quickly, it picked up speed and was swallowed by the grey sky and grey water.

He had eyes like a hawk, and he was certain she hadn't come back on deck. Why hadn't she?

He was very vain and couldn't believe she hadn't wanted a last glimpse of him. The realization was aggravating and sad. When he recognized how pathetic he was being, he staggered away and went to find George.

Chapter Four

"No, absolutely not."

Sheridan glared at his father, Neville, but Neville could never be shamed or cowed. His expression was bland and infuriating.

"Why would you automatically refuse?" Neville asked. "You haven't heard me out."

"I don't intend to hear you. Your badgering won't work on me."

"Are you sure about that?"

"Yes, I'm very sure."

They were sequestered in a parlor at his father's newly-inherited town house, seated side by side on plush chairs and drinking a brandy. A fire burned in the grate to ward off the evening chill. Sheridan had arrived in London several hours earlier, and servants had finally located Neville and whisked him home from his gambling club.

They hadn't seen each other in over a year, and for the moment, it was comforting to be back, but Sheridan had barely sat himself down before his father had begun harping that Sheridan should get married—and he should proceed immediately.

For once, they were alone, which was odd. Neville liked to wager at his favorite haunts, especially *Ralston's,* the posh club where he was a premier member, so it was an unusual interval for Sheridan. He was trying to cherish it, but he and Neville had a difficult relationship, so their interactions were never smooth.

Neville had been a worthless parent, and Sheridan's mother had died when he was a baby. He and his brothers, Hunter and Warwick, had grown up at Neville's country estate of Stone Manor, while Neville had caroused in London.

They'd been rambunctious boys who'd been wild and incorrigible. There had been no challenge they wouldn't accept and no feat they wouldn't attempt. They were much too brave and never careful. To curb some of their more reckless impulses, Hunter and Warwick had enlisted in the army. Sheridan had chosen the navy instead, then had become a spy and privateer.

Of the three of them, he was the most ruthless and impetuous, and his negligent conduct was only matched by his immoral tendencies. He possessed all of Neville's worst traits and very few of his good ones. Actually, Neville didn't have many *good* traits. He gambled and chased slatterns, and he rarely engaged in any other endeavors. Even though he was fifty, he was still a debauched wretch—and proud of it.

"Our situation has changed," Neville said.

"I understand that fact. I'm not a dunce."

"You need to wed. Fast."

"I just got here, after a year away, and that's the subject you're raising? Matrimony?"

"In case you've forgotten, I'm an earl now."

"You don't have to remind me."

"It seems as if I should."

"Will you lecture me about how we have responsibilities?"

"Yes. We have a lineage to protect, and I expect you to help me protect it."

Sheridan bristled. "You've never been concerned about any of this."

"I'm starting to be concerned. I *have* to be."

To the bewilderment of nearly everyone in the British Empire, Neville was suddenly Earl of Swindon. Hunter, as the oldest son, was Viscount Marston and would be the next earl. Sheridan and Warwick weren't anybody, and he was happy to keep it that way.

Neville had never imagined he'd inherit the title, so he'd constantly wallowed in vice and sloth. Sheridan's great-grandfather had been brilliant at commerce, and he'd amassed a fortune. Over the generations, they'd employed skilled accountants who expanded their wealth at an obscene rate, so Neville had always been very rich, but he'd had no future elevation to weigh him down. He'd been able to indulge his basest inclinations.

He was a hideous custodian of the huge windfall of Swindon, but with it being bestowed, he was acting lucid and reliable. Despite *his* abrupt transformation though, Sheridan wasn't fretting over any of it. He supposed he'd tie the knot someday. Every man of his class and station had to bite the bullet eventually, but he was in no rush.

"I have a surprise for you," Neville said.

"If it's awful, can't it wait? I doubt my bags have been unpacked, and you're already making me wish I hadn't visited."

"I'm simply trying to have an important father-son chat."

"We've never had one of those. Not that I can recall anyway. Have you decided to carry on like a parent? If that's what I'm about to observe, I may faint from shock."

Neville sighed, as if Sheridan was being a brat, and Sheridan studied him, thinking he was looking older, as if his decades of dissipation were taking a toll. It was a disturbing realization. Neville was such a fixture in their world. If he ever passed away, how would the sun continue to rise?

"What is your surprise, Neville?" he asked. "Please don't aggravate me with bad news. Let me be glad I'm home."

"This should have you smiling: While you were away, Hunter married."

Sheridan cocked his head, not certain he'd heard correctly. "He what?"

"He met a girl, fell madly in love, and wed her with hardly a thought to the consequences."

"You're joking." Sheridan assessed his father, then blanched with astonishment. "You're *not* joking."

"No, I'm not."

"My goodness," Sheridan murmured. "I'm stunned speechless."

He and his brothers were inordinately close. They'd been reared in such a slapdash, haphazard manner, and he was amazed they'd lived to be adults. Himself especially. Because they'd had no one else to depend on, they'd just had each other. They'd been like triplets, like one person separated into three parts. They were that fond and connected.

How could Hunter have taken such a drastic step without seeking Sheridan's advice or opinion? How could he have proceeded without Sheridan being present for the ceremony? How could Sheridan have stayed away and missed such a monumental experience in his brother's life?

He was horrified and slightly bereft.

"Who is his bride?" he asked. "Is she anyone I would know?"

"It isn't likely you'd have crossed paths with her, but you'll probably recognize her father. Her maiden name was Hannah Graves, and he was the famous mariner, Sir Edmund Graves."

"Huh . . ." Sheridan murmured again. "What's she like? Do *you* like her?"

"She is precious and kind, and she dotes on Hunter. I couldn't be more ecstatic."

Neville was a pretentious snob who liked loose women, the looser the better. He couldn't abide respectable young ladies, so the compliment was bizarre.

"If *you* have been charmed by her," Sheridan said, "she must be exceptional. I'm delighted for Hunter. I am."

Was he speaking the truth? Or was he trying to convince himself?

Hunter had been the most debauched cad in the kingdom. He'd kept mistresses and consorted with tarts, and he'd reveled in his dissolute antics. If he'd married abruptly, if he'd been altered into a contented husband, the world didn't make sense anymore.

"You're about to be an uncle too," Neville said, yanking him out of his reverie.

"I'm what?"

"I just received a letter from Hunter. Hannah is in the family way already, so you're about to be an uncle."

Sheridan sucked in a sharp breath. "This is happening too fast. I wonder if I should climb up to my bedchamber and lie down before I fall down."

"I have another surprise for you too."

"Must you share it? I'm not sure I can stand much more news."

Neville was too eager. "Warwick has wed too."

"No!"

Sheridan felt as if he'd been punched. It was another wedding he'd missed, another major episode that had occurred when he'd been off chasing pirates. If that had been the cost, had his wild, nomadic existence been worth it?

Suddenly, it seemed as if it might not have been.

"Who is his bride?" Sheridan asked.

"Wilhelmina Dobbs?" Neville paused to see if Sheridan recognized the name, but he shook his head. "Her father was the famous painter, Jefferson Dobbs."

Sheridan was astonished again. "I generally view myself as an uneducated dolt, but even I have heard of him. Where did Warwick meet her? When did he marry her? I can't believe any of this."

"Warwick tells me *she* is in the family way too, so you'll be an uncle twice over."

"What is your opinion of her? Do you like her too?"

"I *love* her. She is the most gorgeous, flamboyant siren I have ever encountered, and Warwick was smart enough to snag her for his very own."

"Where are they now?" Sheridan asked. "Are they in London?"

"No. Hannah and Hunter are at Hannah's property of Parkhurst. There have been some problems at the estate, so they're changing staff and hiring employees. Warwick and Wilhelmina are at Warwick's property of Hill Haven. They've made it their home, and they're slowly settling in."

"Warwick bought a country property? He fled London? With a . . . *wife?*"

Sheridan pronounced the word *wife* as if it were an epithet. He and his brothers had agreed on several important facts about themselves: They were bachelors. They were cads. They were rich and entitled, and they could behave in any manner they pleased. They had no interest in monogamy or matrimony. Most of all, they *hated* the country.

Their childhoods, where they'd rampaged through the neighborhood, had cured them of any affection for rural living. They thrived in the city, where the company was lofty, the entertainment intriguing, and sins could be committed with impunity.

He felt angry and forgotten, as if his brothers had moved to the moon and had deliberately left Sheridan behind. He hadn't even had a chance to decide if he'd like to tag along.

He staggered over to the sideboard to refill his glass. He gulped down the contents, then returned to his chair. His leg was aching, as if his woe had landed there, and he couldn't keep from limping. Neville, who was usually a negligent slacker, honed in with annoying precision.

"You're limping," Neville said, stating the obvious. "Why are you?"

"It's nothing," Sheridan claimed, which was his typical response to questions about the injury. His world was one of tough, violent men. A fellow didn't whine or complain. He endured whatever was thrown in his path.

"Tell me!" Neville's tone was steely.

Sheridan waved a vague hand. "I was in a skirmish. I was wounded."

"How dire was it?"

"Not dire at all. It just hurts occasionally. I took a saber slash to the thigh."

"Did it have to be sewn?"

"The scar runs from my knee to my hip. I seem to remember the surgeon saying it was forty-five stitches."

"Forty-five!"

There was a fraught silence, as Neville scrutinized him, and Sheridan stared at the flames in the hearth, pretending not to notice.

"You look weary," his father finally said.

Sheridan shrugged. "My work is hard. You're aware of that. I'm not involved in a child's game. I play for high stakes, and there can be terrible consequences."

"Have you thought about quitting?"

The suggestion reverberated around the room. It lodged in Sheridan's chest, igniting a surge of exhilaration, and before he could bite down the reply, he said, "Yes, I think about it constantly."

He was astounded to have admitted it aloud. So far, he'd mused over it privately. If he wasn't out on the water, captaining a ship, who would he be?

He was acquainted with too many sailors who'd tried to settle down, but couldn't. The sea was a lure they couldn't resist. They had wives they never saw, children they didn't know, yet Sheridan didn't suppose he could continue for much longer. When he wasn't in perfect condition, he endangered his crew.

At what point would he stop? Would it be when crew members were imperiled because he couldn't pull his share of the load?

"If you retired," Neville said, "what would be your plan?"

"I would . . . would . . ." Sheridan broke off. "I have no idea what I'd do. I guess I'd wed like my deranged brothers. If they can manage it, I expect I can too."

"I'd like you to resign and come home." Neville's comment was a surprise. "We could all be together."

"You would not like it. You've never wallowed in *family* moments or gatherings."

"I'm mellowing in my old age."

Sheridan smirked. "You're not old, you're not mellow, and you can't persuade me that you're changing your habits."

"Hunter and Warwick are very happy," Neville said.

"So you say."

"They are! You'll see for yourself. I'm traveling to Swindon Hall in two weeks to celebrate my birthday and my elevation. I'm hosting a grand house party, and they're attending and bringing their brides. You'll get to meet your sisters-in-law."

"Oh, goody." Sheridan was being much too snide.

"Don't be a snot about it. I'm lucky that your brothers made such excellent choices. And now, to have grandchildren about to arrive!"

Neville drew a kerchief out of his pocket and dabbed at his eyes.

Sheridan was aghast. "What is wrong with you?"

"I'm happy. Why shouldn't I be? It's been such a marvelous year."

Maybe Neville was mellowing a bit. Maybe, after decades of being a degenerate rogue, he was wishing he was closer to his three boys. It could happen. Couldn't it?

Pigs might fly someday too!

Sheridan scoffed with derision. "You've told me so many odd details, and you're behaving so strangely, that I feel dizzy."

"If you retired, you could marry too. It wouldn't kill you."

"It might."

"With your health so deteriorated—"

"I'm fine!" Sheridan testily insisted.

"I don't believe you. Will you keep on until you can't sail anymore? Or will you be murdered by some villain who doesn't deserve the honor of being the fiend who slays you?"

"I'm too tough to be cut down and I have nine lives."

"Haven't you used all of them?"

Sheridan chuckled miserably. "I'm betting it's been more than nine."

Neville extended his glass, wanting more liquor, but there was no servant hovering, so Sheridan had to fetch the decanter. He tried to conceal his limp, but couldn't. Neville focused in like a hawk sighting a rabbit.

"I need a favor," Neville said as Sheridan sat again.

"I'll consider it, but don't tender a horrid request."

"I'd like you to meet a young lady."

Sheridan had just raised his brandy to his lips, and he froze. "What kind of young lady?"

"A possible bride."

"No. Absolutely not." They were going around in circles. Wasn't it time to head up to bed?

"Hear me out." Neville was practically begging.

"Why would I?"

"Hunter and Warwick wed quickly, without any argument, and now, it's your turn."

"They're already busy filling their nurseries, so I fail to see why I have to pitch in. I'm positive they'll supply you with plenty of grandsons."

"You aware of how fickle Fate has been with our bloodline. We can't jeopardize what our ancestors have built."

"You sound as if you're being halfway responsible."

Neville shrugged. "The burden of the title is weighing on me. I can't deny it, and you have to step up."

"By shackling myself to a woman I've never even met?"

"I'd simply like you to visit her. If you like her, we can discuss a contract with her mother, and if you don't, we can look at other families. I'm being deluged with letters from parents about their daughters."

"Well, becoming an earl can make a fellow more popular, but it's a mystery to me why any sane father would give his daughter to me."

"You're more suitable now because *I* am more important. People are knocking down my door to inquire about you."

Sheridan sipped his drink, staring at Neville over the rim of the glass. He was rattled again by the fact that his father was older. He viewed Neville as a sort of god who floated above mortals, but no. He was very human, and he was aging.

Apparently, Sheridan was a weak, fickle creature. Neville sought a favor, and he was suddenly dying to oblige him, but he managed to say, "I'd be an awful husband."

"Probably," Neville agreed, "but you can't keep sailing forever. You can't keep boarding ships and fighting pirates."

"I know."

"Have I ever asked you to do anything for me before? Ever?"

"Not that I can recall."

"I'm asking this: I would like you to travel to the country to be introduced to her. You can spend a few days and discover if a bond might develop."

"If lightning struck, and I realized I couldn't live without her, what then?"

"Then we'd enter into marital negotiations."

"I like being a bachelor," Sheridan caustically said. "It's been the defining aspect of my existence. I'm a spoiled, rich cad who never thinks of anyone but myself. I'd be hideous at matrimony."

"I never wanted to wed either, but men of our class have to break down eventually. If we didn't, how would we continue to rule the world? We'd have no sons to come after us."

Sheridan sat for several minutes, gazing into the flames. His mood was low, and he was feeling poorly. His physical condition was annoying. It was satisfying to contemplate a change that would slow his life down.

And if he married, but determined later on that he couldn't abide domesticity, he could pack his bags and take to the High Seas again. That's how sailors escaped when they couldn't tolerate what was happening. They ran away to their first love: the ocean.

He couldn't tamp down his curiosity. "How do you know the family?"

"I was acquainted with the father as a schoolboy, but he passed on recently. I met one of his daughters too, and I was quite charmed by her. It's the mother who wrote to me, and I told her we'd notify her when you were next in port. Are you *in port?*"

Sheridan pondered for an eternity. Why not? It wasn't as if he was being forced to propose. It wasn't as if he had to commit to any action. It wasn't as if a leg-shackle was about to fetter him. He could socialize with the blasted girl and form an opinion. Where was the harm in it? What if she turned out to be perfect?

"What's her name?" he asked.

"Aurora. Miss Aurora Newton. She has a fine dowry, with their estate of Riverglen being given to her husband once she's wed. If you like her, you could have a wife with hardly having had to search, and you'd receive her property, so you could retire immediately and settle down."

It was a pretty thought, and it niggled at a spot buried deep inside him. He'd grown up with his rampaging brothers, and he'd always mocked the notion of family, home, and hearth, but secretly, he'd assumed it would be wonderful to belong somewhere, to have people counting on him.

In the past, when had he ever had that?

"Would you do this for me, Sheridan?" his father asked. "Please?"

Neville appeared particularly woeful, and Sheridan couldn't keep himself from saying, "Yes, I'll go, but I won't make any promises. You can't raise any expectations on their end, and it has to be my decision. If I don't like her, that will be that. You have to swear you won't nag or try to push me into it."

"I won't nag or push, and if you don't like her, we'll find another candidate who's better. I have a desk full of letters you can read. We'll choose someone with scarcely any effort at all."

"Not bloody likely," Sheridan muttered.

"Could you call on them next week? You can get the lay of the land, then journey to Swindon for my party. May I write and tell the mother you're coming?"

Sheridan took a breath to calm his racing pulse. He was twenty-eight, and adult men *married*. He was no different or more special than any other fellow. It was time to put away childish things and proceed into the future. Yet if he was truly amenable, why did he feel as if he was suffocating?

"Yes, it can be next week," he said. "You may write and inform her I'm about to arrive."

Chapter Five

"I have exciting news."

"What is it?"

Aurora Newton stared at her mother, Millicent, who was lying on her fainting couch and reading her afternoon mail. Millicent was a dedicated hypochondriac who, after experiencing the littlest twinge or cough, was convinced she was dying. She was hale and healthy though, so her worries were preposterous.

She never left her bedchamber, and whenever she made an attempt, she instantly claimed she was too anxious and dizzy to carry on. She'd slither back to her fainting couch as quickly as she could. Her behavior created enormous burdens, particularly for the servants who had to lug every meal and bath up and down the stairs, simply because she refused to exit her room.

"I've heard from Lord Swindon," Millicent told her, "and his son will visit us."

"Which one?"

"Sheridan. The ship's captain."

"The older ones have married then?" Aurora asked.

"Yes, they've been snatched up already."

There had been brief notices in the London newspaper that Hunter and Warwick Stone had wed, but Millicent had insisted they might not be true. Aurora had deemed the opinion to be idiotic. Lord Swindon was hardly the sort to falsify a nuptial announcement.

"Their swift marriages are so unfair," Millicent said. "They didn't give girls like you a chance to grab one of them. At least Sheridan is still available. We should be glad for small favors."

"I don't care that I didn't have a shot at the oldest brother. I wouldn't have liked to ever be a countess."

Her mother tsked with annoyance. "Don't be silly. Every female in the kingdom dreams of being a countess."

"Not me."

"Even if you're reduced to catching the younger brother, there is never a detriment to joining an earl's family."

Aurora wasn't overly interested in matrimony. The whole notion was tiresome, and men were such tedious creatures. Who would want one of them as a husband?

Apparently, there were numerous foul physical acts a bride had to perform as a wife, and she couldn't imagine it. Then again, a young lady married. It couldn't be avoided, and she was twenty-two. If she put it off much longer, she'd be declared a spinster and the opportunity would pass her by.

"Miles won't like Captain Stone to bluster in," Aurora said.

Millicent waved away the comment, as if Miles was irrelevant. "He'll get over it."

"That's easy for you to say. You'll be languishing up here in your room, while *I* will have to deal with him as he pouts and struts with offense."

"If he grows too petulant, send him up. I'll talk to him."

"Yes, I'm certain that will have him shaking in his boots."

Miles Bernard was a fixture in the family, but he wasn't family. Decades earlier, his father and hers had been school chums. His father had perished when Miles was a boy, and her father, Oscar, had been named his guardian. He'd come to their home of Riverglen as an adolescent, and he'd never departed.

As the years had sped by, and Millicent had failed to deliver a son, Oscar had started to view Miles as his son. Miles had gleefully leapt into the role, and once he was an adult, he'd become the estate agent. He ran the huge property and managed their finances, having shrewdly wedged himself into a position where he was indispensable.

In her father's Last Will, Oscar had placed Riverglen in a trust, and he'd arranged for it to go to his son-in-law, with him figuring that Aurora or her sister, Caroline, would wed Miles. Miles was counting on an engagement, but so far, Aurora and Caroline hadn't obliged him.

Caroline had ruined herself, then had been banished to France in disgrace, so if he was to ever receive Riverglen, Aurora had to agree to be his bride. The plan had been delayed by Caroline and her father dying. Aurora had been in mourning and not in any condition to contemplate a betrothal, so she'd evaded the marital noose, but things were back to normal. She had to proceed—or not.

Miles had just turned thirty-five, so he was impatient, but she hadn't exactly been in a hurry. If she could find a better candidate, she thought she might let him sneak in and seize Miles's spot. She supposed she was a bit of a romantic at heart, and she'd like to be swept away by a handsome knave, but the only fiancé ever offered to her was steady, boring Miles Bernard.

After Millicent had learned that Neville Stone had inherited his title, she'd immediately contacted him about a possible match between Aurora and one of his sons.

Millicent hadn't mentioned the overture to anyone but Aurora. Aurora hadn't breathed a word either, so Miles wasn't aware of Millicent's plotting. He had such high hopes of glomming onto Aurora, so he could be a landed gentleman. If it didn't occur, he'd never recover from the shock.

"When will Captain Stone arrive?" Aurora asked.

"On Wednesday."

"So soon? It's in two days!"

"Yes, so the housekeeper must speak with me. We have to make sure the manor and grounds are spectacular. We'll open the blue bedroom suite for him, so he can look out over the park. That should impress him."

Aurora was already feeling exhausted over the brouhaha that was about to ensue. "What if I don't like him? Will you act as if it's the Middle Ages and force me into it?"

"Actually, *he* gets to decide. If you charm him—and I'm positive you can—he'll propose. If you don't, he'll head to London and choose some other lucky girl."

Aurora scowled ferociously. "Why should it be up to him? What about what I want?"

"It's always up to the man, Aurora. You have to accept that fact, or you'll have a very difficult time being a wife."

"What shall I tell Miles?"

"You'll think of something."

"You toss every problem in my lap. It would be nice if you could pitch in for once."

Her mother frowned. "Who do you imagine runs this monstrosity of a house?"

"Me and the housekeeper? If Captain Stone shows up, you might have to come down to greet him. He'll expect to see you sitting at the supper table."

"Well, of course, I'll come down. Why wouldn't I?"

Aurora gaped at her mother. The ridiculous woman hadn't left her bedchamber in months. Or had it been years? She'd attended her husband's funeral, but other than that, Aurora couldn't remember when she'd last stepped outside.

Millicent was like a ghost, like a fairy. At forty, she was still beautiful, her hair blond, her blue eyes clear and bright, but she was thin to the point of being gaunt. When she walked, she seemed to float, her robe dragging behind her, so she could have been a tragic character in a gothic melodrama.

"You'll have to socialize with Captain Stone," Aurora said. "I can't entertain him on my own. If you don't put in an appearance, he'll assume we have a madwoman locked in the attic."

"I'm not mad," her mother said. "I'm ill."

Aurora sighed with aggravation. "Will there be anything else? I should get on with my day."

"Has there been any news from Sophia?"

"No. Miles might hire an investigator to check on her."

"I hope she hasn't suffered a mishap."

Aurora scoffed. "You liar. If she and the baby vanished, you'd be delighted."

"Don't be absurd. Caroline's baby is my granddaughter and your niece. Why would I want that?"

"Why would you, Mother? There's a question for you to ponder. Don't forget that I was eavesdropping when Caroline's predicament was revealed. I overheard you apprising Father that you were shamed to the marrow of your bones. You were elated when Father kicked her out."

"It was the only viable solution. You remember how insolent she was being, so she couldn't have remained here. Not with such a scandal brewing."

"You can't claim you're on pins and needles, wondering where Sophia is. I'll never believe you're concerned."

Suddenly, the door slammed open, being pushed so forcefully that it whipped around and crashed into the wall. Aurora and her mother jumped, and when Aurora saw who had barged in, she blinked and blinked, being certain she was hallucinating.

"Sophia?" she finally sputtered. "Is it really you?"

"Yes, Cousin Aurora, it's me. I'm betting I've surprised you."

"Why would I be surprised? Welcome home!"

"Am I welcome?" Sophia smiled an evil smile that threatened all sorts of retribution, then she altered it into a semblance of cordiality and settled it on Millicent. "Hello, Cousin Millicent. Let me tell you where I've been."

Millicent nearly slid off her couch onto the rug. "Have you . . . you . . . brought the baby?"

"Yes," Sophia said, "I've brought her, and she and I are staying."

Aurora swallowed down a gasp. Captain Stone was about to visit, so they couldn't have Caroline's bastard on the premises. What would he think?

"The child is here?" Aurora asked, feeling as if she might faint.

"Yes. Do you have a problem with that?"

Sophia advanced on Aurora, and she was so angry that Aurora hurriedly said, "No, I don't have a problem with it."

"Good." Sophia whirled on Millicent. "How about you, Millicent? Do you have a problem with it?"

"No!" Millicent looked as if she'd crunched down on broken glass. "I'm absolutely thrilled."

"Good again," Sophia said. "It appears we understand one another."

With that, she spun and stormed out.

"Where have you been?"

"Where would you suppose? In France."

Sophia glared caustically at Aurora.

It was evening already, and they were seated at the supper table in the dining room and eating their meal. They were the only two present. Miles hadn't staggered in, and Millicent never did. Emily and Pierre were in the nursery and being fed there, with a housemaid tending them.

Pierre had been incensed by the arrangement. He was ten, but he didn't view himself as a boy, and he didn't like being treated like one. She'd whispered that he had to always watch Emily, to be sure she was safe. It wasn't that Sophia didn't trust her cousins, but she *didn't* trust them.

Caroline had been banished, with her parents declaring her a disgrace to women everywhere, and as far as Sophia could see, her mother hadn't mellowed in that opinion. Sophia hated to be suspicious, but she was terrified she might fail to focus someday and swiftly find that Emily had been delivered to an orphanage or put up for adoption.

The realization was infuriating, and it had imbued her with the courage she needed to track down Emily's father. If it killed her, she would locate the rich, obnoxious oaf and nag at him to pitch in and raise Emily. Until that moment arrived, she'd have to be on guard.

She was trying to be glad she was home. She'd returned, like a wandering nomad, but in the interval she'd been away, nothing much had changed except that Caroline and her father were deceased. Millicent was still locked in her bedroom and pretending she was sick. Aurora was still princess of the manor, as gorgeous, snooty, and exasperating as ever.

Miles was still in residence too, a fixture who had established such deep roots they could probably never be dug out. Sophia was twenty, Aurora twenty-two, and Miles thirty-five, so he was old enough to be their father. He acted like he was too. He bossed them constantly and chastised them over how they comported themselves.

When Caroline had been alive, she and Sophia had bristled over his officious, conceited conduct, but he'd been Oscar's favorite, so he'd ambled along on a very loose leash. Oscar was gone now, and Miles was in charge, but without Oscar to peek over his shoulder and rein in his worst excesses, there was no predicting how awful he'd grow to be.

She should have felt sorry for him. He'd given his entire life to the Newton family, with the expectation that he'd wed a Newton daughter and be a landed gentleman, but Fate hadn't cooperated. Caroline had gotten herself ruined and had died. Aurora was in no hurry to be a bride, and Oscar hadn't included any bequests to Miles in his Last Will.

He could have named Miles as his heir outright, but apparently, he hadn't completely believed Miles would take care of Aurora and Millicent. Aurora's union with him would guarantee he was bound to protect and support them. It wouldn't be left to Miles's discretion; he'd have a duty imposed by marriage.

He wasn't having any luck though. He and Aurora were both still single, and he had such a massive ego. Aurora's lack of haste had to be galling.

"You know, Aurora," she said, "I'll eventually learn what happened to my rent and my stipend."

"What are you talking about?"

Aurora stared at her, looking innocent as a lamb, but she was an adept liar. It was difficult to deduce if she was genuinely confused.

Her cousin was very beautiful. She resembled Millicent exactly, just as Caroline had: slender, lithe, ethereal. With her blond hair and blue eyes, she was too striking for words, and men drooled over her.

She exuded an air of woe and distress, as if she was on the verge of collapse, as if she needed a strong knight to hover close by to steady her. Sophia supposed she'd inherited the trait from her mother. Millicent exuded the same despairing air, but she'd elevated it to an absurd level where she'd convinced herself she couldn't stand on her own two feet.

"After Oscar died," Sophia said, "our money stopped."

"My goodness. I had no idea."

"Really? I wrote you a dozen times, begging for help."

"We didn't receive any letters."

"Were you hoping to leave me stranded in France so I couldn't bring Emily home?"

Aurora huffed with offense. "What a perfectly ridiculous notion. Why would I be upset? She's my dead sister's child. She's welcome here."

"I intend to hold you to that promise."

"In the past, you were such a fun girl, but while you were away, you became angry and harsh."

"If you had the slightest clue of what I've endured recently, you wouldn't be quite so annoying. I'm not the little brat I was when I slithered off to France. I've grown up since then, and you cross me at your peril."

Aurora frowned. "You just proved my point. You always had a penchant for the dramatic, and now, you're on the verge of hysteria. You should figure out a method to calm your surly mood. It's so unnatural and unladylike."

"Yes, I'll begin working on it immediately. Thank you for the advice."

Evidently, they'd bickered enough. They started eating. A pair of footmen lurked behind them, and their ears were probably burning. They'd be eager to run down to the kitchen to gossip with the rest of the staff.

Sophia didn't know if anyone was aware of why Caroline had skulked off to France. That sort of thing frequently occurred—a daughter suddenly vanishing. People pretended they couldn't guess why, but it was always for the same reason: A cad had misbehaved with a maiden.

There had been no unique aspect to Caroline's situation, except that she'd perished during her exile.

Sophia peeked up at Aurora, and the silence was too oppressive, so she struggled to find a topic they could discuss that wouldn't cause a quarrel.

"How has your mother been?" she asked.

"The same."

"And how is Miles? Where is he anyway?"

"I can't imagine. I thought he was joining us."

As if she'd conjured him by mentioning his name, he burst in and marched straight to the head of the table. It could seat ten comfortably, so she and Aurora were sitting across from each other at the end. He was a man, so of course, he assumed he should lord himself over them.

She studied him and couldn't keep from comparing him to her hero and champion, Captain Stone, who'd been tall, dashing, and handsome. He'd swept into her life and had fixed what was wrong. He'd been possessed of every stellar attribute: power, authority, generosity, kindness, intellect, and an astute ability to manage and mend any dicey dilemma.

In contrast, Miles was short, plain, chubby, petty, arrogant, and obnoxious. He was only thirty-five, but his brown hair was mostly grey and thinning on the top. He tried to distract from it with a bold set of muttonchops that covered most of his cheeks, but his face was too round, so the extra facial hair made him look like a fat squirrel.

His grey eyes were the most disturbing. They were steely and cold, assessing her in a dismissive way that was exasperating.

He believed he was smarter than she was, more important than she was, but in reality, they'd both been reared as wards of Oscar Newton, and Sophia's bloodline was much higher than his. She'd never understood why he acted so superior, but then, it was Oscar's fault for treating him like a favored son.

His pomposity had always irritated her, but it had blossomed into full-on loathing. He ought to be careful with her. Her temper was on such a fine edge that, if he was an ass to her, she truly couldn't predict how she might respond.

"Sorry I'm late," he said as a footman rushed over to pull out his chair. "Sophia! When I heard you were back, I was astounded. Where have you been? We've been expecting you for months."

"Have you?" she snidely asked.

He chuckled, his tone snide too. "The same old Sophia, I see. You were such a child when you sailed for France. I had hoped your sojourn might have smoothed over your more unpleasant impulses."

"I don't suppose you'd like to explain what happened to my rent and my allowance."

"First of all, it was Caroline's rent and allowance. Not yours. Second of all, why would you pose that question? Your stipend was sent regularly, although after Caroline passed away, I considered stopping it, but I didn't. I don't particularly like you, but I wouldn't have stranded you in a foreign country."

"Yes, you've been a veritable saint through the entire affair."

"What took you so long to return?" he asked. "Caroline has been dead for ages, yet you chose to tarry."

"Since I had no funds, my trip was a tad more hazardous than I had anticipated."

"Whatever do you mean? What became of the money? From how you're glowering, it appears you never received it."

Sophia scoffed with disgust. Miles was lying like a rug.

"I didn't *receive* it," she fumed, "because you never sent it. I'll dig up the proof too, and when I have, you'd better watch out. I'm not the naïve ninny I was when I was here before. I've learned how the world works, and I can be especially vengeful when vengeance is required."

Miles shared a conspiratorial glance with Aurora, then he snorted with annoyance. "If the funds never arrived, then I must presume some shrewd Frenchman snatched my letters, and he's a lot richer than he was previously."

"You'll pretend your letters were stolen?"

"It certainly sounds like it."

"And what about the letters *I* wrote to Millicent and Aurora? I begged for help over and over again. I could barely scrape together the coin to bury Caroline, let alone pay my passage across the Channel. Will you claim a sneaky Frenchman stole the ones I mailed in your direction too? The fellow must have been quite devious."

Miles shrugged. "The post is so unreliable. I can't fathom why you'd blame me for any missing correspondence."

Sophia stared at him, stared at Aurora. They stared back blandly, as if they'd plotted out her future and knew she wouldn't like it. In another year, when she was twenty-one, she'd be free of Millicent's custody and control. For the moment, Millicent had a legal duty to support her, but after that?

She'd like to assume Millicent wouldn't cast her to the winds of fate, and she probably wouldn't—if the decision was left up to her. But Millicent never emerged from her bedchamber. If Miles evicted Sophia, if he sold her into indenture, if he locked her in a convent or a mental asylum, she might vanish, and Millicent would never realize she had.

Hadn't Sophia earned a bit of a reward by accompanying Caroline to France? She'd stayed by her cousin's side, had tended her through thick and thin, but no one was grateful, and their disdain underscored her need to find a situation for herself. It would have to include Pierre and Emily.

The Newton family didn't want Emily, and there was no guarantee Sophia could convince her toplofty father to take her. She'd never met the man and couldn't count on him riding to Emily's rescue. Then and there, she resolved to spend every second implementing some plans, and they had to carry her far from Riverglen.

What were her options? Maybe she could drum up a beau and wed. Or maybe she could land a position as secretary to a noblewoman or . . . or . . . as a teacher at a girl's school. Yes, perhaps she could teach! Or maybe she could persuade Emily's father to hire her to be Emily's governess. Could that be the solution to her dilemma?

"Would you excuse me?" she said. She tossed down her napkin and pushed back her chair. "I seem to have lost my appetite."

She started out, and Miles called to her, "You brought a French boy with you. And the baby. They'll be your responsibility, so don't pester the staff to assist you with them. They have other chores."

Sophia answered without stopping. "Trust me, Miles, I wouldn't permit any of you to be within a thousand feet of either of them."

Aurora piped in with, "Could we not fight?"

If Miles replied to her, Sophia didn't hear him. She walked out of the room and down the hall, and she bristled with frustration and regret.

She'd thought she could return to Riverglen and things might have changed for the better. She'd told herself her horrid memories were exaggerated, but the place was just as awful as she recollected, and it wasn't *her* place.

What was she going to do?

Miles shooed the servants out, and he was silent until they'd vanished, then he smirked at Aurora. "It sounds as if Sophia suffered many difficulties in France, so I'm stunned she made it back, but then, she always was incredibly resourceful."

"You shouldn't be so cruel to her," Aurora said. "She's Mother's ward, and Millicent has a duty to her."

"Not for much longer. She'll be twenty-one very soon, and we'll be shed of her."

"Why must we be shed of her? She's kin, and she's a female with no dowry or prospects. It's a dreadful conundrum. I feel sorry for her, and I've never comprehended the animosity you harbor toward her."

"She's never been civil to me, and she's too impertinent. I shouldn't have to tolerate her insolence. In my view, your father was too lenient with her, and I have been too. Now, as a final affront for our many kindnesses, she's dragged home Caroline's bastard. How am I to assess such a scandalous circumstance?"

"Our having the baby here doesn't affect you at all. It's not as if it's your child or your niece. We'll deal with it."

Miles was shocked by Aurora's comments. Normally, she agreed with him on every issue. She didn't argue or complain. He was in charge of the estate and the finances, having been Oscar's most cherished ward, so she was easy to manipulate. She never questioned him, never countermanded, never opposed him.

He didn't own the property though, and her mother was ostensibly in charge. Yet Millicent was completely incompetent and never exercised any authority, so Miles had free rein to carry on without her interference, and he blustered forward unimpeded.

In reality, Millicent could fire him and hire a different manager. Not that she realized she could. He was so indispensable that the notion had never occurred to her, but he wasn't safe. He might have been on an untethered raft and careening down a river. The sole way he'd truly be protected was to wed Aurora. Then his spot would be secure.

"You're being a tad snotty this evening," he said, but he smiled to cut the sting of his criticism.

"I've been thinking about Sophia, about her being alone in France, with Caroline deceased and the baby to feed. I'm very impressed with how she maneuvered through the debacle, and I'm embarrassed over how she's been treated."

He sighed dramatically. "We've debated this frequently, dear. Sophia isn't family. She doesn't deserve any special consideration from us."

"She *is* family, Miles. She's my cousin."

"Your very distant cousin." He reached over and patted her hand. "We've supported her for a whole decade. Isn't that enough? Will she be a drain forever?"

"She's a nuisance, but she's not a drain."

"We should have your mother arrange a marriage for her."

"I wonder if Sophia would like that." Aurora frowned and pondered, then she said, "Who would agree to have her? She doesn't have a dowry, and she's feisty and obstinate, which husbands never like to observe in a wife. It would be hard to find the right fellow."

"Your mother could pick a suitable candidate. I'm sure of it. Perhaps we could chip in a few pounds as a dowry. There's probably a farmer nearby who would jump at the chance."

Usually, he wouldn't waste a penny on Sophia, but Riverglen would be his shortly. Once he'd slipped a ring on Aurora's finger, *he* would decide who resided with him and who didn't.

Sophia didn't respect Miles, didn't show him any deference, and she could never mind her manners. He wouldn't have such a harpy in the house. There was the added benefit too of getting even with her for her many insults.

She and Caroline had never been polite or submissive to Miles, and he was very petty. He never forgot a slight or snub, and he retaliated for any transgression. If he could shackle her to an oaf she loathed, an oaf who would abuse her and crush her spirit, he would celebrate that ending.

"This has been a long day," Aurora said, and she stood. "I think I'll head up to bed."

"It's only eight o'clock. I thought we'd read by the fire."

"Maybe tomorrow. I'm too tired tonight."

He bit down a churlish retort. With each passing month, she was acting more insolent. She knew what her father had intended. As a reward for Miles's devotion, he would wed Aurora and become the owner of Riverglen. No one had ever worked more diligently to earn such a gift.

He was enraged that the blasted man hadn't bequeathed it to Miles directly. He'd promised he would, and it would have solved every problem. If Riverglen was his, he could have commanded Aurora to proceed. If she'd refused, he could have threatened to marry someone else, then she and her mother would have had to leave the estate so his bride could move in. That possibility would have yanked her to her senses quickly enough.

But no, Oscar had tied them into a desperate knot that couldn't be unraveled unless he and Aurora walked down the aisle. She was being so cruel, so selfish and juvenile, and his patience was exhausted. How could he force her to hurry?

"I guess I'll see you in the morning then," he said. "Will you join me for breakfast?"

"If I rise in time, I will."

He pushed himself to his feet, having to be courteous and stand as she waltzed out. As she reached the door, he sat down again, prepared to finish his meal. She didn't wish to eat, but he wasn't about to starve simply because she was being a shrew.

"Oh, by the way," she suddenly said, "Mother has company coming on Wednesday."

His shoulders slumped. Millicent never had guests. What would be the point? She wouldn't drag herself downstairs to greet them.

"Who is it?" he asked.

"It's one of Father's friends. Actually, it's his son. He'll be traveling through the area, and his father wanted him to stop by. Mother felt pressured into being gracious."

He tsked with aggravation. "I hope you'll assume the role of hostess. You're aware that your mother won't socialize with him. Don't make me pick up the slack. I have no desire to fraternize with a stranger she shouldn't have invited."

"I'll be delighted to pitch in. He's a ship's captain, so he'll be interesting."

"Yes," Miles sneeringly said, "he'll overwhelm you with tales about navigation and waves."

"Well, it will be a nice change. The neighbors can be so boring, and I'm excited to have a fresh face to entertain me."

She swept out, and as he dug into his food, it dawned on him that she'd deftly avoided another discussion about setting their wedding date. He grumbled with frustration. Why allow her to quibble and delay? It was autumn already, and a Christmas wedding would be lovely.

At breakfast, he'd raise the suggestion, and he wouldn't let her slither off until he had a firm commitment. His future was on the line, and he'd been much too accommodating. She had to clearly learn that lesson.

Chapter Six

"It was kind of you to come."

"Your mother caught me at just the right moment. I returned to England a few days ago. If she'd written a bit earlier or later, she might have missed me."

Sheridan smiled at Aurora Newton, realizing he was pleasantly surprised. She was beautiful, in an airy, almost carefree way. She was blond and blue-eyed, like most every British girl, but she exuded an aura of languor that was very sensual in its appeal. She seemed to float rather than walk, and he kept leaning toward her, as if she was about to fall and he'd need to prop her up.

When his father had asked him to visit Riverglen, he'd assumed it would be a huge waste of time, but so far, he hadn't had to endure any shocks.

He'd been in residence for several hours, and it had been a quiet arrival. Miss Newton had been the only one to greet him, so he hadn't had to suffer a room full of grouchy, elderly aunties. Nor had her mother made an appearance, which was fine by him. He was in no mood to charm a mother.

The staff had gotten him settled, then he'd joined Miss Newton in the front parlor. She'd offered to give him a tour, and the suggestion of a stroll had been wise. They hadn't had to linger on the sofa, trying to figure out what to discuss.

The manor wasn't the grandest house in the kingdom, but it was quite acceptable: three stories high, constructed of a sand-colored brick from a local quarry. The driveway was swept, the lawns swathed, the gardens manicured. The servants were capable and busy, smartly-dressed and courteous to a fault.

It looked well-run and well-tended, indicating that the family had money and spent it shrewdly. He was very rich himself and was accustomed to quality and opulence, and he was struggling to envision himself cozily shackled to her, sleeping in the master suite or eating in the dining room, but he couldn't picture it.

If he had to wed and retire to the country, Riverglen might be the ideal spot. Then again, the tedium and silence might drive him mad.

They were behind the manor, ambling down a groomed path. It was a crisp autumn afternoon, so they were bundled against the weather. Her nose was rosy from the cold, her cheeks too, so she was even more alluring.

"Why is the estate called Riverglen?" he asked her.

"There's a river, and apparently, there used to be a glen. The river wound around it to form a grassy meadow, but that was in the ancient past. Now, there's just a river with no glen attached."

He chuckled. "It's an exquisite property."

"I've always thought so."

"Are you happy here? Or do you constantly wish you could move to London?"

"We travel to town occasionally, and I enjoy it, but Riverglen is home to me. I know the neighbors and enjoy watching the seasons change."

It was an intriguing response. He had friends who'd wed rural maidens, only to discover that they didn't want to remain in the country. They'd presumed matrimony would be a means to escape their fetters, and it created strife in the unions.

If Sheridan ever broke down and wed, he would never bicker. If he had to marry in order to garner a home for himself, the place would have to be his peaceful sanctuary, his flawless castle, and he would be the king of it.

He switched topics. "My father apprised me that your father has passed away."

"Yes, last winter."

"Who is managing the estate for you? I wouldn't imagine it's you and your mother."

"We have a land agent. Miles Bernard? He was orphaned as a boy, and my father was his guardian. He was raised with us."

"How old is he?"

"Thirty-five."

"Is he competent? Are you satisfied with his efforts?"

"I'm satisfied enough. I've never really been interested in the finances or the property. Father never deemed it appropriate for a female to involve herself, and Miles loves being in charge."

Her comments posed two issues, one difficult and one refreshing.

The thorny one had to do with Mr. Newton's ward, Miles Bernard, who'd had free rein for years. How would he cope with Miss Newton bringing in a husband to take over?

Mr. Bernard would have to be terminated, but he was probably viewed as family. If Sheridan blustered in and sent him packing, he would stir controversy and generate hostilities.

The encouraging one was her declaring herself to be a modest woman who deferred to the men in her life. She wasn't like that brazen tart, Sophia Cantwell, whom he'd met in France. Miss Newton recognized her lower role, that she should submit to a man's advice and guidance. She would never sass, trick, or deceive a fellow. She definitely wouldn't ever waltz about in trousers, with a pistol in her pocket!

As the memory of Miss Cantwell wafted by, he tamped down a grin. She'd been a fascinating piece of work, and he wondered what had happened to her. Despite himself, he'd relished her flighty conduct and her penchant for trouble.

Maybe *she* was the sort of spouse he needed. Maybe, instead of pursuing a female who would never rock a boat and who would bore him to tears, he should be searching for a feisty, spirited vixen. Wouldn't he be more content with that type of bride?

He shook away the ridiculous notion. He was at Riverglen to assess Miss Newton for a possible engagement, and he was a very British male. He understood the kind of woman who would make a proper wife for a man of his station, and most likely, Miss Newton would turn out to be perfect.

He had no idea how a nuptial visit was supposed to unfold, but he'd never been one to dither and debate. He gazed at her and said, "Do you know why I'm here?"

She smirked. "Should I pretend to be confused and claim I can't fathom why? Or should I reply honestly?"

"I prefer honesty."

"Well, then, I will tell you that my mother wrote to your father to inquire about a match between us."

"I'm glad you're aware of that. I didn't want to tiptoe around you, insisting I'd come to examine the flowers."

"Are you ready to settle down, Captain Stone? You're a sailor, and I've always heard they have a hard time being landlocked."

It was his utmost concern, but his qualms were his own business. "I hadn't thought I was ready, but with my father's elevation to earl, our situation has changed. I don't have the choices I had previously."

"May I brashly ask how many young ladies you'll be interviewing? Or is that too forward?"

"It's very forward, but I don't mind answering. Yours is the only introduction my father scheduled, but that's because I just arrived home."

She laughed prettily. "So you didn't rush here due to my reputation as an irresistible goddess?"

He laughed too. "Will it hurt your feelings if I confess that I don't know anything about you? My father was acquainted with yours when they were boys at school, and I guess he's met your sister too. He was quite taken with her."

Her smile slipped. "Yes, I had a sister, but she died last winter too."

"I'm so sorry. It appears you've had a year of losses."

"Yes, it was a terrible year, but then, life is never easy, is it? There are no guarantees that it will roll along in a smooth way."

He couldn't argue with that. His leg was aching, the chilly air making it throb. He couldn't recollect a period when he'd felt hale and fit.

"How shall we spend our week together?" he asked. "What would you suggest? I've never participated in an appointment like this before. Are there rules we have to follow?"

"I don't believe there are any rules. We should just chat, share stories, and decide if we like each other."

"That sounds like a plan, and if we decide we *don't* like each other, can we agree to part as friends? If we determine we wouldn't suit, I would hate for this to conclude awkwardly."

"You are wise to request it," she said.

"I'll leave next Wednesday. Can you put up with me for seven whole days?"

"I shall try to bear up, and to spur us into some vigorous socializing, I've arranged a supper on Friday night with some neighbors and the vicar."

He grimaced; he was not pious. "I promise not to offend him with my heathen habits."

"And Saturday, we'll have a party—with dancing. Are you a dancer?"

Normally, he loved to dance, but with his leg in such a painful condition, he doubted he could perform the required steps. He didn't mention it though. He'd save that explanation for another day.

"Yes, I'm a dancer," he said, "and a country house revel will be a marvelous treat for me. I'm out of England so often that I haven't attended one in ages."

They were headed toward the barns. He was eager to walk through the stables, to see how the horses were tended, to check the cleanliness of the stalls. A lot of problems at a property could be hidden, but not a messy horse stall, so a tour would provide vital information.

They were passing a row of small cottages that looked as if they might be lodging for the upper-level servants. Suddenly, from inside one of them, there was shouting, curses hurled, and to his great astonishment, a gunshot blasted.

"What the devil?" he muttered.

"Oh, dear," Miss Newton said. "That might be Miles and Sophia, but I hope it isn't. I'd be mortified to have you meet them when they're fighting."

Sheridan dashed off to investigate, not pausing at the name *Sophia.* The reference simply didn't register.

Sophia was standing in the cottage Miles used as his office. It was at the end of a row of houses, where the butler and housekeeper resided. He also had a suite in the manor where he lived like an anointed king, and he'd claimed some of the nicest rooms, assuming it would add to his power and authority.

The servants were wary of him because no one was certain of his role. Yes, he was the estate agent, but was he a fiancé? So far, the answer was *no,* and the staff quietly grumbled that he was merely an up-jumped orphan.

She had the account ledger on his desk, and she was perusing the columns of numbers. Miles was an idiot, but he kept the records current, so it was easy to find the date of the final disbursement of the stipend that had been sent to France. It had occurred the week before Oscar's death. None had been mailed after that. She'd also located a copy of a letter he'd written to her French landlord, advising him that the Newton family was relinquishing the cottage and the lease wouldn't be renewed.

Caroline had been dead by then, but Sophia and Emily had still been tenants, yet why would Miles have been concerned over their fate? Why would he have cared if her lodging was yanked away without warning?

He could be very cruel, so it was typical that he'd stopped the money after Oscar died. Her only question was whether Aurora and Millicent were aware of what he'd done. Had he acted on his own? Or had he sought their opinion and received permission? Had they colluded with him to imperil Sophia so Emily could never be brought home?

She didn't want to suppose that was the case, but the possibility created numerous issues with regard to Emily. Sophia had asked Millicent to spend some time with Emily, but she'd refused. Clearly, Millicent was angry that Sophia had returned with Emily, so what now?

She pushed away the aggravating thoughts and focused on Miles. While she was away, he'd had his portrait painted, and it was hanging behind the desk. It was an obnoxious piece of art, with his hand on a silver-tipped cane and a hound at his feet—but he didn't even have a hound!

She was surprised he hadn't hauled it into the manor and hung it over the fireplace in the front parlor, but unfortunately for him, Oscar's portrait was still there. She figured—once he married Aurora—Oscar's picture would be put up in the attic and Miles's displayed instead. He was just that conceited.

The door opened and he blustered in. On witnessing her with her nose buried in the ledger book, he blanched. It was obvious her presence unnerved him.

"Why are you snooping, Sophia?" he demanded as he stomped over. He shoved her away and closed the book with a determined snap.

"I'm simply searching for proof that you cut off my money to strand me in France. I found it too."

He smiled his weaselly smile. "You're not intelligent enough to read a ledger and know what it indicates."

"I'm sure it will astound you to discover that I am absolutely intelligent enough. I also stumbled on the letter you wrote to my French landlord." She waved it at him, then stuck it in the bodice of her dress. "I need to keep it for a few minutes, so I can show it to my guardian. Who would that be? Oh, that's right, it's Millicent. She should be apprised of how I was endangered by you."

"You will not tattle to Millicent about me. I am not an ill-behaved child."

"No, you're an ill-behaved adult."

"You are not welcome in my office. Don't let me catch you in here again."

"Don't worry your pretty little head about it. I'm leaving, and I won't be back."

"You think you're so smart," he fumed.

"Yes, actually, I do think I'm very smart."

"You think you can carry on however you please, but we'll see about that."

Sophia sighed with exasperation. "Don't you ever get tired of being such an ass? You've devoted your whole life to Riverglen, and it's been a losing proposition. Maybe if you were kinder and less exhausting, people would like you."

"I will be lord and master shortly." His teeth were clenched so tightly that she was amazed he didn't crack a tooth.

"Really? When will that transpire? I haven't noticed Aurora being in any rush. Why is that? I would hate to suppose you've waited all this time for nothing."

His temper exploded, so it was immediately evident that she'd crossed a line by mentioning Aurora.

"You're about to be twenty-one," he said, "so I won't have to tolerate you much longer."

"Won't that be a grand day for you?" she blithely retorted.

"You don't realize the power I've accumulated in your absence. I am in complete control, and I can arrange any ending for you."

"Are you threatening me, Miles?"

"Yes, definitely. I could lock you in a convent or send you to a mental asylum, but a better plan would be to have Millicent wed you to a farmer. If you had to live in squalor, with a dozen brats tugging at your skirt, you wouldn't be quite so impertinent."

If she'd been a weak, feckless sort of female, his comment might have alarmed her. A man could implement any horrid conclusion for a woman, and Sophia wasn't exactly in a strong spot. She didn't have any allies either, but if she knew one thing about Miles, it was that he was all talk and braggadocio.

He liked to throw his weight around, but he had no authority over her, and in reality, his status in the world wasn't much different from hers. Not unless he married Aurora. If that never happened, what would become of him?

He had no money or prospects, just as she didn't have any, and she smirked. During her ordeal in France, she'd learned a lot about surviving in desperate circumstances. If he was ever fired and evicted, she would be able to provide him with advice on how to stagger through calamity.

"You don't scare me, Miles," she said, "and it's so annoying when you boss me. Who did you pick on when I was away? There must have been someone. You're a bully, and I wish you'd shift your attention back to whomever you were harassing before I arrived."

She started out, and he said, "Where are you going?"

"I already told you. I'm showing this letter to Millicent."

"You will not speak to Millicent. I forbid it!"

He shouted the remark, and she rolled her eyes. "You *forbid* it? Should we review our situation? I'm not your ward, your cousin, your daughter, your wife, or your sister. You have no connection to me whatsoever. You have no right to order me about, and I have no duty to obey you."

"Give it to me!"

He raced toward her, being in such a hurry that he knocked over a chair, and it crashed to the floor with a loud bang. He grabbed her arm forcefully enough to leave bruises. He wasn't that tall, so he didn't tower over her, but he was portly and wide, so he could jostle her with ease.

He reached for her chest, as if he'd stick his hand inside her dress and retrieve the letter. It would have been a shocking development. She jerked out of his grasp and pulled her pistol out of her pocket.

"Don't touch me ever again," she warned.

At observing her weapon, he flinched and lurched away. "You bloody shrew! What are you thinking? Have you gone stark raving mad?"

"Yes, I'm quite deranged these days," she said.

"You wouldn't dare shoot me!"

"You have no idea what I've endured due to your belligerence, just as you have no idea what I'm capable of perpetrating."

"If you suffered difficulties, it's your own fault. Don't blame me."

"That is the precise reply I could have expected from you."

She had the barrel pointed directly at him, her finger on the trigger. She'd fantasized about murdering him. She'd dreamed about it. She'd gleefully pictured him lying dead at her feet, but apparently, she wasn't a homicidal maniac. She couldn't kill him simply because he was an arrogant prig.

Then again, she'd been angry for an eternity.

She yanked the gun away and aimed at his portrait instead. It was a good second choice, and in her opinion, she was exercising enormous restraint. The bullet hit the target, plunging right through the center of his chest where his black heart would have been located—if he'd had a heart. The frame rocked, and the nail wrenched from the wall, so it fell to the floor, generating another loud crash.

"What have you done!" he shrieked. "You *are* insane. You are! I knew it!"

The room was filled with smoke, and her ears were ringing. Miles looked as if he might burst into tears, and he was so astonished that his knees gave out. He reeled over to a chair and plopped down. She had to admit that she was a tad astonished too, and it had been foolish to lash out in such a juvenile way.

Was it juvenile?

It was behavior a man might have exhibited, and more and more, she thought she should act like a man. If she acted like a woman, she was constantly mocked and maligned.

She wasn't inclined to let Miles regroup and assault her, and she would have marched out, but suddenly, the door was flung open. A large man loomed in, and when she saw who it was, she was so confused that she had to blink over and over to be sure she wasn't hallucinating.

"Captain Stone?" When he answered her, she was astounded by the sound of his voice. She'd been that certain he was an apparition.

"Miss Cantwell?"

In unison, they asked, "What are you doing here?"

He didn't wait for her response. He stomped over and seized her pistol, and when he spoke, there was accusation in his tone. "You haven't changed a bit. Why am I not surprised?"

"I told you in France that men should stop making me angry."

"Yes, but that doesn't explain why you're at Riverglen and shooting your gun."

"This is my home. It's where I live."

"You . . . what?"

Aurora bustled in behind him, and she was very upset. "Sophia! Miles! We have company, and you're carrying on like a pair of spoiled toddlers."

"She shot at me!" Miles whined.

Sophia tsked with offense. "I didn't shoot *at* him. I wanted to, but I controlled myself."

Captain Stone swallowed down an irked chuckle. "Didn't I tell you, when I put you on your ship, that you were not to cause any trouble in England?"

"Are you acquainted with her?" Aurora asked him. "How can that be?"

Sophia ignored her and said to the Captain, "I promised to tamp down my worst impulses, but Miles and I have a bad history, and it seems to be flaring." She frowned at Aurora, then asked him, "Why are you at Riverglen? You can't have been following me. Please swear you're not that mentally unhinged."

"Gad, no, I wasn't following you." The Captain was being rather snotty. "You are the last person who's been on my mind. I came to meet Miss Newton." Without his pausing to wonder if some discretion was warranted, he added, "We're considering whether to engage ourselves."

"Engage yourselves . . . as in get married?" Sophia stammered.

"Yes, as in get married," the Captain admitted.

Sophia couldn't decide who was more rattled by the news: her or Miles. Miles leapt to his feet and said, "Aurora, tell me this isn't true!"

Aurora squealed with dismay, and Captain Stone peered back at her and said, "I'm sorry, Miss Newton. Is our objective meant to be a secret? If so, I didn't realize it was, and I apologize."

"You and Aurora?" Sophia murmured, not able to process the disturbing declaration.

"Ah . . . yes?" he said.

Sophia peeked over at Miles, feeling a wave of unusual sympathy for him. What was Millicent thinking? What was Aurora thinking? How could they have invited Captain Stone without giving Miles fair warning?

Captain Stone wasn't aware of the conflicts that swirled in the Newton household, and Aurora was a coward, so she wasn't about to tarry and clarify what they were. She said, "I should . . . should . . . probably inform Mother that Captain Stone has arrived. And Sophia, she has to hear about this incident. It's really beyond the pale. What if you'd killed Miles?"

Sophia scoffed. "Don't be ridiculous. I didn't even aim at him."

Aurora flitted out, leaving Captain Stone to his own devices. He glared at the spot where she'd been, then he whipped his furious glower to Sophia.

"You and I had better have a little chat," he said.

"As always, Captain, I'm at your service."

He stuck her pistol in his coat, then escorted her toward the door. Miles was over by the desk, a dazed, miserable creature whose world had just been smashed to pieces. Sophia thought she should stay and commiserate. If she didn't, who would?

She was incredibly moved by his wretched expression, but Captain Stone whisked her out of the smoke-filled room without her getting a final glance in Miles's direction.

Chapter Seven

"Talk and talk fast."

Sheridan glared at Miss Cantwell, and the impertinent vixen grinned impishly and asked, "Have you missed me?"

"I'm stunned to have stumbled on you, but why would I have missed you? You're absurd to think I have pondered you a single minute."

He'd dragged her into a nearby barn, and they were huddled in the shadows. She was leaned against the wall, and he was standing in front of her, their proximity setting off sparks. He'd forgotten the attraction that sizzled between them. It was so powerful that it was downright scary.

She was pert and pretty as ever, dressed like the young lady she was, with nary a trouser in sight. With her wearing a green gown, the shade enhanced the color of her eyes so they twinkled with mischief.

Though it was very strange, he was inordinately thrilled to see her again. He'd claimed he hadn't been pondering her, but humiliating as it was to admit, she was always out there on the fringe of his rumination.

He often found himself chuckling over her antics and wondering what had happened to her after they'd parted.

He was delighted to have crossed paths with her, and there was the eeriest sense of destiny in the air, as if the universe had arranged their meeting. She was a magnet, and he was metal, and he wasn't strong enough to evade her steady pull.

Unfortunately, he was at Riverglen to court her cousin, and with her present, the entire visit would be extremely awkward. While he was supposed to be focused on Miss Newton, Miss Cantwell would constantly distract him.

It was simply a fact that, when she was in the room, he couldn't stop staring at her. She fascinated him; she made him laugh, and he could never wait to discover what she might do next. She was a showoff and scalawag who liked to be the center of attention, and when she was placed beside her beautiful, modest cousin, she would completely outshine the other woman.

"You might have told me you were a Newton from Riverglen," he said, as if she'd hidden the bothersome detail for nefarious purposes.

"Why would I have mentioned it? First of all, I'm not a Newton. I'm a Cantwell. And second of all, why would you follow me home? I could have sworn, when you shoved me onto that ship in Boulogne, that you intended for us to separate forever. Now, you've blustered in like an unexpected storm."

He tsked with annoyance. "Have I ever pointed out that you're much too sassy?"

"I seem to remember a complaint like that."

"Well, you are. Sassy, I mean, and would you stick to the subject?"

"Which is . . . ?" she asked.

"Who is that fellow with whom you were fighting and why shoot at him?"

"Why must I keep explaining myself? I didn't shoot *at* him. I deliberately missed."

"Praise be, but who is he, and why were you provoking him?"

"Why would you automatically assume it was my fault? Why can't you consider that he might have been the cause?"

"I know you, Cantwell. If there was a spat brewing, I'm sure you started it."

She blew out a heavy breath, as if he was being ridiculous. "He is the fiend who cut off my money. After I arrived home, I confronted him about it, but he claimed he'd sent it regularly, and it must have been lost in the mail. I was checking the account ledger to verify my suspicions."

"He must really, *really* not like you."

"No, he never has."

She deflated a bit, as if the stress of the moment had rattled her, and she staggered over to a bench and plopped down. She was particularly woebegone, and it had a peculiar effect on him. When he was close to her, he yearned to leap in and assist her in whatever way she required.

"Who is he to you?" he asked. "Is he a relative?"

"No, he's the estate manager, Miles Bernard."

On hearing the name, Sheridan concealed any reaction. He was the man Miss Newton had described when they were walking. He'd run the property for years and, if Sheridan trudged forward and proposed, would have to be evicted.

Mr. Bernard was a short, portly little oaf, and Sheridan already disliked him. He never liked to see a woman abused, and he was incensed on Miss Cantwell's behalf. What sort of man would behave as he had? What sort of man would maliciously put a woman in such jeopardy?

"He and I came here as wards," Miss Cantwell said. "Aurora's father, Oscar, was our guardian when we were children. I'm not of age yet, so Aurora's mother, Millicent, has control of me."

"Ha! She's not doing a very good job."

"No one has ever been able to rein in my impulsive tendencies."

"That, Cantwell, may be the truest words you've ever spoken. Why doesn't Mr. Bernard like you? And don't lie about it. I'll know if you are."

"He's always lorded himself over me, and I can't abide how he struts and preens. I might occasionally be a snot about it."

Sheridan snorted with amusement. "You *might* be? For pity's sake! You shot at him."

"Will you get it through your thick head? I shot at his portrait. Not at him. Did you see that blasted painting? It deserved to be wrecked."

He was gradually sidling over to where she was sitting. He hated to be so far away from her, and it felt as if a rope was drawing him nearer. She peered up at him, looking tired, ill-treated, and very young.

"Mr. Bernard stranded you in France due to your ancient bickering?" Sheridan's tone was incredulous. "I can't accept that version of events."

She gazed up at him, seeming morose and regretful, as if she might confess to fibbing, but instead she said, "Will you betroth yourself to Aurora?"

He couldn't bear to admit his purpose, and she'd be hurt if he was candid, but that notion was patently absurd. He had no connection to her, and they were practically strangers—except that they were more intimately bonded than they should be.

He shrugged. "I have no idea what I intend. I only just rode up the lane, and I was immediately distracted by you almost killing someone."

"There are . . . *issues* here, and I guess—if you're about to wed my cousin—I should shut my mouth. We have a lot of skeletons in our closet, and it wouldn't be appropriate for me to blab about them."

"Nice try, Cantwell, but tell me what's going on. I don't like to be kept in the dark."

"Oh, all right, you big bully." She tsked with exasperation. "My cousin, Caroline, was Aurora's sister."

"She's the one who died in France?"

"Yes. The family was aghast over her ruination, and they were determined to hide it. She's dead, and I've strolled in with her bastard. They're not happy about it."

"Who isn't happy? Miss Newton? Her mother? Mr. Bernard?"

"None of them are happy. Miles planned for me to vanish in France so Emily would vanish with me. It's why he cut off my funds. I haven't figured out if Aurora or her mother were complicit. I haven't had a chance to fully interrogate them."

"Are you sure that's what transpired? You spew the most fantastical stories, and I'm convinced you're exaggerating."

She withdrew a letter that she'd tucked in the bodice of her dress, and she gave it to him so he could read it. After he scanned the contents, he scowled ferociously.

Evidently, her tale was true, but what did the news indicate about Miss Newton? If she wasn't aware of Mr. Bernard's shenanigans, why hadn't she at least been a bit worried about Miss Cantwell's slow return? Shouldn't she have been?

Miss Cantwell was the poor relative, and natural children like Emily were common. If he engaged himself to Miss Newton, did any of the pathetic history matter? Did Miss Newton's possible cruelty matter? Did Miss Cantwell's dilemma matter? Did the baby matter?

If he could become the owner of Riverglen and swiftly get his nursery started, should the problems of a poverty-stricken cousin prevent him from proceeding?

On the spur of the moment, he couldn't decide.

He gave the letter back to her, and she slid it into her gown. Her expression grew even more woeful, and he had to look away. He couldn't abide her distress, and it was clear she had no allies in the house. Should that fact bother him?

"Do you believe me now?" she said.

"Yes, I believe you, and it's obvious you and Emily aren't welcome. You might be better off somewhere else. Have you realized that?"

"Where would I go?" she asked.

There was such a plaintive tone in her voice, and he was greatly moved by it. He rested a comforting hand on the top of her head, as if she were a toddler who'd dropped her candy in the dirt. He shouldn't have touched her though.

Those pesky sparks sizzled again, and he was suffering from the most powerful urge to take her in his arms and kiss away her anguish. Was that to be his constant state when she was near?

The prospect didn't bear contemplating.

She shook him away and said, "I should return to the manor. Aurora will have tattled to her mother. Miles too. I have to put in an appearance and provide my side of the story—as if we're still ten."

He smirked at that. "If I remember correctly, you spin a good yarn."

"Will you come with me? You're a guest, so I shouldn't abandon you in the barn."

She stood quickly, eager to escape, but he was hovering much too close. She stepped around him, and she was off balance, so she tripped slightly and bumped into him. Suddenly, her body was crushed to his all the way down. At the intimate positioning, his own body celebrated.

He could feel her breasts, her flat tummy, her shapely thighs, and lust shot to his loins, a fierce wave of desire pummeling him. How could he be so physically attracted to her? Gad, he didn't even like her!

As if he was observing from a high perch, he was horrified to find himself dipping down and kissing her. He hadn't meant to commit such a folly. Or maybe he had. She generated such bizarre emotions that he couldn't figure out what he wanted from her.

It seemed like the most ordinary thing to kiss her, but it also seemed like the most deranged. What was wrong with him?

In the whole history of kisses, it wasn't all that passionate. He simply brushed his mouth to hers. He didn't linger, so it ended practically before it had begun. As their lips parted, she grinned up at him in such a fetching manner that his heart flip-flopped in his chest.

"Why, Captain Stone," she said, "if I didn't know better, I'd think you were sweet on me."

"You should be so lucky."

"Why would you kiss me? You don't even like me, do you?"

"No, I don't like you, but when I'm around you, I behave like a lunatic."

She laid a palm on the center of his chest, and it set off numerous strange sensations.

His world was a world of men and always had been. There were very few women in it, and those who were never exhibited genuine affection. Displays of fondness were purchased with hard money, in brothels, where a trollop was paid so her customer would presume he was virile and charming.

It was a rare occasion when a female extended honest affection, and the gesture ignited an attack of absurd yearning.

"How long are you staying with us?" she asked.

"Too long probably."

"Will you court my cousin right in front of me? Will I have to watch you?"

"I guess that's my plan."

"Couldn't you have humored me and denied it?" She snickered miserably. "If you're determined to proceed, you shouldn't be dallying with me out in the barn."

"It wasn't my best idea."

"I'm glad you did though. I liked it."

"Well, *I* didn't like it, and I can't imagine what came over me."

"Haven't you heard? I drive men wild with lust."

She laughed, and he laughed too and said, "Yes, I'm sure that's it. You are a vixen of the highest order."

"It's how people always describe me."

He laughed again, then he brazenly kissed her again. He loitered too, holding her tight, inhaling the smell of her hair and skin. There was an aura or scent that hovered about her, and it tantalized him. It called to him on an almost feral level, and he suspected it could get him into loads of trouble.

He drew away and pointed to the house. "Why don't you go inside, so I don't make an even bigger fool of myself."

"Is this you, being foolish? I kind of like it."

"I don't."

They shared a conspiratorial smile, and she said, "Will you walk with me?"

"No. I can't let your family see how I look at you."

"How is that?"

"Like I want to gobble you up. I intend to avoid you for my entire visit."

"I'll avoid you too. After all, I have a reputation to protect."

"What reputation?" he said. "In my view, no one thinks much of you."

"True, but I can't have my status lowered further by you dragging me into dark corners."

"I'll try to restrain myself," he facetiously retorted.

"I appreciate it. I am an innocent maiden—"

"There's nothing innocent about you."

"Despite what you assume, I'm not the sort of female who can be swept away by a handsome cad."

"Go!" He shamelessly put a hand on her bottom and pushed her toward the door. She took a few steps, then stopped to glance at him over her shoulder. She was so delectable, and he said, "I mean it. Get out of here so we're not found together. I only just arrived, and I can't have your family worried that I've been enticed by you."

"What if they ask where you are?"

"Tell them I'm snooping through the stables to discover how they tend their horses. I'll be along directly."

"May I have my pistol?"

"No, now go!"

She bristled, then continued on and quickly vanished. He went over to the bench where she'd been sitting, and he collapsed down on it. He tarried, so his desire could cool, his thoughts calm.

To his great disgust, he was wondering where her bedchamber was located and whether he dared sneak into it. Why did she have such a stunning effect on him? It made no sense.

Women never overwhelmed him. They never drove him to insane heights of yearning, so it was clear Fate was toying with them. He was as superstitious as the next fellow, even more so because he was a sailor.

He believed in portents and signs, and usually, he wouldn't disregard a destiny that was thrown in his path, but he would have no difficulty disregarding *her.*

She was a walking calamity. She was tragedy and drama. She was bad luck, rolled into a pretty package, and he needed to stay as far away from her as possible. She tempted him to madness, but he didn't have to succumb. He was at Riverglen to woo her cousin, and she couldn't interfere with that goal.

He had a marriage to pursue, a bride to consider, a dowry to ponder.

Miss Sophia Cantwell was naught but a distraction, and she couldn't be allowed to divert him a single second.

"I SUPPOSE YOU SHOULD explain yourself."

"I'd be glad to."

Millicent watched as Sophia marched over and handed her a letter. She didn't care what it said and only pretended to read it. The afternoon hours exhausted her, and she wouldn't waste energy refereeing a fight.

They were in her bedroom suite, and she was relaxed on her fainting couch. She'd been trying to nap, but she kept being interrupted.

First, Aurora had blustered in to inform Millicent about the quarrel Sophia had started with Miles. Then Miles had stormed in to complain about the same incident. He'd also demanded to be apprised about Captain Stone, and his haughtiness had been infuriating. He often forgot his place when addressing her.

It was Oscar who'd been determined that Miles marry one of their girls, but Millicent had never thought it was a good idea. Caroline had loathed him and would never have agreed, and Aurora wasn't keen either. She was so beautiful, and she was a wealthy heiress besides. She deserved the chance to be courted by a few dashing swains.

Miles had accused Millicent of duplicity, of ignoring Oscar's final wishes. He'd claimed she would endanger the estate by bringing in a stranger to run it, that he understood the workings of the property better than anyone else could. He'd been so adamant that Millicent had had to feign a weak spell so he'd leave her alone.

Now, Sophia had stomped in, and she was eager to vent her rage about Miles, but Millicent couldn't bear to listen. Sophia was smart, funny, and kind, and when she'd grown up with them, she'd been full of mischief that Caroline had exploited with humorous consequences. Millicent should have liked her more, but she wasn't a very maternal person.

The house had been much quieter after Sophia and Caroline had moved to France, but Sophia was back, and Miles was already having problems with her. Evidently, they would carry on no differently from how they had as children.

Miles was pushing forty. He should have matured and learned how to deal with Sophia, but he was incredibly thin-skinned.

"What do you think of that?" Sophia asked about the letter.

Millicent was fatigued, and she returned it with a languid grace. "What does it say, dear? My eyes hurt, so I can't read it myself."

"When I was in France, Miles cut off my money so I'd be trapped there and unable to travel to England."

"Why would he treat you that way? It seems needlessly cruel."

"I realize you'd like it if Emily had never been born, but did you order him to imperil me?"

Millicent had sporadic meetings with Miles, but she didn't like to chat with him. She didn't *like* him, really, and he could be so officious and domineering. After Oscar had died, she'd advised him to seize the reins and manage things however he pleased. It kept her from having to speak with him on a regular basis.

Had he nagged at her about Sophia's money? She couldn't recall.

"I don't believe he and I discussed you," she said. "I don't remember it anyway, but you can't needle him as if you were still a girl. You especially can't shoot at him with a pistol."

"I didn't shoot *at* him. I shot at his portrait."

"That's as may be, but I can't condone such violence."

"I had planned to murder him, so in my opinion, I exercised considerable restraint."

"You're so adept at justifying your actions."

Sophia looked crestfallen. "Don't you care that I was stranded? Don't you care about what might have happened to me? You're my guardian, aren't you?"

Millicent waved a weary hand. "You're back safe and sound, Sophia. Why harbor a grudge?"

"Why indeed?" Sophia murmured.

A lengthy, morose silence wafted between them, and Millicent said, "I've been contemplating you recently and wondering how your future should unfold."

"Well, that comment makes me shudder."

"We should find you a husband."

"Is this Miles's plot to be rid of me? Or is it yours? Why am I certain it was Miles?"

"He might have mentioned it, but I agree with him. Every young lady weds sooner or later. Wouldn't you like to have a home and family of your own?"

"No, thank you. I can't have them without the husband being included, and I deem men to be fools and fiends. I won't be given to one of them or I'd wind up miserable forever."

Millicent frowned. "You didn't even ponder the notion. You just automatically refused."

"I don't have a dowry, so I can't buy a fellow who could provide me with a suitable life. What sort of man would be available to me?"

"You're fetching and interesting. I'm betting we could dig up a candidate you'd like."

"I tremble simply from imagining who you might select."

"You'll be twenty-one next year. If you don't wed, what is your plan?"

"I will . . . will . . ." Sophia trailed off. "I can apply for some jobs. Maybe I could teach or . . . or . . ."

She trailed off again, recognizing how difficult it was for a woman on her own in the world. If a female had money, she could shun matrimony and wallow in a bohemian existence. She could move to London with a companion, could host salons where intellectuals and artists stopped by to drink her wine.

But for a female in Sophia's position, marriage was the only choice.

"Harry Roland has always liked you," Millicent said, "and he's still a bachelor. Shall I inquire about him for you?"

Sophia tsked with disgust. "If I wed Harry, he would quickly come to despise me. I'm not the bride he needs, and I would never torture him."

Mr. Roland was a young man from the neighborhood. He was older than Sophia, thirty already, and whenever he'd attended events at Riverglen, his fondness had been obvious, but she'd never returned his regard.

He was very different from her: mature, quiet, observant. He worked as a clerk for the brewer in the village, and apparently, he was very good with numbers. He was a man on the rise, establishing a reputation as a skilled accountant.

He wasn't flashy or loud, wasn't handsome or dashing, didn't ever put himself forward. He was simply stable and steady, which meant he was the exact kind of husband Sophia should have. He could rein in her more raucous tendencies.

She started for the door, and Millicent said, "Where are you going? We're not finished talking about Harry. Should I send a note to his mother and ask him to call on you?"

"I would throw myself off a cliff before I'd encourage him, so don't you dare write to her."

"That's a very harsh attitude to have, and I hate that you're being recalcitrant. As far as I can see, marriage is the sole option for you. We should strategize to figure out a viable conclusion."

"We can meet about it again—when you're feeling better."

With that snotty remark deftly hurled, Sophia stomped out.

It was an insult; they both knew it. Millicent was never *better.* No one believed she was suffering though. People accused her of faking, that her misery was all in her head. Even the doctor said so. They didn't understand how she ached and fretted, how her anxiety soared at the very idea of being downstairs.

She was safer in her room. Why not stay in it?

Her discussion with Sophia had used up a pile of her energy, but she wasn't completely exhausted. Despite how Sophia assumed she was unappreciated and unsupported, Millicent had her best interests at heart.

Millicent was her guardian, and she thought Sophia should be a little more grateful for Millicent's continued affection. What if Oscar had shifted the responsibility to Miles? What if Oscar had designated *Miles* to arrange her future?

Sophia probably hoped she could loaf at Riverglen forever. After all, she'd moved in with them when she was ten, and she viewed it as her home, but Aurora was about to marry—by Christmas if Millicent could organize a wedding that fast.

By the time Aurora marched down the aisle, Sophia had to be lodged elsewhere. If she wasn't dispatched to a distant location, she'd be a recurring annoyance.

If Aurora bit the bullet and settled on dreary, grumpy Miles, Sophia would constantly fight with him, so Aurora would never have any peace. And if Aurora was lucky, and Captain Stone proposed, Sophia especially couldn't remain.

Millicent wasn't the greatest mistress of the manor, but she'd learned a very important lesson from her mother: Never keep a pretty girl in the house when there was a man in residence who might notice her and get himself into trouble. Because of that unmentioned rule, she never hired pretty housemaids. They had to be plain and ordinary.

Sophia was feisty, funny, and fetching. Men watched her and wondered—when she was so boisterous—if she might be a tad loose. Millicent would never let her be a temptation to Captain Stone, so she had to leave.

She was lively and spirited and needed a husband who would tamp down her vivacity. Had Harry Roland heard Sophia was back?

Millicent had a writing tray within easy reach, and she pulled it onto her lap and penned a letter to him. They were having a supper on Friday and a dance on Saturday, and he hadn't visited Riverglen in ages. With Sophia in the mix, Millicent was certain he'd like to join them.

Chapter Eight

"I CAN'T BELIEVE I let you drag me to the park."

Sybil Jones smiled at her friend, Neville Stone. They were strolling down a groomed path, arm in arm, as if they were adolescent sweethearts.

The park wasn't that busy. It was sunny, but chilly, and sane people were huddled inside by a warm fire. His coach was trudging along behind them, his servants waiting to be useful. It was the middle of a work day, and she was loafing as if she were a lady of leisure, but when he'd asked her to accompany him, she'd decided to be frivolous for once.

She'd known him for years, through her gambling club, *Ralston's,* that she'd started with her prior ward, Caleb Ralston.

Currently, it was the most posh, entertaining spot for London's premier gentlemen to amuse themselves, and she strove to keep it that way. Neville and his friends were some of the kingdom's most infamous scoundrels, and they'd become her earliest members.

She'd always been charmed by him. He was a flamboyant, amiable rogue, the best-dressed man in any room he entered, and even though he was fifty, he hadn't slowed down a bit.

"How could you have refused to walk with me?" he said. "It's a lovely October afternoon. How many more will we have before winter sets in and it's too cold and rainy to enjoy the weather?"

"I'm busy," she told him, her tone scolding. "I don't loaf and play as the women in your world are so fond of doing."

"I had to lure you away from the club. When you're there, you never focus your attention on me, and you're aware of how spoiled I am. You ignore me, and it crushes my ego."

"Are you about to nag over your party?"

"Yes. I insist you come to Swindon and be my hostess."

His birthday had arrived over the summer, but he'd been overwhelmed by personal issues, so he hadn't celebrated the milestone as might have been expected. First, his remaining nephew had passed away, so he'd inherited the family's earldom and been installed as earl. Then his oldest sons, Hunter and Warwick, had married in a hurry.

Matters had finally calmed, and he was planning an ostentatious fête at Swindon Hall. It was one of England's grandest estates, with one of its finest manor houses, and he wanted her to join him for the two-week revel.

He'd been begging her for weeks, and she'd declined over and over, but he was wearing her down. While he had a reputation as a wastrel and laggard, he could be quite steely when he was intent on a certain conclusion.

She had to admit she'd like to travel to Swindon and see the extraordinary place for herself. She'd risen from humble beginnings, with her father being a navy sailor, so she'd grown up in Jamaica. He'd died, then her mother shortly after, when she was just eighteen, so she'd taken a job as a housemaid for another British woman.

After her employer had died too, Sybil had brought the woman's sons, Caleb and Blake Ralston, to England and had delivered them to their relatives. She'd stayed in England so she could be close to them and ensure they were treated appropriately.

She was forty and Caleb thirty, so she hadn't been his substitute mother. She'd been more like a stern, strict sister. She'd gotten him enlisted in the navy, and when he'd mustered out, they'd built *Ralston's* together. They had a knack for commerce, and their endeavors had left them obscenely rich.

But her role of watching over Caleb and Blake meant she'd never married, that she'd never had any children. Most women her age were grandmothers, but she was wed to her business. Her children were her employees. Her grandchildren had to be the pretty money that flowed into her bank account, but she was starting to have some regrets.

Should she have trod a different path? With her sliding into her later years, would she be happier if she'd had a husband? How about if she'd had some children who could have given her grandchildren?

More and more, she caught herself debating those kinds of questions.

"You're a bully, Neville," she said to him.

"Yes, and I'm adept at coercion too. Am I having any luck at grinding you down?"

"Maybe."

He chuckled. "I hate how you toil away."

"As opposed to you, I like working. I don't view it as a chore."

Neville was renowned as a lazy cur. He'd spent his life wagering, chasing slatterns, and being as slothful as possible. He was actually an aristocrat who could afford it though. One of his ancestors had invested in shipping and imports, and the family had shrewdly managed its fortune, so he was wealthy enough to malinger.

She, on the other hand, had had to earn what she'd accumulated. She liked to be productive, liked to have people counting on her.

She was also very vain, and she liked to prove to men that she could out-perform them at any venture.

Recently though, she was feeling lonely, and she wasn't receiving as much satisfaction from the club as she had previously. Over the prior summer, Caleb and Blake had both wed. Blake was in the navy and stationed out of Gibraltar in the Mediterranean. He'd moved there with his bride, and Sybil didn't know when he'd be able to visit again.

Caleb's fiancée had loathed gambling. In her opinion, it was a terrible stain on the nation that ruined families, which it did, and she'd been reluctant to marry him when his income was generated from such an immoral source. He loved the dear girl so much that he'd signed the place over to Sybil, so she owned the whole thing outright. Then he'd trotted off to the country with his new wife.

Why not go to Swindon with Neville? Perhaps a holiday out of the city would lift her spirits, and she'd return to town in a livelier mood.

"I will shock you," she said, "and agree to come along."

She'd surprised him, and he stopped and grinned. "You will? Really?"

"Yes, I will. A sojourn away from London will be perfect."

"Marvelous!"

They were facing one another, and it was very strange, but as he smiled at her, a burst of affection swirled between them. They were friends and were fond, but suddenly, it seemed as if they might be more than friends. Was that likely?

If Neville had a *type* of female he fancied, Sybil wasn't it. He adored loose tarts, the looser the better, and he was a handsome libertine who couldn't calm his roving regard. A woman who assumed a romance was bubbling up with him would have to be insane to suppose that's what she was witnessing.

She was a spinster, but not a virgin. She'd had two chances to wed when she was younger, chances she'd declined, and she'd also engaged in a passionate affair when she'd been thirty. Those experiences had furnished plenty of amorous knowledge, so she recognized when a man was gazing at her with desire.

"You old roué," she said. "Don't look at me like that."

"Why shouldn't I? I've always thought you were very beautiful. Haven't I ever told you before?"

"No, I don't think you ever have."

She'd been attractive in the past and could once have boasted of being very fetching, but she was *forty*. She was short and sturdy, with brown hair and brown eyes. Her eyes were still bright and merry, but there were strands of grey in her hair, her age definitely showing.

She was flattered that he'd complimented her, but it was depressing too. When he chose a paramour, it was someone youthful, sillier, and much more dazzling.

Then again, Sybil was logical and sensible, competent and pragmatic, and she was loyal to a fault. Lust got in the way with Neville, so he made bad amorous decisions. Was he growing weary of the girls he chased? Was he viewing Sybil's maturity as a benefit rather than a detriment?

That couldn't be true, and she smirked with amusement.

"If you don't watch that sly tongue of yours," she said, "my head will swell."

"I'm so glad I've convinced you about Swindon. I'm very happy."

"I'm delighted to hear it."

She took his arm again, and they strolled on.

"Sybil Jones!" a man called from farther down the path. "Is that you?"

Sybil glanced over, finding that it was Caleb's half-brother, Jacob Ralston. He was with his wife, Joanna. They waved and bustled up.

It had been a summer filled with matrimony, with Jacob recently tying the knot with Joanna, so technically, they were newlyweds. Sybil had been invited to their wedding, and it had been a quiet joy for her. She didn't know Jacob all that well, but he was trying to have a better relationship with Caleb, so she was trying to have a better relationship with *him.*

"How lovely to see you," she said to him. "I didn't realize you were in town."

He motioned to his pretty bride. "You remember Joanna, don't you?"

"Yes, of course. How are you, dear? Are you settling into married life?"

"I'm getting the hang of it, Miss Jones," Joanna said. Jacob coughed out a snort, and she laughed and tartly added, "My husband might disagree with that assessment though."

Sybil turned to Neville, prepared to introduce the young pair to him, but he was gaping at Joanna so oddly that Sybil was unnerved. Her immediate worry was that Joanna might be an old paramour, and Neville was face to face with her spouse, but she suspected it was more than that. He was startled, and he'd never been startled by anything.

"Neville," she said to him, "this is Caleb's brother, Jacob Ralston. I don't believe you've ever met him."

"No, I haven't." His gaze was still locked on Joanna.

Sybil continued. "This is his wife, Joanna. Jacob and Joanna, may I present my very good friend, Neville Stone, Lord Swindon?"

Joanna gasped and staggered slightly, and Jacob reached out to quickly steady her.

"Are you all right?" he asked her.

"Yes, yes, I'm fine," Joanna hastily said.

She and Neville glared at each other, and Sybil was puzzled by their reaction. Finally, she inquired, "Are you two acquainted?"

Neville was unusually bewildered as he asked, "Mrs. Ralston, by any chance was your mother, Belinda James?"

To Sybil's great shock, Joanna didn't answer him. She simply said to her husband, "Jacob, could we go?"

Jacob blanched at her rudeness. He was as mystified as Sybil, and he replied, "Well . . . ah . . . yes, I suppose we can."

Joanna spun and practically ran off. Jacob hurried after her, pausing once to peer back at Sybil. He shrugged and mouthed, *Sorry!*

Neville watched them until they disappeared, then he lurched over to a nearby bench and eased down. He was so pale that she was scared he might faint. She rushed over and plopped down next to him.

"What on earth is wrong with you?" she said.

"I'm . . . I'm . . ." He cut off. "Just give me a minute to catch my breath."

Neville was the most self-centered, carefree rogue in the world. He was never at a loss for words, so his condition was extremely concerning. She glanced over at his carriage, and the driver and outriders were studying them, looking as alarmed as she was.

"That was the most awkward encounter I've ever observed," she said. "Who is Joanna to you?"

"Sybil, it is a wise man who recognizes his own child."

"Joanna is your daughter?"

"Yes, I'm afraid so."

He drew a kerchief from his coat and dabbed at his eyes, and she stared at him, then stared down the path where Jacob and Joanna had vanished around a corner.

She should have been offended to learn that he'd sired a bastard, but she wasn't. He was a dedicated philanderer, and if he ultimately admitted he had a hundred natural children, she wouldn't be surprised.

"Was this the first time you ever spoke to her?" Sybil asked.

"I knew her when she was little, but I haven't seen her since she was three or so." He frowned up at the sky, as if seeking divine forgiveness. "Her mother was so exotic, a gorgeous, red-haired vixen, and I was absolutely obsessed. I couldn't leave her alone."

Sybil patted his hand, and he grabbed hold and linked their fingers. It was an intimate gesture, and they were right out in the open, but she didn't pull away. He needed to grip something solid, and she was delighted to be a rock he could lean on.

"Did you support her and her mother?" she asked. "Did you help them?"

"No, I was terrible—as is my wont. My wife grew weary of my seeming bewitchment, and she chased them away. I never discovered how she coerced them or what they endured." He blew out a heavy sigh. "They simply moved one day when I was away from home. I came back and they'd fled."

"I don't imagine you searched or fretted." She was quite exasperated.

"Oh, I fretted a bit, but then, I carried on with my life. I was twenty-five and an irresponsible dandy. I found other girls to entice me, and I forgot about them. My fixation on her mother had stirred such quarrels with my wife that I merely wanted some peace and quiet."

"You've never liked to quarrel."

"No, but I always wondered what became of her. Does that wipe away any of my sins? Gad, she's so beautiful! Didn't you think she was beautiful?"

"Yes, she's very pretty."

"I have a daughter," he mused, sounding stunned.

"And your sons have a sister."

He shook his head with disgust. "I'm so despicable. It's clear she hates me, and I don't blame her. What must she have suffered after my wife took after her mother?"

Sybil had learned Joanna's story. The whole kingdom had, but she didn't mention it. Currently, he was much too morose to hear it, so she'd tell him later, when he wasn't so distraught. She was already speculating whether she shouldn't begin planning a proper introduction between him and Joanna.

A daughter should know her father, and a father should know his daughter, and Sybil was an optimist.

"I doubt she hates you," Sybil said. "I'm certain she was simply astonished to bump into you without any warning."

"I'm astonished too, and I'm so overwrought that I feel as if my heart might quit beating. Why am I so awful? I've never been sorry for any of the trouble I've caused."

"You can change your ways."

"Do you truly believe that?" he asked. "I've been dreadful for so long. I can't picture myself being a better person."

"I could probably help you with that situation."

"Could you whip me into shape? Are you that brave?"

"Yes, I'm brave, tough, and stubborn. I'm a fighter too. If you stopped being such a wretch, I might like you a bit more."

He chuckled, then sat quietly, lost in thought, then he murmured, "I wish I hadn't been so horrid to my children. I wish we were close and that they liked me. It's been bothering me as I age. I have so many regrets."

"Well, you're not dead. If you're having regrets, you can work at improving your relationships with them."

He dipped in and astounded her by kissing her on the cheek, and she told him, "Let's get you home. You've had an atrocious shock, and you could use a brandy."

She tugged him to his feet and guided him to his carriage. He was wobbly and weak, as if he might collapse, and the servants were aghast. They puttered around, steadying him, settling him on the seat.

As to Sybil, she was plotting, contemplating Joanna. The minute Sybil was alone, she would pen a letter to Jacob. If she could bring Neville together with his daughter, it would be such a good deed that it might guarantee her a ticket into Heaven just when she needed it the most.

"I MOST HUMBLY APOLOGIZE."

"For what transgression?"

"You were forced to observe my relatives when they were quarreling. I pray it won't cloud your assessment of us."

Sheridan gaped at Aurora, struggling to comprehend her words, but he couldn't focus on her. He was completely disoriented, but then, Sophia Cantwell could do that to a man.

He'd barely arrived at Riverglen, and he'd wound up kissing her out in the barn. He'd like to *still* be kissing her, which was utterly deranged. If he wasn't careful, she'd drive him insane with her nonsense.

He was back at the manor, ensconced in the front parlor with Miss Newton. Sophia was nowhere to be found, but his entire attention was on her. He kept expecting her to waltz in, to be silly and chatty and to annoy him beyond his limit, but she didn't appear.

"My cousin, Sophia, is very immature," Miss Newton was explaining, "and she has a temper. I'm embarrassed that you had to witness her ridiculous display."

"I didn't mind. I crossed paths with her when she was in France, so I'm aware of her proclivity for mischief."

"It seemed as if you were acquainted with her, and I'm relieved that you are. It means you won't be disturbed by any of her antics."

"No. She can't disturb me. Who was the fellow she shot at?"

Sophia had clarified who he was, but Sheridan couldn't reveal that fact to Miss Newton. He had a thousand questions about Mr. Bernard, mostly regarding the family's fondness for him. He'd definitely been startled when Sheridan had divulged that he was considering a betrothal with Miss Newton.

Might Bernard assume he had a hold on her affection?

Sheridan was trying to figure out how to inquire about it, but there wasn't a polite way to delve into the subject. It dawned on him that he had an excuse to interrogate Sophia about it. She could provide the details.

When he realized how fervidly he was anticipating the opportunity to speak to her again, he nearly scoffed with disgust. He had to tamp down his unruly emotions. He would not be infatuated!

"The man is Miles Bernard," Miss Newton said. "He was a ward of my father's, as Sophia was. He's a pompous oaf, and they've never been cordial. She's been in France and has only just returned, and their old animosity is flaring."

Sheridan smirked. "It certainly is."

"He's our land agent."

"Is he good at his job?"

"Good enough. Mother likes him and that's what matters. He deals with everything so she doesn't have to be bothered."

The comment was exasperating. It sounded as if Bernard had unfettered control, and that type of authority was difficult to yank away.

"Is your mother at home?" he asked. "Will I meet her?"

"She's . . . ah . . . indisposed. She might eat supper with us, but I'm not sure. I'll check on her to discover how she's faring."

"I hope it's not serious," he said.

"No, she simply tires easily, and the squabble between Sophia and Miles wore her out."

How was he to evaluate the remark? It wasn't as if her mother had had to intervene in the row. Why would she be exhausted? Was she ill? What was her malady? If she was sick, why wouldn't Miss Newton inform him of the problem? Why hide it?

Suddenly, a whirlwind erupted at the parlor door. They peered over as a tempest of blue, white, and starched petticoats bustled toward them. Then tiny hands were lifted up, and Emily cried, "Cap! Cap!"

Without thinking, he leaned down and scooped her up, and he was amazed at how happy he was to see her. He was so curious about the roué who'd seduced Caroline Newton. Who could have sired the pretty little angel?

The conundrum would furnish him with yet another excuse to pester Sophia. She claimed her cousin had never identified the father, but he thought that was probably a lie. Was it someone he knew? If that was the case, he wouldn't be surprised.

Emily was fetching and precocious, so there had to be plenty of blue blood coursing through her veins. He had no doubt her father was an aristocrat. He balanced her on his hip, as she babbled like a brook, talking in her indecipherable language. She seemed to be asking him where he'd been, scolding him for abandoning her.

Miss Newton was offended by Emily's arrival, and she clucked her tongue. "I apologize again, Captain Stone. Let me summon a housemaid. I'll have her removed."

"It's all right," he said. "Miss Emily and I are old friends."

The baby cast such a dismissive glance at Miss Newton, as if telling her to butt out, that Sheridan laughed. "You are being very naughty, Miss Emily. Where is your nanny?"

The irksome fiend, Pierre, popped up in the doorway, and he said, "She doesn't have a nanny, Captain Stone. *I* am supposed to be watching her, but she heard the maids mention that you were here, and she ran off to find you. I couldn't catch her."

Pierre hastened over and reached for her, but she wailed with dismay and wrapped her chubby arms around Sheridan's neck.

"For pity's sake," Miss Newton fumed. She jerked Emily away, plopping her on the floor very hard, then she said to Pierre, "Take this child away at once, then send Sophia to me. She promised to keep her out of sight, and if she's shifted the chore to you, it's clear you are completely incompetent at your responsibilities."

Sheridan ignored Miss Newton's sharp tone and asked Pierre, "How are you, Pierre? How are you liking England? Have you been picking any pockets? Or have you been behaving yourself?"

"I have been behaving, *monsieur.* I would not engage in any conduct that would anger Miss Sophia."

"Good boy," he said.

Emily had curled herself around Sheridan's leg, and she gazed at him with her striking blue eyes. He was rattled again by how much she resembled him. His brothers too. She looked just like his kin. A tad anxiously, he wondered if she might be the bastard daughter of one of his brothers. Or perhaps one of his deceased cousins. She couldn't be *his.*

He'd never met Caroline Newton, and he'd been out of the country when Emily would have been conceived, so he wasn't the culprit. But who was?

If Hunter or Warwick was her father, it would mean she was his half-sister. Was that why he felt such an affection for her? Could it be possible?

As rapidly as the notion arose, he shook it away. If they were related, what were the odds of him stumbling on her in France? Then stumbling on her again at Riverglen? The whole idea was too preposterous to ponder.

Sheridan pulled her away and said, "Why don't you go to the nursery with Pierre? I'll be here for several days. I'll visit you very soon."

It was obvious she didn't believe him, and the glower she flashed was so woeful that he chuckled. She was so spoiled, and she reminded him of his father. It was the exact expression Neville displayed when he didn't get his way.

"Come, Emily," Pierre said. "You have gotten us both in trouble. Not that you care."

He dragged her away, and she frowned at Sheridan over her shoulder until she was yanked into the foyer. She was a foaming ball of outrage, aggrieved at his failing to treat her as she'd expected he would. He'd never spent time with a little girl. Did they all act in such a forward manner?

She was . . . what? Two? Three? Did they all flirt and fawn to obtain what they wanted?

After the room quieted, Miss Newton was very incensed, which was silly. Emily had simply rushed in when she shouldn't have. It wasn't the end of the world.

"I can't devise enough versions to tell you how sorry I am," she said. "What must you think of us? The manor seems to be a madhouse full of lunatics."

"It was nothing. Really. I find her very charming, and I'm not upset that she barged in."

"Well, I'm sorry anyway."

He'd like to ask what the family planned for Emily, but he wasn't in any position to pry. Sophia had brought her back from France, her father unnamed and her mother dead, but from Miss Newton's dour scowl, it didn't appear Emily was welcome. Nor was Sophia, and the rancor was sad to witness.

If he wed Miss Newton, would this sort of acrimony be common? Or had he arrived at a dramatic moment? He'd hate to wedge himself into a group of people that fought constantly. When he and his brothers were boys, they had suffered through too much vitriol in their own home.

Sheridan's mother had bickered relentlessly with Neville. She'd been livid over his philandering and gambling. It was why his father had resided in London, and his sons had grown up like orphans. Sheridan had always told himself, if he ever married and had children, he wouldn't live like that. He wouldn't be a stranger to them, so what type of circumstance was he facing at Riverglen?

His wound began to ache, as if his vexation had made his leg throb. It indicated he'd been standing too long, and the realization was depressing. It forced him to accept the fact that his life of sailing was swiftly drawing to a close.

Retirement might not be so dreadful, and the dilemma with Sophia and Mr. Bernard was peripheral to the choice confronting him. Why didn't he just propose? He ought to put himself out of his misery. If he dithered, he'd invent excuses to convince himself he was hale and healthy, but he wasn't.

Once the property was his, he'd be lord and master over it. If Sophia or Miles Bernard annoyed him, he'd send them on their way so the estate could become the haven he was seeking.

Why not wed in a hurry? He was sure, in such a beautiful spot, his stamina would quickly return.

"Will we dress for supper?" he asked her.

"Yes. We always do."

"The afternoon has flown by, so I should head to my room to wash and change."

"I should too."

"Who will be joining us?"

"I've invited some neighbors. You shouldn't have to stare across the table at me alone. It might have been too awkward."

"Will Miss Cantwell and Mr. Bernard be included?" he asked. "I'm afraid that might cause some very loud fireworks."

"Oh, my, I hadn't considered how unpleasant the meal might be if they attend. I will have them dine in their bedchambers. We shouldn't encourage another argument."

He nodded in agreement. "What time shall I come down?"

"How about seven? We'll have wine, then supper will be served at eight."

"That sounds perfect. I'll see you then."

He walked out to the foyer, breathing a sigh of relief to have escaped.

The autumn days were short, night falling early, so it was already dark outside. It wouldn't take him long to change, and he figured he had a few minutes to swing by the nursery to flirt with Emily. He'd like to pepper Pierre with questions too. The boy was canny and perceptive, and no doubt, he could provide plenty of information about the estate that Sheridan couldn't obtain from anyone else.

He went to the stairs and started to climb.

Chapter Nine

"HELLO, CANTWELL."

Sophia glanced over her shoulder to find Captain Stone lurking in the doorway. Before she could stop him, he marched into her bedchamber, shut the door, and spun the key in the lock. He stuck it in his pocket. She didn't have a fancy suite like the rest of the family. It was just the one room, with no separate sitting or dressing room, so there was no extra space where she could escape him.

It was nearly midnight, and she was ready for bed, wearing her nightgown and robe, a pair of woolen socks on her feet. She was seated at her dressing table, trying to tug a brush through her hair, but it was impossible. The thick, curly strands refused to be tamed.

"What are you thinking?" She sounded a tad hysterical.

"You didn't join us for supper."

"Of course I didn't. First of all, I was *dis*invited by your fiancée who told me not to show my face at the table. And second of all, why would I eat with you and her? Why would you want me to? Are you hoping to flaunt your betrothal and make me jealous?"

"She's not my fiancée. Yet. I'm simply pondering the situation."

"Are you certain Aurora knows you're merely pondering? She's not the sharpest nail in the tool box, so her mother has probably already drafted the contracts." She flashed a furious glower, then turned back to the mirror. "You should be careful. Your father and her mother will have you fettered before you have a hint it's about to occur."

"My father won't proceed unless I tell him he can. We discussed it prior to my traveling here. The decision is totally up to me, *and,* Miss Smarty-Pants, your cousin has been apprised that nothing is official."

"Thank you for that important clarification. Now then, I'm tired and it's late. Will you leave so I can crawl into bed?"

"No," he said like the bully he was.

He simply took up too much space in any room he entered. It was like having an African elephant wander in, and the best route to encourage his departure was to ignore him. Once he realized she wouldn't drool over him, he'd slink away without her having to figure out how to evict him.

She began tugging on the brush again. For a moment, he loafed behind her, silently observing, then he stepped over and yanked it out of her hand.

"Hey!" she complained. "Give me that!"

"No. You're the most inept female I've ever encountered. You can't even brush your hair. Is there any chore at which you're competent?"

"No, none."

"My point exactly."

He started brushing for her, and he was much too good at it, indicating that he was a libertine who'd likely had a thousand paramours. It was probably regular entertainment for him to dawdle in women's bedchambers. It was probably how he spent every evening.

His brash conduct was outrageously intimate, but shockingly pleasant too. She could have tarried there all night, letting him behave precisely as he shouldn't, but her better sense finally prevailed. She slid off the stool and leapt to her feet.

"You can't just . . . just . . . brush my hair," she said.

"Well, you can't do it yourself. Watching you try is like watching a turtle flounder on its back. I can't fathom how you've survived for two decades."

"I'm fine."

"No, you're hilarious."

He went over to the bed, where he promptly flopped down and stretched out.

"Get off of there!" she scolded.

"I had too much brandy after supper. My head is spinning. I need to rest a minute, then I'll sit up and go."

"Are you a drunkard, Captain?"

"I don't drink much, so *no,* I'm not a drunkard, but your relatives are driving me to it."

"You are being obnoxious, and you're scaring me."

"I'm not scaring you."

"Yes, you are! You might commit any sin, and I couldn't stop you."

"You generate no passionate interest in me," he said. "You should be so lucky to capture my amorous attention."

"And you should be so lucky to capture mine."

"Tell me something," he said.

"If I can, but there are no guarantees."

"Why are you lodged in this tiny bedchamber in this deserted wing of the manor?"

"It's where they put me when I first arrived."

"How old were you?"

"Ten."

"Evidently, you haven't managed to ingratiate yourself. Does anybody in this blasted house like you?"

"For your information, I could have moved to a bigger suite, but I like this room. It's comfortable."

"Sure it is."

"It's convenient too. I'm just down the hall from the nursery, so I'm close to Pierre and Emily."

"How are you connected to that little fiend, Pierre? He appears to have latched onto you pretty tight. How could you allow it to happen?"

"His mother was our housemaid in France. She and Caroline died the same week, of a virulent influenza. It was an incredibly traumatic period, and he didn't have any family to take him in. I couldn't kick him out on the road."

"You're too nice," he said, sounding irked. "You don't have two pennies to rub together, so you can't accumulate an entourage of lost souls who require tending. You can't afford it."

"I'd rather be kind and caring than a braggart and tyrant like you."

He sat up, suddenly not looking intoxicated in the least. She was still over by the dressing table, her back pressed to the wall, as if she wished a hole would open so she could fall through it.

He extended a hand to her and said, "Come here."

"Why?"

"Because you're much too far away."

"I'm in my nightclothes, Captain, and you're presuming on my good nature. I ought to scream."

He snickered with amusement. "You won't scream. You don't dare be discovered with a man in your room. You have such a low reputation among your kin that they would immediately assume *you* lured me in. I'd exacerbate the situation by insisting you invited me. You'd be in trouble. Not me."

"Thank you again for your wise advice. It's so sweet of you to smother me with your pompous guidance."

"You're a female, and I'm a male. You're supposed to listen to me."

She bristled with aggravation. "You are so insufferable, which is my view of every man I've ever met. Why am I not surprised to find you're exactly the same?"

He huffed with mock offense. "There are no men like me, so you can't claim I'm like every other one."

"How are you different? I'm dying to know."

"For starters, I'm disgustingly rich. My whole family is. You wouldn't ever have crossed paths with a person as wealthy as me."

"Who is your family? You never told me."

"You never asked." Blithely, as if tossing walnut shells on the ground, he said, "My father is Neville Stone, Lord Swindon."

She sucked in a sharp breath. "Your father is Neville Stone?"

Neville Stone was a cad and gambler, a charming ne'er-do-well, who seduced young maidens for sport. He had constant affairs, and his amorous exploits were legendary.

That beast, that scoundrel, was Sheridan Stone's father? Earlier, she'd wondered if there might be a distant relation. Now, he was boasting about being the exalted man's son. The prospect was riveting and exhausting, and she certainly understood why he was so arrogant.

He snorted. "It's clear you're enthralled by the news, and you should be. My brother, Hunter, is Viscount Marston, so you see, Cantwell, I am descended from a lengthy line of aristocrats, many of whom have helped to rule England for centuries."

"What is your spot in the grand scheme of things?"

"At the moment, I'm not important. I'm simply a spy and privateer who serves King and Country. I risk my life every second."

"A spy? Really? You're not merely a felonious smuggler? It's the biography I would write for you."

"I am a decorated navy veteran, and I am lauded in the highest circles of the land. Are you in awe of me yet?"

She scoffed. "I will never admit to being in awe of you. You are too conceited, and I won't fan the flames of your massive ego."

Her mind was awhirl as she absorbed the shock of learning that he was Lord Swindon's son. How could she use the information to her own advantage?

"If you're such a famous hero," she said, "why are you at Riverglen and skulking after my cousin? Why aren't you out on the High Seas, increasing your notoriety?"

He wrinkled his nose, his expression a tad despairing. "I was wounded, remember? I'm tired."

"Where were you wounded? I mean, what were you doing when it occurred?"

"I was boarding a pirate ship."

"You were not. Don't tell me stories like that. I might start to like you."

"You should like me, and I *was* boarding a pirate ship. I was slashed in the leg in the fighting. It hasn't healed as much as I'd like, so I'm not as hale as I was previously."

It had to be a stunning confession for him. He was such a manly man, full of strength and vigor, but apparently, beneath the bluster, he was in daily misery. It made her fret for him, fear for him. All of those emotions were ridiculous, and she tried to shove them away, but couldn't.

"Will you quit?" she asked. "Is that it? I've heard that being a sailor is difficult. Are you thinking you can't continue anymore?"

"Yes, I'm beginning to think that, so I'm contemplating my future."

It was another stunning confession. He was very proud, and she couldn't envision him blabbing such a terrible secret to just anyone. She was thrilled to have him share it with her.

"If you wed Aurora," she said, "you could settle at Riverglen. It might be a good path for you. You could rest and recuperate."

"That would be my goal, yes. Her father arranged his final affairs so her husband will inherit the estate. I could glom onto it by marrying her, but it would be a big change for me, and I'm debating if I could bear it."

She stared at him, struggling to figure out the ramifications of him moving to Riverglen and staying permanently. It would kill her to watch him with Aurora. Then again, she was leaving in the next year. Hadn't that alteration been determined?

Millicent didn't want her to remain, and Sophia had bragged that she could find a situation for herself. Why would it bother her if he wed Aurora?

"When will you decide whether to propose or not?" she asked.

"I'll tarry until Wednesday, then I'm heading to my father's Swindon property to discuss it. He's traveling there himself to celebrate his fiftieth birthday."

The accursed roué was fifty already? She bit down a scathing retort, asking instead, "Is he throwing a huge party?"

"Yes. The mansion will be packed for two weeks, with his old compatriots joining him. My brothers will be there too, and I haven't seen them in ages, so I'm excited about it. I told my father I'd give him my answer about Miss Newton once I arrive."

"So Aurora is auditioning for the role of Mrs. Sheridan Stone?"

"Basically, yes."

She snorted with disgust. Aurora would be perfect for him. She was a gorgeous heiress, and she exuded an aura of helplessness, so men ran to her rescue. Sophia had never understood why men were attracted to weak, defenseless females, but they slathered over her.

Life was hard and short, and tragedies arose without warning. Just look at her own history! Her mother had perished birthing her, then she'd staggered after her wistful, impractical father who'd passed away when she was ten. She'd had to grow up very fast, had had to develop a thick skin.

Why didn't men want a tough, cunning female like her, one who could survive in desperate circumstances? Why were they tantalized by frailty and frivolity?

"You should beware of Miles Bernard," she said. She probably should have avoided the whole mess, but she was more despondent by the minute.

"I meant to inquire about him. When he discovered my purpose for visiting, he seemed quite shocked."

"He expects to marry Aurora himself. Her father, Oscar, viewed Miles as the son he never had, and he planned for Miles to wed Caroline or Aurora."

"Caroline ruined herself, so she was off the table."

"Yes, and Aurora has never been in any hurry."

Captain Stone snickered. "I can certainly see why. He's an arrogant dolt, but if Oscar Newton was so fond of him, why didn't he simply bequeath the place outright? Why make the inheritance contingent on his snagging a daughter?"

"I'm guessing he didn't completely trust Miles to take care of Millicent and Aurora unless he was forced to assume the obligation by marriage."

"Mr. Bernard isn't happy that I'm here."

"No. He's extremely enraged."

"I imagine you'll be delighted to have him fuming and fretting."

She nodded gleefully. "I will be tickled pink."

"Why haven't I been introduced to Mrs. Newton? Is she hiding from me? Is she afraid of me? What's keeping her away?"

Sophia sighed. There were so many issues swirling, and she shouldn't have to be the one to explain them. "Aurora's mother is erratic and silly, and she believes she's dying—but she's not. She has attacks of anxiety, where she can't breathe and she's sure she's suffocating, so she rarely leaves her room."

"That's peculiar. I'm curious if she isn't actually a lunatic who's been locked in the attic. What kind of family is this?"

"Aren't we just like every other family? Don't they all have their faults and odd ducks?"

"Not mine. We're handsome, dashing scoundrels. We act as men are supposed to act. We don't have parents who cower in bedrooms and are scared to peek out the door."

Sophia shrugged. "It's a problem you have to evaluate as you ponder matrimony. If you're ever Aurora's husband, you'll have to deal with it constantly."

He must have heard her petty tone, for his gaze narrowed, and he grinned his devil's grin. "Will you be upset if I wed your cousin?"

"Why would I be upset? I don't know you, I don't like you, and I have no connection to you. If Aurora winds up shackled to you, I will feel sorry for her forever."

"You will not. You wish *you* were the one I fancied."

"You're being ridiculous. As you previously mentioned, I don't have a penny to my name. How could I entice a fellow like you? Aurora can flaunt an estate as her dowry, and I don't have a dowry, so why would you be interested?"

Voiced aloud, her predicament sounded pathetic, so she figured she should shut up. There was no benefit to comparing herself to Aurora. How could Sophia hope to compete? And there was no reason to compete.

Her current goal was to meet with Emily's father, to carry out Caroline's deathbed request by convincing him to support Emily. After that, she had to find a position. It was clear, if she loafed at Riverglen much longer, Millicent would marry her off to a country idiot who would crush her spirit and grind her down with rules and routines.

She was a dreamer and schemer—as her father had been. She wanted to travel, write poetry, and rub elbows with fascinating intellectuals. She wanted to invent things and be acclaimed for her brilliance. She wanted to be noticed and lauded for her exceptional attributes.

She *didn't* want to be fettered to a man who would view it as his duty to rein in her worst impulses. If that happened, she might become invisible.

"Come here," he said again.

"No. I'm not joining you on my bed."

"You'll like it. I promise." He was seductive as the snake tempting Eve in the Garden of Eden.

"I've been much too patient with you, and you have to go."

She went over to the door and spun the knob, but she'd forgotten it was locked. She whirled and frowned at him. "Give me the key."

"No. I snuck in because I missed you at supper, and evidently, I haven't had my fill of you yet."

Quick as lightning, he moved off the bed and loomed in so swiftly that she had no time to register his intentions. He lifted her, twirled them around, and tumbled them onto the mattress. It occurred so fast that she wasn't able to protest or react.

She was frozen with alarm, but with excitement too. He was stretched out atop her, his large body pressing her down, and it was incredibly thrilling. But as rapidly as she rejoiced, she just as rapidly realized she'd been pitched into a dangerous quagmire.

They were sequestered in an isolated room at the end of a deserted hall. He could ravage her, and she couldn't stop him. She sensed no menace though. In France, she'd been trapped by libidinous rogues, so she'd learned the signs for when a cad was planning to seize what he wasn't allowed to have.

Captain Stone exuded none of those signs. His eyes were merry, as if he'd played a great trick on her. She had no idea what he might be thinking, but he opened his mouth and said, "I'm going to start calling you Sophia."

She chuckled quite miserably. "You've attacked and frightened me, and *that's* your only comment?"

"I haven't attacked you, and you're not frightened."

"Yes, I am."

"No, you're not, and you will call me Sheridan."

"I might—when we're alone, but I can't have people assuming we're friendly."

"Why not? I'm a friendly person."

"They might wonder exactly how well we were acquainted in France."

He smirked. "If anyone ever inquires, I will insist I knew you *very* well."

"Don't joke about it. I have enough trouble fitting in, so you can't be horrid. Not when you're about to betroth yourself to my cousin."

He smirked again. "Ha! You are jealous."

"Oh, you are so obnoxious."

"Would I like being her husband? What's your opinion?"

"You are a cruel beast to pester me about it."

"Who else should I ask? Her mother who never leaves her room? Miles Bernard who yearns to wed her himself?"

She tsked with exasperation. "If you marry Aurora, you'll be very, very happy. There! Are you satisfied?"

"Why don't you like her?"

"I like her very much, and she'd be a perfect bride for a roué as annoying as you."

"Are you wishing I'd pick you instead? Is that why you're angry?"

"I'm not angry!" she said, sounding very angry. "I think men are fools, so I have no desire to be a wife."

The remark bewildered him. "Doesn't every woman hope to wed? If you don't, what will become of you?"

"I'm certain it will shock your amazing male self, but women can have a full and interesting life without dragging along behind a man."

"Name a woman who shunned matrimony and wound up glad." She scowled, trying to conjure someone, and he laughed. "It's unnatural to remain a spinster. It's an accepted fact."

"You are so absurd that I can't decide where to begin in dissecting the flaws in your assertion."

She thought he'd launch into a diatribe about why he was correct, but he said, "Have I told you that you talk too much?"

"I don't talk *too much.* I talk just enough."

"No, you chatter like a magpie, and it distracts me."

"From what? What do you mean?"

"Sophia? Hush."

At hearing him use her Christian name, she beamed with pleasure, so she wasn't paying attention as he dipped in and kissed her. He'd kissed her earlier in the barn, so it wasn't their first foray into romance, but this embrace was much different than that prior one had been.

His lips captured hers in a way that tickled her innards and rocked the foundations of her world. He seemed to drink her in, to want to be connected to her forever, to never be separated. He was carrying on as if she was unique and special, as if he'd been searching for ages and had finally located her.

The entire interval was wrong and immoral, but she'd never participated in such a wicked, exhilarating experience. Why not revel in it?

She leapt in with excessive vigor, and the encounter swiftly heated to a sizzling temperature. They scrapped, fought, and grappled for purchase, as if they were shipwreck survivors, floating in the waves and about to sink under them.

She hadn't realized a man and woman could generate such intense passion, and it made her understand why young ladies were so carefully chaperoned. She was sliding down a perilous slope where she might commit any sin he suggested.

Eventually, they slowed and stopped, and he cockily said, "I guess I've discovered how to get you to pipe down."

"I let you proceed because I couldn't bear to hurt your feelings. You're so spoiled that you would have pouted if I'd refused."

"Have you always been sassy or is it just *me* who brings out your impertinence?"

"I've always been sassy, but around you, I behave worse than usual."

He shifted away from her and sat up, his back to her, and she took the opportunity to scramble off the mattress and escape. She staggered over to the dressing table and plopped down on the stool, her knees too weak to hold her up.

"I shouldn't have snuck in," he told her, "but I'm delighted I did."

"I *might* be delighted too, but that's the only time I'll ever admit it."

"Where will you be tomorrow? Will you stay out of sight so I don't have to rescue you from any mishaps? Or will you strut into every room I enter and constantly throw yourself in my face?"

"I'll hide. If I had to watch you fawning over Aurora, I'd grow too nauseous. How can you loaf in my bedchamber and kiss me senseless when you're supposed to be courting her?"

He shrugged. "Didn't you know? I'm a cad. All of the men in my family are cads. We're renowned for it. I can kiss one woman, then another, without batting an eye."

With what she'd learned about his father, she could hardly argue the point.

"Are you bragging about it?" she asked.

"I'm not bragging. I'm just stating the facts."

He pushed himself to his feet, and she noticed his limp, so maybe his story about being injured and forced to retire was true. He straightened and walked to the door.

He stuck the key in the lock and spun it, then he glanced over at her and said, "I still don't like you. Don't think—just because I kissed you—that I've changed my mind about that."

"I don't like you either, so *no,* nothing has changed."

They shared a fond, almost conspiratorial smile, one that rattled her, one that terrified her. Then he tiptoed out without checking that the hall was empty. She probably didn't need to worry. It was very late, but still!

She crept over and peeked out to wave goodbye, but he'd already vanished around the corner. She breathed a sigh of relief, then she went to the bed and laid down. His scent was on the pillow, on the blankets, and her body was on fire with a hunger she didn't recognize.

She felt as if she'd been scrubbed raw, as if the blood no longer flowed through her veins correctly. She was giddy, flustered, and too excited for words, and she wondered if he'd visit her again while he was at Riverglen. That was a deranged notion, but she hoped he would, so she scolded herself.

He had her wishing she was a tad loose. If she was, what sorts of antics might they have attempted? She couldn't wait until she saw him again. What would they say to each other? Would they chat as if naught had occurred? Would he be able to conceal his infatuation? Would she?

He was simply so amazing, like a comet streaking across her personal sky. He was fun, joy, and desire wrapped into a handsome package, and she yearned for him to shower her with gifts she couldn't describe.

My, my, but wasn't she in trouble?

Chapter Ten

"AURORA!"

Miles called to her, and it was clear she'd heard him. For a brief second, her shoulders stiffened, then she continued down the hall. Since Sheridan Stone had arrived, he hadn't been able to corner her. She'd deftly avoided his every attempt to discuss the man's appearance.

The prior evening, she'd even ordered him to stay away from the supper table, lest Sophia show up too and instigate a quarrel. They'd had neighbors over for the meal, people Miles had known most of his life, yet he'd had to cower in his suite and eat off a tray. In all his years at the estate, he'd never been treated so shabbily, and he wouldn't stand for it. He had to reestablish his control, but he wasn't certain how.

He tried again. "Aurora! Wait up!"

He was closing in on her, so she couldn't pretend to be deaf. She spun to face him. "Oh, hello, Miles. Were you searching for me?"

"Yes, I was bloody well searching," he crudely told her.

He was never short or impolite with her or her mother. He never chastised them or used foul language. But honestly!

His path with her had been laid down by her father. They were to wed, then Miles would own Riverglen and take care of Aurora and Millicent forever. Had Aurora forgotten that pertinent fact?

Apparently yes.

They were next to an empty parlor, and he grabbed her arm and dragged her into it. She stared at him, her expression innocent and questioning, as if she had no idea why he'd be raging.

"Would you like to explain yourself to me?" he said.

"On what topic?"

"As if you didn't know." He scoffed with disgust. "Why is Captain Stone here?"

"Mother invited him. She didn't ask my opinion first."

"That's your story?"

"What other story could there be?"

"The oaf assumes he's about to be betrothed to you!"

"I'm confused as to why he claimed that. I was as surprised as you were."

"I don't believe you. Are you scheming behind my back? Is that it?"

"No!"

"Your father intended for us to marry. You are to be *my* wife, Aurora. Riverglen is to be mine, so I can watch over you and your mother. Now then, I've been too accommodating over your delays, and I insist we pick the date. How about a Christmas wedding? What do you think?"

"Christmas? I'm not sure we could arrange it by then."

"The date, Aurora! What is it to be?"

"You should talk to Mother about it. She wouldn't like me to select it without her input."

He was still holding her arm, and she jerked away and stepped into the hall, which incensed him beyond his limit.

"Aren't you listening to me?" he said. "You will not trot off without our resolving this."

"We're having company tonight, so I have to confer with the housekeeper about the menu. I just checked on Mother. She's up and has had her breakfast. Why don't you speak with her?"

She vanished like smoke, leaving him to fume by himself in the empty parlor. His alarm was rising. His entire future was dependent on Aurora being his bride. If she didn't follow through, he would remain an employee, a functionary, a lackey.

He stormed out and went to the stairs, and he climbed to Millicent's bedroom suite. The door was open, so he didn't have to knock and beg admittance.

The servants were bustling in and out, cleaning, laying out her clothes for the day. She was in a nightgown and robe, lounged on her fainting couch in the middle of the sitting room. She blandly observed them, like an indolent queen who was too posh to lift a finger to tend herself.

Everything about her irritated him: her hypochondria, her fake spells of weakness and anxiety, her declarations that she was failing, that she was dying. If it had been up to Miles, he'd have locked her in an asylum like the lunatic she was.

He marched in, and the servants froze. There were six of them, and he snapped his fingers and said, "Everyone out!"

They glanced at Millicent, and she nodded imperiously, giving them permission to depart. They flitted by him, and Millicent said to them, "Our conversation will be very brief. Please return as soon as he and I are finished."

She gazed up at him, looking frail and fragile, and he wondered—as he often had—how Oscar had tolerated her. Yes, she was very beautiful, but her quirks and ailments were legendary and exhausting. After Miles was fully in charge, there would have to be some changes.

"You're angry Miles," she said. "What's wrong?"

He shut the door and came over to her. He wasn't that tall, but she was reclined on the fainting couch, so he towered over her. He didn't mince words. "Why was Sheridan Stone asked to visit us?"

With no equivocation, she said, "He's pondering an engagement to Aurora."

"Why would you encourage him? Aurora is mine! She's always been destined to marry me. Don't pretend that's not the case."

"I don't exactly see you exerting yourself to win her. It's never been guaranteed that she would agree to have you."

"It was all arranged! It's what Oscar wanted."

She shrugged, as if his life wasn't hanging in the balance. "Oscar is no longer with us, so we don't necessarily have to obey him."

His jaw dropped in astonishment. "You're not serious."

"In my view, you've grown too complacent. You simply presume Aurora will be yours, without your having to make any effort, as if you're entitled to be her husband. I decided she should have a chance to be courted by some other gentlemen who will treat her with more respect." She flashed an obnoxious grin. "Once you realize other men are interested in her, maybe you'll stop being so confident. Maybe you'll work a little harder."

"I shouldn't have to work at it. It was settled ages ago."

As he voiced the complaint, he sounded extremely petulant, but didn't he deserve Aurora? In light of how he'd ingratiated himself to Oscar, wasn't he due a reward? It was supposed to be Aurora. It was supposed to be Riverglen.

Rage swept over him. Could Millicent truly imagine he would gracefully step aside? That he would let Aurora slip away? That he would allow a handsome, dashing sea captain to strut in and seize what belonged to Miles?

Millicent was deranged if she expected she could yank away his prize at the very last minute.

She must have noted his fury because she waved it away. "Don't worry so much, Miles. Captain Stone will never covet our paltry rural property. He's a nautical man, and they never like to be landlocked. Plus, the Stone family is very rich. He can purchase any estate he likes *and* he can wed any young lady in the world. With how his father has been elevated—"

Miles interrupted. "How was he elevated?"

"He's Earl of Swindon now, so Captain Stone can choose a duke's daughter or even a foreign princess. He doesn't have to lower his standards for a country mouse like Aurora."

Miles's teeth were clenched so tightly that he could barely speak. "Then why invite him to Riverglen?"

"I told you: You're too smug, and Aurora ought to be wooed. You should try it. Perhaps you'd have more luck."

"I demand we pick the wedding date. When would you like it to be?"

She laughed her twinkly laugh. "How could we select the date when the two of you aren't betrothed yet?"

He gaped at her, and his anger bubbled up to such a high temperature that he clasped his hands behind his back, lest he slide them around her throat and strangle her to death. He was that livid. He was that aghast.

He didn't dare open his mouth or he would hurl comments he could never retract. Despite his lofty aspirations, he was just an employee, and unless he became Aurora's husband, he'd never be more than that.

He whipped away and stomped out without another word.

SHERIDAN SAT AT THE desk in the cottage that served as the estate office. It was where Sophia had shot at Miles Bernard, and Sheridan probably should have requested permission before entering, but he hadn't been eager to deal with Bernard. He'd wanted to peek at the account ledgers without Bernard hovering over his shoulder.

He had a good head for numbers, which was why he was such an excellent gambler. His mind clicked like an ancient abacus, and he could calculate the odds and predict the outcome with an uncanny reliability. If he hadn't been such a violent, masculine brute, he could have been a mathematics professor at a university.

He usually concealed his ability though. It seemed like such a frivolous skill, and he never liked others to realize he was very smart. It kept his enemies off balance, and people always underestimated him.

The portrait of Mr. Bernard was on the floor behind him. It hadn't been removed or repaired. There was a huge hole burned in the center. Sophia had admirable aim, and Bernard should be glad she'd pointed at the picture rather than the person. If she hadn't exercised some restraint, they'd be planning his funeral.

Without warning, Bernard stormed in the door and slammed it. He glanced over and saw Sheridan where he shouldn't have been. Obviously, Bernard was furious, and Sheridan wondered why. He hoped Sophia hadn't stirred a new spat with him. The blasted girl had to learn to control her worst impulses.

"May I help you?" Bernard's tone was cool and unfriendly.

"We haven't been introduced. I'm Captain Sheridan Stone."

"I know who you are. Is there something you need? I don't mean to be rude, but I'm busy this morning."

Sheridan gestured to the ledger book. "Your records are neat and tidy."

"Thank you."

Bernard marched over, snatched up the book, and put it on the shelf. Then he spun on Sheridan, glaring, visually advising Sheridan to get out of his chair. Sheridan could be a real ass though, and he didn't budge. He raised a brow and said, "Your records are orderly, but I could swear there's money missing."

"Yes, I'm sure you're an accounting expert," Bernard snidely retorted.

"It's occasionally claimed that I am." Sheridan shrugged, as if the talent was irrelevant. "I didn't have time to factor many of the numbers, but from what I could tell, they didn't add up."

He watched Bernard closely, and the oaf wasn't easily intimidated. If he was stealing a bit here and there, he didn't reveal it by so much as the blink of an eye.

In Sheridan's opinion, underlings had to be supervised. There had to be standards, then regular assessments. Millicent Newton was hiding in her room and had given Bernard free rein, so it would be a simple matter to pilfer a few pounds.

Bernard sighed exaggeratedly. "It's clear you stopped by with a purpose, Captain. What is it?"

Sheridan flicked his thumb over his shoulder, indicating the ruined portrait. "Too bad about your fancy picture. It looks as if Miss Cantwell doesn't like you very much."

"Miss Cantwell is an annoying child, and beyond that description, there is no reason for me to discuss her with you."

"You're fortunate she aimed at the wall instead of your chest."

"Yes, if she'd killed me, I'm certain you'd have been bereft."

"Were you aware I met her in France?" Sheridan said. "I know you deliberately stranded her there."

"It is a bizarre rumor Sophia has spread in an attempt to mask her failure to appropriately spend the funds we sent. She's a renowned liar, and you shouldn't believe her on any topic."

"I don't like to see a woman harmed."

Bernard bristled. "If Sophia landed herself in a jam, I can guarantee it was one of her own creation. She has a habit of getting herself into trouble."

Sheridan wholeheartedly agreed, but he didn't admit it. "In the future, I wouldn't like to hear you were awful to her."

He pushed himself to his feet, straightening to his full height so he towered over the petty tyrant, but Bernard was a cocky dolt. He studied Sheridan with a great deal of disdain, and he didn't step away, so he was either very brave or very stupid.

Apparently, he was weary of talking about Sophia, for he changed the subject. "Mrs. Newton tells me you're courting Aurora."

"We've scooted past courting already," Sheridan said. "I'm considering an engagement."

"You haven't been informed that Aurora is promised to me and has been for over a decade."

"You've been officially bound? Really?"

Bernard's cheeks heated, and he replied, "It's not official, no. Her father arranged it before he died, and it will happen soon. We're merely working out the details."

"I'll keep that in mind."

"Mrs. Newton is toying with you. She thinks I'm too smug about Aurora, so she's using you to spur me into being less complacent."

"Is that so?" Sheridan chuckled with amusement.

"Yes. I just spoke with her, and she confessed her ploy."

"You know, Mr. Bernard, if I decide to wed Aurora, there won't be a spot for you at Riverglen. I won't retain you as my estate agent. Have you pondered that possibility? Perhaps you ought to make some alternate plans—just in case."

For an instant, Bernard's arrogant expression fell, and Sheridan witnessed his dismay. He understood his position was in jeopardy and that Sheridan was a huge hazard.

If Bernard had been more of a man, Sheridan might have been worried about how the dilemma would resolve, but Bernard was a coward, the type who liked to pick on a female who couldn't defend herself. He didn't have the courage to pick a fight with someone who could fight back, and Sheridan had never been afraid of anything.

He wasn't a helpless female, and he loved a good brawl.

His task complete, his threats delivered, he whirled away and strolled out.

"It's nice to have you home, Miss Sophia."

Sophia smiled at Harry Roland. He was thirty and a very ordinary fellow, slender, short, brown hair, brown eyes, average features. He would never be described as handsome or dashing. He dressed conservatively and was tidy in his appearance.

His comportment matched his profession as accountant for the local brewer. It was a thriving business, and he earned a fine salary. He'd recently bought a house in the village for his mother, and he was still a bachelor. He'd be an excellent catch for some lucky girl. Not Sophia though. Despite what Millicent was hoping, Sophia could never view him in a romantic fashion.

She was exasperated with Millicent for stirring this unwelcome pot, but she didn't blame him, and she would never be rude.

"Yes, it's a relief to be here," she said.

"How are you settling in?"

"It's been tricky. While I was away, I grew up quite a bit. An entirely different person has returned to Riverglen."

"I wanted to tell you how sorry I am about Caroline's death."

His sympathetic comment was the first one offered since she'd been back. Everyone else acted as if Caroline had never existed.

"Thank you for that," she said. "It's kind of you to mention her."

"I hear you brought a . . . a . . . daughter with you?"

"She's not mine!" Sophia hastily insisted.

His cheeks reddened. "I wasn't inferring any misbehavior on your part." He stopped and shook his head. "I shouldn't have raised the issue, but the whole neighborhood is gossiping, and I thought I should learn the truth rather than listen to stories. When the two of you left for France, there was plenty of speculation as to why, but we couldn't confirm any of the rumors. Now, they're swirling again."

She sighed with frustration. "Caroline was ruined and increasing. It's why we went. To hide it."

"But she's deceased and the baby is with us in England, so I guess the attempt at concealment wasn't very successful."

She smirked. "No, it's been a disaster."

"I don't suppose the family is too keen to have the baby here. How are you dealing with it? Has it been difficult for you?"

"I'll muddle through," she said. "We all need an interval to come to grips with the tragedies of the prior year."

"You certainly do, and many of the burdens have fallen on your shoulders."

Supper was over, and they were in a rear parlor. Dancing was about to start.

Usually, the salon was used as a music room, but it was also a social hall when they hosted larger events. There were several dozen people present, but her focus was on Sheridan and Aurora. They were over by the door and chatting with their guests. They looked happy and at ease with each other, as if they were already married.

They were a striking couple, and she couldn't stand to watch them, yet she couldn't yank her gaze away. Sheridan seemed positively enchanted by Aurora. How could that be? How could he have kissed Sophia so passionately the night before, then shift his attention to another woman?

His conduct was maddening and distressing, but then, he'd boasted about being a cad. A cad, by his very nature, had few scruples in his amorous affairs.

He was limping slightly, but he was being a good sport, pretending he wasn't injured. Was she the only one who'd noticed? She yearned to walk over and tell him to sit down, but in the middle of the soiree, she was a spectator. Any display of concern would be odd.

Harry had her trapped in a corner, and she couldn't escape. From the minute he'd arrived, she'd been avoiding him, but he'd finally caught her unawares.

She grasped what Millicent expected to occur, but she couldn't imagine being married to him. All her life, she'd had such big dreams.

Her father had planted them in her head, always tossing out silly remarks such as, *Why be normal? Why be the same as everyone else?*

She'd taken those words to heart, and she struggled to be abnormal. Harry was the most placid, methodical man she'd ever met. He was her exact opposite, and if she wound up wed to him, she would view it as a huge failure.

She was only twenty. Could she accept such a small ending when she was still so young? Wasn't it possible that better choices were hovering just beyond her horizon? Shouldn't she search for them?

The notion that Millicent assumed they'd be a suitable match underscored how little Millicent knew about her. Millicent had no idea of the sort of husband Sophia should have. Not that she wanted a husband. But Harry Roland? Really? Was that the best Millicent could do?

Millicent and Miles were weary of supporting her, so she had to make some decisions. She had Pierre and Emily to consider, so any road she selected had become much more convoluted. Any situation she found had to include them.

"I hate to bore you," he said, "but have you heard my news?"

"No, sorry. What is it?"

"I've been promoted. In fact, my employer's uncle is negotiating to hire me away. I shouldn't brag, but my name is being bandied in certain circles."

"That marvelous, Harry." She truly meant it. She liked to have good things happen to good people.

"A man should strive to improve himself, and I was wondering . . ."

He puffed himself up, appearing as if he was about to pose an important question. No doubt he'd suggest a cozy carriage ride the following afternoon or perhaps he'd ask to escort her to church on Sunday. At Millicent's urging, he would be pondering a courtship that would never commence.

"Would you excuse me?" she said, interrupting him. "It's chilly this evening. I should fetch a shawl from my room."

"Yes, yes, of course. I . . . ah . . . apologize for bothering you."

"You're never a bother, Harry. Please don't think you are."

She dashed away before he could delay her further. He was very modest and never touted his achievements, so it was a sign of his intentions toward her that he'd been eager for her to discover how he was thriving. She'd like to grab him by his lapels, shake him, and say, *I could never shackle myself to such a stable, steady fellow! Why can't you understand that?*

But she would never hurt his feelings. She simply had to flee the party, had to flee from the sight of Sheridan and Aurora together. If she watched them another second, she might explode.

Sheridan Stone wasn't hers, and he never would be, but it crushed her to see him wooing her cousin. She wasn't a glutton for punishment, and she refused to continue suffering.

Sophia flitted away, and if Harry had been more assertive, he might have chased after her, but he wasn't brazen or aggressive. He was thoughtful and kind, reflective and industrious, which were qualities a spirited girl like Sophia could never appreciate.

Unless maybe she was in trouble. Unless maybe she needed help. Unless maybe she was out of options. Then her opinion might change.

When Mrs. Newton had written to apprise him that Sophia was back, he'd immediately realized what she was telling him. She wanted him to woo Sophia, but obviously, it was a lost cause.

He'd always worried over what would become of her, and he'd never supposed the Newton family would be very diligent about arranging her future. Yet he'd also supposed she would never seriously consider him as a beau. On receiving Mrs. Newton's invitation to supper, he'd debated over whether he should oblige her. Sophia had never reciprocated his interest, so why humiliate himself?

From the time he'd first met her, when he'd been twenty and she'd been ten, newly orphaned and bewildered by the death of her beloved father, he'd liked her. She'd brimmed with traits a female wasn't allowed to exhibit, being funny, brash, and full of pluck and vigor.

Her cousin, Caroline, had egged her on into most of the mischief she'd perpetrated, but he'd enjoyed the antics the boisterous pair had instigated. Sophia was so different from the type of person he was, so much braver and confident. He'd yearned to be more like her.

As they'd grown up, he'd remained quiet and studious, but she'd blossomed into a beautiful young lady. He'd begun to speculate as to how he—boring, ordinary Harry Roland—could entice her into a more permanent relationship, but there didn't seem to be a way.

In the end, he'd dragged himself to Riverglen for supper. He'd cornered her and had tried to chat, but she'd been completely unenthused over what he had to say. And though she'd valiantly struggled to conceal her fascination, she'd been totally fixated on Aurora's swain, Captain Stone.

Harry wasn't surprised that she'd moon over the Captain. He possessed every attribute Harry lacked: height, handsome features, brawn, charm. In comparison, Harry was . . .

Well, there was no comparison.

She was probably hoping Mrs. Newton would find her a fiancé like Captain Stone, but he doubted Mrs. Newton would work that hard at choosing someone appropriate, so what would happen to her?

He couldn't imagine, but he wasn't what she needed, not as a husband or even a friend really. He sighed and headed to the foyer. He'd have the butler retrieve his coat and hat, then he'd start the lengthy walk home. It was a cold autumn night, and the cool air would clear his mind and center his thinking.

He shouldn't dream of what could never be. He shouldn't reach higher than he was meant to go. He was British to the bone, and he believed a man should recognize his place and stay there. Any other path simply fueled longing, bitterness, and discontentment.

He was busy, his career on the rise, but it would be a very small rise. Sophia Cantwell could never be part of the narrow road he was destined to travel, and he had to stop wishing she was.

What was the point?

Chapter Eleven

"Hello, Captain Stone."

"It's Sheridan, remember?"

"Yes, I remember."

Sheridan quietly shut Sophia's door and spun the key in the lock. It was late, after midnight, and he couldn't imagine anyone might bluster in after him, but he couldn't take any chances. If he was discovered with her, it would barely cause a ripple in his conscience, but her life would be ruined.

"I figure it would be futile to order you to leave," she said.

"Yes, it would be futile."

"Have you any idea of what would happen to me if you were caught in my room?"

"I have a fairly good notion of the consequences."

She scoffed with disgust. "Yet you barged in anyway?"

She was seated on a chair by the window, gazing outside and looking very melancholy. She was ready for bed again, so it was the second night in a row that he'd stumbled on her when she was undressed. He should have been ashamed of himself, but he wasn't. The prior evening, he'd had too much to drink, and he'd used alcohol as an excuse for his foolishness. What was his excuse on this occasion?

"You vanished after supper," he said, "and I had to find out why."

"I'm sure you'll be stunned to hear that I don't like to socialize with my relatives." Facetiously, she added, "With my being so *close* to them, it's such a joy."

"I didn't like you to sneak off without my being aware."

"Oh, yes, I'm positive I was front and center in all your musings."

"You scarcely spoke two words to me before you left." He sounded as if he was pouting.

"How could I have? You were busy with your fiancée, and I was too courteous to interrupt."

"How many times must I tell you? She's not my fiancée."

"I bet *she* believes she is."

He grinned. "Are you jealous?"

"I'm . . . something, but I can't decide what it is. I don't like you enough to be jealous, so what could it be?"

"Do you wish I was courting you instead?"

"I don't think so. Or maybe I do. I contemplate you, and I simply wind up befuddled and annoyed."

"I feel exactly the same when I contemplate you."

He pushed away from the door and went over to where she was sitting. He stood next to her, leaned on the sill, and he stared out. It was grey and cloudy, so there wasn't much to see.

They were silent, lost in thought, and he couldn't guess what was rattling through her deranged head, but as for himself, he was trying to deduce his purpose with regard to her. He was growing convinced that Miss Newton would be a fine bride, so where would Sophia fit in that nuptial scenario?

He could wed in a hurry, become a property owner, and settle down. He'd retire from government service, declare himself a gentleman farmer, and learn to be content. Why shouldn't he proceed? Why not?

Except that, when he was with Miss Newton, he constantly wondered if Sophia might flit by. When he was with Miss Newton, he'd bizarrely wonder how quickly he could creep away and track her down. His behavior was dangerous and preposterous, but he couldn't keep his focus on Miss Newton where it belonged.

"How is your leg?" she asked.

"It's all right." It was the answer he repeatedly gave when people inquired.

"Liar. You were limping when you danced with Aurora."

"I always limp."

"If that's the case, then you shouldn't be up on your feet so much. You certainly shouldn't be dancing. How will you ever get better if you don't rest your injury?"

"I doubt I'll ever get better," he murmured.

She had an uncanny ability to drag confessions out of him, and she recognized how difficult it had been for him to utter the comment. She slipped her hand into his and squeezed his fingers. It was a show of kindness that thrilled him, that soothed him. That irked him.

He didn't want displays of kindness from her. He didn't want understanding or compassion. When she extended feminine comfort, it seemed as if they were more firmly attached than they actually were. He didn't dare be attached, but evidently, he possessed an important affection for her.

It was bubbling below the surface, and he knew he shouldn't act on it, knew he shouldn't flirt with her, but then, he didn't know either.

He was descended from a long line of cads, and when a pretty female captured his attention, he made bad choices.

It was the pathetic story of the men in his family. They seduced young ladies and were ensnared in amorous mishaps. It was always wrong and hazardous, yet he didn't pull away.

"I hate to hear that you're hurting," she said.

"I'm not hurting. I'm just wounded. The pain comes and goes. I'll survive."

"But probably not as a sailor?"

"Probably not."

She was yanking admissions out of him that left him too morose, and he refused to be gloomy. These few minutes by her side were the best of the whole day, and he wouldn't waste them feeling sorry for himself.

"You're so glum," he said. "Why are you sitting here and staring out the window?"

"I had planned to wish on a star, but it's too cloudy."

"What would your wish have been?"

She chuckled. "I have such a lengthy list that I'd have to babble until dawn to tabulate them all."

"What's at the top? What is your biggest dream?"

She considered, then said, "I suppose I'd like to be fantastically rich, so I could carry on however I please."

"It's marvelous to be rich. I highly recommend it."

"I'd like to journey to new places and rub elbows with intriguing strangers in foreign lands."

"I've done all that, and it's very fun. It's why I can't picture myself retiring to the country. The notion of rural living holds no appeal to me whatsoever."

"My father was a poet," she said. "He filled my head with wild ideas, so I yearn in ways that are foolish. I keep thinking I should be able to arrange the type of future he envisioned for me, but I can't fathom how I would."

"It's hard to be a woman."

"Yes, it is," she agreed, "and you're so lucky you were born a man."

"I've always thought so."

She gazed out for a bit, then she said, "Millicent has demanded I marry."

The announcement was like a punch in the gut, which was very odd. The prospect was none of his business, and of course she should wed. It was the only sane route for her, and with her being in such a dire fiscal condition, she'd be fortunate to have the chance.

He scowled. "Has she picked someone?"

"A neighbor who's sweet on me. Now that I'm back, Millicent is encouraging him."

"Would you like to wed him?"

"He's very nice, and he has steady employment and a house of his own. Could you imagine me trapped in a small, tedious life like that? With an ordinary spouse like that? I'd throw myself off a cliff first."

He realized he should tread carefully and shouldn't offer an opinion that would discourage her. If she could glom onto a husband and escape Riverglen, she absolutely should. There was the added, very selfish benefit that—if he wed her cousin—she would be gone from the property, so he wouldn't have to bump into her whenever he turned a corner. But still, the prospect of her being given to another man was alarming.

"What other option do you have but marriage?" he asked.

"There isn't one. I'll be twenty-one next year, so Millicent's guardianship will terminate. She believes she should shackle me before she's finished."

"Was your beau at supper?"

"He's not my beau, but yes. Millicent invited him."

"What's his name?"

"Harry Roland. If you met him though, you wouldn't remember him. He's very forgettable."

Sheridan searched his mind, and she was correct. He couldn't recall the fellow, but then, he'd been introduced to several dozen people.

She peered up at him and changed the subject. "It hurts me when you dote on Aurora."

"I already figured that out."

"I don't know much about romance, but could you explain this to me? How could you kiss me last night, then today, act as if nothing happened between us?"

His cheeks reddened with chagrin. "What can I tell you? I'm a cad. Bad behavior is practically expected of me."

"What if you marry Aurora? What if I'm still here after your wedding? Would you continue to sneak into my bedchamber? Would you constantly kiss me, then ignore me later on?"

It was the most awkward conversation he'd ever had with a female. Generally, his amorous forays were with whores or doxies. When he was traveling, they entertained him at brothels in port towns. When he was in England, he amused himself at upscale brothels in London.

He'd never wooed a respectable maiden. He'd also never envisioned himself a fiancé, then a husband. He'd never worried about issues like fidelity and monogamy, but he had to begin worrying about them.

He was such a huge dunce! "The possibility of me walking down the aisle with your cousin is so far down the road that it's like a peculiar dream. I haven't pondered any of the consequences that might ensue."

"I couldn't tarry at Riverglen as this unfolds. It might be quite a few steps beyond my ability to tolerate."

"You and I are just flirting, Cantwell. You shouldn't read too much into it."

"Yes, it's flirting," she said. "Inappropriate, dangerous flirting. I don't see this ending well. Not for me anyway."

"I could pretend to be gallant and claim I'll stay away from you, but I'd probably be lying. Doesn't it seem as if there's mischief afoot and Fate is toying with us?"

"Yes, it seems exactly like that."

"We keep crossing paths, and I keep getting dragged deeper into your life."

"I picture it the opposite way: *I* am being dragged into yours."

He smiled. "It's not so terrible though, is it? Your paltry existence is wretched. You're lucky I've barged in to enliven it."

"You're sufficiently vain that you'd presume I'm viewing it like that."

She looked so despondent, and he couldn't bear to observe her woe. The exhausting fact was that he liked her more than he should.

Of the two women at Riverglen—her and Miss Newton—*she* was the one he should be courting. She made him laugh. She made him happy. She amazed and infuriated him. He'd never have a dull moment with her, but she was poor as a church mouse. She brought no assets to the table, and a man didn't marry for friendship or fond feelings.

He wed for status, for property, for wealth. He wed to increase his position in the world, to wind up higher than where he'd started.

What could Sophia Cantwell provide that would satisfy any of those requirements?

He couldn't think of a single thing.

He dipped down and kissed her. He shouldn't have, but he couldn't resist. For a brief second, she participated, then she drew away and said, "I can't do this with you, or I'll begin to crave in a manner that's pointless. I'll yearn for you to be mine, but I don't even want you."

He chuckled at that. "You are such a ridiculous ninny."

"Yes, I've always been ridiculous."

"I was teasing, Cantwell," he gently said. "You're sweeter than you let on."

She shook her head. "I'm not. I'm just as silly as you've assumed."

"I stand corrected."

He kissed her again, more fiercely, and he tried to pull her to her feet, so he could maneuver them over to the bed and tumble them down onto it, but she had better sense than he did. She squirmed away and scampered across the small room to hover by the dresser.

"You're too much *man* for me," she said.

"I'm too much man for every woman who's ever known me."

"I can't involve myself like this. I can't pursue a reckless amour. I don't have the fortitude to stagger through it unscathed."

"I like tiptoeing in to be alone with you. I can't stop."

"You have to. You can't tempt me like this."

She tempted him too, in insane ways, and he was totally enthralled by her. The cord that bound them was firm and tight, and he didn't have a knife sharp enough to cut her loose and free himself.

"I have an idea," he blurted out before he could persuade himself to be silent.

"From the gleam in your eye, I'm scared to hear what it might be."

"How about if you come to London with me."

"As your what . . . ?"

"As my mistress."

She scoffed dejectedly. "I could never do that, and I'm embarrassed that you would suggest it."

"What is your alternative? After all, if you tarry here, it appears your guardian will marry you—against your will—to a tedious dolt who will make you miserable forever."

"So I should jump at a lewd proposition instead? My cousin would get to be your bride and I'd get to be your doxy? Is that what you're telling me?"

He winced with dismay. "When you put it like that, it sounds horrid. I'm sorry."

"I can't believe you view me as being that debauched."

"I don't view you as debauched. I simply can't imagine never seeing you again. That seems . . . bizarre, I guess."

"Even if I was interested," she said, "I have Pierre and Emily to consider. You wouldn't be gaining a paramour. You'd be fettered to a woman with two children to raise."

"I forgot about them, didn't I?" He grinned to lighten the somber mood he'd created. "I apologize. I insulted you, and I shouldn't have mentioned it."

"Apology accepted."

"In my own defense, I was reared like a wolf pup in the forest, and I've spent my adult life as a sailor. I've had very few social graces pounded into my head."

"You have enough of them rolling around to make you charming." She tossed the compliment to him like an olive branch.

He snorted. "You think I'm charming?"

"Yes, you sly devil."

Without pondering or planning, he'd thrown out his offer that she be his mistress, but she was smarter than he was. She could never have agreed. It was the sort of secret that always leaked out, but evidently, he was searching for excuses to be close to her.

What was wrong with him? He couldn't enter into a passionate arrangement with her, then wed her cousin. That would be deranged conduct.

"When are you leaving?" she asked.

"Wednesday."

"You're traveling to Swindon for your father's party?"

"Yes."

"He'll be there? You're sure?"

It was an odd query, but then, she was an odd female, so he didn't dwell on it. "Ah, yes? It's his birthday celebration, so he'll definitely be there."

"I'll remain out of sight until you depart. Don't stop by in the future. Don't look for me."

"You don't have to hide."

He felt weirdly panicked at the prospect of her avoiding him, and as usual, she was being absurd. He would absolutely sneak into her bedchamber again. If that little pleasure was off the table, what fun would he have at Riverglen?

"You should go," she said.

"I don't want to."

"I don't want you to either, but it's for the best."

"Says who?"

"Says me," she saucily retorted.

"Well, Cantwell, I've always thought you were very silly, so why would I listen to you?"

He sauntered over and drew her into his arms. He kissed her for an eternity, not able to resist, then he eased away.

"I'll see you tomorrow," he said, and he tapped a finger on the tip of her pert nose. "Keep out of trouble until then, will you?"

"I'll behave. I swear."

He smirked with amusement. He was completely besotted and much too fascinated. Where would it lead? Where would it end?

Nowhere good, he was positive.

He had to physically yank himself away; her hold on him was that strong. He went to the door and crept out without glancing back. He was anxious to glance back, but that was an unhinged impulse, and he couldn't yield to it.

For pity's sake, they'd be together again the next morning.

He continued down the hall to his own bedroom, where he should have been tucked away all along.

Chapter Twelve

"Does the King of England live here?"

Sophia shook her head at Pierre and said, "No."

"Might he stop by? Might we see him?"

"I can guarantee the King will not stop by."

She couldn't be certain though. Why wouldn't he visit?

She was nestled in her carriage and staring out the window at Swindon Hall. The mansion looked like the sort of place where royalty would reside, so she could completely understand Pierre's question.

It was four stories high, constructed of a sand-colored stone. The wings went on forever in both directions, and there seemed to be a thousand windows gleaming in the afternoon sun. The grounds were immaculate, the gardens impeccable. Every detail blatantly indicated the wealth attached to the Swindon title.

Sheridan had bragged that they were very rich, but she'd simply thought it was male boasting. This exquisite building was his family's main seat of power. It was an unabashed monument, meant to underscore their magnificence.

Why would he bother with a paltry estate like Riverglen? Why would he marry Aurora? With his father being this grand, why wasn't he hunting for a princess bride?

She felt quite foolish. While they'd been kissing in her bedchamber, she'd begun to wonder—in a silly, feminine way—why she couldn't have him for her very own.

Well, Swindon Hall was why.

When he'd crowed about his affluence, he'd actually been warning her. It was ridiculous for her to have pondered an amour with him. He was a cad who ruined ninnies like her for sport. He'd likely viewed their pathetic flirtation no differently than he'd have viewed a romp with one of the scullery maids. In fact, he'd probably romped with the scullery maids! She was lucky he hadn't slipped her a penny every time he'd snuck into her room.

She was mortified and sad, but relieved too that she hadn't behaved stupidly. Her heart was a bit bruised, but that was her sole injury, and it would heal.

She hadn't said goodbye to him or even hinted that she was leaving, and when she returned home, he'd be gone. He was staying until Wednesday, then making his own trek to Swindon Hall. She'd handle her business, then depart before he arrived. They'd pass each other on the road, and he wouldn't realize it.

She'd crept away from Riverglen without an explanation to a single soul about her mission or destination. She'd penned a bland note to Millicent, apprising her that she'd be away for a short jaunt, but she'd provided no other information.

It had taken a day and a half to reach Swindon. They'd left on Saturday morning, so it was Sunday afternoon. The house was massive and overwhelming, and suddenly, she wasn't sure she should have appeared unannounced. How would she breach the walls of such a majestic spot? What had she been thinking?

Should she have written first? No. That hadn't been an option, for she was positive her overture would have been ignored. Emily was precocious and lovely, like an angelic cherub. People were always charmed by her, and Sophia would use the child's allure to gain the access she was desperate to have.

A footman whipped the door open and said, "Welcome to Swindon."

He set the step, then stuck his hand into the vehicle and helped her out. Pierre clambered down on his own, then Emily strutted into the doorway. She extended her arms to the footman, imperiously demanding he lift her down.

"Hello, little Missy," the young man said to her as he swung her out. "Aren't you pretty as a picture?"

Emily preened at the compliment, smiling as if his adulation was her absolute due.

For once, Sophia had fussed incessantly over Emily's clothes so she'd be perfectly adorable. She was wearing a white dress, a blue pinafore over the top. Her black shoes were polished, her petticoats starched and crackling when she walked.

Sophia had even tied a bow in her hair, the blue ribbon matching her pinafore and enhancing the sapphire of her eyes. At the moment, there could be no more gorgeous girl in the entire kingdom.

The footman yanked his gaze from Emily and said to Sophia, "Are you here for the party, Ma'am?"

"I'm not a ma'am. I'm a Miss, and no. I'm not here for the party. I should like to confer with Lord Swindon. I have an important topic to address with him. I recognize I'm being very forward, but might he be available to speak with me?"

Sybil Jones marched down the hall toward the private parlor behind Neville's library. The butler had come to find her, and he'd been very distraught. He'd stashed an uninvited visitor in the rear salon, so she couldn't blab her purpose to any guests before someone in authority—that being a family member—talked to her.

The butler had worked at Swindon for forty years, and he could perceptively diagnose catastrophe when it was brewing. A Miss Sophia Cantwell was asking to meet with Neville. She had a toddler with her and in the butler's astute opinion, the girl was a Stone daughter.

Sybil knew Neville and his sons, knew their risqué habits and their reckless tendencies. If one of them had sired a bastard, she wouldn't be surprised.

Disappointed, yes. But surprised? No.

She was speculating over whose it would turn out to be. Neville's? Hunter's? Warwick's? Both boys had just gotten married, so the prospect would create problems with their brides. Or maybe it was Sheridan's. He was still a bachelor, but he was off on a nuptial scouting trip. Would the first news he shared with his wife be that an unwanted bastard had surfaced?

She halted at the parlor door, took a deep breath, then entered the room. Miss Cantwell was seated on the sofa. A boy stood behind her, seeming stern and protective, but she didn't see the toddler anywhere.

Miss Cantwell was twenty or so, with curly dark hair and big green eyes. She was obviously Quality, attired in an emerald gown that was sewn from an expensive fabric and tailored to accentuate her petite anatomy. She looked fetching and interesting, smart and shrewd, and she exuded a calm air that was a relief to witness. Sybil wouldn't be negotiating with a frivolous ninny.

"Hello, Miss Cantwell," she said, as she swept in and sat in a chair across from her. "I am Miss Sybil Jones. I am a dear friend of Lord Swindon's, and I am his hostess as we celebrate his birthday. The butler thought I should speak with you."

"Hello, Miss Jones. Thank you for bothering with me. I'm being very bold in seeking out the Earl, but I'm plagued by a rather delicate matter, and I don't suppose I should reveal it to anyone but him. What would you predict the chances are of my obtaining an audience?"

"I guess that depends on what *I* decide to tell him about you. Why are you here?" Miss Cantwell stared implacably, not awed or daunted, and Sybil said, "You can confide in me, Miss Cantwell. If you have any hope at all of seeing Neville, you'll have to convince me that I should allow it."

Miss Cantwell gnawed on her cheek and sifted through her replies, trying to pick the one most likely to succeed. The boy fidgeted, anxious to comment, but Sybil figured Miss Cantwell had ordered him to be silent.

Before Miss Cantwell could choose her response, a tiny bundle of energy scooted out from behind the sofa. She was blond, blue-eyed, and pretty as a porcelain doll. Sybil instantly concurred with the butler's conclusion: A Stone daughter had arrived. But who was the father?

The toddler bustled over to Sybil and perched at her knee, a hand on her thigh, as she spewed a flurry of words that sounded like a combination of French and English that was very difficult to comprehend. It seemed as if she was complaining that she'd come a very long way in a carriage and that it had been very boring.

She was delightful and mesmerizing, and Sybil was immediately smitten. She wasn't a maternal person, but she was keen to snuggle the child on her lap. What would Miss Cantwell think of that?

"This is Emily," Miss Cantwell said. "She believes she's the center of the universe, and she's never accepted the admonition about how children are to be seen and not heard." To the girl, "Miss Emily! You are to behave, remember? Sit down!"

Miss Cantwell patted the spot next to her on the sofa, and the toddler debated whether to obey. Then she went over as Miss Cantwell had demanded. The boy lifted her onto the cushion, and he kept a palm on her shoulder so she couldn't wiggle away.

Sybil sighed, but with what emotion? Exasperation? Dismay? Resignation?

Men had affairs, and they sired children when they weren't careful. Gad, they sired them when they *were* careful. It was simply a fact that babies were born when the adults didn't expect them. She wasn't naïve about it. The only part that ever angered her was how the father acted, how the mother was treated.

When a woman was seduced, it was always the man's fault, and Sybil thought they should step up. In the world she inhabited, they rarely did though. They were too elevated and grand to follow the rules laid down for common people.

"Now that I've met Emily," Sybil said to Miss Cantwell, "I won't inquire as to your purpose. It's clear what it is." Sybil gestured to the boy. "Is this your son? Your brother? May we talk frankly in front of him? Or should I have the butler take him to the kitchen for a snack?"

"I apologize for leaving you confused about us, Miss Jones." Miss Cantwell nodded to the boy. "Pierre is my servant. His mother died recently, so he's become my responsibility. I don't have any children."

"So you're not . . . ah . . . Emily's mother?"

"No. Her mother was my cousin. She passed away too, the same week as Pierre's mother."

"My goodness," Sybil murmured, "but you've had a rough go of it."

"It's been very rough, and I was left with custody of Emily."

Sybil said to the boy, "Hello, Pierre. I'm sorry for your loss."

"Merci, mademoiselle."

He'd answered in French, so evidently, Miss Cantwell had an intriguing story to share.

"We can talk in front of him," Miss Cantwell said. "He was with me through the entire debacle that I have to address."

Sybil didn't dither. "I assume Emily is a Stone daughter?"

"Yes, she is," Miss Cantwell firmly stated, "and I appreciate your not arguing or denying it. I've been worried over how we'd be received. I have a birth certificate as proof. It's in French though."

"May I see it?"

Miss Cantwell produced the document and handed it over. Sybil wasn't fluent in the language, but she could figure it out sufficiently to identify the mother and father.

"Caroline Newton," she mused, but the name meant nothing to her. She traced a finger across the name of the father, and she smirked and shook her head. Of course it would be him.

A flurry erupted in the hall, and she heard Neville approaching. He was with the butler, and the butler was valiantly trying to slow him down, but he wouldn't be delayed.

"Sybil?" Neville called. "Where are you? There's a problem with the champagne that's being shipped from Paris. I need you to . . ."

He sauntered in and slid to a halt, frowning at Miss Cantwell.

"Pardon me," Neville said to Sybil. "I didn't realize you were busy."

"Neville, we have guests, and you should join us for this discussion. It concerns you." Sybil said to Miss Cantwell, "Miss Cantwell, your wish has been granted. May I present Neville Stone, Lord Swindon?"

Miss Cantwell leapt to her feet and curtsied, displaying some very pretty manners. Then Sybil said, "Neville, this is Miss Sophia Cantwell. She's come to confer over a very important subject. Why don't you sit down? I'm afraid, when you discover what it is, you might faint."

There was no opportunity for Neville to absorb the strange scene or remark on it. Emily squirmed to the floor and hurried over to him.

"Papa?" she asked, and she extended her arms so he'd lift her up.

Without thinking, without blinking, Neville picked her up and hugged her to his chest.

"What should I say to you? I'm not sure."

As Sybil posed her question, Neville peered up at her, and for once, he was at a loss for words.

He'd lived a life of debauchery and vice. He was renowned for his romantic foibles, for his bad marriages, for his gambling and foul habits, but normally, he committed his sins with other men who were just as wicked as he was. They were rich and entitled, so who could have stopped them? Who would have dared?

He was vain and imperious—and obnoxiously self-centered. He never thought he should have to defend himself, and he never did. Except that Sybil was his dearest friend.

She wasn't like the demur, tedious wives who populated his lofty world. Nor was she like the fallen angels of the demimonde. She was part of the demimonde, where he thrived, but she hadn't been corrupted by it. She understood the rules and routines, understood the characters and rogues, and she was never shocked by any antic or activity.

"I always hope you have a high opinion of me," he told her, "and I'm embarrassed to have landed you in the middle of this fiasco. I'm glad I don't have to maneuver through it by myself. I'll make much better choices with you guiding me."

"I have a high opinion of you, but it's a realistic opinion too. You're a cad, and you've reveled in the designation, but there are consequences to your larks and frolics. One of those consequences has just appeared on your stoop."

They were still in the parlor where Neville had stumbled on her during her meeting with Miss Cantwell. When Emily had called him *papa,* he'd been so stunned that he'd nearly fainted—as Sybil had warned him he might.

Sybil had had the butler escort Miss Cantwell and the children to the kitchen to be fed. Neville and Sybil were huddled privately and deciding how to proceed. Neville was seated on the sofa, and Sybil in the chair across. She'd poured him a brandy, and he was drinking it with quaking hands.

"Is Miss Cantwell telling the truth?" Sybil asked. "Did you have an affair with her cousin?"

"Yes, I had an affair with the blasted girl. I shouldn't have," he muttered. "How can I discuss it in a manner that won't sound awful? I was careful with her, and I can't fathom how I wound up planting a child."

His cheeks heated to such a hot temperature that he was amazed he didn't ignite.

Sybil watched him fidget and spew justifications, and she said, "It doesn't take much effort to plant a babe in a girl's belly. A man can be incredibly cautious and still be caught. Weren't you aware of that fact? I'm the spinster in this relationship. I shouldn't have to explain the details of carnal couplings to you."

He chuckled miserably. "Are you scolding me? If you are, I deserve it."

"I'm not scolding you. I'm simply trying to figure out how we should move forward with this debacle. It's awkward timing, what with your guests arriving for the party. We're about to have dozens of acquaintances filling up the bedchambers, and I can't imagine dealing with Miss Cantwell too."

"What does she want from me?" he asked. "Has she apprised you?"

"You blustered in before she had the chance, but I presume she'll request parental recognition and support." Sybil scowled ferociously. "You're not about to reject her claim, are you? She showed me a birth certificate where Caroline Newton declared you to be the father."

"You saw Emily when I was holding her. You viewed the two of us together. Can you seriously expect I would state, with a straight face, that she isn't mine?"

Sybil nodded. "Good. I'm delighted to have you admit it. I've been struggling to deduce how I'd respond if you denied her."

"Had I pretended innocence, you'd have laughed me out of the room."

"Yes, I would have, but first, I'd have ordered you to stop being an ass. Did you have any idea you were a father again?"

"No! I dabbled with Caroline—twice!—when she was in London for a few weeks. She'd come to town with her mother's friends; they trusted her and didn't chaperone her. She was recklessly flirtatious, and she snuck out of their house at night to dally with me. Then they went home to the country. I never heard from her again."

"I don't suppose you ever thought about her again either."

"No, I didn't. I'm a sorry excuse for a man, aren't I? I hate to have you witness this side of me."

"I've always seen this side of you, Neville. You are not a mystery to me."

"I'm a mess, darling," he said. "I'm mortified and bewildered. What should I do? What would you advise?"

She rose from her chair, and she nestled herself next to him on the sofa. She clasped his hand and rested her head on his shoulder.

"It's not the end of the world," she said. "Bastards are common, and you're negligent. Didn't you tell me you had four others?"

"Yes, four, but I've never been thrust into an encounter like this. To have Miss Cantwell strut in without any warning! It's beyond the pale."

"In London, we bumped into your natural daughter, Joanna Ralston, in the park. You told me then that you wished you'd been kinder to your children."

He sighed. "Yes, but I never suspected a second daughter would immediately stroll in. She's just a baby! I'm too old to start over from scratch."

"Maybe this is the universe giving you an opportunity to do exactly that. Maybe you can atone for some of your sins."

"If I had a century to try, I couldn't fully atone."

"Well, it's always good to walk down a new road."

"I simply wanted to have a lovely celebration with my friends." He sounded petulant. "I didn't want to spend two weeks, rearranging my entire life."

"I like the notion of having a baby in the house. It's been many years since I lived around a toddler."

"I've *never* lived around one," Neville said. "I didn't have the patience for their rambunctious clamor, so the result is that I barely know my boys."

"And they barely know you. They constantly complain about it, so you're being offered another chance—and to orchestrate a different conclusion."

"Am I interested though? At the moment, I'm happy with the way things are."

"Perhaps Emily will make them even better."

"Perhaps," he mumbled, but he was dubious.

"How about this, Neville? Let's invite Miss Cantwell to tarry for a few days. We'll put them up in the nursery. They'll mostly be out of sight from your guests. We can confer with Miss Cantwell to learn what she'll solicit from you, then we'll determine if you should provide it."

"If we determine that Emily should stay with us, how will we proceed?"

"We'll raise her, you clueless oaf." Sybil laughed. "I wouldn't let you dump her on the servants as you did with your boys. Look how they turned out!"

"My boys are fine."

"They don't think they are, and I agree with them, so if you assume custody of Emily, you'll have to be a parent for a change, which means you and I will have to have a long talk about the future. You might have to keep me around for the duration."

"Are you proposing marriage?" he asked.

"I might be," she said.

He smirked. "You would never wed me. My awful habits would drive you mad."

"Probably, but I won't permit you to have Emily unless *I* can have her too. I'd never abandon her to your wastrel ways."

"Aren't we getting ahead of ourselves?" Neville said. "We don't even know if Miss Cantwell wants to give her to me."

"I don't care what Miss Cantwell wants. You and I will decide what will happen to Emily. Miss Cantwell's wishes are irrelevant."

Sybil stepped into the nursery. Pierre and Emily were playing in the corner. Miss Cantwell was seated on a chair by the window. She looked lonely and wistful, as if she'd like to be anywhere but Swindon. Pierre and Miss Cantwell stared at Sybil, and they were braced for disaster, as if they were certain they were being kicked out.

Emily scarcely bothered to glance up. She was totally at ease, as if she belonged right where she was and she wasn't about to depart.

"Papa?" she asked Sybil, apparently wondering if Neville was about to arrive.

"He'll visit in a bit," Sybil said.

She couldn't predict if he would. He wasn't an affectionate man, and he definitely didn't consider himself a father. He might acknowledge Emily, but as to how the actual issue of parenting would unfold, she couldn't guess. She couldn't see him bonding with Emily or bringing her into the bosom of the family, but Sybil was forming her own ideas about the situation.

The past few months, Neville had been hinting that he'd like a closer connection to Sybil. She'd teased him in return, pretending she might be interested, but she couldn't imagine having him as a husband. She wouldn't wed a philanderer, and she couldn't picture him settling down and practicing monogamy. He might be fifty, but he still viewed himself as thirty and a rake who could entice any girl who tickled his fancy.

Sybil was forty, and subjects like fidelity and loyalty mattered to her. She might be a modern, independent woman who'd earned a fortune from the reckless dandies of the demimonde, but at her core, she had a very moral center. She wouldn't have a faithless spouse.

Occasionally, Neville had claimed he could be the husband she needed, but he was only fooling himself. He might swear he'd improve. He might even utter vows in a church, but he'd never keep to them. Of that fact, she had no doubt at all.

But what about little Emily? Had she altered Sybil's opinion? Had she altered Neville's? Time would tell, she supposed. If Neville didn't want Emily, Sybil might. What would Miss Cantwell think of that possibility? Sybil was very wealthy, and she could give a child a grand life.

She was friends with Neville too, and she could layer on guilt when necessary and force him to behave as Miss Cantwell was hoping. If Sybil wound up in charge of Emily, Emily would frequently visit her father. She'd grow up around him and would get to know him. Wouldn't that be marvelous?

"Might we speak privately, Miss Cantwell?" she asked.

"Yes, of course." She glanced at Pierre and said, "Mind Emily for me."

Pierre replied in French, and they exchanged a flurry of comments. Emily ignored them and peered up at Sybil, as if asking, *Well? Will you treat me as I'm expecting or not?*

Sybil exited into the hall, and Miss Cantwell followed her. The nursery was located in a wing of smaller bedchambers, where the less illustrious guests would be housed. Most of the rooms had been opened and aired in preparation for the party. Sybil led her into one of them.

The autumn afternoon was chilly, the fire not lit, so the temperature was frigid. They went over to the window, yearning for sunshine to break through and warm them.

For such a young person, Miss Cantwell was very confident, very self-possessed, and she started the conversation. "Are you about to inform me that we're leaving? If that's the case, the day is waning, so could we go in the morning? We can remain in the nursery until then. You won't even realize we're on the premises."

"You're not leaving," Sybil told her. "Not yet anyway. The Earl would like you to tarry briefly while we figure out a solution. What is it you seek with regard to Emily? He wanted me to inquire."

Miss Cantwell's response was an odd surprise. "Have you ever been burdened by a deathbed promise, Miss Jones?"

"No, I can't say that I have."

"Emily's mother, Caroline, was my cousin, but she was more like a sister to me. When we found out she was increasing, her parents were livid. They sent us to France to hide her shame."

Sybil winced. "It happens, Miss Cantwell. Family members don't always deal with scandal in a rational way."

"The whole debacle was very traumatic for Caroline's father," Miss Cantwell said. "I never blamed him for banishing her, but he was incredibly enraged because she wouldn't name the scoundrel who'd ruined her. She bit her tongue—until she was dying."

"Why wouldn't she tell anyone?"

Miss Cantwell shrugged. "She was naïve and foolish. She thought he would miss her and come for her. She had concocted a fantasy where he'd arrive on a white charger and they'd ride off into the sunset together."

Sybil tsked with exasperation. "I've been acquainted with Lord Swindon for years, and if that's what your cousin believed, then yes, she was a terrible fool."

"He was also married back then."

"Ah, yes, he was. In the interim, he's been widowed."

"Caroline learned he was married," Miss Cantwell explained, "and after that revelation, I imagine she was too mortified to identify him. In the end, she made me swear that I would contact him and ensure Emily was raised in the style to which she's due. Her mother asked it of me with practically her last breath."

"A deathbed promise . . ." Sybil murmured.

"Yes, so I'd like to request that he recognize and support Emily."

"What is in it for you, Miss Cantwell? You must want something."

"Not really." She paused and frowned. "Well, my own affairs are quite tangled. If he intends to hire a nanny, I suppose I could beg for it to be me. I don't have many maternal qualities though. I might not be very good at it."

Sybil chuckled. "If that was a job interview, I can't claim you've convinced me you'd be a viable candidate."

"I'm an orphan and spinster. I don't have a dowry, and next year, I'll come of age. My relatives aren't too keen to have me residing with them. If I could stay with Emily and watch over her, I would do that—for her mother."

"If we don't wish to employ you? Then what?"

"Then . . . I . . . I . . . will probably wed a farmer and be miserable forever."

Sybil chuckled again, being very charmed by her. "And if we decide Emily is *not* his daughter, what would your opinion be about that?"

Miss Cantwell's jaw dropped. "But I showed you the birth certificate! I told you about Caroline's deathbed confession. Will Lord Swindon pretend I'm lying?"

"I can't guess what he'll choose. He is a rich, important man. He's brought many children into this world, but he's never parented any of them. It's difficult for me to predict how this will resolve."

Miss Cantwell's shoulders slumped with defeat, and she stared at the floor as she processed Sybil's blunt remark, then she said, "I realized it would be hard to travel here and even harder to persuade you. I'm stunned that you and the Earl met with me. I shouldn't expect much more beyond that opportunity."

"Don't worry. We'll devise an acceptable conclusion. If he doesn't want Emily, there might be another option."

Sybil might like to raise Emily herself. It would be the chance to have a daughter, without having the bother of a husband.

"What alternative are you envisioning?" Miss Cantwell said. "I wouldn't let you shuffle her off to a tenant farmer who was paid to take care of her. You can't abandon her in an orphanage. If that's your idea, I'll have to keep her with me."

Sybil barely knew Miss Cantwell, so she wasn't about to clarify her plan. She would hover on the edge of the situation, and if Neville didn't step up, she'd suggest her own custodial arrangement.

"Never fear," Sybil said. "It wouldn't be horrid. It would be what she deserves, and it would please you very much."

Miss Cantwell gazed outside, her mind whirring, then she said, "All right. I can tarry until early Wednesday, but then, I'm . . . ah . . . needed at home. I can't remain any longer than that, so we'd have to work it out by then."

"We'll get it settled to everyone's satisfaction."

They walked back to the nursery, and as they approached the door, Pierre was standing in the hall. He pressed a finger to his lips, urging them to silence, then he moved away, so Sybil could peek into the room.

To her great astonishment, Neville was sitting in the rocking chair. Emily was splayed across his chest, sucking her thumb and fast asleep. He looked perfectly comfortable, as if he'd rocked a baby to sleep every day of his sorry, unrepentant life.

He flashed a sheepish grin at Sybil, as if to apprise her that he wasn't certain how he'd wound up where he was. She grinned back, thinking everything might turn out just fine.

Chapter Thirteen

SHERIDAN SHRUGGED OFF HIS coat and handed it to his valet and bodyguard, George Barnes. They were both in a foul mood.

It was Monday evening, and he was ensconced in his bedchamber at Swindon. Over the years, he'd visited the spot when his uncles, then his various cousins, had been earl. But it was the first occasion he'd strutted in the front door when his father was earl, and every facet of the situation was strange.

He'd meant to tarry at Riverglen until Wednesday, but he'd been chafing and bored and had decided to leave early. He wouldn't admit that he'd departed because Sophia had left too. On Saturday, he'd kept watching for her to stroll by and entertain him. He'd stopped by the nursery too, thinking she'd be there or that he could chat with Pierre, but she and the children had been noticeably absent.

Finally, he'd eavesdropped on a pair of housemaids who'd mentioned that she'd taken a carriage and had snuck off. She hadn't provided any information as to her destination, so her purpose was a mystery, but Sheridan was certain it would be for some ridiculous pursuit.

He'd suffered through a quiet, exhausting Sunday, and by Sunday night, he'd invented a pretext to flee, claiming Neville needed him sooner than planned. He'd packed his bags and had raced away at dawn.

George had been staying with friends on the route to Swindon, and the arrangement had been for Sheridan to pass by on Wednesday, with George accompanying him to the party. Sheridan's premature arrival had upset George's schedule too. George hadn't been invited to Neville's celebration, but was attending as Sheridan's servant. He had a rare knack for managing a fellow's wardrobe, and he'd refused to allow Sheridan to waltz into any of the events unless he looked like the son of the aristocrat he now was.

It had been a miserable day for traveling, rain drizzling the whole trip, wind lashing them. They were wet, cold, and weary, but they couldn't relax. Sheridan had a role to play. The downstairs parlors were filled with people, so socializing was in progress, and supper would be served at nine.

He was required to put in an appearance, so he had to adjust his attitude, dry off, wash, and don apparel appropriate for the moment. His brothers weren't in residence yet, so he was the only son to stagger in. He'd asked after his father, but the servants hadn't been able to locate Neville, so Sheridan hadn't seen him.

"Let's get you ready," George said.

"You're as drenched as I am," Sheridan told him. "You should repair yourself rather than worry about me."

George would lodge with the groomsmen who had an apartment over the stables. He was a navy veteran who was used to sparse quarters and would be comfortable there, but he hadn't had a chance to rest. His focus was on Sheridan.

"I have the entire night to regroup," George said. "You, on the other hand, have an audience awaiting you."

"Well, my father's audience awaits anyway. From what I observed when we entered the house, it's mostly his closest chums who are here. They're a collection of aging, immoral wastrels."

"Which is what I assume you will be in a few decades, so you shouldn't be so derogatory about their habits and choices."

"I'm trying very hard to walk a different road."

"By becoming a married man?" George asked.

So far, George hadn't uttered an opinion about Sheridan's nuptial foray. And why would he? Even if he thought the notion absurd, every man wed sooner or later. It was the way of the world.

"Yes, by marrying," Sheridan said. "It should keep me from being viewed as an unrepentant roué when I'm older."

"Aren't all of the Earl's friends married? I don't believe matrimony has had much of an effect on whether they were libertines or not. It seems to me that a wife never prevented any of them from behaving badly."

Sheridan snickered. "You're correct. They even brag about it. You ought to hear the stories they tell. It's embarrassing to listen to them, and none of them has slowed down in the least. Most especially my father."

"Perhaps you'll be a better husband than your father ever was."

"That is a very low bar."

They chuckled and went to work, getting Sheridan into what George deemed an acceptable condition. A footman stoked a roaring fire, and they huddled by it to warm themselves on the outside and sipped whiskey to warm themselves on the inside.

George had dressed Sheridan for years and quickly had him garbed in his formal evening clothes. They added some jewelry: gaudy diamond rings on his fingers, gold cufflinks on his sleeves, a sapphire-studded pin to secure his cravat.

George gave him a final once-over, declared him magnificent, then pushed him toward the door.

"Head to your own room and your own supper," Sheridan called over his shoulder as he left.

"I will. First, I have to be sure the rest of your clothes are unpacked and hung properly."

"Don't come back to the manor tonight. I won't need you. I can put myself to bed."

"I'm glad you're feeling up to it. I shall enjoy myself, and I won't fret over you a single minute."

Sheridan offered a mock salute, then hurried off.

Swindon Hall was a massive place that had been gradually remodeled over the centuries. New wings had been cobbled together, so there were spaces that made no sense. The building was filled with unnecessary alcoves, with winding halls that ended abruptly. It wasn't unusual for a visitor to get lost.

When a gathering was being hosted, it was common for footmen to loaf in central locations so they could guide people to their destinations if they grew confused. Normally, he didn't have a problem finding the main stairs that led down to the public salons, but he was distracted, thinking about Sophia, thinking about Aurora Newton, thinking about Riverglen.

Because he was woolgathering, he wasn't paying attention to his surroundings, and eventually, he stopped and glanced about. He had no idea where he was, and he dawdled, trying to pick a direction, when he heard a woman approaching.

She was humming to herself, and he hoped she would be a housemaid who could point him to the correct stairs. But as she rounded the corner, and he saw who it was, the sight was so peculiar that he assumed he was hallucinating.

Sophia Cantwell? Why the devil would she be strolling through the ostentatious mansion?

He shook his head quite vigorously, desperate to dispel the vision, but no. She was standing right in front of him. What ploy could the little minx possibly be pursuing?

Evidently, she was bewildered to bump into him too. She froze, her eyes wide, as if she couldn't fathom what she was witnessing.

A strange interval wafted out between them, where Time seemed to stretch out, gluing their feet to the floor so they couldn't move. He was the one to break the mystifying silence. "Sophia Cantwell! What the bloody hell are you doing at Swindon?"

"What are *you* doing?" was her snotty reply. "You're not supposed to be here until Wednesday."

"I arrived early, and I ask you again: Why are you here? I'll never believe it's for an honest purpose."

Without clarifying, she spun and dashed off. He chased after her, not hesitating to wonder why he would. He prayed he wouldn't pass any of Neville's acquaintances. He could supply no explanation for his actions that wouldn't sound emasculating.

He caught her immediately, and he grabbed her arm and yanked her to a halt.

"Why are you running from me?" he asked.

"Ah . . . no reason. I was simply startled to see you, that's all."

"Really?" His tone was incredibly dubious.

"Yes, really. I wasn't expecting you. Why aren't you at Riverglen, courting your fiancée?"

It was futile to mention yet again that he wasn't engaged to Aurora Newton. He countered instead with, "Why aren't *you* at Riverglen where you belong? According to the housemaids, you snuck away without a word to anyone, and now, you're lurking in my father's home." Facetiously, he added, "I can't imagine why I'd be suspicious of that fact. Can you?"

"I'm not lurking," she responded. "I'm a guest."

"You didn't slip in a rear door to steal the silver when no one was watching?"

"No, Mr. Obnoxious, and that's all I have to say to you."

She stuck her pert nose up in the air and tried to saunter off, but he wasn't about to let her go until he had some acceptable answers that would clear up her current mischief. Who could guess what she might be fomenting? He certainly hoped Neville hadn't been sucked into her scheme.

He leaned in and pressed her to the wall, his much larger body holding her in place so she couldn't escape. Those annoying sparks, the ones that sizzled when they were together, were flaring, and it occurred to him that he was thrilled to see her. Actually, he was ecstatic to see her. His anatomy, down to the smallest pore, was rejoicing. He didn't understand it, but when she was near, he felt better. He felt happier and more in control.

Who cared why she was present?

Without pausing to think, he dipped down and kissed her, and the instant their lips connected, he tumbled into a well of delight and lust. It was his perpetual state when he was with her. She agitated his masculine instincts to a dangerous level, and suddenly, he was terrifyingly close to throwing her over his shoulder and hauling her into an empty bedroom.

He was that overwhelmed, which was so exasperating. He simply looked at her, and his common sense flew out the window.

He was sufficiently cognizant of his aroused condition to recognize that he had to pull away or he'd behaved even more ludicrously. He slowed, then drew away, and she grinned up at him, appearing sassy and impish.

"You missed me," she said.

"Maybe I did and maybe I didn't."

"Ha! It's obvious you've been pining away since the moment we parted."

"You left Riverglen without telling your cousins where you were going. Why must you always act like a lunatic?"

"Why would I share my plans with them? They don't worry about me, and I'm an adult. If I want to jump in a carriage and travel to another location, I'm fully capable of accomplishing it."

"You're twenty, but you're so petite you could be ten. The highways are packed with rogues and criminals who would view you as easy bait. Any foul incident could have arisen while you were away from home. How would you have alerted your family that you were imperiled?"

"I'm fine, so it's silly for you to fret. If you hadn't taken my pistol, I could have been armed. Will you ever give it back to me?"

"Are you mad? You are not a woman who should be allowed to brandish a weapon."

"I hate it when you scold me, and you are not my father, brother, or husband. You have no authority over me, so you have no right to command me."

"Someone should. You bluster about as if you're invincible."

"And you don't?"

"I'm a man, you ridiculous creature. It's appropriate for me to carry on as if I'm invincible, so you are being as illogical as ever—and don't change the subject."

"What was it again?" Her expression was innocent and irritating. "If I can't recollect what it was, how could I have changed it?"

"Why are you at Swindon? You better have a very good excuse or, first thing in the morning, I'll have your pretty behind in a carriage, and you'll be on your way to Riverglen."

She sighed as if he were a great burden. "Why don't you ever listen to me? I'm a guest. I'm probably not a *welcomed* guest, but I'm a guest just the same."

"Who invited you?"

"No one. I barged in unannounced."

"For what reason?" A horrifying possibility rattled him. She was exactly the sort of tart who would tickle Neville's fancy. "By any chance, are you acquainted with my father?"

"I wasn't in the past, but I am now."

He lurched away from her as if she'd grown too hot to touch. "You're having an affair with him?"

She gaped at him, then laughed uproariously. "No, I'm not having an affair with him. Ick! Why would such a preposterous idea lodge itself in that deranged male brain of yours?"

At her denying it, he shuddered with relief and said, "My father tries to seduce every girl he meets. He's the most notorious libertine in the kingdom."

"He's been a perfect gentleman with me. Besides, isn't he engaged to be married?"

His father, a gentleman? His father, engaged again? Sheridan scoffed. "No, he's not engaged. He's a widower, and he pictures himself as God's gift to the females of the species. If he hasn't attempted any mischief with *you,* it's because he hasn't had an opportunity."

She batted her lashes. "I'll be sure to remember that."

"Now then, I'm tired of fussing with you. Tell me why you're here and don't you dare lie. You chatter like a magpie, and you can't keep a secret to save your life, so why not merely admit your scheme?"

"I'm on a discreet mission, Captain Stone, and I am not at liberty to divulge what it is."

"What is that supposed to mean? You could be speaking in riddles."

"If you're determined to learn my purpose, you should talk to the Earl. If he would like to inform you, he will. Otherwise, I have nothing to say."

He was on one side of the hall, and she was on the other. She was glowering at him, and he was glowering back.

Apparently, she felt she'd hurled a sufficient number of snotty comments because she flitted away. He grabbed for her, but she was too quick. He could have chased after her again, but he managed to restrain himself. She had a keen ability to goad him into behaving in maddening ways, and he had to pull himself together.

He went in the opposite direction, and eventually, he figured out where he was in the large mansion. He started down toward the lower parlors, and as he reached the landing, a footman was ascending.

The young man called, "Captain Stone, there you are! Your father had me find you. He'd like to see you for a few minutes prior to your heading down to supper. He's in the master suite. May I escort you to him?"

"Would you? I hate to bother you, but I'm completely turned around."

"It could never be a bother to assist you, sir."

They marched off, the footman leading him up to the next floor, then down a series of winding halls. The master suite was at the end, the doors open, the lamps lit. The footman rapped once, stuck his nose in, and said, "It's Captain Stone, my lord."

"Wonderful!" Neville said. "Send him in!"

Sheridan thanked the fellow, then walked by him and into the sitting room of the grand chamber. He couldn't recollect ever being in it previously, but he'd expected it to be very posh, and he wasn't disappointed. His relatives had been aristocrats for several centuries, and they enjoyed their luxuries.

Before he could fully assess the lavish décor, a familiar voice cried, "Cap! Cap!"

Emily barreled over and threw herself at him. He lifted her up so they were nose to nose, and he asked, "What are you doing here, Little Missy?"

Then it dawned on him that Sophia had fled Riverglen with Pierre and Emily, so it probably wasn't a surprise that he'd bump into her. But in Neville's private quarters? His father was many things, but he was *not* and never had been fond of children.

Neville was seated on a sofa, and Sybil Jones was snuggled beside him. There was an obvious affection emanating from them, as if they were suddenly devoted partners. What was happening? The whole scenario was bewildering.

With his holding Emily, the extra weight had his leg aching, so he went over to a chair and eased onto it. Emily was perched on his lap, and she was patting his chest, playing with the buttons on his coat, and generally being a cute pest.

"You arrived early," his father said, "which indicates you left Riverglen early. I'm not sure if that's good news or bad." He didn't wait for Sheridan's reply, but said, "You remember Sybil, don't you? She's the hostess for my party."

"Yes, of course I remember her," Sheridan said. "Hello, Miss Jones."

"I didn't want to oblige him," she said, "but he nagged until I couldn't refuse."

"He's adept at nagging." Sheridan had endured plenty of it himself.

Neville tipped a glass in Sheridan's direction. "We're having a whiskey. Will you join us?"

"A whiskey would be perfect. I had a wet ride, and I haven't had much of a chance to warm myself."

A footman was hovering, and he poured a drink for Sheridan and brought it over, as Neville smiled at Sybil and said, "I think he should call you Sybil. May we make that jump? Or would you rather delay a bit?"

"Yes, he can call me Sybil. I don't mind."

Neville squeezed her hand, right while Sheridan was watching them. It was an intimate gesture that astounded him. They looked cozy as an old married couple, and Sheridan's sense of bewilderment grew.

His brother, Hunter, had once mentioned that Neville might be having an affair with Sybil, but Sheridan had hardly listened to the story. At the time, Neville had been wed to his second wife, Susan, and if he'd been cheating on her, Sheridan hadn't been anxious to speculate.

Yet Neville wasn't a husband anymore. Had his relationship with Sybil blossomed to a different level? Were they romantically involved?

They appeared to be, but why would Sybil want him? She seemed to be smarter than that. Then again, Neville could charm the bark off a tree. Perhaps she couldn't resist.

"It's clear," Neville said, "that you're confused about what's occurring. I will state that I am confused too. Evidently, you and Emily are fast friends. Did you meet her at Riverglen?"

"No. I met her when I was last in France. She was there with a young lady named Sophia Cantwell who, by the way, I just stumbled on out in the hall. She claims she's visiting you, but she wouldn't tell me why. She insisted she had clandestine business with you that she couldn't reveal."

"Yes, I asked her to keep it a secret until Sybil and I decide how to proceed."

"How to *proceed* with what?" Sheridan inquired. "Do you . . . ah . . . know Miss Cantwell very well?"

"She's definitely an interesting character." Neville motioned to Emily and said to her, "Come!"

Emily obeyed immediately, exhibiting an unusual burst of deference. She slid away from Sheridan and hurried over to Neville. He picked her up and settled her on his lap. In all of Sheridan's twenty-eight years, he'd never seen Neville hold a child—or even notice one really.

He gaped at his father as if he was staring at a total stranger. Neville and Emily were completely comfortable with each other, and as Sheridan studied them, the most terrifying realization arose: They looked exactly alike.

"I have some news," Neville said, "and I'm positive it will shock you, but Emily is my daughter."

"Whoa! What?" Sheridan had deduced on his own that the announcement might be made, but still, it was distressing, and he was very skeptical.

Neville didn't note Sheridan's incredulity. He simply continued speaking. "Since she's my daughter, it means she's your sister. You never had a sister, but you have one now."

"Actually," Sybil put in, "he has two sisters." She peered over at Sheridan and said, "Are you acquainted with Jacob Ralston? He's retired, but he was in the navy for years."

"Yes, I know Ralston."

"His wife, Joanna, is your sister too. I invited them to the party, but I haven't heard if they'll accept or not. Joanna isn't too keen to befriend your father. He was awful to her in the past, so I don't blame her."

"I'm determined to redeem myself," Neville said to her.

Sybil smirked at that. "The jury is out as to whether you'll succeed. You'll have to change significantly before I'll be impressed."

Sheridan scoffed with disgust. "You imagine that Neville could change? Are you joking?"

"No," Sybil said, "and you're about to faint. I guess we've been too blunt. We didn't take any steps to soften the blow, and we probably should have."

"I won't faint. I'm simply stunned."

Neville grinned in an exasperating manner. "It's become obvious to me, as I've grown older, that I should atone for some of my sins. Emily showed up at just the right moment."

Emily liked having him mention her. She leaned in and patted his cheeks, saying, "Papa!"

Neville beamed with pride, and on witnessing it, Sheridan was floored.

"Will you publicly acknowledge her?" Sheridan asked.

"Absolutely," Neville replied. "Sybil and I will raise her, and—if I'm very lucky—we'll be married as we're doing it."

Sheridan's jaw dropped in astonishment. "You might wed again?"

Neville shrugged. "I'm still trying to convince her, but she doesn't think I'm much of a catch."

There were several facets about Neville that were incontrovertible truths: He would never wed a third time, and he wasn't fond of children. His metamorphosis was so baffling that Sheridan felt dizzy.

"And Miss Cantwell," Sheridan said. "How does she fit into all of this?"

"She brought Emily to me and asked me to recognize and support her."

"Has she requested a financial reward for her bountiful act?"

Neville glanced at Sybil. "Maybe I should pay her a reward. As you pointed out, her personal life is wretched. I could improve her fortunes."

Sheridan's mind was awhirl, as he struggled to figure out what was transpiring. He'd only known Sophia for a few weeks, but what he *did* know wasn't good. She was a schemer and trickster. She was a liar and a fraud. What game was she playing with Neville? Was Emily really his daughter? From how similar they looked, she probably was, but Sheridan didn't suppose Sophia had an altruistic bone in her body.

Had she produced a shred of evidence to back up her claim? Why was he suspecting she hadn't? If she walked away with a monetary prize in the end, it would certainly solve many of her problems. Could she be that devious? That deceitful?

Well, yes, she could be. He had no doubt at all.

He downed his drink, then stood and started out.

"Where are you going?" Neville asked.

"I have to speak to someone. I'll meet you down in the receiving parlor."

He hurried out, not willing to let his father delay him. He would find a servant who could direct him to Sophia's bedchamber. The bloody girl had some explaining to do, and she had better be ready to talk fast.

Chapter Fourteen

Sophia was standing by the window and staring out at the night sky. She was tucked away in the small bedchamber that had been supplied to her by the Swindon housekeeper. It was next to the nursery, so she was close to Pierre and Emily. They were in a quiet wing of the mansion, and her room was one where an unpleasant cousin or governess might have been lodged.

She'd promised Miss Jones that she'd hide from the Earl's guests, but she was chomping at the bit to go downstairs to the party. She yearned to join in the merriment. Her life was so dreary. Didn't she deserve a spot of fun?

But no. She was lonely, trapped, and having to pretend she didn't mind, but she suspected some of the men in attendance might have known her father. He'd attended university with the sons of the aristocracy, and while he hadn't achieved fame with his poetry, several collections of his work had been published to critical acclaim.

His old acquaintances recalled him fondly, and it would be nice to have them share their kind memories.

No one at Riverglen ever did. There, among her relatives, he was only ever derided as a spendthrift who'd negligently squandered his meager inheritance, and thus, had left no funds for her support. They never gave him credit for the beautiful words he'd strung together and didn't care that he'd toiled so hard to be amazing.

To her great annoyance, her isolation furnished her with too much time to ponder. Her panic was rising over how she hadn't fully assessed the ramifications of approaching Lord Swindon. It was her habit to behave rashly and without debating consequences, but when Sheridan had mentioned that his father would be at the estate, it had seemed like a sign she couldn't ignore.

The Earl would very likely take Emily from Sophia, and after that, Sophia wouldn't have a say in what happened to her. How would she feel about that conclusion? She wasn't a mother, and she didn't exactly *mother* Emily. In that regard, she carried on more like a very disinterested nanny.

As it currently stood, she didn't have any legal authority to make decisions for Emily, and she wasn't sure Lord Swindon should be in charge. To top it off, Sheridan had arrived early and had instantly bumped into her. It was a complication she hadn't sought or planned on, and she couldn't tarry when he was in residence too. Every minute in his presence was torture.

Initially, she'd apprised Miss Jones that she would depart on Wednesday, but she had to leave immediately. The Earl needed an interval to consider the predicament with Emily, so Sophia would return home and let him consider. He could write when he'd reached a verdict as to how he'd like to proceed.

Behind her, the door opened, and she knew who it would be. She sighed with resignation. It was as if she'd conjured him just by contemplating him so intensely.

She glanced over her shoulder and said, "You can't be in here."

"I already am, so your complaint is moot."

Sheridan shut the door and spun the key in the lock, and she sighed again. "Is there some reason you constantly harass me?"

He marched over to where she was leaned on the windowsill, and he leaned on it too, arms crossed over his chest. He glared down at her, looking irked, as if she'd been placed on the Earth merely to aggravate him.

He was garbed like the wealthy scoundrel he was, wearing formal black evening clothes, his hair combed back, his appendages glittering with expensive jewelry. It was difficult to remember he was the sea captain she'd met in France, the one who'd appeared so ferocious that she'd figured he was a pirate. Any trace of that villainous rogue had vanished.

As to herself, she was dressed in a plain grey gown, a woolen shawl over her shoulders to ward off the chill in the air. Compared to him, she might have been a scullery maid sent to light the fire, and she'd never noticed the differences in their stations quite so strongly.

"I just had the most intriguing conversation with my father," he said. "I'm certain you're aware of the story he told me."

She shrugged. "It depends on which part he shared."

"He claims you waltzed in and *voila!* I have a baby sister."

She frowned. "Well, yes, I guess you're right. Congratulations."

"Tell me, Cantwell, and tell me true. Are you playing some game with Neville?"

She tsked with offense. "You think I'd trick him into believing he has a daughter when he doesn't? You actually suppose I could be that cruel?"

"Yes, I absolutely think that. Your conduct can be so outrageous and convoluted that I can't imagine how you might act."

"You really feel that way? You *really* do?"

"My father, in his entire life, has never so much as looked at a child. He doesn't *like* children. If you've deceived him somehow, I will wring your silly neck."

She was inordinately crushed by his opinion. It was simply a fact of his marvelous existence that he took up too much space in any room he entered. He was big and brawny, and he towered over her in a manner that was tough, dashing, and magnificent. She'd never previously encountered a man like him, and she'd definitely never been kissed as he kept kissing her.

Occasionally, he seemed to be charmed by her, so she'd convinced herself that he'd observed her unusual flare, that he realized she wasn't like other girls, that she was *special*. But he thought she was scheming on his father? He thought she'd brought Emily to Swindon as some sort of ruse to . . . to . . . what? To blackmail the Earl? To demand money in order to remain silent about Emily's birth?

After all, Lord Swindon had seduced Caroline, but he was hoping Sheridan would betroth himself to Aurora. Clearly, the Earl hadn't been candid with his son about his indecent connection to the Newton family.

Sophia had traveled to Swindon to honor Caroline's dying request, and it had required an enormous amount of courage—and gall—to seek an audience with the pompous aristocrat. She'd risked all to obtain the recognition Caroline had begged for Emily to have.

Lord Swindon could have called Sophia a liar, could have had her jailed for slandering him. Noblemen frequently lashed out like that at commoners, yet Sheridan Stone had the nerve to accuse her of bad motives?

She eased away from him and went over to the bed. She perched on the edge of the mattress, her elbows on her knees, her face buried in her palms. She was on the verge of tears, but she wouldn't let him witness her distress. He was a bully, and if she hadn't been so furious, she might have broken down and wept for a week.

A fraught interval festered, then his feet appeared on the floor in front of her. Why couldn't he leave her be? Why torment her like this? He probably enjoyed making her miserable. He probably reveled in it.

"What's wrong?" he said.

"Would you go away?" she morosely responded.

"No. Are you upset? By what? By me?"

"Yes, by you, you ridiculous oaf."

"I'm simply prying some answers out of you. You vanished from Riverglen without an explanation to anyone, then I show up at my father's home, and I discover you're here too. How am I to assess such a peculiar turn of events?"

"I don't care how you assess it."

He viewed himself as God's gift to the world, so her comment had to have incensed him. He laid a hand on her shoulder and pushed her back, so she was forced to peer up at him. Her eyes were brimming with tears; she couldn't help it. She was young and alone, and she was trying to assist and protect Emily, but she had no idea what the best ending should be.

She was relying on his father to point out the correct path, but the Earl was a notorious libertine. How could she trust him? After he shoved her around a bit, she'd head to Riverglen, where Millicent and Miles would beat up on her too.

She wished she could sprout wings and fly away like a bird. She'd continue on forever, until she landed in a good place, a safe place, where people liked and wanted her.

"Are you crying?" he said, aghast.

"Not yet, but if you keep glaring at me like that, I will bawl like a baby just to annoy you." She swiped at her eyes, wiping away the evidence. "I'm sure a manly fellow such as yourself would be completely emasculated by such a feminine outburst, so you'd better flee at once."

"Very funny."

"Who's being funny? You might not survive the sight of my woe, and I would hate to be blamed for harming the masculine aura that makes you so splendid."

He snorted in a way that might have meant anything, then he grabbed the only chair and sat down, scooting it very close so their legs and feet were tangled together.

"Why are you so sad," he asked.

"It doesn't matter why."

"Yes, it does. Spit it out. What's vexing you?"

She fumed and stewed, then said, "How dare you accuse me of duplicity!"

"What am I to think of your being here? I have spent many days in your company, and you never mentioned that Emily is my half-sister. Then, suddenly, you sneak to Swindon and blab the news hither and yon."

"I didn't blab it! I told your father—in private!—so he can decide how he'll proceed."

He leaned in so they were nose to nose. "He believes you! But I don't. He hasn't had the pleasure of wallowing in your dubious presence, so he doesn't understand what a little vixen you are. I'll have to explain it to him."

"Why didn't you already?"

"He was too busy, being a happy family man."

His tone was very sarcastic, very jarring, and she said, "Is that what's bothering you? You had to watch him dote on his daughter and you're jealous? Is that it?"

For an instant, he scowled, as if she'd hit a sore spot regarding his relationship with his father, but his expression was quickly masked. He shifted away, so there was more space between them.

They stared, both of them angry, both of them exasperated. It was a typical exchange for them. They were either fighting, kissing wildly, or insulting each other. There wasn't a smooth center where they could interact like normal adults.

Eventually, he visibly reined in his temper. "Why didn't you ever admit my connection to Emily?"

"Why would I have? It was a secret my cousin took almost to her grave. I wasn't about to reveal it to you; it wasn't any of your business. Besides, I didn't learn you were Neville Stone's son until we were at Riverglen. You're such a conceited ass that you never apprised me of how grand you are."

He scoffed facetiously. "That's not right. I informed you of how grand I was from the very start."

"You're correct. You never shut up about it."

He studied her, pondering, and his next question had her assuming his doubts were waning.

"How old was your cousin when she was ruined?"

"Seventeen."

"And you're positive Neville is the culprit? You swear?"

"Yes, I swear."

He winced. "She was barely out of the schoolroom. It makes him sound like such a lecher."

"If it sounds as if he's a lecher, that's because he *is* a lecher. He was married at the time! So let's call him an adulterer too."

"He's always been spoiled, so he never had to be loyal or faithful. In his dealings with women, he never presumed he should have to be."

It was gradually dawning on her that she couldn't leave Emily with Lord Swindon. He was an undependable, irresponsible wastrel. Emily had charmed him for the moment, but he didn't bond or care about anyone but himself. He probably viewed Emily as he would a new puppy, one he'd hand over to his Hound Master after he grew tired of playing with it.

Who would he hand Emily to after he tired of her? What sort of lazy nanny would he hire to raise her? Could Sophia risk that conclusion? If she permitted it to occur, wouldn't she be failing to carry out Caroline's last wish? Wouldn't it be better to ask Lord Swindon for a stipend, then raise Emily herself? At least then, she'd know who was in control.

Yes, maybe she'd do that. Maybe that was a wiser course, and she'd have a lawyer or vicar intervene and speak on her behalf. She had to enlist an older, smarter man to accomplish it for her. It's how men expected the world to work. She always forgot that fact.

"There's a detail about this quagmire that you haven't realized," she said, "and I suppose I should point it out so you can address it with your father." She paused and frowned. "Actually, you and your father are such scoundrels. Perhaps it doesn't matter to you."

Her comment irked him, and he snapped, "What is it? Just tell me."

"Your father ruined my cousin, but she never named him as the perpetrator. Yet you're about to marry Aurora."

"I'm not about to marry her," he testily said. "I'm considering it."

"Right. You're considering it, but there's an awkward link among all of you. Caroline birthed Lord Swindon's bastard—who happens to be your half-sister. Aurora and her mother aren't aware of the situation. Before you walk down the aisle, you'll need to have a difficult chat with them."

"Gad, I hadn't even thought about it." He'd muttered the remark more to himself than to her.

"I don't imagine Aurora would be too concerned that he seduced her little sister. She's vain and self-centered, and to her, the tragedy seems like ancient history. Her mother might be a tad irate though, so you'll have some issues to resolve with your mother-in-law."

A muscle ticked in his cheek, his mind whirring, as he struggled to process the dilemma. He wasn't the type of rogue who liked to have thorny conversations with others. Particularly women. He blustered forward like a bull in a china shop and pictured himself like a god on a plane up above mere mortals.

He assumed all females should bow down to his magnificent male self, and his haughty posturing had her weary and very troubled. Why couldn't he leave her alone? She needed some privacy while she figured out how to extricate herself from the property without causing a huge uproar.

He rubbed his forehead, as if their discussion had given him a fierce headache, and he said, "You exhaust me."

"Well, I can't claim you're a ray of sunshine in my life either."

"Why do I keep running into you? Why can't the universe let me be?"

"I won't debate the question when we're locked away like this. Would you go? You received the answers you were seeking about Emily, so there's no reason for you to tarry."

"I've barely begun to interrogate you."

He scooted the chair back and stood, and she watched as he paced across the tiny room. In three quick strides, he reached one wall, then in three quick strides, he reached the other, so it was a ridiculous journey that provided no ease.

She'd eaten supper on a tray, delivered by a housemaid, and it was still on the dresser. The kitchen had included a glass of wine that she hadn't drunk. He grabbed it and helped himself to the contents, as he glared at her quite caustically.

When he finally opened his mouth and spoke again, what would he say? Would he hurl more insults? Would he call her a liar? Would he declare that he would send her home in the morning?

He wasn't keen to have her dawdle at the estate, and in that regard, they were in complete accord. She would depart as rapidly as she could. She'd simply like to have a better situation awaiting her at Riverglen.

He finished the wine and smacked the glass down on the tray with a determined clunk, then he said, "Why do you suppose we met?"

"I have no idea. I'm sure Fate likes torturing you."

"What about you and Fate?" he asked. "Are you being tortured?"

"Yes, definitely."

They shared a charged visual exchange, and she was braced for anything, but she hoped he'd storm out. Then again, she hoped he'd stay all night. She would return to Riverglen shortly. What if this was the very last occasion they were ever together?

The prospect left her breathless with dismay.

He looked bewildered, and before she grasped his intent, he stepped over to her and swept her into his arms. He tumbled them onto the mattress, and it happened so fast that she didn't have a moment to protest his brash move. And she didn't really want to protest it.

He rolled them so she was beneath him, and he was stretched out atop her. He was crushing her in a manner that should have been uncomfortable, but he didn't feel heavy. He felt grand and glorious, and she yearned to remain tucked away with him forever.

Apparently, they were done talking, for he dipped in and kissed her desperately. She leapt into the fray with an equal amount of enthusiasm. She didn't pause to worry about her virtue, about consequences, or any other topic that should have mattered.

They continued on for a lengthy period, and as with every other of their dalliances, it was ferocious and out of control. They bit and nipped, tugged and pulled, but gradually, it slowed and altered into a sweeter encounter. By the time he drew away, she was overcome by fond emotion. She liked him much more than she should, and there was no place to put her festering affection.

She was suffering from an incredible quantity of lusty desire too. Her cousin, Caroline, had furnished plenty of details about carnal conduct. She'd deemed it her duty to warn Sophia of what could transpire if she wasn't cautious, so Sophia knew more about physical amour than a maiden ought to know.

In light of the sensations he'd stirred, she couldn't deduce why a female would want to behave. Her body was on fire with longing, and she was lucky he hadn't pushed her to a reckless conclusion.

She should have been relieved by his reticence. After all, if it had been her decision, she'd likely be begging him to rush forward to disaster. It was her typical mode of staggering through life. She was negligent in her choices, but he'd saved her from folly.

He was gaping at her as if he was confused as to why he was lying on a bed with her. He shook his head and said, "I'm constantly amazed by how I bother with you."

She scoffed with disgust. What had she expected from him? Poetry? Romantic sonnets? "You sure make a girl feel special."

"It's one of my best traits." He scoffed too, then slid away from her.

He sat on the edge of the mattress, his feet on the floor, while she loafed behind him like a contented cat. She rested a palm on the center of his back, meaning it as a tender gesture, but he shrugged her away.

Evidently, they could be intimate when *he* was interested, but once he'd had enough of her, their tryst was over. His attitude was infuriating and hurtful. She didn't comment though. What would be the point? He had a monumental capacity to be an ass, so she'd fume after he left.

"My presence is required downstairs," he said.

"Don't let me keep you."

He must have heard a snotty tone in her voice because he glanced over his shoulder and frowned at her. She gazed back innocently, not providing the merest hint that she was livid.

"I might stop by later," he said like a threat.

"I wish you wouldn't, but I imagine it would be futile to tell you that you can't."

"Yes, it would be futile. Stay in this room. Don't roam the halls. While I'm eating my supper, I don't want to have to worry that you're getting into trouble."

"It's so aggravating when you scold me. I'm not ten, and you're not my father."

His heated focus dropped to her lips. "No, I'm definitely not your father."

She waved him out. "Go away, before you annoy me beyond my limit. You always tarry a minute too long. I just start to like you, then you ruin it by being arrogant or idiotic."

He set his finger between her eyes, then he traced it down her nose, over her mouth, her chin, down her neck, only halting when he arrived at the bodice of her gown. They froze, on the verge of a more risqué event, but he recognized the danger bubbling up.

As if she'd suddenly grown too hot to touch, he yanked away, stood, and went to the door. He didn't open it though. He simply stared, pondering her.

Ultimately, he said, "I may have sounded grouchy, but I'm not. Grouchy, that is. I'm glad you're at Swindon so I know you're safe. When I found out that you'd fled Riverglen, and that no one was concerned about you, I was frantic. I'm delighted to have stumbled on you. I'm not angry."

"Don't continue talking or you'll say something perfectly kind, and it will shatter my illusions about what a pompous prig you are."

He smirked. "You could have told me about Emily. You could have confided in me."

"You wouldn't have believed me."

He smirked again. "Probably not."

Then he tiptoed away without first peeking out to ensure the hall was empty. Yet why would he care if he was observed?

It didn't matter if he was seen sneaking out. He was an earl's son and a notorious scoundrel. If he chose to visit a young lady in her bedchamber, who would tell him he couldn't? Any disdain would fall on her. Not him.

She flopped onto the pillow, listening as he departed, and it dawned on her that he hadn't invited her to come down to supper with him. She couldn't have done that; there wouldn't have been a seat for her at the table, but she could have joined him for the merriment after the meal was over.

Clearly, he was happy to creep into her room, to kiss her when there were no witnesses to what he was perpetrating, but he wouldn't be caught dead, flirting with her in front of his father's fancy friends.

It was a galling realization. When they were alone, it seemed as if they belonged together, but he hadn't asked her to come down. No doubt it had never occurred to him to ask, and she had to always remember that fact.

Chapter Fifteen

SHERIDAN WAS IN HIS bedchamber. Evening had arrived too quickly, and George had laid out his clothes, so he could dress for supper. Drinks were being served in the receiving parlor, and he had to join in the socializing, but he was being a sluggard and couldn't force himself to get moving.

He'd spent the day out of the manor and roaming the massive property. He was in a disgusting state of confusion, and he'd needed some peace and quiet to ponder recent events without being interrupted every two seconds.

His father might wed again, which was incredibly strange. He was an earl now, but he might pick Sybil Jones? The pragmatic, no-nonsense woman would probably be the perfect wife for him, but she owned a gambling club! Didn't that make her exactly the wrong choice?

Shouldn't Neville seek out a debutante with stellar bloodlines? It's what a nobleman was supposed to do. He shouldn't proceed willy-nilly, without concern for the consequences, to an inappropriate female he simply *liked* very much.

Yet he was fifty, and he'd already produced three strapping sons to carry on the family name. With that conclusion in place, did Sybil's position matter? Neville's first two marriages had been horrid. If he could find happiness later in life, with a different kind of bride, shouldn't Sheridan welcome that development?

Children had been stirred into the mix. Sheridan had a baby half-sister and an adult half-sister too. Siblings were popping up much too rapidly, and it was provoking odd emotions with regard to his father.

The main aspect that defined Sheridan's life, as well as his brothers' lives, was their convoluted history with Neville. It had shaped them into spoiled, reckless men. They blamed him for their dissolute habits, and they constantly chastised him for having been such a worthless parent.

Neville never denied that he'd been detached and awful, but what if he changed and became responsible? How would Sheridan view such a peculiar alteration?

He was also fretting over his nuptial decision, wondering what it should be. How could he propose to Aurora Newton? Neville had seduced her sister, had sired a bastard on her, then had strolled away without a backward glance. The tragedy hung over all of them, so should Sheridan wedge himself into the Newton family? Why would they want him?

Neville's behavior wasn't a secret that could be kept. Not if he recognized Emily as his daughter, so Sheridan would have to apprise them of what had occurred. Then what?

And what about Sophia? Where did she fit into the debacle, and how could he pluck her out of it? When he was on the road to marrying her cousin, why had he tarried in her bedchamber the prior night?

Even if Sophia left Riverglen and went to reside elsewhere, he'd see her occasionally at holidays and other gatherings. How could he bear to be around her, but not have her for his own?

She was the chief reason he'd stayed away from the manor for hours. It was insane to have dallied with her, to have kissed her so passionately, and he couldn't risk going farther than that, perhaps deflowering her. His only genuine option was to avoid her like the plague.

Suddenly, the door banged open, and Hunter and Warwick blustered in. Sheridan wasn't aware they'd arrived.

"If it isn't the notorious Captain Stone!" Hunter called. "Can you really be my baby brother?"

Sheridan beamed with delight. He was closer to them than anyone, and with how they'd been raised, they'd grown up more firmly attached than siblings typically were.

Hunter marched over and hugged him, which was bizarre. They weren't huggers, and as he pulled away, Sheridan thought Hunter seemed very happy. Could it be that marriage agreed with him?

Warwick appeared to be very happy too. In fact, both brothers looked grand, while he was worn down by his injury, limping, and perpetually dithering over the direction he should travel.

A footman was hovering, George too, and George had the boy pour them a round of whiskeys, then he guided the boy out of the room. As he tiptoed away, he gestured to Sheridan and mouthed, *I'll be back in a bit.*

Sheridan nodded that he understood. His brothers were dressed to head downstairs, but Sheridan was still in his riding clothes and he hadn't washed.

Once they were alone, they toasted themselves with the salutation they always used: *To us! We're still alive and kicking!*

They were always surprised they'd lived to be adults. None of them had assumed they would.

They drew chairs over to the fire and sat in front of it, and Sheridan suffered a swell of affection for them that was astonishing. He supposed, with his almost being killed in the battle where he'd cut his leg, he had to stop taking certain things for granted, most especially his brothers who were his favorite people in the world.

"I sail off for a year or two," he said to them, "and I come home to discover that you wed without waiting for me so I could attend your ceremonies."

"The weddings happened too fast," Hunter said. "There was no time to wait for you."

Warwick added, "If we'd postponed, we were afraid our brides would change their minds. It was tricky business, convincing them to shackle themselves."

"Then they're very smart," Sheridan said. "A little bird informed me that Neville is about to be a grandfather twice over."

"That old sot never could keep his mouth shut," Warwick grumbled.

"So he wasn't lying?" Sheridan asked. "You both got busy with filling your nurseries? Neville was enthused about it, but when did you become so obedient?"

Hunter said, "He was an absolute monster about dragging us to the altar. With his inheriting the title, he's pretending to be responsible and reliable."

"How long will this odd trend last?" Sheridan inquired.

"Not long."

The three of them snorted and clinked their glasses.

"Now that you're home," Warwick said, "he plans to nag at you too. He wants you fettered by Christmas."

"He's already started in on me," Sheridan told them. "The very first day I staggered off my ship, he was pestering me."

Hunter and Warwick winced, and Hunter asked, "Has he lined up a girl for you to meet?"

"Yes, he claimed he'd found the perfect fiancée, and I trotted off to the country to be introduced to her." At the comment, his brothers whooped with amusement, and he asked, "What's so funny?"

"He found the *perfect* girls for us too," Warwick said, "but we ignored him and picked better candidates."

"Who has he picked for you?" Hunter asked. "Would we be acquainted with her?"

"I doubt it. Aurora Newton? She's an heiress. If I wed her, I'd be given her family's estate of Riverglen."

"What would you think of that?" Warwick asked as Hunter said, "What did you think of her?"

"The property is spectacular," Sheridan said. "If I have to settle down, it would be a good spot."

"But *you,* a gentleman farmer?" Hunter said. "I can't picture it."

"You two managed the transition from soldier to civilian," Sheridan said.

"Just barely," Warwick muttered.

"Why couldn't I do the same?" Sheridan asked, more to himself than to them. "I hurt my leg, and it's been bothering me. I'm not sure how long I can continue at my job. Sailing is such hard work, and a man has to be vigorous."

He shrugged dismissively, as if his reduced health was of no account. He didn't clarify how he was fretting over the future, but he didn't have to. His brothers could decipher what he was actually telling them, and Hunter had been critically wounded himself when he was in the army. He understood about slow recuperation and difficult choices.

"Father mentioned that there had been an incident," Hunter said. "What happened?"

"I was teaching some pirates a lesson, and I took a saber slash to the thigh."

"It's still plaguing you?"

Sheridan waffled his hand, as if it was a minor problem. "It's better than it was, but I'm not as strong as I was in the past."

He was stunned to have admitted the failing. He viewed himself as a tough, valiant brawler, and his brothers viewed him that way too, so they would grasp that he was quietly declaring his condition to be a bit more dire than he'd let on to their father.

"I'm not worried for myself," Sheridan said. "I'm generally fine, but I worry about my crew. When we're in an ominous situation, I have to be able to pull my own weight. I couldn't bear to ever imperil them."

Hunter and Warwick peeked at each other, indicating they'd gossip about him once they were by themselves. He hated that. He was the youngest, so they treated him as the *baby* brother, as if he needed them to be his nanny.

They never liked to focus on bad news though, and Hunter rallied, lightening the mood and asking, "You like the estate that's been offered, and it might be worth a marriage, but what about the woman? Would she be worth it? If she's not precisely who you want, but she comes with an excellent property, you could probably make some allowances."

"She's beautiful, pleasant, and elegant," Sheridan said.

"My goodness," Warwick said. "I can't believe Father selected a suitable person."

"There are issues with her though," Sheridan told them, "and I'm debating whether they matter or not."

"Would you be happy with her?"

With the question, Hunter sounded like a romantic, but he didn't have a romantic bone in his body. What had *happiness* to do with matrimony?

"I'd be happy enough," Sheridan said.

"High praise indeed." Warwick snickered. "What are the issues with her? Tell us and perhaps we can guide you in the right direction."

"I sincerely doubt it. Have you spoken to Neville yet? We've been discussing *me*, rather than him, so I'm betting you haven't."

"What's he done now?" Hunter was instantly on alert. Neville, and his antics, were legendary. He never surprised them.

"Brace yourselves," Sheridan said, "but we finally have a half-sister."

His brothers gasped, and Warwick stammered, "We what?"

"I guess we have two of them," Sheridan explained. "One is Joanna Ralston. She's married to Jacob Ralston. I know him from my service in the navy."

"I know him too," Hunter said. "How old is Joanna?"

"I didn't inquire, but isn't Jacob your same age of thirty? If I have to speculate, I suppose she's in her twenties. Sybil invited them to the party, but they weren't all that excited to come, so I can't predict if we'll meet her or not. But . . ."

"Uh-oh," Warwick said. "Why am I certain I won't like how that sentence ends?"

"That's because the other girl is at Swindon. You'll definitely meet her."

"You're joking!" Hunter said, and he and Warwick moaned in unison.

Over the years, they'd argued over the likely number of Neville's bastards. They'd always been prepared for a knock on the door, where a half-sibling would arrive to seek assistance. It was only to be expected that their luck had run out. After Emily and Joanna were welcomed into the fold, how many more would appear in the future?

"How old is the one who's here?" Hunter asked. "Is she an adult too?"

"No, she's a toddler. Two, maybe? Neville would have sired her when Susan was still alive."

Susan had been Neville's second wife, a debutante he'd ruined and whose male relatives had dragged him to the altar. The naïve ninny had been thrilled to snag Neville, but no one had informed her that he was a spoiled brat and philanderer. He'd driven her to an early grave with his adultery and vices.

"What's this toddler's name?" Warwick asked.

"Emily. Emily Newton." Sheridan paused and frowned. "Or would she be Emily Stone?"

Sheridan provided a quick recitation of Neville's seduction of Caroline Newton, of her refusing to identify him as the father, of her being banished to France, how she'd birthed the child there, then died later on.

"Caroline's cousin, Sophia Cantwell, accompanied her to France," Sheridan said. "I stumbled on her and Emily when I was about to sail to England. She was trying to book passage across the Channel, and I paid her fare to get them home."

"You didn't bring her yourself?"

Sheridan scoffed with derision. "Gad, no! Miss Cantwell is such a nuisance. I wouldn't have let her set foot on my ship. The Fates would have cursed my vessel."

"When you were in France with them," Hunter said, "were you aware of your connection to Emily?"

"No. Miss Cantwell didn't apprise me. She simply waited until she was in England, then she traipsed to Swindon—with Emily—and demanded Neville recognize and support her."

"From your tone, it's clear you're dubious about her claim. Are you persuaded Emily is his daughter?"

"Initially, I was skeptical, but when I was chatting with her in her bedchamber last night—"

"Ho-ho!" Warwick crowed. "You were in her bedchamber? As you started this story, I pictured Miss Cantwell as an elderly spinster. Why am I suddenly suspecting she's young and beautiful?"

Sheridan couldn't believe his gaffe, and his cheeks flushed bright red. His brothers were gaping at him so curiously that he was compelled to add details. "She's not an old crone. She's twenty, and I imagine some men might describe her as fetching."

Warwick grinned at Hunter. "Look at him! He's blushing like a besotted boy. He reminds me of you, when you were falling for Hannah."

They chuckled in an annoying way, then they glared at Sheridan in a manner that made him feel ten again and about to have them pound on him for being an idiot.

He was determined to seize control of the conversation. "What I'm struggling to explain—and where I'd like your advice—has to do with my possible engagement to Aurora Newton. You haven't realized that Caroline was her little sister, and Neville seduced her."

Hunter scowled. "Neville seduced one sister, and he's scheming for you to wed the other? I'll need an opportunity to reflect so I can deduce if that's perverted or not."

"Can I marry the sister," Sheridan asked, "when there's a bastard daughter in the middle? What is your opinion? Is the situation weird, disturbing, or irrelevant?"

"Why don't you avoid the whole dilemma," Warwick asked, "by marrying Miss Cantwell? You've already been lurking in her bedroom. Wouldn't you be happier with her?"

"Miss Cantwell is poor as a church mouse. *And* she's a liar and confidence artist. She'd drive me mad with her nonsense."

Warwick glanced at Hunter and said, "Me thinks he doth protest too much."

Sheridan rolled his eyes in exasperation. "If you can only sit there quoting Shakespeare, rather than supply me with useful guidance, we should head down to supper."

Hunter, as the big brother, liked to act as if he was smarter and wiser than they were. "You don't have to marry for money, Sheridan. You could marry for love instead."

"Well, I suppose I could," Sheridan snidely retorted, "if I thought *love* was an actual emotion a man could suffer. In the meantime, I'll glom onto an heiress for the property in her fat dowry."

George poked his nose in. "I hate to rush you gentlemen, but I was just informed that your father would like you to attend him. He plans for the three of you to promenade down the stairs with him, and Captain Stone has to finish dressing."

They couldn't argue with that edict. They stood and gulped their whiskeys, then Sheridan ushered them to the door. He didn't notice he was limping, but Hunter did.

He pointed to Sheridan's leg. "Your injury appears worse than you've let on."

Sheridan shrugged, not keen to discuss his condition in front of George. "The pain is intermittent. Mostly, I'm fine."

"I had a letter recently from an army chum," Hunter said. "He wasn't aware I'd wed, and he was wondering if I'd like to accept a government post in Gibraltar. I could write to him about you. Maybe you could retire and take it for yourself."

"I wouldn't be interested in that."

Sheridan peeked at George, but his expression was unreadable. Then he glowered at Hunter, urging him to drop it, but evidently, Hunter didn't care if George overheard.

"You wouldn't have to become a gentleman farmer," Hunter said. "Somehow, I can't envision you being content that way. Out of the three of us, you were the one who liked action and adventure the most."

Sheridan snorted. "I can't envision me as a government functionary either."

Hunter patted him on the shoulder. "We can debate it more thoroughly while we're here. I'll ask Neville about it."

"Please don't. I wouldn't like to learn his view on any topic. He's too busy harping at me about matrimony. I won't give him other subjects about which to harangue."

Warwick asked George, "Are we to meet my father in the master suite?"

"Yes. Your wives are already there and waiting for you."

His brothers started out, but Warwick peered back at Sheridan and said, "I realize, with Mr. Barnes's assistance, you'll show up garbed like the vainest dandy, but would you not dawdle too long over your outfit? I'm starving, so don't delay our meal simply because you must dither over selecting the correct cravat."

"Go!" Sheridan pushed them out and shut the door.

An awkward interval arose, where he spun away from George, and they didn't speak. George went into the bedroom, to where Sheridan's clothes were arranged on the bed. As he fingered the coat he'd picked for Sheridan to wear, he asked, "Are you thinking of retiring? Is your leg bothering you that much? I wasn't sure."

"No, I'm not thinking that," Sheridan hurriedly claimed. "Hunter was just being obnoxious."

"If you decided to quit"—George's tone was much too casual—"you'd give me some warning, wouldn't you? So I could find another position?"

"Of course I would, but don't fret. You're stuck with me. I'm not going anywhere."

"We've been to Gibraltar, and it's a beautiful spot on the globe. The weather there is lovely. It wouldn't be the worst place to end up."

"I'll keep that in mind." Sheridan was anxious to talk about anything else. "I forgot to mention that Sophia Cantwell is here."

"What? No!"

"She's brought Emily and that little fiend, Pierre, too."

George scowled. "Why would she have?"

"Well, let's get me dressed, and while your hands are occupied, I will regale you with a tale that will light your hair on fire."

George scoffed. "Where Miss Cantwell is concerned, you couldn't possibly astonish me. Whatever mischief you describe, I will absolutely believe it."

"He looks awful," Hunter said to Warwick, referring to Sheridan. "That limp is really worrying to me."

"You just watch. It will turn out to be much more serious than he's admitted."

"Yes, he's always been too tough, and he never complains."

"Do you suppose he's even seen a physician?"

"Probably not. You're aware of how stubborn he can be."

They were walking down the hall, strolling slowly, enjoying the chance to be together. Once they reached Neville's suite, their quiet conversation would conclude. Their wives would join them, Neville too, then they'd head down to supper. It would be loud, hectic, and busy, with guests eager to chat with Hunter and Warwick about their marriages and the babies that were coming.

For the moment, they were alone and could address the issues that mattered most, particularly their youngest brother. It was the two of them, gossiping about the third. They butted their noses into each other's business, with Warwick and Hunter feeling entitled to manage Sheridan's life for him.

"We could have Neville order him to visit a doctor," Warwick said.

"Sheridan would laugh in Neville's face."

"Perhaps *I* could drag him to a medical examination, whether he's willing or not."

"I'd be glad to help you," Hunter said.

"What is your opinion of our having a half-sister?"

"I think Neville should learn to keep his trousers buttoned."

"We should sit him down and force him to spill the gory details. I want to hear about the toddler who's arrived, but I'm also curious about Jacob Ralston's wife. What was her name? Joanna? I wonder when Neville sired her. Who was her mother, and was *our* mother alive when Joanna was conceived?"

"I'm sure she was," Hunter said. "Matrimony never deterred Neville, but are you certain we should waste our breath interrogating him? He'll simply lie and rationalize his conduct."

"He insists he's mellowing in his old age. Maybe he'd be a tad forthcoming."

"You're hilarious to imagine he would be."

They continued on, and Hunter said, "I'll reply to my friend about that government post in Gibraltar. It would be the ideal situation for Sheridan. He could reside in a foreign locale and pretend he hadn't settled down. It might be a viable beginning as he transitions to civilian life."

"He's about to betroth himself. Would his bride be keen to move there? That might be a problem."

"Is he about to betroth himself?" Hunter asked. "He didn't seem all that enthused to me. If I remember correctly, he was much more attached to her property than to her."

Warwick nodded. "That's how I read it."

"If he's intent on proceeding, we should meet the woman. Sheridan assumes she's a fine candidate, but when has he ever made a good decision? We can't have him shackled to someone horrid."

"He has to pick a girl we can abide when we gather for family events."

"I'd just like him to be happy," Hunter said. "Did he look happy to you?"

"No, he looked grouchy, but his injury might be keeping him surly."

"The only time he was the least bit animated was when he mentioned that Miss Cantwell."

Warwick raised a brow. "She's here at Swindon. We ought to take a peek at her. If we like her, we can throw them together to see what happens."

Hunter chuckled. "I didn't realize you had skills as a matchmaker."

"Well, we can't leave this choice to Sheridan and Neville. They'd muck it up completely. You and I selected our own brides, and it turned out grand."

"Yes," Hunter said, "and I want Sheridan to wind up in the same perfect spot."

Chapter Sixteen

"Tell me about yourself, Miss Cantwell."

Sophia gaped at Sheridan's brother, Hunter, who was Viscount Marston, and she couldn't fathom why he was even talking to her, let alone fishing for information. She supposed he'd learned about Emily's existence, and he'd want to find a chink in Sophia's armor that would indicate she was a liar.

The whole blasted family exhausted her!

She was in the ballroom, and a festive dance was in progress. The participants were promenading down the center, but she was huddled in a corner with Viscount Marston. They'd just danced, which had been fun, but very odd. Shortly after they'd been introduced, he'd practically dragged her out onto the floor.

Once the set had ended, she'd expected to slip away to join the wallflowers, but he'd escorted her to the beverage table so they could share a glass of wine.

She hadn't intended to still be loitering at Swindon, but the Riverglen servant who'd driven her to the property had notified her that there was a problem with the wheel on their carriage. It wasn't serious, and the estate blacksmith would fix it, but her departure had been delayed by a day or two.

She'd assumed she would spend her time huddled in the nursery, but to her great surprise, she'd received a note from Sybil Jones, inviting her to socialize after supper was over. Then Miss Jones very graciously had a housemaid visit to inquire whether Sophia had appropriate attire to wear at the party.

When she'd confessed that she didn't, the girl had scrounged up some lace, ribbons, and a fan to embellish the only gown she'd brought that was the least bit fancy. The girl had styled her hair too, so—while she wasn't the most glamorous woman in attendance—she didn't look as if she'd staggered in from the barn either.

She didn't understand what had occurred to restructure her position in the house. Her father was a poet, and she was cousin to Aurora Newton who would likely wind up as a member of the Stone family, so Sophia wasn't exactly a barbarian.

She had the ancestry, education, and personality to bluster into the middle of a bunch of posh aristocrats and fit in just fine, and she was delighted that Miss Jones had included her. She'd already chatted with a man who'd known her father and remembered him fondly, so the whole trip had been worth it merely to have had that experience.

"There's not much to tell," Sophia claimed in answer to the Viscount's question. "My father was the poet, Richard Cantwell, and we're kin to the Newtons of Riverglen. I'm Mrs. Newton's ward until I turn twenty-one next year."

She didn't add that Sheridan was considering marriage to Aurora. If Viscount Marston wasn't aware of that fact, Sophia didn't imagine she should apprise him.

"Your father was a poet?" the Viscount said. "I'm sorry, but I don't recognize his name."

"It's all right. He never achieved any fame, but he published several volumes. He thought he was very good, and I like to honor him by insisting he was."

"As well you should. I hear you delivered a little gift to my father."

Again, she had to tread cautiously. Was he referring to Emily? If he hadn't been told about her, Sophia wasn't going to speak up.

"What gift do you mean?" she asked.

"Evidently, I have a new sister."

"Oh, yes. Emily. She's my cousin Caroline's daughter."

"May I meet her?"

"Of course. Stop by the nursery. We have her tucked away up there. She's a handful, so we can't have her waltzing around in the downstairs parlors while your father's friends are in residence."

The Viscount snorted at that. "His friends are cognizant of his amorous foibles, and they're a group of notorious scoundrels. None of them would be shocked to discover that a natural child had knocked on the door."

Sophia had no idea how to respond to the comment, so she said, "Emily is cute and precocious. She'll charm you."

"I'm sure she will." He sipped his drink and studied her meticulously, as if he was searching for something he couldn't locate. Finally, sounding very sly, he said, "I've been informed that you and Sheridan are cordial."

It was a peculiar remark, and she felt as if she was tiptoeing in a bog where a wrong step would suck her down into it.

"Yes, I stumbled on him in France. Emily's mother and I were living there, and she passed away. I had an interruption of my funding from home, so I was in a financial bind and trying to devise a way to get to England."

"Sheridan admitted he paid your fare, and I'm stunned to find he was so generous. He rarely is with anyone."

"He talked to you about me?" The query popped out before she could swallow it down.

"Yes, and he seems very enamored of you too."

She shook her head. "He holds many opinions about me, but *enamored* is not one of them. If he was forced to declare a sentiment, he'd say I'm a nuisance and a troublemaker."

"Are you?"

"Definitely."

He laughed. "What is your plan for the future, Miss Cantwell? Are you engaged? Have you a sweetheart who's eager to wed you?"

"Gad no. First of all, I have no dowry, so what sane fellow would notice me? And second of all, I was reared by my father who was a dreamer and traveler. He filled me with wanderlust. If I had my druthers, I'd jump on a ship and journey around the world."

"Will you?" he asked.

"No." She scoffed with amusement. "I'm fairly certain nothing amazing will ever happen to me." She astonished herself by adding, "If I'm really unlucky, my guardian will wed me to a farmer so she can be shed of me. I can be that much of a bother."

"You poor girl. I can tell that would be a fate worse than death for you. How would you survive it?"

"I wouldn't, so I'll probably remain a lonely, exhausting spinster who's naught but a drain on her family."

He tipped his glass, motioning across the room to where Sheridan had slipped in the door. Like a besotted ninny, she'd been watching for him every minute, but he hadn't arrived.

He was dressed elegantly again, wearing another formal suit, his cravat sewn from the finest Belgian lace, his fingers adorned with expensive jewelry. He was simply too handsome for words, and on seeing him, her pulse raced with excitement. What would he think of her prancing about with the other guests? She suspected he wouldn't like it, and she hoped he wouldn't raise a fuss.

"There's my brother," the Viscount said, "deigning to make an appearance. You should dance with him. Shall I wave him over?"

It was another strange comment she didn't understand, and she felt as if she was in the middle of an employment interview, with her applying for a job and being completely confused as to what that job entailed.

"He shouldn't dance," she said. "Because of his injury? It pains him too much. It would hurt his leg to twirl and spin."

The Viscount's assessment grew even more probing. "You know about his injury? He's discussed it with you?"

"Ah . . . yes?"

"Interesting," he mused. "What did he confide about it? He never likes me to worry, and I've been afraid it might be much more dire than he's let on."

"You're right to fret. He works very hard to hide his condition, but he can never totally conceal it. Not from me anyway. I doubt he'll continue to sail much longer. With his physical stamina so reduced, I fear he couldn't manage it."

The Viscount glared at her as if she were an exotic creature he'd never previously encountered. "It sounds as if the two of you have had some intimate conversations."

She kept her expression blank, but her cheeks heated, so she was positive he would assume she was loose with her favors.

"We became close when we were in France," she said. "I was experiencing numerous difficulties there, and I couldn't fix them on my own. I needed a knight to ride in and rescue me, and your brother grudgingly played that part. He was very gallant about it too."

"Sheridan was gallant?" the Viscount asked. "I am absolutely astounded to learn of it."

In unison, their gazes drifted across the packed salon so they were both staring at Sheridan, as if trying to figure him out.

He was leaned in the doorway, as if deciding whether to tarry or not. For a moment, the crowd shifted, and he was staring directly back at them. He couldn't miss that she was loafing with Lord Marston, and he scowled, then whirled away and departed into the hall.

The Viscount smirked. "He didn't like to see us talking. I'm sure he's aware we were talking about *him*."

She shrugged. "He's a pompous menace, and I don't care what he thinks."

"A pompous menace . . ." the Viscount murmured. "That describes him perfectly."

The dance set had ended, and a new one was starting. He downed the remnants of his wine and put the glass on a nearby tray.

"Will you excuse me, Miss Cantwell?" he said. "I've promised to partner with another young lady. She'll be wondering where I am."

"Go, go!" She shooed him away. "I can't fathom why you lingered with me in the first place."

"It was an intriguing and satisfying discussion, and I'm delighted that we had it. I hope we'll chat a bit more in the future. I'd like to introduce you to my other brother, Warwick. He'll be as fascinated as I am."

"I have no idea why that would be the case, but yes, I'll be around."

She couldn't predict if that would turn out to be true or not. Miss Jones had invited her to that evening's entertainment, but did it extend to other events? Who could guess? Besides, she was leaving as soon as her carriage was repaired.

"You can stop by the nursery," she said. "I'm usually there in the day. You can meet Emily."

"I will do that."

He nodded, then sauntered off. She dawdled for a few minutes, struggling to decipher the bewildering exchange. She imagined he was probing her veracity, but it had seemed too as if he was prying into her relationship with Sheridan.

"Good luck with that," she muttered to herself.

Who could clarify what was happening between them? They were intimately bound, but if she'd explained it to the Viscount, he'd have thought she was deranged.

She left the ballroom and wandered through various parlors. The guests all knew each other, so she was the stranger, the outsider, and she realized how alone she was in the world. The notion had her morbidly nostalgic, which was exasperating. Why couldn't she ever simply be content in the moment?

The prior night, she'd pouted because she hadn't been invited to the party. Now, she'd been invited, and she was feeling sorry for herself.

She went onto the rear verandah. It was cold, the temperature bracing, but the fresh air was invigorating. She walked to the balustrade and gazed out at the park. Lamps were lit and people were strolling. She would have liked to stroll too, but she didn't have a cloak, and it was too chilly without one.

She was about to head back inside when she noticed Sheridan skulking over in the shadows. He was smoking a cheroot and watching her like a hawk. She should have ignored him, but where he was concerned, she could never pick the saner route.

"Well, well," he said as she ambled over, "if it isn't Miss Cantwell."

"Hello, Captain. It's lovely you could drag yourself down for the festivities."

"I was here for supper, but after the meal, I hid for a while."

"Is your leg bothering you?" she asked. "Is that why you slithered off?"

"Yes, you little busybody. My leg is hurting."

He flicked his cheroot out into the grass, then he slid an arm around her waist and pulled her close. He dipped down and kissed her, and it was thrilling and disturbing. Yes, they were huddled in the shadows, but anyone out in the garden could observe them.

She didn't suppose she should have the guests speculating over who she was or why she was kissing Sheridan Stone on the Earl's verandah.

"What's wrong?" she said as he eased away. "It's more than your leg, isn't it? You're very sad too."

"Yes, I'm very morose, and I was positive—if I kissed you—I'd feel better."

"Did it work? Have I cured what ails you?"

"No. You've only made things worse."

"Thank you, Captain. You're such a sweet-talker. When your pretty compliments flow over me, I find myself quite overcome."

He chuckled. "You silly girl. Aren't you freezing without a cloak?"

"I didn't intend to tarry, but you've waylaid me."

He opened his coat and tugged the lapels around her, snuggling her even closer. She could have stood with him forever and died a happy woman.

"Why are you at the party?" he asked. "I can't believe no one saw that an interloper had snuck in."

"If you must know, I was invited by Miss Jones."

"Really? If she included you, she must be losing her mind."

Sophia tsked with offense. "How is she connected to your father? Are they engaged or merely cordial?"

"She runs a popular gambling club in London. My father is a premier member."

Sophia's jaw dropped. "She gambles?"

"No, she's a businesswoman. In certain circles, she's notorious because she's a female. Everyone was convinced she'd fail at the endeavor, but she's been wildly successful."

"My goodness. I wasn't aware she was involved in such a dicey enterprise."

He shrugged. "She's an important person who's acquainted with London's best citizens. If she's befriended you, it wouldn't necessarily be a detrimental development, so don't be a snob about her."

Sophia scoffed. "I've never been a snob in my life."

Even as she uttered the remark, she was worrying about Miss Jones. If Sophia could persuade Lord Swindon to publicly recognize his paternity of Emily, what sort of impact might Miss Jones have on Emily's upbringing? Sophia had already decided that Lord Swindon would be a poor guardian. With Miss Jones stirred into the mix, wasn't the problem increasing?

"Your father is very attached to her," she said. "Are you about to have a new mother?"

"Gad, don't even say it. His last marriage was to a debutante, and it played out like a bad carriage accident. Luckily, I was out to sea for most of it, so I wasn't present as the debacle unfolded. If he could shackle himself to a pragmatic woman like Sybil Jones, it might be a benefit. She might be the only female in the kingdom who could coax him into better behavior."

They were quiet for a bit, and she reveled in the silence. She was in a perfect spot, nestled to his chest, his heart beating a steady rhythm under her ear.

After a lengthy interval, he said, "You were chatting with my brother, Hunter, in the ballroom. What did he want?"

"I'm not sure. The entire encounter was totally bizarre."

"Were you discussing me?"

"Yes, and I view it as absolutely typical that you'd be vain enough to think so."

"How did he corner you? Why did you let him?"

"He asked me to dance, and I don't understand why. I should have refused, but I couldn't figure out how. Then, after the set was finished, he dragged me to the beverage table, where I had to politely drink a glass of wine with him while he peppered me with questions about you."

"What kind of questions?"

"Mostly about your leg and your health. He's concerned about you."

He huffed at that. "He's not concerned. He's always been a damned meddler. He acts as if I'm still ten and can't blink without him giving me permission."

She pinched his waist. "Don't curse. In your foul dealings around the globe, I'm positive you've committed many sins, and you shouldn't add to the list by spewing vulgar words."

He huffed again, but didn't apologize. "What did you tell him about me?"

"I claimed you're completely crippled and barely able to hobble about, and your condition is so hideous you should be confined to your bed and never allowed to roam among normal people."

She could sense him smiling. "You did not say that."

"No, I didn't. I told him I was worried about you too because you're such an arrogant beast that you don't take care of yourself." She pulled back to peer up at him. "He agreed with me."

"About me being an arrogant beast?"

"No. About you not taking care of yourself."

"I take care of myself," he testily complained.

"Liar. Your limp has gotten worse just in the short time I've known you."

"It's not worse. I'm just favoring it more than usual."

"Point made, Captain Stone."

"Hunter believes I should retire and accept a government job."

"Would that be so awful?" she asked.

"How could it be any different from becoming a farmer and wallowing in rural tedium?"

"Don't denigrate rural tedium. Most of us are trapped in the country, and we don't like you to poke fun at us."

He sighed, as if the world was weighing heavily on his shoulders. "I can't picture me away from my ship. I try to envision it, but I can't. If I wasn't a sailor anymore, I might simply be invisible."

It was such a poignant comment, and she was quite moved by it. For some reason, he shared confidences with her she was convinced he never shared with anyone else. It caused her to feel more attached to him than she actually was, and it had her imagining endings that could never be.

He saw a future for them, but it was an illicit relationship, with her as his mistress. She saw a future, and it involved church bells and a vicar reciting marital vows. They weren't destined to walk the same road.

"You could never be invisible," she told him. "You're too brash and dashing for that to ever occur."

"I'll keep telling myself you're right."

"You're not the first person in history who's had to change course and reinvent himself. It happens constantly. Take me for example. The past decade, I've resided at Riverglen and have been supported by my cousins, but I'm about to be an adult. My life will be transformed in significant ways."

"Why would anything have to be transformed? They won't kick you out the minute you turn twenty-one, will they?"

"It's not that. I just couldn't remain there after you wed Aurora, so I have to make other plans for myself."

She waited on tenterhooks, expecting him to utter any number of various replies: that he hadn't fully decided about Aurora, or that Sophia shouldn't have to leave Riverglen over him, or that it would be awkward to have him marry Aurora, but they'd muddle through.

But he didn't offer a single platitude or inanity about how she was being either silly or hysterical. He didn't insist she was incorrect or that she'd misconstrued the situation. He simply stared down at her, and whatever thoughts were filling his thick male head, she couldn't decipher them.

He snuggled her to his chest again, and while she couldn't have predicted what his next remark would be, the one he chose was ridiculous.

"Please don't ever discuss me with my brothers. Or with my father. I'm none of their business."

"They think you are."

"They're wrong. If Hunter pesters you again, tell him to stuff it."

She doubted there would be a subsequent opportunity for Viscount Marston to chat with her. She was departing shortly, but she didn't admit it. She couldn't guess what Sheridan's opinion would be about a departure, but she wouldn't give him a chance to stop her.

Apparently, he was finished conversing. They hovered together until, from behind them, a man said, "Sheridan! There you are. I've been searching everywhere. Father needs us for a toast."

To Sheridan's credit, he didn't leap away from her, as if he was embarrassed to have been caught with her. No, he merely slid away and spun around. She spun too and casually stepped away from him. With her losing his body's heat, goosebumps careened down her arms, and she shivered.

It was Viscount Marston who'd called to Sheridan, and there was a smirk in his gaze, as if she'd behaved precisely as he'd figured she might. By morning, it would be all over the mansion that she was a bit of a tart.

Sheridan spoke to his brother. "You know Miss Cantwell, don't you?"

"Oh, yes," the Viscount replied. "She and I are very friendly. We danced and she's excellent at it. You should escort her out onto the floor yourself."

"If you want information about my condition," Sheridan said, "you can ask me directly. You don't have to bother a stranger."

"Is she a stranger?" Lord Marston snickered. "It doesn't look like it to me."

Sheridan didn't answer the charge. Instead, he peeked down at her and said, "I have to go. Try to stay out of trouble."

She batted her lashes like a coquette. "Why would I? If I start to act like a saint, you'll never have reasons to lecture me."

He snorted with amusement, then sauntered off with his brother. Sheridan went in first, and Lord Marston paused to glance back at her.

He assessed her too thoroughly, so he probably didn't like that he'd stumbled on her with Sheridan.

His heightened attention could never be to her benefit. He would spend the evening warning Sheridan that it was inappropriate for him to be flirting with her, to be leading her on, that she would misinterpret his signals.

Well, she and Sheridan understood all of that. They hardly had to be scolded over the fact that their liaison was misguided and ill-advised.

She hurried inside, but through a different entrance. The two brothers had sucked the fun out of the party, and she was eager to hide from them. She wouldn't lurk in the crowd and drool over handsome, dashing Captain Stone. Nor would she beam delightedly as their father lifted his glass in a toast. She didn't care what Neville Stone had to say about any topic.

She found a rear staircase and climbed to her bedchamber. She checked on Pierre and Emily, and they were sound asleep. Then she tiptoed to her own room, and she locked the door. She didn't suppose Sheridan would sneak in later on, but she had to stop encouraging him.

He wanted something from her. He *needed* something from her, but despite what it was, she simply couldn't supply it.

SHERIDAN RAN ACROSS THE lawn, sprinting as if he was hale, healthy, and had no lingering wound.

It was a beautiful autumn afternoon, the air crisp, the sky blue, and he felt better than he had in ages. He'd awakened in a brilliant mood that had made him wonder if he wasn't improving. The doctors had counselled that it would take a long time. Was it finally happening?

The younger male guests were rough-housing, kicking a ball in a wild game where hands couldn't be used; just feet. When they'd asked him to join one of the teams, he hadn't been able to resist, most particularly because Hunter and Warwick were on the opposite team.

The three of them were very competitive, and he relished the chance to beat them at any endeavor. Coats were off, shirt sleeves rolled back. They were elbowing, shouting, and tripping each other. It was heady sport, the type he hadn't enjoyed since his years in boarding school. He seemed bracingly alive, free from worry or responsibilities.

The female guests were seated on chairs, watching from the sidelines. They had their favorites, and they cheered and clapped when a jarring tackle was successful. Sophia wasn't present though, and he kept peering over, wishing she'd arrive.

The prior evening, he'd trifled with her again, right out on the verandah where they could have been observed by others. Hunter had dragged him away from her, which had been the only logical conclusion, but as the festivities had worn down and people had slunk off to their beds, he hadn't proceeded to his own bedchamber. No, he'd marched to the wing where her room was located.

He'd yearned to talk to her and had been suffering from an absurd impulse to explain why he'd marry her cousin. She had to comprehend why it was for the best. In the end though, he'd reined in the bizarre whim. He hadn't knocked on her door. He hadn't visited her, but he'd spent the rest of the night regretting it.

He had to ignore her, but he was being overwhelmed by the most terrifying impression that his time with her was dwindling, and he was eager to revel in all of the Sophia *moments* he could before they were gone forever.

He was focused on her so avidly that he wasn't paying as much attention as he should have. The ball bounced in front of him, and as he leapt toward it, a brawny fellow rushed up to steal it away.

Their bodies collided violently, then the other man jumped and kicked, and his foot landed—full impact—directly on Sheridan's thigh. The pain was sharp and brutal, and to his great mortification, his leg gave out and he fell to the ground.

Evidently, he'd blacked out for a minute or two because once his vision cleared, it was dreadfully silent, the game having abruptly halted. His brothers were leaned over him, and Hunter was patting Sheridan on the cheek and quietly saying, "Sheridan! Sheridan! Are you there? Can you hear me?"

The other players were hovered in a circle, all of them shifting nervously, and he was incredibly embarrassed to have so many people gaping at him.

He swatted Hunter away. "Yes, yes, I'm fine. Don't be so annoying."

"Is it your wound?" Warwick asked. "Have you re-injured it?"

"I'm *fine!"* Sheridan repeated more tersely. "It was simply a hard blow. Don't wring your hands as if you're my nanny."

"What do you need?" Hunter asked.

"Help me up?" Sheridan said, and he extended his arms.

He was a big man, and it took both his brothers to haul him to his feet. He was nauseous, dizzy and swaying, sweat popping out on his brow.

"Would you like to sit down?" Warwick gestured as if he'd toss a female spectator out of her chair and bring it over for Sheridan to use.

"No, thank you. I'll head to the house and rest there."

"Shall I accompany you?" Warwick inquired, and he was so alarmed. It was humiliating.

"Go back to your game." He waved at the grass, indicating they should resume. "And to my teammates, would you please be sure to beat my brothers? I always like to win against them."

The remark smoothed away the anxious glances, and the men moved away and began milling, kindly pretending they hadn't witnessed the incident.

"I'm walking you inside," Warwick said, his tone brooking no argument.

"I'm not a cripple. I can trudge in without a nursemaid guiding my way."

He was being much too surly, but he couldn't feign a jolly deportment. He hated to have his brothers observe this aspect of his personality, but his wound left him in a constant bad humor, and he was lashing out at them.

To his enormous relief, George bustled up and said to Warwick, "You shouldn't miss out on all the fun, Mr. Stone. I can escort him in for you."

Warwick might have quarreled about it, Hunter too, but George stared implacably, so they wouldn't cause a scene. Without waiting for further comment, George started Sheridan toward the mansion, and he had a firm palm on Sheridan's back that steadied and balanced him.

They didn't hurry, but in reality, Sheridan couldn't have hurried. It required every ounce of strength he possessed to keep from collapsing in agony. Behind him, he could feel his brothers' gazes cutting into him like daggers.

"What happened?" George asked after they were far enough away that they wouldn't be overheard.

"I was kicked in the leg by one of the other players."

George clucked his tongue like a fussy governess. "I don't suppose I should have to tell you that you're in no condition to participate in such a rough escapade."

"I think I'm invincible."

"You *think* you are," George said, "but we know it's not true."

"Don't scold me, George. Just get me to my room and make it fast. If I don't lie down shortly, I might pass out and never wake up."

Chapter Seventeen

Sophia was tiptoeing toward Sheridan's bedroom suite. She realized she was making a serious mistake, but she couldn't stop herself.

She'd spent a frustrating afternoon in the nursery with the children. She'd been waiting for something to happen, for the wheel on the carriage to be fixed, or for Lord Swindon to summon her for a discussion, or perhaps for Miss Jones to summon her instead. But the minutes had ticked by in a slow sort of torture.

She hadn't received a second invitation from Miss Jones to participate in the evening socializing, and no maid had arrived to fix her hair, so she'd decided she hadn't been welcome to attend. She didn't feel slighted exactly, but then again, she felt incredibly slighted.

She'd been pouting and struggling to deduce what the snub indicated. Had Miss Jones forgotten about her? Or was it a more exasperating issue than that? Had Viscount Marston advised Miss Jones to keep Sophia away from his brother? Or had Sheridan warned her that Sophia shouldn't be allowed to mingle with the toplofty company?

He wasn't a cruel person though, so it couldn't be that. Could it?

The prior night, she'd locked her door, but she was fairly certain he hadn't attempted to visit her. Upon waking in the morning, she'd tarried petulantly, expecting him to show up, but he hadn't, and it had distressed her. Her time with him was winding to an end and, very soon, she'd never see him again. She couldn't let an entire day go by without speaking to him.

It wasn't until the housemaids had retrieved their supper trays that she'd heard them talking about his accident. He'd been playing a lawn game, and he'd been kicked in the leg. According to their whispered account, it had been such a dire injury that he'd been rendered unconscious, and briefly, the other players had been afraid he'd died.

She'd asked the chatty pair about his current condition, but they'd had no information. He hadn't come down to supper, so everyone was worried about him.

Pierre snooped and wandered in the large manor, and he'd learned many intriguing details about the place. She'd slyly coaxed him into divulging the location of Sheridan's bedchamber, and after he and Emily had dozed off, she'd snuck away to find out how he was faring. She had no idea how else she could glean any news. It wasn't as if anyone would have rushed to apprise her, and she had to be sure he was all right.

The halls were deserted, with the guests still reveling in the lower parlors, so she hadn't encountered a single soul. She reached his door and pressed her ear to the wood, listening for voices, but there weren't any.

She inhaled a fortifying breath, then spun the knob and peeked into the sitting room. If it had been full of footmen, doctors, or his brothers, she'd have crept away, but it was dark and empty, so she slipped inside.

The inner door was ajar, and there was a candle burning. She could see a bit of the bed, but couldn't tell if he was lying on it or not. She dawdled and debated, wondering if she hadn't gone stark raving mad.

She'd just convinced herself to silently glide away, to exit as quickly and quietly as she'd entered, when he called, "Sophia? Is that you?"

She frowned, then marched over and glanced around the door.

"How did you know it was me?" she asked.

"Your snotty stride is too obvious."

She tsked with offense. "I won't even try to figure out what that means."

He was stretched out on the bed, lounged against the pillows, and looking like the loneliest man in the kingdom. It was a massive piece of furniture, with an ornate, carved headboard and plush feather mattress, and it appeared so grand it might have been designed for the King. Maybe it had been.

He was wearing trousers, but they were a type of garment she'd never previously observed. They were loose and comfortable, sewn from a silky fabric, the sort a sultan might don when entertaining his harem.

He had a robe over top, but had shed his shirt. The belt was untied, the lapels flopping open, so much of his chest was visible. His hair was unbound, the blond tresses curling over his shoulders. Someone had left him a liquor tray, and it was next to him on the mattress. She suspected the decanter contained whiskey, and from how little remained, it was clear he'd drunk a substantial amount.

"I was hoping you'd come," he surprised her by saying. "I wanted to send for you, but I didn't suppose I should."

"I only just heard the maids gossiping or I'd have visited earlier."

"Lock the door to the hall, would you?"

"I will. Give me a minute."

She traipsed through the sitting room and spun the key, and the moment was very strange, as if she was up above her body and watching some other foolish woman behave precisely as she shouldn't.

It was dangerous to be sequestered with him. She understood that pertinent fact, and she couldn't be caught with him, so it was wise to lock the door. He was protecting her from folly. Wasn't he?

She walked back to the bedroom and over to the bed. They shared a charged visual exchange that was so potent, and so filled with longing, that it scared her.

"I stay away from you for one afternoon, Captain Stone," she teasingly said, "and you practically kill yourself when I'm not there to keep an eye on you."

"It's your fault I was hurt."

"I wasn't present, so how could it have been my fault?"

"I was pondering you so furiously that I wasn't paying attention."

"Well, doesn't that make me feel special?" She eased a hip onto the mattress and asked, "What happened? I was told you were rough-housing out on the lawn."

"Yes, with some of the other guests, and one of them kicked me in the leg." He waved a hand, as if he could wipe away the episode. "It was a simple collision, but from how people reacted, you'd think the world had ended."

"They thought you'd died! They were terrified!"

He scoffed with derision. "I fell down; that's it. It throbbed like the dickens, so I limped away and . . . here I am. My father put me to bed and ordered me not to move. I was so astonished to have him exhibit concern for my welfare that I've been as obedient as a puppy."

"You're much more hale than I anticipated. According to the housemaids, you're half dead."

"I'm fine," he mumbled, seeming embarrassed. "My deteriorated condition exhausts me. I've always been such a strong, hearty fellow. It's galling to find myself debilitated."

"I know that about you." She reached over and pushed his hair off his forehead. "I wish I could heal you and chase the pain away."

She started to pull her hand back, but he clasped hold of it and kissed the center of her palm. It was an endearing gesture, and her pulse raced, her alarm spiraling. When he was charming, it was so difficult to erect any barriers between them.

"Have you seen a doctor?" she asked. "Does Swindon have a physician who's not a quack?"

"They have one who *is* a quack," he said, "and I refused to let him touch me. I've already consulted with several doctors. I merely have to rest and recuperate, but it will take an eternity to regain my stamina."

"You're not very patient."

"No, I'm not. I want to bluster forward as if I was never wounded."

"That is a silly attitude to have."

"Yes, but please don't scold me. My brothers have been chastising me for hours. They're treating me like an invalid, and it's extremely irritating. I finally shooed them out and told them to cease their nagging."

"They're worried about you, and you're lucky you have them. Stop complaining."

He sighed, looking very forlorn. "Will you sit with me for a while? And be nice to me?"

"Yes, of course. I'd be glad to. Do you need anything?"

"No, just sit."

He patted the mattress, indicating she should join him on it, but the liquor tray was in the way. She carried it over to the dresser, and as she went back to him, she asked, "How much have you had to drink?"

"I don't remember, but however much I've imbibed, I'm sure it wasn't enough."

"Are you aching? Would you like some laudanum? The housekeeper probably has some in her medicinal box. I could fetch some for you."

"I don't need any laudanum. The whiskey has soothed my senses sufficiently that I'm numb all over."

He extended his arms to her, urging her to tumble into them, and she said, "Will it bother your leg if I climb up?"

"No."

She was careful though. She eased up and stretched out, and he drew her close. Once she was nestled to him, his entire body relaxed, as if he'd been balancing a load of tension on his shoulders and, with her arrival, he'd been able to release it.

He smirked. "I'm better already."

"I'm renowned for my curative abilities."

"Normally, I'd laugh at that, but I'm too worn down to joke with you."

"It tells me your level of misery may be beyond repair."

"Don't you wish we could lie here forever and never have to return to the real world?"

"I will pretend that's a serious question," she said, "but I'm positive, if I dawdle for even a brief period, your ego will flare and you'll be lecturing me about my failings."

"You should be lectured. In light of how recklessly you act, I can't fathom how you've lived to the ripe old age of twenty." He yawned, then asked, "What did you do all day?"

"I waited in the nursery for you to visit me, and I can't believe you stayed away." She peeked up at him and facetiously said, "I'm such a temptation. Weren't you chomping at the bit to come upstairs? Even if you weren't, humor me and claim you were."

"I thought about visiting you," he admitted, "but I was practicing my self-restraint. You have such a strange effect on me, and I'm trying to ignore it."

"Are you succeeding?"

"Since you're with me on my bed, I guess I have to say *no,* I'm not succeeding."

He dipped down and kissed her, then he snuggled her down. She rested her hand on his chest, directly over his heart, and it beat beneath her palm.

"I'm so fatigued," he said, and he yawned again. "I've been shooting you mental messages all evening so you'd sneak in, but now that you're here, I can barely keep my eyes open."

"Will you doze off on me?"

"I'm afraid I might. Will you tarry?" he asked. "Just for a few minutes."

"I will tarry—for as long as you need me."

With that assurance voiced, he fell asleep immediately, his torso slumping as if he'd expended every ounce of energy he could manage. He was so vain, and it had to be difficult to hide his true condition from his relatives. He feigned good health for them, but clearly, it was a losing effort.

The room was cooling, the fire dying, and she slid away and found a knitted throw. She brought it back and covered him with it, then she stretched out beside him again, and they were sealed in a toasty cocoon.

She didn't want to forget a single aspect of the intimate interval, and she catalogued every detail. It seemed as if she had a special obligation to watch over him as he slumbered, and she felt lucky.

No one else had offered to remain with him. No one else had realized he might be lonely and forlorn. No one else had figured out that he required some affectionate tending. *She* had realized it, and she'd arrived to provide it.

It was the most wonderful occasion of her life, and she was glad she'd dared. The dim, quiet room was hypnotic though, and she started to doze off too. She knew she shouldn't, but he'd asked her to tarry, and she'd promised she would. She'd have a quick nap, then tiptoe to her own room.

Her eyes fluttered shut and sleep swept her away.

SHERIDAN STOOD BY HIS window, staring out at the night sky. It was dark, drizzling rain, and clouds blocked the stars. What was he trying to see anyway?

He was particularly morose, being landlocked with too many miles between him and his ship, between him and the sea. Why was he at Swindon? While he liked having the chance to visit his brothers, he didn't give two figs about his father's old chums. Why didn't he depart?

Depart to where?

The question rang in his head. He could scarcely walk, and he was chafing over what was forfeit, which was very petty. So what if his career was ending? So what if he had to marry and settle down? It happened to every sailor sooner or later. Why should he be allowed to escape that fate?

He glanced over to where Sophia was asleep on his bed. The ribbon had fallen from her gorgeous hair, so it was spread across the pillows. She looked like an angel, like the worst sort of coquette, and her presence was a gift and a danger. She was such a lovely, foolish girl, and she was tucked away precisely where she shouldn't be.

She assumed he wouldn't take advantage of her, but she was wrong about that. If he'd been a gentleman, he'd have awakened her and sent her to her room, but he wasn't that gallant.

When he stumbled on something he wanted, he reached out and grabbed it. He *wanted* her in a manner he'd never wanted any woman, but he had no viable options with regard to her. They couldn't be friends, and she had wisely refused to be his mistress. The only other choice was to wed her, and he pondered for a moment, considering the idea.

It was thrilling in a way that was very peculiar, and he let the exciting sentiment flow through him. He was very wealthy, so he didn't have to wed for property or money, but he was as British as the next fellow. If a man didn't obtain a benefit from matrimony, why proceed?

He wouldn't pretend it was possible to marry for affection. He *wouldn't* do it. If he betrothed himself, it would be to accrue the boons a husband received as payment for shackling himself. It was a cold, brutal attitude to have, but it was true.

Where did it leave him with her? It was obvious they shared a destiny, and he couldn't bear to have their relationship conclude without knowing her more intimately.

He went over and laid down beside her. He tugged a blanket over them and pulled her into his arms. She lurched up on an elbow and peered around frantically, not sure of where she was.

When she focused in and saw him smiling at her, she chuckled and plopped down. "Ooh, I was sleeping so hard, and you're a fiend to have roused me. What time is it?"

"It's late."

"I should go to my room. I can't believe I loafed in here. We're lucky I wasn't caught."

At her mentioning she should go, he suffered a wave of panic, but she didn't budge, so it swiftly faded.

Instead, she grinned and stretched, appearing delectable and comfortable, and he leaned over and kissed her quite fiercely. He couldn't ever kiss her any other way. She simply stirred his passions to an insane degree that he couldn't control. And why should he control them?

He'd been kind and incredibly patient with her. Didn't he deserve a reward for his efforts? Well, *no,* he didn't. That was the lust talking, but he was sad, glum, and still half-intoxicated. Alcohol was giving him excuses to rationalize bad behavior.

He rolled on top of her, and her pertinent feminine areas were crushed to his torso: her soft breasts, her flat tummy, the mound cradling her woman's sheath. His phallus was so happy that, if it could have wept with joy, it would have.

She leapt into the embrace, and as always occurred when they were together, the interval grew too raucous to manage. They were wild for one another, and there was such a perception of immense fondness that the whole bloody event seemed appropriate and absolutely allowed.

She was a willing partner so, very rapidly, he was in over his head. He couldn't slow down or retreat as was required. He needed to be closer to her, needed to be skin to skin, so he rose up onto his knees and shed his robe. He was wearing just his trousers, his chest bare, and she tsked with exasperation, as if he was a boy who was being very naughty.

"You can't disrobe," she scolded. "I'll snuggle with you for a bit, but we're not removing any of our clothes."

"That wasn't *clothes.* That was a robe. It's an entirely different garment."

"You are a scoundrel, so you would split hairs."

"You're complaining, Cantwell," he said, "and I don't think you mean to. Not when we've stolen this very private moment for ourselves."

"No, I definitely don't mean to complain."

He clasped her wrists and placed her palms on his chest, and her touch was so erotically charged that he was surprised he didn't ignite. He was still on his knees, and she drew him down to her, saying, "Isn't your leg hurting? Don't put pressure on it."

"You've made me forget all about it."

"I'm a miracle-worker." She laughed her sensual laugh. "Everyone has always told me so."

He began kissing her again, and matters escalated at a very fast rate. There was no time to contemplate their direction. She was a maiden, so she couldn't have been expected to contemplate it, but he was an experienced libertine, and he knew better. He was aware of how easy it was to flaunt the rules.

A man couldn't blithely fornicate with a female. The Church declared it a depravity. The Law deemed it a crime. Society forbade it. With those obstacles erected, there were huge roadblocks to prevent folly. If she didn't scurry out soon, they were marching to perdition, but he wasn't about to suggest another route. He was excited for what was transpiring, and he wouldn't call a halt.

He kept her busy, distracting her as he unbuttoned her gown, loosening it, raising the hem of her skirt. He was delighted to find that she'd taken off her corset before sneaking to visit him, so that impediment was missing. If she'd still been wearing it, he'd have had to exert more energy to get her naked.

Was that what he was planning? To get her naked? Apparently so.

He tugged on the bodice of her dress, exposing a breast, and she didn't notice how quickly the debacle was spiraling. He'd never previously pushed her onto a carnal ledge, and he realized he ought to temper the pace, but he couldn't be more cautious.

He blazed a trail down her chin, her neck, to her bosom. He didn't pause, didn't hesitate, but sucked a nipple into his mouth. Finally, she recognized how far they'd traveled, and she yanked away and glared at him as if he'd lost his mind.

"What are you doing?" she asked.

"I am making love to you."

"That felt so good. Is it a sin?"

He grinned. "The preachers claim it is, but I've never been especially pious, so I've never paid attention to them."

"I've learned what happens between men and women," she said. "My cousin, Caroline, informed me, so I can guess what you want to do."

"Might I hope *you* want to do it too?"

"I don't believe I should."

He studied her. She was halfway ruined already. In a few more hasty minutes, they'd be finished, and he couldn't picture himself stepping off the cliff where they were perched.

"Shall we stop?" he asked. "Is that your wish? Will you slip away and return to your quiet, lonely room? Could you bear to leave right now?"

He was an expert at obtaining what he sought from other people, and she was no exception. He stared at her, grinding her down with the force of his personality. He was playing on her sympathies too. She pitied him and would like to please him. Why shouldn't they continue?

"I can't decide what's best," she said. "I'm not eager to leave, but I'm scared about what will occur if I stay."

"You needn't be scared. We won't attempt any antics that would distress you."

"That's the problem I'm having. You could convince me to participate in many risqué acts I shouldn't consider. Where you're concerned, I'm a complete milksop. You could solicit any favor, and I'd agree."

"Well, then, aren't I lucky?"

She moaned with a kind of agonized despair. "You overwhelm my better sense."

"Good."

"Can we talk about this? I'm not sure where we're headed." She halted and frowned. "I should rephrase that. I'm absolutely sure of where we're headed, but I'm not certain we should go there."

He smirked like the cad he was. "You'll like it; I promise."

"You would say that, you bounder."

"Take a chance, Sophia. Let's see where we wind up."

Her frown deepened. "You're about to marry my cousin. When that's to be your ending, we can't proceed."

It was a perilous spot for him. He understood the reply she was anxious to have. She yearned for him to declare his interest in her cousin to have vanished, that he would wed her instead, but he never would.

She was pretty and fun, but with her being so poor, she could never be the bride he deserved. It was a horrid view of the situation, but there it was. What was she saving her precious virginity for anyway? Would she ultimately bestow it on some rural dolt who'd make her miserable forever? Why shouldn't she give it to Sheridan? Why not?

He groaned with dismay and slid onto his back. He gazed at the ceiling and struggled to identify his purpose. He'd desired her so desperately for so long, and a feral impulse was lurking below the surface, urging him to grab her, to satisfy himself and damn the consequences. He was terrified to move, lest he leap on her like a wild beast.

She shifted onto her side, and she peered at him, looking fetching and confused. He should have offered a placating comment, but he didn't dare open his mouth to speak, for he couldn't fathom what remark might emerge.

"What's wrong?" she asked. "Have I upset you?"

"No. You just arouse me beyond my limit, and I'm trying to calm down."

She assessed him for an eternity, then asked, "Could you ever imagine picking me rather than Aurora?"

"Yes, I imagine it constantly."

He was positive he meant something very different from what she was envisioning. She would be pondering matrimony, while he would be pondering furtive assignations in deserted parlors.

"If you're really thinking you'd choose me," she said, "then I'd like us to finish this."

"Yes, but you're a flighty female who's much too young and inexperienced to be here with me. I shouldn't drag you any farther down this road."

"Don't call me young and inexperienced," she huffed. "I may only be twenty, but I'm not naïve about what's happening."

Oh, but she was so naïve! "I'm merely stating the facts. If a person is swept up in a lusty dalliance, it's easy to forget the rules that govern our conduct."

She flopped onto her back and gazed at the ceiling too. There was a ball of gloom rolling between them, and eventually, she said, "What should we do?"

"You should depart or I can't be responsible for my actions. Would you go?"

~

Sophia heard Sheridan clearly. Evidently, he was so overcome that he couldn't control himself, but he'd dangled a proposition that was riveting. He'd changed his mind about Aurora and was picturing a future with Sophia. She could be his wife! She hadn't thought she'd like to ever be a bride, but with him as her husband, it would be very grand indeed.

He was adept at bed sport, and he'd tantalized her anatomy to an ecstatic point. She was dreadfully keen to have him demonstrate the type of marital behavior Caroline had described. And wouldn't it be smart to continue?

If they forged ahead, they'd have to marry. The issue would be resolved. After all, a gentleman couldn't blithely seduce a maiden, then walk away. Well, a cad like Lord Swindon could be that brash, but Sheridan wasn't his father. He wasn't callous and cruel.

He was kind and affectionate. He was besotted with her, and if they proceeded, they'd both be fettered. She wouldn't be able to second-guess in the morning. Nor would he. They would be completely ensnared.

Wouldn't he be happier that way? He was such a lonely, solitary man. They could become a family, and he'd quickly be a husband with two children to parent: Emily and Pierre. His qualms about his lost career would be wiped away, and she would help him move to the next phase of his life.

It was an excellent plan—for everyone but Aurora. Yet Aurora had always been bound to wed Miles, and she ought to follow the path that had been laid out for her.

Sophia had never put her foot down with her relatives, had never demanded any boons for herself, but apparently, she was ready to engage in some demanding. She wanted Sheridan for her very own, and Aurora couldn't have him.

Before she could talk herself out of it, she stretched out on top of him. For an instant, he stiffened, then he scoffed with disgust and pulled her closer.

"We're not stopping," she said.

"You shouldn't tease me, Cantwell."

"Who's teasing?"

"I'm serious. If we start in again, I will rush to the end whether you wish it or not. If you panic and beg me to desist, I won't listen."

"I won't panic. If we keep on, we can be together. You just claimed you're contemplating that conclusion." He didn't reply, and she said, "What is it you expect from me, Sheridan? Can you let me return to Riverglen, then vanish? Are you content for us to be split apart? It doesn't feel right to me, but I'd love to hear your opinion about it."

They were nose to nose, his eyes searching hers as he struggled to devise a response, but he was too bewildered to deliver one. She would admit to being a tad bewildered herself. She constantly wound up in jams because she didn't first evaluate the consequences, and she could never have predicted that she would be leading them in an amorous romp.

He was the male in their paltry duo, so *he* should have been coaxing her to perdition. Why was she in charge and practically ordering him to ruin her?

He stared forever, then seemed to arrive at a decision. He flipped them so she was on the bottom, and he could control the encounter. He was in quite a hurry too, as if afraid—should he delay—his courage would fail him.

He began kissing her yet again, massaging her breasts, playing with her nipples. He pinched them, suckled them, toyed with them, and on this occasion, she didn't exhibit any alarm as she had previously. She forced herself to relax, to let him guide them down the road she was determined to travel. She couldn't suffer a fit of the vapors that would send him careening onto a safer route.

Her nagging had provided him with renewed energy, and he was much more intent on reaching their destination. The lively pace was a benefit too because it kept her from focusing on what was occurring.

His hand was drifting down her tummy, lower, lower, to her drawers. He slipped under the fabric and continued on to the mound between her legs. He slid a finger into her womanly sheath, then a second one, and he stroked them in and out, in and out. He didn't give her an opportunity to acclimate or complain. He simply pushed forward in a manner that was thrilling.

Desire coursed through her, and her hips flexed instinctively. Finally, when she couldn't stand the torment any longer, he latched onto her nipple, as his thumb flicked on the sensitive spot at the crest of her thighs.

Suddenly, she was soaring to the heavens, flying up and up to a sort of apex, then she tumbled down and landed in his arms. He was grinning, his expression smug and delicious, and she thought—if she died that instant—her whole life would have been worth it.

They didn't regroup or chat about the intimacy they'd just shared. He immediately jumped to arousing her again, shrewdly distracting her so she couldn't concentrate on their risqué conduct. Things were spiraling so fast that they were still dressed. He was wearing his trousers, and she her gown, shoes, and stockings, although her bosom was exposed and her skirt shoved up nearly to her waist.

He was working her drawers down and off, and he tossed them on the floor. Then he centered his torso, and he was fussing with his trousers, tugging them down, baring his flanks. He grabbed his phallus and placed it at her body's opening.

She understood, in a technical fashion, what was transpiring, but in spite of it, she quailed with a bit of virginal fear. It felt peculiar and scary, and her anatomy was balking. She didn't mean to tense up, but she couldn't help it.

He noticed her negative reaction and said, "What's wrong?"

"I guess I'm not as brave as I imagined."

"You're very brave, Cantwell, but this doesn't take courage. This is a very natural human behavior."

"It's not like anything I've ever attempted before though."

"You trust me, don't you?"

"No."

He tsked with amusement. "In most cases, that would be very wise, but you can always trust me when we're lying on a bed."

"It will be all right in the end, won't it? We'll be together forever?"

There was the slightest hesitation in his reply, the slightest frown that swept across his brow, but it swiftly vanished. He smiled and firmly stated, "It will absolutely be all right."

As a vow of commitment, it was very tepid, and she shouldn't have accepted it as being even remotely true, but she was too overwhelmed to think clearly. She convinced herself he was sincere, that they would marry and live happily ever after.

How could he not want that? How could he not realize how perfect it would be? With him about to be her husband, she wouldn't ascribe bad motives to him. They would *marry.* They would!

He started in, and he was flexing with his hips, his cock pressing into her most private area. He was wedging it in a little at a time, then a little more, then, with a sharp thrust, he burst through her maidenhead.

Although Caroline had instructed her in the particulars, the reality was much more unusual than she could have grasped. They froze, the significant event rocking them both.

"I didn't hurt you, did I?" he asked.

"No, I'm not hurt. I'm . . . I'm . . ." She cut off her sentence. She couldn't describe what she was.

"I need to finish this." He sounded a tad desperate. "Wrap your arms around me. Hold me tight."

"Like this?"

"Yes, exactly like that."

It was all the conversation he could manage, and a wild, raucous adventure commenced. He would push in very far, then pull out to the tip, then push in again. He was very deliberate, very precise, his movements thrilling her, baffling her, leaving her breathless with worry and anticipation.

Initially, it was awkward, but she gradually got the hang of it. Much before she was ready, he pushed in all the way, then he groaned and spilled his seed against her womb. It was shocking and riveting, and she was completely stunned.

It dawned on her that he hadn't withdrawn at the end. Caroline had explained that it was a method to prevent a babe from catching. Had he known about that? He was a skilled roué, so he must have. Why hadn't he protected her?

She was a novice at sexual endeavors, so she hadn't suggested it. Then again, they were about to wed, so how could it matter? She would have a ring on her finger very soon, and at the moment, she was too befuddled to fret over it. She felt like weeping, which was bizarre. She was very, very glad, so why be morose?

He was very still, his torso hovered over hers, then he collapsed onto her, his heavy weight crushing her in an exhilarating manner. But then, he shifted away, their bodies separating. They turned onto their sides so they were nose to nose, and he kissed her so sweetly that tears flooded her eyes.

He looked aghast. "You're not sad, are you? You can't be."

"No, I'm not sad. I'm happy."

"So am I," he delighted her by claiming.

"You're stuck with me for good," she said.

He laughed. "You blurted that out like a threat."

He rolled onto his back and draped her over his chest. It was the most wonderful part of it, this quiet interval after their ardor was spent. Caroline had mentioned that it could be very special, that it made the physical portion worth the bother—just for the cuddling that came after.

"What do we do now?" she asked.

"We rest a while, then we try it again. If you're not too sore?"

She stretched her legs, sensing a twinge in her womanly spots, but she fibbed. "I'm not sore."

"That's my girl," he murmured, and he yawned.

"Are you falling asleep on me again?"

"I think so. If I doze off, don't sneak out. Promise?"

"I won't. I like watching over you."

"I like it too."

"When will we arrange everything?" she asked. "Will you talk to Lord Swindon about us or what? He could apply for a Special License so we could hold the ceremony immediately."

She braced, anxious for his answer, but it wasn't voiced. Ultimately, she peeked up at him, but he'd drifted off. He was that fatigued from his injury.

Their lust had been assuaged, so she was able to more carefully assess their remarks. It didn't seem as if she'd received a secure commitment from him. The lack of certainty provided stark evidence of why a female had her father choose her husband. A father could confer with the other father, could discuss terms and dates. A female couldn't orchestrate it on her own.

What if Sheridan didn't follow through? What if, in the morning, he told her she'd misconstrued his every comment? What then?

No, no, no, Sheridan wouldn't treat her like that.

He would take the necessary steps to propel them to where they were meant to be, but there were several problems on the horizon. She'd have to track him down in the light of day. A difficult conversation would be required, without the heat of passion spurring them to quick decisions. She'd have to remind him of their agreement, and she was sure it would work out for the best. She refused to suppose it wouldn't.

Sheridan was her hero, her knight in shining armor, her favorite person in the world. They would marry and be happy forever.

She dawdled until she nearly dozed off too, but she didn't dare. They would be engaged shortly, after Sheridan shared the news with his family. Before that occurred, she couldn't let anyone suspect that they'd misbehaved. If word leaked out, gossip would spread that she was a tart who'd snagged him against his will, and she couldn't allow that implication to circulate. She wanted his kin to be glad he'd picked her, so she couldn't have a cloud hanging over her reputation.

She slid off the bed, and he was so weary that he didn't notice. She stood next to the mattress, filling her eyes with the sight of him.

I love you, she mouthed as she straightened her clothes and tugged on her drawers.

She waited for him to stir, to realize she was leaving, but he didn't. She could have awakened him to tell him she was going, but she didn't have the heart to rouse him. He needed his sleep, and she'd see him in a few hours. They'd work out the details, and in a trice, she'd be betrothed to Captain Sheridan Stone! She was practically bursting with joy.

She spun and tiptoed away. Luck was with her, and she made it to her room without incident. She was exhausted, but ecstatic too. Her nerves were too jangled to relax though, so she didn't lie down.

Instead, she went to the window and pulled up a chair. She gazed out at the dark night, eager for dawn to arrive, for the day to start. Then she would seek out Sheridan and the rest of her life could begin.

Chapter Eighteen

"What is happening?"

Miles glared at Millicent, but she stared back with her typical bland expression.

"As far as I'm aware, nothing is happening," she said. "Captain Stone left for his father's birthday party, and I haven't heard a word about his plans after that."

"Will he return to Riverglen?"

"I have no idea."

She was lounged on her fainting couch, and he was standing in front of her. He wasn't a big man, but with her prone, he towered over her. She didn't exhibit any sign that he scared her, but maybe he should display a few frightening tendencies. Maybe if she was concerned about how he might lash out, she wouldn't taunt him with disaster.

"You'd better not have a scheme in progress," he said.

She scowled, as if confused by the comment. "How would I be scheming?"

"Aurora swears Captain Stone hasn't proposed. Has he?"

"No, he hasn't proposed."

"Are you lying to me?" He leaned down and searched her eyes. "If you are, you should stop it immediately."

She huffed with indignation. "Honestly, Miles, I don't appreciate your attitude."

"Well, I don't appreciate yours. If you give Aurora to that scoundrel, what will become of me? Has that question ever popped into your deranged mind? Where would I go, Millicent? How would I support myself? What future would I have? Oscar was eager to have me remain at Riverglen, so I could watch over you. I was willing to do that. For Oscar. Because I was so devoted to him."

"Yes, in that regard, you were a veritable saint."

Was there derision in her tone? Was there scorn?

"Will you throw me to the wolves?" he asked. "After all I've sacrificed for this family, will you deliver my inheritance to that impertinent rogue, Sheridan Stone?"

"You're being completely ridiculous. As usual. He didn't particularly like Aurora, as evidenced by his departing early."

"If you hand the reins to him," he said, "can you truly expect he'll allow you to loaf in your boudoir as I have allowed? Rumors abound in the neighborhood that you're mad."

She laughed. "If the neighbors are gossiping about me, how can it matter?"

"I have shielded you from their ridicule, but I can assure you that Captain Stone won't be so accommodating. He'll have you locked in an asylum like that!"

He snapped his fingers in her face, but she wasn't fazed by his threat. She laughed again and said, "You have such a flare for melodrama."

"I'm not being melodramatic. I'm warning you about Stone. You presume he would wed Aurora and that things would lope along in the same slapdash manner they always have. But you should beware, Millicent. Sheridan Stone would never tolerate your lunacy."

Millicent sighed. "Oh, Miles, must we quarrel?"

"We're not quarreling. I'm simply telling you how Captain Stone will treat you."

She switched subjects so fast that it made him dizzy. "Has there been any news of Sophia?"

"No, there's been no news, and if she never returns, it will be fine with me."

"I'm still her guardian," Millicent pointed out. "You're not worried about her, but I am. She has a knack for landing herself in jams. Where could she be?"

He inhaled a deep breath, then slowly released it. He didn't care about Sophia! He cared about Riverglen and his marriage to Aurora, but with Millicent shifting them off to a different topic, he was so angry he could barely keep from striking her.

"Let me be very clear, Millicent. Sophia and her petty problems are irrelevant to me."

"I'm sorry I've upset you."

"No, you're not. You enjoy taunting me. You probably spend every minute up here, devising your torments."

"I hate to crush your ego, but I rarely think of you at all."

It was a snotty, infuriating remark, and he whipped away and stomped off. As he reached the door, Aurora was just entering from the hallway. Since Captain Stone had ridden away, she'd deftly evaded him. When she realized he'd been sequestered with her mother, that she'd bumped right into him, she winced with dismay.

"Well, well," he sneered, "if it isn't the invisible Aurora Newton."

"Is there some reason you feel the constant need to be horrid?"

"I've had enough of your delays. We will pick the wedding date one week from today. If you don't have an answer for me by then, I will have to take steps to protect myself."

"What steps? What are you talking about?"

"You'll find out."

He marched out, his temper boiling so hotly that he wouldn't be surprised if he suffered an apoplexy.

There weren't many options that would wrench an affirmative response from her. He had several letters from Oscar that were a sort of unofficial codicil to his Last Will, so Miles could hire a lawyer and try to force her into a marriage. Or perhaps he could sue her for breach of promise.

He could ask a judge to give him the estate as damages, but he doubted he could succeed. Millicent and Aurora didn't know that though. If they believed he could yank the property away from them, then kick them out, might it spur a more amenable conclusion?

He had no idea, but one fact was certain: Sheridan Stone would never wed Aurora. She belonged to Miles. Riverglen belonged to Miles, and Sheridan Stone couldn't have either one.

"Have you decided?"

Neville smiled at Sybil and tsked with regret, "Yes, darling. How could I parent a little girl at my age? It's madness to imagine I could."

They were discussing Emily. When Miss Cantwell had first arrived, he'd been charmed by her, and he'd briefly flirted with the notion of being a man he'd never been destined to be. He'd felt like an actor in a theatrical drama, but it wasn't possible for him to change so substantially. His old chums had convinced him. He was a gambler and cad, and he loved his life just the way it was.

"What's your plan for her then?" Sybil asked, her displeasure obvious.

Neville waffled his hand. He hadn't reflected on it, except to grasp that he'd been insane to ponder fatherhood. Matrimony too. Fleetingly, he'd pictured himself and Sybil happily shackled and rearing Emily together.

But . . .

He didn't want to do that. Not deep down.

"I'll give Miss Cantwell some money," he said, "and she'll figure out a solution. She can hire a nanny or . . . whatever."

"Money, Neville? Really? That's all you're willing to do?"

He sighed. "You can't have assumed I would consider the prospect of becoming a father after all these years."

"Yes, I supposed you would consider it. I foolishly thought you'd make me proud for once."

They were in the master suite and having a private breakfast. They were seated at a table by the window so they could look out at the morning mist that had settled over the park.

The prior evening, he'd tried to persuade her to join him in his bed. They'd never pushed themselves that far, and by adding a carnal dimension to their relationship, he was probably at risk of ruining it. She'd been too smart to oblige him though. She'd insisted she didn't trust him and would never proceed unless she had a ring on her finger.

On hearing her opinion, he'd nearly proposed, but at the last second, he'd come to his senses.

She'd tempted him to wed a third time, but he'd finally remembered two very important things: He'd never liked being a father or a husband. He hated to hurt her, but he simply couldn't supply what she was expecting to receive from him. Hadn't that been the story of his life with women? He was always a great disappointment.

"If you keep on like this," she churlishly said, "you'll die old and alone."

"One of my three boys will hold my hand."

"You'd better hope so." She scoffed. "Don't you care what will happen to Emily? If Miss Cantwell leaves with her, won't you worry? Won't you wonder?"

His shoulders sagged with defeat. Apparently, they were about to quarrel, and he hadn't even finished his meal. "No, I won't wonder."

For an eternity, she glared, but didn't scold him. Praise be! Over the years, he'd driven many women to bouts of fury. He was used to it. He was particularly good at it. He was simply selfish and lazy, and he never exerted himself on anyone's behalf. He was lucky he hadn't coaxed her into his bed. It would have furnished them with another issue about which to bicker.

"Your daughter, Joanna, isn't coming to Swindon," she said. "Her husband wrote to me. They decided it would be too awkward."

"That's too bad." He truly meant it. "She's a beautiful girl, and I would have liked to become acquainted with her."

"You're so blasé about this, and you're fifty already. What if you drop dead tomorrow? How would you explain yourself at the Pearly Gates?"

He laughed. "There's no chance I'll be winging up to Heaven. I'll fly off in the other direction, but I won't mind. My friends will be there to greet me."

"I can't abide this callous side of you."

"I shall tuck it away then, so you don't have to look at it." He flashed his most charming smile. "What's on the agenda today? I'm sure you've scheduled a ton of amusing activities."

"Actually, I've had all the fun I can stand, playing hostess for you."

His smile slipped. "What are you saying?"

"I'm not a lady of leisure, and I detest loafing. I should return to work."

"You're not going to town. I forbid it."

It was exactly the wrong comment, and she scoffed again, with an enormous amount of disgust. "You're not my husband, Neville, and you've reinforced my choice to never wed. Occasionally, I debate whether I should have remained a spinster, and you've convinced me I was wise to stay single."

She tossed down her napkin and stood. It appeared she was departing, and he couldn't believe it.

"You can't desert me," he said. "The party won't be the same without you."

"You should know that *I* will ingratiate myself to Joanna, and as opposed to you, I would love to have a daughter. If I'm nice to her, perhaps she'll invite me to a few holiday dinners."

"I've found holiday dinners to be highly over-rated." He voiced it in a teasing manner, and he'd thought it would make her chuckle, but it didn't.

"I'll devise an arrangement with Miss Cantwell too, so you needn't trouble yourself. Your pathetic assistance won't be necessary." She blew out a heavy breath. "You can be such an ass. I really hate it when you are."

She headed for the door, and he huffed with irritation. "Sybil! You're being ridiculous."

"I don't like you when you act like this. Would you not stop by the club for a bit? Let's say until after Christmas."

"You can't be serious. I socialize there with my friends, and if I didn't pop in every evening, I'd never see them—or you."

"You're aware of my view on memberships. You and your friends can join another club. As for mine, you won't be welcome in it. I'll have my footmen guarding the entrance, so please don't try to cajole your way in. It would be so humiliating to have you cause a scene where we'd have to throw you out bodily."

The snide remark rankled, poking holes in his placid demeanor. "I told you I'd give Miss Cantwell some money! It's not as if I'm kicking her out on the road to fend for herself. I don't understand why you're so upset."

"I realize you don't, and that's the root of the whole problem."

She stomped out, and he was left to fume all alone.

It infuriated him when women didn't behave as he demanded. What bee had gotten into her bonnet? Was she hoping he'd chase after her? To beg her pardon? To swear he'd change?

He wouldn't grovel, and in a burst of insight, he recognized she wouldn't expect him to. She was one of the few females in the world who'd never been confused about the kind of man he was.

She knew him all too well, and she'd had enough.

"You have to retire. I'm afraid I must insist."

"I don't want to retire."

Sheridan glared at Neville. His father was in a very bad mood, and he looked as grouchy as Sheridan felt. What could have happened? Neville was gregarious, amiable, and never peevish.

It was morning, and Sheridan was wondering why he'd come downstairs. His leg was throbbing, and it was clear his many months of recovery were wrecked. He'd have to start over with regaining the strength he'd lost. He'd considered asking George to search for a cane he could use, so he could brace himself as he hobbled around, but he'd tamped down the suggestion before he'd disgraced himself by uttering it.

They were in the library, with Neville seated at the desk and Sheridan slouched in the chair across from him. From how Neville was glowering, Sheridan was reminded of boarding school, when he'd been caught in mischief. The headmaster would give him a stern talking-to, prior to administering a fierce whipping.

He hadn't planned to have a private meeting with Neville, but the minute he'd arrived in the foyer, the butler had grabbed him and escorted him to the room. There had been no chance to debate whether the conversation would occur or not.

So far during Sheridan's visit, Neville had been busy entertaining, so there had been no opportunity to dither over Sheridan's career, his pending marriage, or any of the other myriad of subjects that had to be addressed.

It was an awful time to chat because Sheridan could only focus on Sophia. They'd proceeded to the worst conclusion of all, and he was trying to deduce why he'd fornicated with her. He was blaming his low attitude and the hefty amount of whiskey he'd consumed before she'd snuck in, but it wasn't working.

The damage was done. He'd deflowered her, which had been irresponsible and rash. How was he to unravel it? Unfortunately, he didn't want to unravel it. She was like a disease in his blood, and he couldn't cure himself. He had no desire to cure himself.

She was front and center in his musings, so he had to watch out with Neville. His father was an expert manipulator, and Sheridan was too distracted. If he wasn't careful, there was no predicting what he might agree to do in the end.

"It doesn't matter that you don't wish to retire," Neville said. "You can barely walk. You received a slight kick in the thigh, and the pain was so intense it knocked you unconscious."

"It wasn't a *slight* kick," Sheridan testily retorted. "The oaf who delivered it was massive, and despite what you were told, I wasn't knocked unconscious. I simply fell down."

"You had to be carried up to your bedchamber!"

Sheridan tsked with offense. "Where are you hearing these things? I marched up there of my own accord. Why are you so grumpy? I'm sorry you're so irritable, but don't take it out on me."

"You behave like a child."

"Are we going to sit here and trade insults? If so, I shall leave you to your foul temper and find some breakfast."

Neville never fretted about any issue, but suddenly, he was seething. He blurted out, "Sybil left. She had a tantrum and returned to town. In the middle of my party! With her serving as my hostess too! How am I to assess such rude conduct?"

"What did you do to her?"

The question bewildered Neville. "Why would you automatically assume *I* was at fault?"

"I've known you all my life. You picture yourself as a great Romeo, but you're quite clueless about women. I'm surprised you're lauded for your seduction skills. You don't have any."

Neville was fit to be tied. Apparently, Sybil had driven him into a frenzy of ire. "She expected me to alter myself into someone I'm not!"

"She wouldn't have expected that," Sheridan said. "She's much too astute, and she's aware that you are completely intractable. I'm betting she tendered a modest request, and you're so spoiled that you refused. What was it?"

"She wanted me to be a father to Emily. She wanted us to wed and raise the girl as her parents."

He spat the word *parents* as if it were an epithet, and Sheridan chuckled snidely. "You have never been—and never will be—a parent. Surely she realizes that about you."

"Evidently not, for when I declined to enter into domestic bliss, she abandoned me. She may even revoke my membership at *Ralston's*. As it is, she ordered me not to stop by until after Christmas."

"My goodness. You really managed to enrage her, didn't you?" Sheridan scowled. "I'm confused by this story. I thought you were charmed by Emily and that you would recognize and rear her. Isn't that what you told Miss Cantwell?"

Neville's cheeks heated as if he was embarrassed. "Of course I was charmed by Emily. Who wouldn't have been? She's delightful, so I'll give Miss Cantwell some funds for support. I'm convinced she'll figure out a viable path."

Sophia believed Neville would claim Emily and supply the life she deserved as an earl's daughter. What would she think of Neville's cold-hearted decision? He suspected she'd be crushed and very angry.

Oddly, he felt he should champion her cause, when in reality, he should probably butt out. Neville was very stubborn, and he never changed his mind.

"You might like being Emily's father," Sheridan said. "You should try it."

"I just turned fifty. At my age, I'm not about to bring a toddler into the family. I don't have the energy for it."

"It wouldn't kill you."

"It might, so don't nag," Neville said. "I already swallowed down a bellyful of castigation from Sybil before she stomped out. I made it very clear to her that the notion of my being a husband or father holds no appeal whatsoever."

"Join the club, Neville," Sheridan snottily muttered.

"I did my duty to King and Country by siring you three boys, but you still owe the kingdom a few sons, so you should get busy with filling your nursery. How was your trip to Riverglen? We haven't had two seconds alone where you could describe your visit."

"It's a beautiful property. I'd be lucky to own it."

"That's wonderful to hear. And Miss Newton? What is your opinion of her?"

"She's a terrific candidate: refined, elegant, educated, pleasant in her manners and habits."

"I thought she would be. Her sister was the same."

"I suppose you'd know for certain, what with you having ruined her and all." Sheridan's tone was very sarcastic.

"My dalliance with Caroline Newton has no bearing on your choice with regard to her sister."

"You seriously think that?"

Neville sighed, as if Sheridan was a heavy burden. "Did you propose?"

"Not yet."

"Why not? What's preventing you?"

"I can't imagine retiring and settling down."

"You're not healthy enough to continue at your current post. Your deteriorated condition is obvious. Will you continue until some villain murders you?"

"How could I be a farmer? I can't envision it."

Neville shrugged. "There are many ways to thrive in a smaller existence. You develop outside interests. You find hobbies. You entertain company. Your brothers have managed it."

"They're not *me,*" Sheridan said. "You don't understand how grand my life has been. What is there to entice me into relinquishing it in order to loaf at Riverglen?"

"You have to wed, Sheridan. You know that."

"But Aurora Newton is a stranger to me. How can I be sure she would be a good bride?"

"No husband can ever be positive. You assume you've picked the perfect girl, but once the leg-shackle is attached, the situation can fall apart. She can grow petty or jealous, cranky or cruel, overly pious or preoccupied by personal problems. There are no guarantees."

"At the moment," Sheridan said, "Miss Newton seems sweet and obliging, but what if—as the years passed—I found I couldn't abide her? What then?"

"Then you have affairs with doxies who can provide the excitement you require. It's what a gentleman does, Sheridan. It's how the world works. You select a wife to give you children and a tart to give you joy."

"It's such a cynical view of what's in store for me."

"We have no power to redesign the structures of society. We can only devise methods to thrive within the walls that are erected to constrain us. We marry because we must, then we invent other avenues to be content."

Sheridan pushed himself to his feet, and he went over to the window and stared out at the park. It was a blustery day, with clouds whipping by. He hadn't been outside, but the temperature would be frigid. The leaves on the trees had changed color, and the wind was stripping them from the branches.

The sight stirred his wanderlust, so he wished he was on his ship and sailing south. Why wasn't he doing that? Why was he trapped in England where he was so confused and miserable?

His father was watching him, his eyes like daggers in Sheridan's back, but Neville didn't speak. Despite his being a horrid parent, he knew his sons quite well. He recognized how they thought, how they fretted, and Sheridan's torment was practically rolling off him in waves.

"I just want to be happy," Sheridan finally murmured.

"Every man wants that. It's not an odd craving."

"Aurora Newton would never make me happy."

"Happiness has naught to do with matrimony."

Sheridan glanced over his shoulder. "Have you been informed that I'm fond of Miss Cantwell? You're such a busybody; I figure you'd have heard any gossip."

Neville frowned ferociously. "How fond are you?"

"We met in France when she was there with Emily. We have a . . . connection, I guess. It's incredibly blatant."

"Have you seduced her?" His father never beat around the bush, and he didn't wait for Sheridan to answer. "Right under my roof? You couldn't help yourself?"

"I'd like to wed her instead of her cousin."

Neville snorted with amusement. "Don't be ridiculous. Isn't she the poor relative of the Newton family? I remember learning that somewhere. She delivered Emily to me because she can't support her. What could she bring to the table that would be worth having?"

"She's funny and sassy. She can't stay out of trouble, and I like her pluck and nerve."

"You've just listed several attributes that a man *never* seeks in a wife. When you choose a bride, you look for modesty and chastity. You look for reserved conduct and quiet deportment. You don't want feistiness or vigor. Abrasive traits grow exhausting very fast."

"I like her so much."

"So what? If you're thinking you need a wild trollop in your life, glom onto Miss Newton, then find a spirited mistress to entertain you. It's how a husband wades through this sort of predicament."

"I ruined Miss Cantwell," Sheridan admitted as he limped to his chair and slid onto it. "She's expecting that I'll betroth myself."

"I am your father, so I am charged with selecting your fiancée, and I firmly declare that it absolutely will not be her. I am an earl now, so you are the son of an earl. We have ruled in England for centuries. We don't fetter ourselves to poverty-stricken ninnies. Not when there is money and property being dangled in front of us. We are allowed to pick from the richest heiresses in the kingdom, and Aurora Newton is one of them. You will ride to Riverglen as quickly as you can and get this settled."

Every word Neville had uttered was totally correct. Sheridan was a member of a prominent family, and they joined themselves to other prominent families. They didn't make the peculiar choice, the eccentric choice.

Plus, a fellow never shackled himself for love or lust because they burned away and left nothing sustainable. Down through the ages, that adage had been proved true time and time again. Wealth and property were the solid foundation that guaranteed nuptial success.

He couldn't bear for it to be the case though. Aurora Newton would be a fine wife, but he would die of boredom with her. With Sophia, he'd never have a dull moment. Wouldn't that be better? Why couldn't that be a basis for a sound marriage?

Well, he knew why. A man proceeded to advance himself, to lift himself even higher. Sophia didn't supply any boons he was desperate to have. Except . . .

He was so fond of her. If he failed to follow through on his pillow promises, she would never forgive him. He would never forgive himself. Forever after, he would be a villain in her eyes. That reality would be too hideous to abide.

"What about Sophia?" Sheridan asked. "If I marry her cousin, it will devastate her."

"She'll just have to get over it," Neville coldly said. "If she actually imagined she could stake a claim to you, she's deranged. But then, that possibility dawned on me when she traipsed in the door with Emily. She's a brash meddler who has overstepped her place with both of us."

"She has not," Sheridan mumbled, but without much enthusiasm.

Hadn't he always chastised her for blustering in without thinking? She constantly behaved in a crazed manner that landed her in jams. For pity's sake, she'd snuck into his room in the middle of the night! What did she assume would happen once she was there?

As the rationalization slithered by, he scoffed with disgust. The carnal incident they'd shared had been spectacular, and *he* was the sophisticated roué. In the light of day, it was easy to blame her, but the debacle was his own fault. How could he repair the dilemma so she didn't wind up hating him?

"What should I tell her?" Sheridan asked. "You're adept at wiggling out of messes like this, but I haven't had your experience as a libertine. What would you suggest?"

"I suggest that you not talk to her again. Let's not court more trouble. Stay away from her, and I'll deal with it."

"No. You'd muck it up more than it already is."

"You will leave her alone!" Neville was being unusually recalcitrant. "I have to have a frank discussion with her about Emily, and I'll give her some extra money to smooth over your gaffe. I'll write to Mrs.

Newton too. The woman is her guardian. She'll be able to manage any problems that arise."

"Don't you dare write to Mrs. Newton," Sheridan fumed. "You're in no position to contact her about Sophia."

"In this instance, it's fully warranted. We're planning your marriage, Sheridan! We're arranging your future. If I can't be involved in this situation, where would I involve myself?"

Sheridan was sick at heart. He was too weary to argue with Neville, too sad to complain about his autocratic impulses. And again, he told himself that Neville was correct. Sophia wasn't the appropriate bride for him. Sheridan recognized that fact, and he never should have coerced her into a sexual disaster.

She was counting on him, but he wasn't about to step up. He'd realized it from the moment he'd unbuttoned the first button on her gown. What was wrong with him?

The answer to that question was simple. He was Neville Stone's son. He was just as selfish, vain, and egotistical as his father. He viewed himself as being very grand and important and that he deserved to be showered with the very best of everything.

Was Sophia *best*? No. Compared to Aurora, there was no standard by which she could be considered a suitable candidate. If that was true though, why was he so wretched?

"Are we agreed?" Neville said, yanking him out of his miserable reverie. "You'll retire from government service? You'll hurry to Riverglen and propose to Miss Newton? You'll settle down there?"

"I guess I can do all of that."

Why dither and delay? Shouldn't he get it accomplished as fast as he could? That way, he wouldn't have time to ponder his options. He'd have a clean cut, like a quick amputation.

"I'd like to have the wedding held by Christmas," Neville said.

"I suppose it could be completed by then."

"When can you depart? I want this over, so you can't change your mind."

"I have to speak with Sophia first. I have to explain what's occurring."

"And I forbid it! I assure you she'll be aggrieved over what we've decided. You'll have a terrible quarrel, and it will cloud your memories of her. *I* will handle it for you, and if she sheds a few tears in my library, it won't faze me in the least."

"I have to find Sophia!" Sheridan firmly stated. "I know how horrid you can be, and I'm not about to let you interfere. Once I'm finished with her, then I'll head out."

"I'm warning you that this is a very bad idea."

"Warning received," Sheridan snapped, and he stood and limped out.

Chapter Nineteen

"May we chat, Miss Cantwell?"

Sophia gaped at Lord Swindon, and she struggled to devise a reason to decline his invitation.

"I was looking for Captain Stone," she said. "I have an important message to deliver to him. May I return in a few minutes?"

"I'm certain, whatever you're rushing to impart, my topic is much more vital. Won't you join me?"

He was standing in the door to his library, and he stared her down so imperiously she didn't dare refuse. She forced a smile and said, "I would love to join you. I've been eager to confer about Emily, but you've been so busy with your guests that I haven't been able to catch you alone."

The statement was a bald-faced lie. She'd already decided she shouldn't have bothered the snooty nobleman. What had she been thinking?

Well, she hadn't been thinking. That was always her problem.

She was anxious to talk to Sheridan, but hadn't stumbled on him yet. Why hadn't *he* sought her out? They had so much to discuss!

She'd had breakfast with Pierre and Emily in the nursery, then she'd dawdled with them, expecting he'd visit, but he hadn't. She'd grown too impatient, so she'd snuck to his bedchamber. A gossipy housemaid she'd met in the hall had informed her that he was up, dressed, and had gone down to eat in the dining room.

Sophia had hastened down after him, but unfortunately, the moment she'd descended to the lower floor, she'd run into the Earl.

He appeared to be upset with her, but why would he be? Since she'd arrived at Swindon, she'd barely spoken to him. Mostly, she'd been cooling her heels, waiting to be summoned into his grand presence. Had she committed a blunder? Was she in trouble?

He gestured for her to enter the ostentatious room, and she marched down the hall and hurried in. Her mind was awhirl, as she tried to figure out what was happening. No doubt he'd admit that he didn't want Emily, but Sophia didn't want him to have her either, so in that, they were in complete accord.

He shut the door, then went to the massive oak desk and seated himself. She followed him and sat in the chair across. The space was dark and stuffy, with wood paneling and bookshelves that rose to the ceiling. Books covered every inch, providing stark evidence of his wealth.

There were huge windows behind him, and it was sunny outside. With the bright blue sky framing him, he seemed to glow with an unearthly halo that emphasized how magnificent he was. It made her feel insignificant and totally out of her element.

She seized the initiative. "What did you need? I don't mean to be impertinent, but you're scowling at me so ferociously that I can only assume I've displeased you in some fashion."

At hearing her comment, he reined in his obvious annoyance. "I apologize. I've had some issues plaguing me this morning, and I'm not myself."

"Apology accepted. How can I help you?"

"I have two matters to review with you, and they're both difficult. I hope we can muddle through without quarreling."

"I'm sure we can," she blithely said, but her pulse began to race.

"First, with regard to Emily, I can't keep or raise her."

"Oh." After constant reflection, she'd reached the same conclusion, but still, she was extremely exasperated. "May I ask why?"

"I shall be very blunt and confess that I never liked being a father when I was younger, and in light of my advanced age, I'm too old to be a parent."

She could have argued the point, but from his steely expression, it was clear he didn't intend to have that debate.

"Will you publicly recognize her though?" she asked. "Will you support her? What is your plan? Have you one?"

"I'll give you some money—so you can support her."

Her temper flared; she couldn't tamp it down. "That's it? That's all you're willing to do?"

"I'm not a kind or generous man, Miss Cantwell, so the fact that I've offered any assistance is quite amazing. I was charmed by Emily and delighted to meet her, so I thank you for that, but you shouldn't expect more from me than what I've already supplied."

To Sophia's great disgust, tears flooded her eyes. "I thought you'd bonded with her. I thought you were excited to have her arrive."

"I was excited, but I've had a few days to ponder, and I've come to my senses. If you dumped her on me, she'd be reared by lazy, incompetent servants. It's how my sons were reared, and they never cease to complain about it. I'm positive you'll be a much better custodian."

"You weren't concerned about the consequences when you were seducing my cousin. Those consequences have taken the form of an actual human being, and you couldn't care less."

He shrugged. "What can I tell you? I'm callous and selfish, and I haven't the energy to deal with a child as rambunctious as Emily appears to be. It would exhaust me."

"If that is your opinion, then I shall be very insolent and declare you to be a horse's ass."

He sighed dramatically. "I could swear we agreed not to bicker."

"Yes, heaven forbid that we fight." Her tone was much too snide, and she jumped to her feet. "If you'll excuse me, I'll have my carriage harnessed. I've been waiting for a wheel to be repaired, but I've learned that it's fixed. We'll depart immediately."

Her wayward tongue had gotten ahead of her, and she'd forgotten about Sheridan. They had so much to do! A wedding date to set. Announcements to send. A future to arrange. Why did it suddenly seem as if none of that would occur?

Had Sheridan heard this terrible news about Emily? Had he tried to dissuade his father? Or had he been amenable? Was he wishing, as his father definitely was, that Emily would vanish? Sophia was desperate to ask him those questions, and receive some answers, but she was very wary. There was more transpiring than she understood.

Lord Swindon waved to her chair. "I'm glad you'll leave without a fuss, but please sit. There's a problem we must address before you go."

"Why would I listen to anything else you have to say?"

"You'll listen to this," he pretentiously stated.

She wasn't in awe of powerful men. Her debacle in France had left her too jaded, but he had a disturbing manner of staring a person down, so she couldn't disobey. She plopped onto her chair, her impatience and fury barely contained.

"I would appreciate it if you would be brief," she seethed. "I have no desire to linger in your presence one second longer than necessary."

He chuckled as if she were cheeky and precocious. "You are feisty, Miss Cantwell. Sheridan told me you were."

His mention of Sheridan should have been thrilling, but from how he continued to scowl, she didn't imagine she'd been painted in a good light. What had Sheridan confided about her? Obviously, it hadn't been to her benefit.

"You talked to Captain Stone about me?"

"Yes, and he advises me that an inappropriate attachment has blossomed between you." Sophia didn't respond, and he studied her as if she were a strange curiosity, then he said, "Evidently, you're very fond of him, so I shall be gentle in apprising you that I will never give him permission to wed you."

If he'd pulled out a knife and stabbed her in the heart, she couldn't have been wounded any more deeply. "The Captain is aware of your opinion? He's fine with it?"

"Yes." A hint of commiseration smoothed his features. "I'm sorry, dear. You were counting on him, but you're not silly or frivolous. You have to have recognized that a match is impossible."

"It isn't impossible. He loves me and I love him."

His expression became pitying. "If that's what you suppose, then you have gravely misconstrued what was happening."

"I didn't misconstrue," she caustically spat. "How dare you claim that I'm stupid or blind!"

He smirked. "Men have affairs, Miss Cantwell. They frequently dally when they shouldn't, but with an elevated swain such as Sheridan, it doesn't mean they wed after the damage is done."

He gazed woefully, and he probably thought he looked paternal. He was oozing false sympathy, furnishing her with fatherly counsel that he assumed she urgently needed, but in fact, he was only fueling a pot of rage.

"What is your plan for him then?" she demanded. "Will you shackle him to a boring ninny so he'll be miserable forever?"

"You know what my plan is."

It took her a moment to realize what he was telling her, and she nearly fell to the rug in a stunned heap. "He's marrying Aurora?"

"There's never been a doubt about it really. I regret that you didn't comprehend the reality of your situation—and hers."

"Captain Stone is forsaking me? He's willing to pursue that conclusion?"

"He didn't argue about a single detail."

The tears that had threatened when he'd denied Emily swarmed into such an ocean of despair that she couldn't keep them at bay. They flowed out, and he was distressed to observe her anguish.

Hastily, he said, "Don't cry, Miss Cantwell. I'm sure, after you've reflected, you'll feel you've dodged a bullet. A girl in your reduced circumstances, and possessed of your rather *perky* attributes, could never have made Sheridan happy. Wouldn't you like him to be happy?"

"Aurora is so wrong for him."

"No, she's perfect, and I'm predicting that he'll be very content. Now then, let's wrap up this meeting before it grows too maudlin."

He opened a drawer and retrieved an envelope. He leaned across the desk and offered it to her, but she was too paralyzed to reach for it.

"It's the money to help you with Emily." He smiled a placating smile that was galling. "I've added a bit extra because of your confusion about Sheridan. It will ease some of your current pain."

If she'd had any pride, she'd have refused the funds, but apparently, she had none at all. She snatched the envelope out of his hand. She was exhibiting quite a lot of pique, but he didn't notice. Or if he did, he didn't care. But why would he? She was so far beneath him that she was like a gnat buzzing at his ankle. Her views and actions were irrelevant.

"While we were chatting," he said, "I had your carriage prepared. The maids have packed your belongings, and the children are waiting for you in the front foyer. How about if we get you going?"

"I'm leaving now?"

She was absolutely aghast. She'd come downstairs, thinking she was engaged, thinking she was about to wed Sheridan Stone in a hurry, but she hadn't even had a chance to confer with him.

There would be no marriage? Sheridan had acquiesced to the decision? He was marrying Aurora instead? Sophia was being evicted on the spot? Had that been Sheridan's idea?

"Yes, you're leaving now," the Earl said. "It's best for us to have a clean break. And there's no reason for you to delay, is there? You can't change Sheridan's mind, and I would never allow you to change it."

"May I say goodbye to him?"

"No."

He stood and walked around the desk. He glared down at her, eager for her to stand too, but she was too numb to move. He clasped her arm and raised her to her feet, and he kept hold of her, as if worried she might collapse. She couldn't bear to have him touching her, so she shook him away and stomped off on her own.

"I hate that it had to end this way," he called to her.

"No, you don't," she muttered. "Don't insult my intelligence."

"It's vexing to have you deem me an ogre." His voice grew cajoling. "How about if you bring Emily to visit me someday? I'd always be glad to see her. Why don't we agree to that much?"

She stopped and glanced at him. "I will *never* come back here, and you will never see your daughter again. But then, I can't imagine that would be much of a burden for you."

She reached the door and was about to spin the knob and exit, when someone opened it from the outside. It was Sheridan.

"Sophia!" he said. "I've been searching everywhere for you."

She scoffed with disgust. "Yes, I'll bet you've been in a veritable frenzy."

He was startled by her harsh remark. He peered over at his father, as if he was nervous about what Lord Swindon might have said to her.

"Did you speak to her without me?" he asked his father.

"Yes," Lord Swindon said, "and she's been apprised of our position."

"I told you *I* would do it. You were to butt out."

She was a petite woman, and they were talking over her head. Then again, she was such a lowly person she was probably invisible to them.

"There was no need for you and I to converse," she advised Sheridan. "Your father was very clear about what the two of you had arranged for me."

"It's obvious you're angry," he said. "Why don't we sit down and discuss this a bit more?"

"There's nothing to discuss, and I'm leaving."

"Sophia!" He grumbled her name as if she wasn't behaving as he'd intended. "You don't have to leave. Not until I explain a few details. Won't you let me? I'll send my father away, so you and I can have some privacy."

"I was very blunt with her, Sheridan." Lord Swindon was practically bragging. "There's no pertinent information you can add, and she's incredibly upset—as I warned you she would be. If you try to explain, you'll simply make the situation worse."

Sheridan ignored his father and said to her, "I'm sorry. I didn't mean to hurt you."

"Really? You can say that to my face?"

She slapped him just as hard as she could. He hadn't been expecting a blow, so it landed solidly. He staggered slightly, a red imprint from her hand instantly popping out on his cheek.

To her great surprise, he didn't hit her back. He seemed like the sort of villain who might. Instead, he rubbed his cheek and said, "I suppose I deserved that."

"Bastard!" she raged, using the epithet for the first and only time in her life.

She dashed away, and to her enormous relief, he didn't follow.

"The Earl kicked us out?" Pierre asked Sophia.

"Yes, and he was quite awful about it too."

"Shall I punch him in the nose for you?"

"It doesn't matter how he treated me. He ordered us away, so we don't have a choice but to obey him."

They were in the carriage and rolling down the lane. He was sitting on one side, with Sophia and Emily on the other. Sophia was wedged in the corner and crying quietly. Emily was standing next to her on the seat, chatting in her mix of indecipherable French and English. She was working to cheer Sophia, but Sophia was too distraught to tolerate her.

Sophia peeked at Pierre and said, "Can you manage her for me please? I can't deal with her at the moment."

Pierre lifted Emily over to him and attempted to snuggle her on his lap, but she had other ideas. She held onto the window and gazed out at the manor that was vanishing behind them.

He wasn't sure what had happened. They'd been playing in the nursery, then a bevy of servants had arrived, packed their things, and escorted them down to the foyer. Shortly after that, Sophia had appeared and hustled them out the door.

"Are we returning to Riverglen?" he asked Sophia.

"Yes."

"Are you certain we should?"

"We don't have any other option, Pierre."

"I'm afraid for you there. Your relatives are not kind."

She shrugged. "*You* will be my relative from now on. You and Emily will be my family."

At the comment, he felt a little better. Sophia was scattered in her habits and decisions, but she was very loyal. She'd sworn to Pierre that she would always take care of him, and he'd told himself to believe her.

He simply yearned to be older, bigger, and stronger. His father had been a large, strapping fellow, and Pierre's mother had insisted he'd grow tall and strong too. He wished he could swallow a magic pill to make it transpire immediately so he could protect Sophia.

She was a female, so men took advantage of her. They cheated and tricked her, and Lord Swindon was no different. Pierre was clever and cunning, and he helped her in furtive ways, but he was just a boy. He didn't have any power or authority. How could he truly guard and defend her when he was young and useless?

"What about Emily and Lord Swindon?" he asked. "I thought she was staying with him. I thought it was arranged."

"He doesn't want her after all," Sophia said. "He thinks she'd be too much of a bother."

Emily understood they were talking about her, and she leaned out the window and extended her arms toward the manor.

"Papa?" she said, as if he might swoop in and rescue her.

Pierre pulled her inside and settled her on the cushion. She tried to squirm away, so she could call to her father again, and he kept a firm hand on her shoulder so she couldn't.

"Did you see Captain Stone before we left?" Pierre asked. "He wouldn't like us to sneak away."

"Captain Stone is aware that we departed, and he's glad about it."

Pierre frowned. "That can't be correct. He's sweet on you."

"No, you're wrong, Pierre. He's sweet on my cousin, Aurora. He'll be marrying her very soon."

Pierre gasped. Despite what Sophia claimed about the Captain, they were so happy together. He'd let a fantasy form in his mind that they would eventually wed, that they would become his parents, and they'd be a family.

Then Captain Stone would fix all of their problems. He was very rich, so he'd hire a nanny for Emily and a tutor for Pierre. He'd pay for Pierre to join the navy when he was fourteen, and he'd find a handsome husband for Emily. They would live in a fine house and be safe forever.

Pierre would never admit it to a single soul, but ever since his mother had perished, he'd had trouble sleeping, so he often wandered in the night. Late one evening at Swindon, he'd watched the Captain tiptoe out of Sophia's bedchamber, and he'd been excited by what it indicated.

There was only one reason a gentleman visited a lady in her private quarters and that was for amorous purposes. His discovery had fueled a wave of speculation he couldn't quell. If they'd engaged in illicit conduct, they had to wed. They *had* to. Everyone knew it, so how could he marry snooty Miss Newton?

If that was the case, the world had gone mad. Would Sophia give him up without a fight? They were headed to Riverglen? To the horrid Miles Bernard? To asylum-bound Millicent Newton? What was Sophia thinking?

"Could we not return to Riverglen?" he asked her, his tone pleading. "I'm sure this is a very bad destination."

"We don't have a choice, Pierre, so don't nag."

She closed her eyes and wept silently. Pierre huddled with Emily, both of them too disturbed to interrupt. They simply observed Sophia as she collapsed with grief. The miles sped by, whisking them away from Swindon so rapidly that they might never have been there at all.

"I TOLD YOU *I* would speak with her! How dare you interfere!"

Sheridan was so angry that he felt as if the top of his head might blow off.

Neville was his father, and a son was required to exhibit the proper amount of respect, but he had no illusions. Neville was an egotistical brute. He imperiously assumed that mere mortals—which was just about every person in the kingdom—should constantly bow down. He would have uttered any vile insults to Sophia, and he'd have delivered them in a way that would devastate her forever.

Sheridan had been frantically searching for her, and finally, a footman had mentioned that she was sequestered in the library with Neville. On learning that information, his fury had flared to a dangerous height.

His father and brothers believed they knew and understood him, but they didn't. Deep down, he was a violent man who was used to lashing out ruthlessly. It was why he was so good at his chosen career.

He attacked without warning, and any dunce who tried to fight back was always sorry.

He had intended to talk to Sophia. He'd realized that he needed to be frank, but kind. He'd have had to admit he was a despicable cad, that he hadn't meant any of his promises. And he hadn't actually offered a binding vow, had he? When she'd pushed him for assurances, he'd been vaguely positive, had let her suppose he was attaching himself when he wasn't.

The justifications were quickly mounting, and he smirked with disgust. He liked to pretend he wasn't like his wastrel father, but it was entirely possible he was worse than Neville had ever dreamed of being.

"What did you say to her?" he raged, and he was shouting.

"Calm down," his father blandly responded. "I will not converse with you when you're bellowing at me."

Neville sauntered over to the liquor tray and, even though it was the middle of the morning, he poured himself a brandy. Then he strutted to the desk and sat down. He sipped his drink, his smug expression making it appear as if he was celebrating how effortlessly he'd vanquished Sophia.

"Did I, or did I not, tell you that *I* would deal with her?" Sheridan fumed.

"Yes, you were very adamant about it, but you are too fond of the bloody girl. You could never have broken it off. If you had any sense, you wouldn't have ruined her in the first place."

"You have the gall to lecture me about an amorous affair? Me? After the mischief you've perpetrated over the decades, you imagine I'll listen?"

He marched over to the liquor tray himself and, stunning them both, he grabbed a whiskey decanter and hurled it at the fireplace. It shattered with a satisfying crash. Glass shards and alcohol flew everywhere, creating a huge mess.

Neville clucked his tongue, as if Sheridan were a toddler throwing a tantrum.

"Was that really necessary?" his father asked. "I recognize that you're upset, but I insist you rein in your temper. We will discuss this rationally or we won't discuss it at all."

The butler had heard the commotion, and he poked his nose in the door and asked, "Is everything all right, Lord Swindon?"

"Get the hell out of here!" Sheridan roared, and the man cringed and slunk away.

Neville's temper ignited too. "You will not be rude to the servants. I don't tolerate that sort of conduct under my roof."

"Bugger you and your roof."

He turned to storm out, and Neville said, "Where are you going?"

"Where do you think? I have to find Sophia."

"She left."

"She what?"

"She left. I had her carriage harnessed and her bags packed and loaded. I demanded she depart immediately, and she agreed she would."

"Where is Emily?"

"She took the baby with her." Neville snorted with derision. "For pity's sake, I can't be a father at my age."

"You sent Emily away too?"

Sheridan couldn't believe it. How was he to assess such cold-hearted, uncharitable actions? He would have launched into a vicious diatribe, but before he could start, Hunter rushed in.

"What on earth is happening?" his brother asked.

"Nothing that concerns you," Neville said as Sheridan said, "Neville is trying to run my life, and I won't have it."

"Well, which is it?" Hunter glared back and forth. "Let's figure this out, so the guests don't have to hear you two quarreling. If we're addressing a skeleton in the family closet, I'd rather not have our visitors know what it is."

Neither of them answered. They stared at each other like pugilists in the boxing ring. Hunter scoffed with exasperation, then stomped over and shoved Sheridan onto his chair. He waved at Neville to sit too, his stern scowl providing firm evidence that Neville shouldn't refuse to obey.

Hunter frowned at Neville and said, "I assume this is your fault. What did you do?"

"Sheridan is retiring from government service. His health is too deteriorated to carry on at his current post. He will come home and wed."

"To Sophia Cantwell?" Hunter surprised him by asking.

Neville bristled. "Don't be ridiculous, and why would you even suggest such a preposterous ending? She's completely unsuited to be his bride."

"How is she unsuited?" Hunter inquired.

"She's impertinent and sassy," Neville claimed, "and she has no appreciation of her low position with regard to a man like me. She has no idea how to act in any situation, and she has the manners of a peasant."

"What's the matter, Neville?" Sheridan snidely said. "Did she tell you you were a pompous windbag? It must have crushed your ego to discover she's not in awe of you."

Hunter was eager to keep the discussion from spiraling out of control, and he asked Neville, "If it's not Sophia Cantwell, who is he marrying then?"

Neville replied before Sheridan could. "He will wed Miss Cantwell's cousin, Aurora Newton. She's an heiress with a massive dowry."

Hunter said to Sheridan, "Do you want to marry Aurora Newton?"

"I don't want to marry anyone. I don't want to retire or become a gentleman farmer. I want to continue on as I have been."

Hunter rattled him by resting a palm on Sheridan's shoulder, as if he were a little boy who'd skinned his knee. Sheridan had had such scant sympathetic tending in his life that, if he'd been a weepy type of person, he might have burst into tears.

"It's not possible for you to continue sailing," Hunter gently advised him. "After the incident yesterday, you must understand that fact."

"He ruined Miss Cantwell," Neville blurted out. "Right under my roof! That's why we're quarreling."

"Neville, shut up!" Sheridan snapped. "I won't have you spreading stories about her."

"Your brother should be apprised of how outrageous you're being." Neville slapped his hand on the desktop, the sound echoing off the ceiling. "The foolish girl expects a proposal, but I will not have it! I found the perfect wife for him. She's rich, elegant, and refined. He told me so himself! Those were his words! Not mine! He will not throw himself away on a brash, insolent hussy who doesn't have two pennies to rub together!"

At the insult to Sophia, Sheridan nearly leapt out of his chair, but Hunter blocked him in, so he couldn't. He could have wrestled with his brother and pushed by him, but what was he intending? Would he pound his father into the ground? Was that the sort of son he'd grown to be?

It was common knowledge that Neville had deserved numerous thrashings over the years, but Sheridan wouldn't debase himself by administering one of them.

Hunter turned to Neville and said, "You! Out!"

Neville huffed with offense. "I'm not leaving. I won't have you two conspiring behind my back. Not about this. He has to make the sensible choice, and I shall see to it that he does. It's too important to his future happiness."

Hunter marched over, lifted Neville to his feet, and escorted him out of the room. He sputtered and fumed, but in the end, Hunter won their brief battle. He shoved Neville into the hall, slammed the door in his face, then spun the key in the lock.

Neville was such a vain ass that Sheridan figured he'd shout and demand reentry, but he didn't. He mumbled a vile comment they couldn't decipher, then he stormed off. Once his footsteps faded, and they were sure he was gone, Hunter came over to the desk.

He stopped by the liquor tray first and brought it with him. He poured them both a hefty brandy, then sat in the chair Neville had just vacated.

Sheridan glowered at him, feeling put-upon and abused. His leg was killing him, and he was too grouchy to have a civil conversation. Hunter glowered back until Sheridan grabbed his glass of brandy and gulped down a long swallow. The alcohol immediately soothed him. Not completely, but it took off the sharp edges.

"Tell me about Miss Cantwell," Hunter said after Sheridan was calmer.

"Why should I?" Sheridan was acting like a spoiled brat, and he breathed out a heavy sigh and tried again. "I like her very much. She's different. She's sassy and funny."

"Are you in love with her?"

It was a strange question for a man to ask another man, but Hunter was a newlywed who constantly praised the glories of matrimony. He was a contented husband and thought every bachelor should be one too.

Sheridan accepted it as a serious inquiry. "I don't know if I love her. I've merely been thinking, if she was my wife, I'd be very glad about it."

"That's what I decided when I picked Hannah. Father didn't pick her for me. He chose her sister who was barely out of the schoolroom."

"Neville won't give me permission to wed Sophia. He's determined that it be her cousin instead."

"As far as I'm concerned, Neville can jump off a cliff. What do *you* want? You don't need money, and if you're keen to own property, you can buy an estate that suits you. You could search near Marston, so we'd be neighbors."

"I have no interest in owning property. It sounds too permanent. I shudder with dread at the very idea."

"You're in a bad mood, so this probably isn't a good time to raise this topic, but I wrote to my friend about that government posting in Gibraltar. They haven't filled it yet. We could convince him to offer it to you. It might be a viable transition while you recover your health and figure out what your path should be."

"Maybe," Sheridan grudgingly allowed.

A stint in Gibraltar would be much more exciting than being locked away at a dreary, rainy, rural farm, but he couldn't admit that he would be finished sailing.

"Have you really ruined Miss Cantwell?" Hunter asked. "Or was Neville being hysterical?"

"Yes, I ruined her."

Hunter shrugged. "I ruined Hannah and Warwick ruined Wilhelmina. We couldn't resist, and the fact that you forged ahead, when you shouldn't have, furnishes me with significant information about your feelings for her."

"Don't provide me with justifications for my wicked conduct. I have to remember to be ashamed of myself."

"Warwick and I wiped away our illicit behavior by tying the knot, so what about Miss Cantwell? Could you do the same."

"If I broke down and shackled myself, I'd like it to be to Sophia. And she might have believed I would marry her."

Hunter blanched. "You cad! You tricked her?"

"I didn't *trick* her. I just might not have been totally honest about my intentions." At the confession, Sheridan's cheeks heated to such a hot temperature, he was surprised he didn't burst into flames.

Hunter snorted. "I won't tell my wife this part of the story. I tell her everything, but I won't tell her this. She'd never forgive you."

"I don't suppose I have many options with regard to Sophia."

"You have plenty of options," Hunter said, "but I like to hope you'll select the right ones."

"Neville is so opposed to it being Sophia, and I've never had the best relationship with him. How can I blatantly defy him?"

"Is Sophia the type of girl who'd travel to Gibraltar with you? From my brief discussions with her, I suspect she would be. Could you persuade her to accompany you?"

Sheridan stared out the window, and it dawned on him that he could absolutely picture Sophia thriving there. She'd be ecstatic to escape Riverglen, and she'd make the trip an adventure. What about Aurora Newton?

Somehow, he couldn't see her being very enthused. She seemed a tad stodgy and set in her ways. Would that become the pivotal aspect for him? Would it be that Sophia would move to Gibraltar, but Miss Newton wouldn't? Could it be that simple?

Sheridan nodded. "Sophia would love to travel to Gibraltar."

"Then perhaps she's the bride for you."

Sheridan wasn't willing to commit to any course. "Neville sent her home this morning. It's why we were arguing. He kicked her out."

Hunter's jaw dropped in astonishment. "You're joking."

"No. He had her take Emily too. He's not going to recognize or support her. He gave Sophia a bit of money for her trouble—but that's it."

Hunter blew out an exasperated breath. "Neville is such an obnoxious prig, but then, we've always realized that about him."

"Even Sybil Jones has had enough. She left this morning too, once she found out he wouldn't claim Emily."

Hunter sighed. "This shifts many issues into clear focus for me. You seduced Miss Cantwell, and she assumed you'd propose because of it. I would hate to discover that you're such a scoundrel you won't do that. *And* we have a duty to Emily. She's our sister after all, and she's also an earl's daughter."

"I was fond of her from the start. She's so charming, and it's obvious she has a ton of Stone blood flowing in her veins."

"Can we cast her loose to be buffeted by the winds of fate? You can wed Miss Cantwell so you'll be happy, then *you* can serve as Emily's father. If might help to cancel out some of Neville's sins toward her mother."

Sheridan leaned forward on his knees, his head in his hands. He was weary, both physically and emotionally. He was the lowest, most despicable rogue in the world. He needed to climb on a horse and ride after Sophia. He needed to fall to his knees and beg her forgiveness, but he didn't feel well enough to chase her down.

He wasn't sure what he wanted. The future was rushing at him so fast that he couldn't jump out of the way to keep from being hit by it. Marriage? Retirement? Fatherhood? A new career?

"I'm too bewildered to know what's best," he ultimately muttered, "so it's beyond me to peer down the road and deduce the direction I should walk."

His brother sipped his liquor and studied Sheridan meticulously, as he debated what his next comment should be. Finally, he said, "How about this? Your health has deteriorated to the point where you must quit your privateering. You can't continue in such a risky business, so you should grab the job in Gibraltar."

"Are you telling me I should go there with Sophia as my bride?"

"I'm not ready to say that because I don't think *you* are ready, so you should spend a few days getting your head on straight. Why don't you sneak off to Stone Manor for some quiet reflection?" Stone Manor was their childhood home. "Why not try it? You can give yourself a time limit. How about a week to reach some decisions? Then we'll take the necessary steps to implement them."

"That might work," Sheridan grumbled.

"In the end, if you'd like to wed Miss Cantwell, don't worry about Neville. Warwick and I will bring him around. He was vehemently opposed to Warwick marrying Wilhelmina, but now, he loves her, so don't fret about him. We can change his mind."

"If you believe that, then I have to wonder if you aren't slightly deranged."

Hunter stood and came over to Sheridan. He rested his palm on Sheridan's shoulder again, and he gazed down with a great deal of affection.

"Will you leave for Stone Manor today?" he asked. "I wish you would. Shall I have the servants pack your bags and harness a carriage?"

For an eternity, Sheridan stared up at his brother, then he smiled. "Yes, why don't you have them prepare my things? I'll depart within the hour."

Chapter Twenty

"Where were you?"

"I went to visit an acquaintance."

Sophia stared at Aurora, but didn't clarify any details about her furtive journey.

"You might have told us you were leaving," Aurora said. "We were worried sick."

"I doubt that very much."

Sophia was completely drained, rubbed raw, emotionally battered, but it was her own fault. She'd trotted off to Swindon with Emily, and when she'd departed for the ostentatious property, she'd barely considered whether she should proceed or not.

It was a personal failing for which she'd been castigated all her life. She blustered forward without pondering the consequences and often staggered into disaster. She'd always laughed at the criticism, but perhaps it was time to reassess her attitude.

She'd delivered Emily to her rich, imperious father, having persuaded herself that she would easily convince him to recognize his daughter. Why had she assumed she could succeed? She was such a dunce. She had no magical power or influence, and she'd been tossed out of his home in disgrace.

While she was there, she'd risked all for love, had been ruined, and had presumed she'd wind up with a husband, but it had been for naught. She was trying not to be too hard on herself though. Captain Stone was an experienced libertine, and he'd slyly offered vague promises that she'd embraced as if they'd been carved into a marble slab.

Despite how she hated to admit it, she was simply Sophia Cantwell. An orphan. A spinster. A poor relative. She was no grander or more special than that. She had no wise elders to provide advice or support. She had no friends to commiserate or furnish sympathy. She had no funds of her own, but for the paltry sum Lord Swindon had coughed up. It wouldn't cover six months of rent out in the real world.

She was floating free, with no allies and two children to raise, but no way to accomplish it. She was a naïve, gullible fool, and she had to stop thinking she was better or cleverer than other people.

Captain Stone would arrive shortly to propose to Aurora. A wedding date would be set and wedding plans implemented. The house would be in a frenzy of preparation. Aurora would probably rush to London to purchase a trousseau. She might even beg Sophia to accompany her, and it was such an offensive idea that she snickered with disgust.

"What's so funny?" Aurora asked her.

"Nothing. I was woolgathering."

"You've forced me to mention that you are behaving so strangely. Ever since you took your clandestine trip, you've been morose and on edge. Everyone has noticed. I wish you'd tell me what's wrong."

"I'm tired. I shouldn't have traveled anywhere. It's left me weary."

She was back at Riverglen, licking her wounds and peeking around every corner, being sure more calamity was lurking. She couldn't survive many more emotional blows. The heartache she'd suffered so far was beyond her ability to endure.

They were in the dining room, having supper. It was a typical Newton family meal, the tension horrid, the conversation stilted. No guests were present, so it was just Sophia, Aurora, and Miles wedged together at the end of the long table.

The children were tucked away in the nursery, with Phillip watching Emily like a hawk. He was terrified to take his eyes off her, lest a dire incident occur when he wasn't looking. He hadn't wanted to return to Riverglen and had constantly protested, to the point where Sophia had repeatedly snapped at him.

She understood his reservations. She hadn't wanted to return either, but where else could they have gone?

That was the burning question for her. She absolutely could not stay at Riverglen as Aurora married Captain Stone. They'd be lord and lady of the manor, and she had to flee. But to where?

"I see you brought the toddler back to us," Miles said, his tone snotty.

Sophia wondered how he'd react when he learned about the wedding. She didn't apprise him though. Nor did she explain about Caroline being seduced by Lord Swindon.

She couldn't deduce how her cousins would view the fact that he was Emily's father. Would they deem it a positive development or another mark against her? And where would Captain Stone fit into the story? Shouldn't Lord Swindon have to confess his perfidy to Millicent before the nuptial contracts were drafted? Why should Sophia have to wade into that bog?

"What child would that be, Miles?" she asked, her tone just as snotty. "By any chance, are you referring to Caroline's daughter, Emily?"

"I thought you'd come home without her. I was certain you were conveying her to her father's kin."

"You should be so lucky," Sophia mumbled.

"Honestly Miles!" Aurora chided. "Must you quarrel? We have to figure out what to do with the girl, and I can't believe you were hoping Sophia would dump her by the side of the road as if she were a stray puppy."

Sophia smirked with derision. "I think he'd be excited by that."

Miles was a tad chastened by Aurora, and apparently, he was anxious to nag on a new topic. He spoke to Sophia. "The French boy is still with you too. What are your intentions with regard to him?"

"His name is Pierre. If you're determined to complain, at least be clear about who you're criticizing."

Miles scoffed. "I can agree that we *might* have a duty to provide shelter to Caroline's bastard, but for the life of me, I can't fathom why it would extend to a French orphan we didn't invite to reside with us." He glanced at Aurora. "I trust you'll support me on this issue. Why should we have to welcome him?"

Aurora seemed stricken, as if she couldn't bear to be dragged into the argument, and Sophia said, "Don't worry, Miles. Pierre is my responsibility. I'll supply what he requires, and he's very small. He doesn't eat much or take up much space. I'm sure—with the family being so wealthy—none of you will even notice he's here."

Tears welled into her eyes. She couldn't abide the vitriol that swirled at Riverglen. Was there no place on the globe where people were happy? Where they liked each other? If there was such a miraculous locale, how could she find it?

Aurora had an instant of perceptive attention, and she said, "My goodness, Sophia, what's vexing you? Anymore, you're a virtual watering pot. Don't let Miles needle you. You never have before, and he enjoys tormenting you. Ignore him."

Sophia might have replied, but suddenly, there was a kerfuffle out in the hall. Servants gasped, and one of them dropped a tray of glasses that shattered with a loud crash.

Sophia, Miles, and Aurora whipped around to discover what was happening, and Millicent strolled in. She was wearing a pink nightgown, a filmy robe over the top, and it floated out behind her. Her feet were bare, her hair down. She looked frail and ethereal, like a fairy that had been caught inside the house and couldn't open the door to escape.

"Mother?" Aurora said, as Miles muttered, "I'll be damned."

Sophia had no comment. As with every other facet in the manor, she felt as if she was no longer part of what was transpiring. She was merely a bystander who was being buffeted by the winds that swooshed by the rest of them.

Aurora regrouped first. "Mother! You gave us such a fright. Why are you in the dining room? What's wrong?"

Millicent was clutching a letter, and she waved it at them like a red warning flag. "I have received important correspondence from Lord Swindon. I will share it immediately, but with each of you individually—in my bedchamber."

Aurora stiffened, and Miles blanched. Only Sophia was unmoved. Whatever the fiend had penned, she couldn't care less. He'd likely announced that Captain Stone would propose to Aurora. So what? Why would Sophia be interested?

"What did he say?" Miles demanded. "Tell us at once. I insist."

Millicent shook her head. "I need each of you to join me in my boudoir. Aurora will start. Then Miles. Then Sophia."

Sophia bestirred herself to inquire, "Why must I be apprised of any message? If Lord Swindon has furnished information to you, I fail to see why I should have to hear it."

"It will affect all of us, and we must begin to prepare." Millicent nodded at Aurora. "Come with me, dear, won't you?"

She vanished as rapidly as she'd arrived, and a grave silence settled in. The servants were frozen in their spots, stunned by the strange incident. Miles appeared pole-axed, while Aurora appeared nervous and even a bit afraid.

Miles broke the taut moment, asking Aurora, "What nonsense is she pursuing? What could Swindon have told her?"

"I can't imagine, but I better talk to her."

"Tomorrow is your deadline." Miles's remark sounded like a threat. "We're supposed to pick the date, so don't get any wild ideas. Your mother is always chasing rainbows; you know that. She's deranged, and she can't derail our plans."

"I'm certain it's nothing," Aurora said, but from how swiftly she skedaddled out, Sophia figured Aurora was aware of what was approaching.

Sophia actually felt sorry for Miles. What would become of him? He'd never peered down his personal road and seen any destination except for his being Aurora's husband and owner of Riverglen. If neither of those happened, what would he do?

He wouldn't accept the situation very gracefully, and she couldn't deduce why Millicent had sought a different engagement for Aurora. It was petty and cruel, and Sophia had thought Millicent liked Miles. Evidently, she'd been wrong.

She mustered the energy to offer a consoling comment. "Don't fret, Miles. You pointed out that Millicent can be very silly, so you shouldn't work yourself into a lather until you unravel her ploy. You can deal with it then."

"Bugger off, Sophia!" he crudely spat.

He tossed down his napkin and raced after Aurora. As to Sophia, she was in no hurry to confer with Millicent. She waved her wine glass at a footman, and he bustled over and filled it to the rim.

"What is it, Mother? You've always had a flare for the dramatic. I hope your little performance downstairs was worth it."

Millicent grinned at Aurora and said, "Captain Stone will betroth himself to you."

"He what?"

"He was charmed by you, and he deemed Riverglen to be magnificent. He'll return in two or three weeks to discuss the details. We have to wait for his father's party to be over."

"I can't believe it. When he left early during his prior visit, I assumed it was a bad sign."

"His father is hosting a huge gala at Swindon. Captain Stone probably didn't want to be late for it. The weather can change so quickly this time of year, and he couldn't have risked being delayed by mud and rain."

Millicent was stretched out on her fainting couch, and she watched as Aurora staggered over to a chair and eased down. Her daughter was very pale, as if she was alarmed.

"Please tell me you're glad about this," Millicent said.

"I guess I'm glad. It's just a bit of a shock."

"You're twenty-two, Aurora." Millicent tsked with offense. "We can't continue to dither."

"But . . . *marriage*. It sounds so permanent. We've put it off for so long that it's started to seem as if it would never occur. Will Captain Stone be happy with me? He's so masculine. I can't imagine how he and I will get on."

"Husbands are a mystery, but wives learn how to manipulate them. You will too."

"I will pray you're correct."

Millicent chuckled. "I handled your father, didn't I? You and I will have to have some chats about matrimony. I'll supply you with some tips on how to manage him."

"My head is spinning."

"Which isn't a surprise."

"Miles will be so angry," Aurora said.

"Leave him to me."

"Are you sure we should have proceeded? He wasn't expecting it, and after Captain Stone takes charge, I doubt he'll be keen to have Miles tarry."

"Miles is entirely too confident about his position in this family, but he's not *in* this family. Oscar should have found a post for him—somewhere else—ages ago. I never understood why we had to keep him here after he turned twenty-one."

"I thought you liked Miles," Aurora said.

"I never did. Now then, why don't you go to your bedchamber and jot down some lists? I would like to hold the ceremony over the Christmas holidays. Could we arrange it that fast? I think we can. I'm not certain who would be willing to travel to Riverglen in December, but we'll find out."

"The Earl might like to have the wedding at Swindon. Or maybe even in London. Shouldn't we check?"

Millicent nodded. "I'll reply to him and inquire about his preference. In the meantime, I'll meet with Miles and explain what's transpiring. Why don't you hide for the next few days? We should give him a chance to calm down, and I won't have him badgering you. If he tries, send him to me, and I'll set him straight."

"Thank you. I can't bear it when he's in a temper."

Aurora walked out, and Millicent said to her retreating back, "You should lock your bedroom door at night. Until our affairs are not quite so heated."

"I will lock it. I can't have him barging in. When we quarrel, it's so exhausting."

Millicent would have counselled her that she'd misconstrued the reason for caution, that any entrance by Miles might be for a nefarious purpose, one that would end up with Aurora being forced to wed him, despite Captain Stone's interest, but they had no opportunity for that conversation.

The door slammed open, and Miles stormed in. She smiled a placid smile that she knew would infuriate him, and she waved to the chair Aurora had just vacated.

"Won't you sit, Miles? I'll share my news, and I promise to be quick about it."

"How COULD YOU DO this to me?" Miles demanded of Millicent.

"I'm not doing it to you," Millicent ridiculously stated. "I'm doing it *for* Aurora. She would never have been happy as your wife, so I'm saving both of you from decades of misery."

"She is supposed to be mine! Riverglen too!"

"If that's what you presume, then you are incredibly confused."

"Oscar wanted it for me! Doesn't that matter to you?"

"If Oscar had truly wanted you to inherit, he would have named you owner in his Last Will. I won't speculate as to why he didn't name you, but you were never guaranteed the conclusion you were convinced should be yours. Oscar assumed you would woo and win Aurora, but you've never expended any energy to garner what you craved. You felt it would be automatically handed over to you."

Tears flooded his eyes. Normally, he was much too manly to be driven to weeping by a woman. Especially by Millicent. He'd always viewed her as stupid, dull, and flighty. How could she have schemed like this behind his back? Why hadn't he watched her? Why hadn't he intervened?

The damage was done. Lord Swindon had written to verify the engagement. Before the month was out, Captain Stone would arrive to propose. The pompous sailor had previously informed Miles that he wouldn't be allowed to remain after the wedding, so Miles would have to move on.

Where would he go? How would he find other employment?

Suddenly, he comprehended how a person could be goaded to commit a homicide. If he'd been holding a pistol, he'd have shot her. As it was, he could barely stop himself from bending down, wrapping his fingers around her slender throat, and strangling her to death.

There was a burly footman standing in the corner though, and he was studying Miles in an insolent, caustic way. Miles received the distinct impression that she'd invited the fellow to be present so she wouldn't be alone with Miles. It only proved that she recognized how livid he'd be.

"Does a heart still beat in that chest of yours?" he asked. "Captain Stone's first act will be to fire me. If you were so eager to be rid of me, why not fire me yourself? Why torture me like this?"

"We can't be positive that the Captain will fire you. You've been a very competent manager. Why wouldn't he keep you on?"

She stared blandly, as if she sincerely believed it, but she was a cunning witch. She knew precisely what she'd set in motion. The process would have him evicted, but she wouldn't have to take the awkward steps herself. No, she'd let Captain Stone carry it out for her.

Miles was absolutely stunned by her duplicity. He'd assumed she was fond of him. How could he have misjudged her so egregiously?

"I can see you're distraught," she said. "Why don't you go for a ride and clear your head? We can chat again after you return. For now, send Sophia to me. I must speak with her too."

She waved him out, the gesture imperious and galling, as if she were a princess dismissing a peasant.

"You've yanked everything away from me," he muttered.

"I didn't *yank* a thing. You simply didn't earn it, and I won't debate it with you. Could you locate Sophia for me? I'd like to finish these discussions before I grow too fatigued."

A few tears slipped down his cheeks, and he swiped at them, then leapt to his feet and marched out. He truly thought he'd creep in after dark and kill her. He was that enraged.

He was about to exit into the hall when she said, "Oh, and Miles? I'll be having various housemaids stay with me. I've been having bad dreams, and they'll sleep with me at night so I won't be by myself.

Please don't think they're slacking off on their other duties. If they're up here with me, it's because I insisted on it."

He glanced at her over his shoulder, and her expression was cool and steady, but his was visibly lethal. Obviously, she'd been aware of how violently he might react to her treachery, but with her having a constant companion, he wouldn't be able to murder her. She'd made sure of it.

He stomped off, and his rumination was pathetic and humiliating. If he graciously acceded to her scheme, what would he have left? Nothing. Could he bear it?

No, no, no . . .

Riverglen and Aurora were his. Would he permit Captain Stone to trot in and seize them?

No, no, and no again . . .

If Sheridan Stone assumed he could have Riverglen without a fight, then he was mad. And Miles would show him there were dire consequences for wallowing in that sort of lunacy.

"Sit down, Sophia."

Sophia entered Millicent's bedchamber. She was lounged on her fainting couch, and Sophia went over and eased onto the chair across from her. She might have been out of her body, as if she was up in the sky and gazing down at some other hapless, unlucky woman as she was about to learn terrible news.

Ever since she'd stood in the library at Swindon and listened to the Earl bloviate about how unworthy she was to be Captain Stone's wife, she'd been frozen on the inside. And she ached on the outside, as if she'd been pummeled with clubs. She couldn't concentrate on any topic.

She recognized that time would pass and her sorrow would wane, but for the moment, she might have been deceased and walking in a realm where humans couldn't tread. She wanted the conversation to conclude quickly, so she started it, hoping to spur Millicent along.

"What did you need to tell me, Millicent?"

There was a footman lurking in the corner, and Millicent shooed him out. Evidently, whatever she was about to impart, it was so hideous the servants couldn't hear it.

"In the letter I received from Lord Swindon," Millicent said, "he astonished me by sharing some comments about *you*."

Sophia blanched. "About me?"

"Yes, and they were very derogatory. It appears you've ruined yourself with his son, Sheridan. I'd appreciate it if you wouldn't deny it. That way, we don't have to skirt the issue or pretend it didn't happen."

Sophia's cheeks flamed bright red. She felt small, stupid, and very wretched. "No, I won't deny it."

"Good. I would have been aggravated to tiptoe on the edges of this. You can't imagine my shock upon being apprised of this incident. To think that you snuck away from Riverglen merely to pursue a torrid affair with that scoundrel!"

Sophia's eyes narrowed. "The Earl claimed that was the purpose of my trip? He has such gall."

"I won't chastise you for your misconduct."

Sophia scoffed. "It certainly sounds as if you are."

"No, I understand why you would be fascinated by Captain Stone. He's quite dashing, and I have no doubt he flaunted himself to you. A girl in your situation would be overwhelmed. I won't automatically accept the Earl's account."

"Thank you. Neville Stone is an arrogant prig, and I can categorically state that he doesn't have my best interests at heart."

"I agree, so I will declare this to be Sheridan Stone's fault."

"I wasn't an innocent victim, Millicent. I know right from wrong, and I shouldn't have participated."

"I'm relieved to have you admit it. I've been acquainted with you for a whole decade, and I'm glad I've instilled a bit of moral guidance."

Sophia tamped down a smirk. No one had provided any moral guidance in her life. Not her extravagant, silly father, that was for sure. He'd insisted a person should carry on however he pleased. Once she'd come to Riverglen, the Newton family hadn't attempted to alter her views or habits. Any ethical leanings she'd developed had been acquired on her own, with her stumbling around and making mistakes—until she'd made less of them.

Perhaps her better tendencies were instinctual or perhaps she'd inherited them from her dead mother. She didn't mention any of that though. Millicent had a message to deliver, and Sophia had to keep her on track.

"What is your point, Millicent? If you'd like me to apologize, I will. I'm very ashamed."

Millicent patted Sophia's hand. "I'll bet you're heartbroken too. Aren't you? You wouldn't have involved yourself unless there was an expectation of matrimony afterward. Did he promise to marry you?"

"Yes, he promised he would." She had no idea what he'd intended, but it was simpler to avoid that explanation. "He's about to propose to Aurora, so it's clear he wasn't serious."

"The word *swine* isn't strong enough to describe him, is it?"

The remark surprised Sophia. Millicent was being so considerate, and her attitude was unsettling. Sophia had committed the same sin that had gotten Caroline banished to France, so why was Millicent being so sympathetic?

Caroline had been Millicent's daughter, so maybe Caroline's disgrace had wounded her more deeply. Maybe, because Sophia was just a distant cousin, it didn't matter if she was a tart. Who cared? Not Millicent.

"Lord Swindon would like me to deal with you," Millicent said, "so we must review our choices."

"What do you mean?"

Millicent's expression became consoling. "You can't stay here. It wouldn't be fair to Aurora, and we can't furnish any temptation to Captain Stone."

"You think I'd philander with him again?"

"I would hope not, but he has a reputation as a cad, so I can't have you around and underfoot. He'll need a lengthy interval to figure out how to be a husband rather than a bachelor. I'm not being an alarmist when I confide that he'll regularly cheat on Aurora, but we needn't open the flood gates so he can easily accomplish it."

Sophia was gaping, struggling to focus on Millicent. The problem was that, since she'd returned, she'd been so distressed. She was terribly confused and couldn't follow any conversation.

"Are you kicking me out?" she asked. "Is that what's happening? Am I to depart immediately?"

"No!" Millicent chuckled, as if the notion was preposterous. "We have to make some plans for you, but then, that's been my opinion for quite a while. Have you wondered how you'll manage if you're increasing?"

It took Sophia a moment to decipher what she was asking. "Increasing . . . with a baby?"

"Yes. What if you and Captain Stone have created a child together?"

She was such a dunce! The possibility hadn't occurred to her. "I swear, Millicent, if that's the case, I will buy a pistol, hunt him down, and shoot him. He confiscated my other pistol. The one I used when I shot at Miles's portrait? I'll purchase another one and kill him with it."

Millicent clucked her tongue. "Murder isn't an option."

"Why isn't it? It sounds like a grand idea to me."

"Please don't be flippant. I'm trying to have a frank discussion with you."

Sophia reined in her insolence. Millicent was being very compassionate, and Sophia was at fault. How could she be a brat about any part of it?

"I'm sorry," she said. "I'm mortified and bewildered, and I'm being unusually surly."

"I realize that, but you have to marry in a hurry." Sophia must have looked as if she'd argue because Millicent held up a palm, forestalling any comment. "We've addressed this dilemma before, so it can't be news to you."

Numerous replies raced through Sophia's head: *But I've just been madly in love and I'm still in love! I was devastated by amour, and I'm not ready to move on! I might be increasing! What sane man would want me?*

She didn't voice any of those protests though. She stared at Millicent and waited for the axe to fall.

"Harry Roland might still be willing," Millicent said. "I could send him a note. I could talk to him."

Sophia winced. "I'm ruined, Millicent, and it would be so duplicitous to throw myself at him. Would we confess my folly right up front?

Or would we hide it? I can't imagine either of those scenarios, and I can't ask him to save me. Not after how I've always been so awful to him."

"Men are very simple creatures. They can be persuaded of almost anything, and I would like you to whisk Caroline's daughter away from Riverglen. I can't have her in residence when Captain Stone is here too. I won't toss our scandal in his face every minute of the day."

Sophia sighed with regret. Captain Stone knew about Emily, so what was the point of concealing her? Yet she said, "I'm bereft to hear you won't allow her to stay."

"It also appears you've dragged home a French boy, and I won't shelter an orphan who has no connection to us. You should have had better sense than to let him accompany you."

"He didn't have anywhere to go, and I couldn't abandon him."

Millicent ignored the pitiful remark. "We can bribe Harry with a bit of a dowry. He's very kind and perhaps, with a financial incentive, he'd take all three of you. The servants have been gossiping that he's accepted a position out of town. His mother is very upset about it, but he's rising in the world, so he's leaving."

"Good for him," Sophia mumbled.

"A girl like you, a girl with no money and no prospects—who is disgraced and maybe in the family way—would be lucky to latch onto him."

Millicent's gaze was eager and optimistic, as if Sophia could just consent and Harry would bluster in and fix what was wrong. Was this to be her fate? Would she shackle herself to a glorified clerk to wallow in tedium and drudgery, with a spouse she didn't particularly like?

She'd been so sure she was meant for a bigger destiny than that. Her father had insisted she was, and she'd believed him, but that was a childhood fantasy, stirred by a parent who'd been deranged on so many levels. And hadn't it been proved, over and over again, that she was a naïve idiot?

She wasn't unique. She wasn't special. Wasn't Harry Roland the highest pinnacle she could attain? Why would she ever have yearned for more?

"These past few weeks have been very hard on me," she said. "I'm not in any condition to make important decisions."

"I understand that you're hurting, but we're in a rush. I'd like the betrothal with Harry arranged before Captain Stone arrives."

"It seems so absurd, I guess. I thought something different would happen to me."

"No female can hope for more out of life than a stable marriage to a steady fellow." Millicent's expression turned harsh and flinty. "I'll pen that note to Harry, shall I? I'll invite him to supper."

"Whatever you pick is fine with me."

Millicent clapped delightedly, as if they'd agreed to host a fancy party. "Wonderful! It will all work out for the best, Sophia. I'm older and wiser than you, and I've discovered how these debacles should be handled. Eventually, you'll recognize that this was your only viable choice, and you'll learn to be content with it."

"Yes, I'm certain I will."

She stood and staggered out.

Her whole world was wrecked, but she'd brought it on herself. Sheridan Stone would marry Aurora, and they'd live happily ever after. Sophia couldn't be on the premises as that future played out, and she grasped that fact.

Why, then, did it feel so unfair that the shame had fallen on her slender shoulders? Didn't Captain Stone bear any responsibility for what had occurred? He'd behaved despicably toward her. Shouldn't there be penalties imposed on his end?

Clearly, the punishment would land on Sophia, but wasn't that how these matters always resolved? The woman paid forever, but the man was permitted to blithely wed an heiress—as if he'd committed no sins.

How could she have expected any other conclusion?

Chapter Twenty-One

"Let's switch places. You can sit in the carriage, and I'll ride your horse."

Sheridan stared at George, and he could see George hesitate.

George was Sheridan's valet and bodyguard. He wasn't Sheridan's nanny, so it wasn't his role to dissuade Sheridan from any conduct. Yet George had been by his side for over a decade, and he understood more about Sheridan's whims than anyone ever could.

In his quiet manner, he counseled restraint or caution, and in his careful assessment of dicey situations, he'd saved Sheridan from committing numerous follies.

George raised a brow. "We decided you would travel in the carriage because your leg is killing you. There's no reason for you to climb onto my horse. It will simply aggravate your injury."

"I can't bear to plod along like this. All of a sudden, I'm in a hurry."

"We're almost there. You need to exercise your patience for another hour or two."

"I've never been patient."

Sheridan opened the carriage door and leapt down. He landed with a jarring thud and had to bite down a fierce grimace. He didn't want George to notice how painfully he was ailing, but then, George noticed every detail.

"May I state for the record," George said, "that you are in no condition for this?"

"You can state it, but I won't listen, so don't nag."

George dismounted, and Sheridan gritted his teeth and pulled himself up onto the animal's back. Thankfully, George was kind enough to glance away and pretend he hadn't noted Sheridan's stiff movements.

His being kicked during the lawn game at Swindon had significantly reduced his vigor. He'd spent a frustrating week at Stone Manor, yearning for the time to pass faster. While he'd loafed, he'd expected a miraculous recovery, but he'd been a fool. The original wound had been too deep, and he had to face the fact that it would never heal completely.

Sheridan peered at their driver and said, "You know the way?"

"We'll find it, Captain. Don't you worry about that."

He grinned down at George. "I'll see you shortly. Don't get lost."

"We'll be right behind you. If your leg starts to ache, just rein in. We'll catch up to you, and you and I can lock ourselves inside the carriage. I'll entertain you with my stellar personality so you're not bored."

"You think I'm mad, don't you?" Sheridan asked.

George was too polite to answer truthfully. Instead, he said, "You're aware of my opinion about women and matrimony."

"That both are deranged?"

"Yes. I've never met a woman worth the bother, and I've never met a happy husband."

"Maybe I'll be the first."

George chuckled. "I will cross my fingers."

"Have I ever failed at anything I set out to do?"

"Not yet."

"This will be good for me. I'll show you." Sheridan couldn't determine if he was convincing George or himself. "I can't let her fend for herself, can I? The world can't stand that much chaos."

"In that, you and I are in total accord." George nodded down the road. "Why don't you head out? I'll be there directly."

"Wish me luck!"

"I'd rather wish you some common sense, but that bird seems to have flown."

Sheridan laughed and galloped off. The horse had been plodding after the carriage for hours. It was eager to run, and they cantered off at an exhilarating pace, the animal's hooves eating up the miles. The elevated speed kept him from pondering his actions too closely.

After his quarrel with Neville, he'd taken Hunter's advice and had snuck off to Stone Manor, which had been beneficial, but idiotic too. He hadn't been firm with his father about the ending he desired, and apparently, he was a coward who had some serious issues with Neville.

Neville had never been much of a parent, but Sheridan tried to respect him as a son should. He'd been incredibly disturbed by the notion of disobeying the annoying oaf, but so what if he disobeyed Neville? His father was an ass, so why heed him?

It was the main realization he'd garnered during his sojourn: He didn't care what his father thought on any topic. Neville had never had Sheridan's best interests at heart. He'd never fretted about Sheridan or his brothers. They'd always been on their own, just the three of them, staggering forward without recklessly killing themselves.

Neville had hurt and insulted Sophia. He'd sent her away with barely any warning that she was being kicked out. Then he'd insisted to Sheridan that she was too far beneath him to be his wife, but when Neville understood so little about Sheridan, why pay attention to him?

If Neville's conduct toward Sophia hadn't been solid evidence of his foul character, then his disavowal of Emily certainly was. How could the conceited dolt refuse to embrace her? Neville didn't want her, so Sheridan would raise her instead, and Neville could choke on a crow.

Once Sheridan had reached that point in his ruminations, the rest had been easy.

George had accompanied him to Stone Manor. He'd hovered in the corner, being as unobtrusive as possible and supplying a comment when Sheridan had dragged one out of him. George viewed Sophia as an impertinent troublemaker. Sheridan concurred, but her outlandish tendencies pleased him beyond measure.

With his decision in place, he'd left for Riverglen, and he supposed his appearance would create quite a stir. When he was observed trotting up, they'd assume he was visiting Aurora, but they would be wrong.

Before he knew it, he was at the gate to the property. He slowed so the horse could catch its breath, but also to calm himself down. He couldn't race up to the front door like a madman.

Sophia could be such a pest, and it would be completely typical of her to announce that he wasn't forgiven and she wouldn't depart with him. But they were leaving together—whether she liked it or not. Emily and the petty criminal, Pierre, were coming with him too. He would whisk them away, and he'd devise a plan later on.

He had started down the long lane that led to the manor when a male voice rang out from behind a tree.

"Captain Stone! Stop where you are!"

Sheridan was so distracted that, at first, he figured he was imagining it. He would have continued on by, but suddenly, the fellow materialized in the middle of the road, appearing so abruptly that his horse shied with fright. Sheridan had to grip the pommel on the saddle so he didn't lose his seat.

"Miles Bernard?" he said, wondering if he wasn't hallucinating.

"Yes, it is I, Miles Bernard. We've been expecting you. Ever since your father's letter was delivered, I, especially, have been watching for you."

"What letter? What do you mean?"

"Don't pretend to be confused," Bernard spat with derision.

He looked a tad deranged. His color was high, his collar tight, his coat askew. Most peculiarly, he was clutching a pistol. Sheridan suspected it was primed and loaded. There was no reason to brandish it otherwise. It dangled at his side, but if he was provoked, he might use it.

"It's clear you're angry with me," Sheridan said, "but at the moment, I can't deal with you. Perhaps we can chat in a bit, after I've finished my business." He was excited to get to the house and speak with Sophia.

"You scoundrel! You are not wanted here!"

"You can protest all you like, but you can't dissuade me."

"You presume you can saunter in and seize what's mine."

Sheridan grumbled with frustration. "What are you blathering on about? I don't have the patience for this."

He nudged his horse forward to circle around Bernard, but the move rattled him, and he lifted the weapon.

"Stay where you are, Captain Stone! I'll shoot! I will!"

"Don't be ridiculous. You're not shooting me. I have to confer with Miss Newton, then I'll be on my way. My calling on her doesn't affect you in the least."

"You will not talk to her!"

"Oh, for pity's sake. Are you insane?"

It was the second time he'd arrived at Riverglen when someone was wielding a pistol. There had to be something in the water that scrambled peoples' wits. The sooner he spirited Sophia away, the better.

He jumped down and whirled on Bernard, marching toward him as he commanded, "I will not fuss with you. Give me the gun! This very instant!"

He was only a foot or two away, and Bernard was frozen in his spot, stunned by Sheridan's aggressive approach. He hadn't been prepared for Sheridan to dismount, to bellow orders, to loom up in an irate manner.

Sheridan reached for the weapon, thinking he'd pluck it away, but there was a rut in the dirt. He stepped wrong, and a jolt of pain coursed up his bad leg, so he staggered slightly. Bernard pulled the trigger, and because Sheridan had tripped, he was off-balance, so he wasn't hit in the center of the chest, which probably would have killed him immediately.

He was standing so close that the force of the blast drove him back. He fell down very hard, his skull cracking on the ground. He was staring up at the blue autumn sky. He told himself to leap up, to fight, but he was paralyzed. Smoke clouded the air, and his shoulder was burning, both from the shot, but also because his shirt was on fire.

Bernard leaned over him and hissed, "Aurora is mine! You will never have her! I swear it!"

"I'm not interested in her, you dolt."

"Liar!"

Bernard raised the pistol and brought the butt down on Sheridan's head. The world went black, and he remembered nothing more.

"COCKY BASTARD!" MILES MUTTERED.

The smug oaf had underestimated Miles. He hadn't believed Miles would have the courage to proceed. Well, Miles had shown the grand and glorious Captain Sheridan Stone!

Aurora was his. Riverglen was his, and Captain Stone had been a fool to suppose he could waltz in and claim them for his very own.

From the minute Millicent had apprised Miles of her marital scheme, he'd been furiously plotting. He'd snuck out to the lane every day, being certain that the brash fiend would swiftly bluster in.

He'd arrived earlier than Miles had anticipated, but he'd been promptly dispatched to the Great Beyond. When Stone never followed through on the engagement, when his family began hunting for him, Millicent could truthfully say that he'd never come to Riverglen.

Then, after a sufficient interval had passed, Miles would coerce her into admitting that she shouldn't have considered another swain for Aurora. She'd have to see that *he* was the only viable choice. And if he couldn't convince her of that?

The servants couldn't watch her constantly. If she refused to behave as he was demanding, there would have to be consequences. With his mustering the fortitude to commit a murder, he wouldn't hesitate to commit a second one.

Stone's horse was gaping at Miles as if he couldn't figure out what was happening. Miles had never previously involved himself in a violent act, so he hadn't understood the contingencies that would have to be managed.

The animal was an expensive thoroughbred, and it would be recognized by those who knew horseflesh, so it would have to disappear too, but Miles didn't have enough hands to accomplish every required task. He would have grabbed the reins, but the uncooperative beast bolted and raced off toward the main road.

"Dammit!" Miles cursed.

He'd have to deal with Stone's corpse, then he'd have to saddle his own horse and find the runaway one. It was an aggravating detail, but then, homicide wasn't meant to be easy.

He gripped Stone by his coat and hauled him into the forest. Stone was very large, and with him being deceased, he was literally *dead* weight. Miles could barely move him. He yanked and tugged, swore and sweated. He'd already dug a grave in the woods, in a deserted section where Stone would never be found, but he wasn't making any progress.

He'd just wrestled the body into the first line of trees, when suddenly, a carriage approached. A man was calling, "Captain! Sheridan! It's George! Where are you? Answer me!"

The cretin kept hollering the same words over and over, each repetition like a blade to Miles's heart. Miles would have to tiptoe away, then return later to finish the job. He'd have to hope the dunce would continue on by without noticing Stone's boots sticking out of the grass.

Why couldn't anything go right? He couldn't even commit the perfect murder and have it resolve correctly!

He spun and fled, hurrying to the manor. Shortly, George would be asking after Captain Stone, and Miles needed to be sitting in his office, the competent functionary who had nothing to hide.

~

George walked slowly in front of the coach, shouting for Captain Stone, listening for a reply, but not hearing one. He was checking the dirt of the road, looking for scuff marks that would indicate where he'd fallen.

His driver had been nearing the entrance to Riverglen when George's horse had galloped toward them, but Captain Stone hadn't been on it. He was an excellent equestrian, and even with his leg plaguing him, it wasn't likely he'd lose his seat. The animal had been extremely agitated, as if it had suffered a terrible fright. What could have happened?

Finally, he stumbled on the signs for which he'd been searching. He could see where the Captain had dismounted, where the horse had bolted. George sniffed the air and could smell gunpowder. Gad, had a gun been fired?

When he traveled, he was always armed. He retrieved his pistol out of the carriage. He had a knife on his belt too.

"What is it, Mr. Barnes?" the driver asked. "Can you smell gunpowder? What's amiss?"

"I have no idea, but pull out your musket. Be wary."

"Where will you be?"

George motioned to the trees. "The Captain has been dragged into the woods, and I have to locate him."

It only took a few steps. He'd been shot in the chest, and he'd received a hard blow to the forehead too, as if he'd been knocked unconscious with a club. The head wound had bled copiously, so there was blood everywhere.

A good share of his shirt had burned away from the blast, so his skin was smoldering and blistered. He was mortally still, giving every sign that he'd perished.

"Oh, my lord!" George breathed, as he dropped to his knees.

He placed a palm on the Captain's heart, an ear to his lips, and joy flooded him. There was a faint pulse, as well as a wavering exhale. Sheridan Stone was the toughest man George had ever met, and he had nine lives. He couldn't have used them up already, but he'd come close.

George was so relieved he almost collapsed. He glanced around, the thick forest particularly ominous, and he could sense a malignant presence, as if a dangerous predator was watching his every move.

"Captain!" he quietly murmured. "Captain, are you still with me?"

He patted the Captain's cheek, each tap growing more forceful. Eventually, his eyes fluttered open, and he frowned at George, his confusion evident.

"What's wrong?" he asked.

"You were riding my horse to Riverglen."

The Captain considered, then said, "Yes, I remember."

"You were shot. Did you see who it was?"

His befuddled mind worked it out, then he nodded. "Yes, I saw him."

"Marvelous. It means we'll straighten it out without too much investigating." George spat out a furious laugh. "Bloody hell, you arrogant oaf. I can't leave you alone for a single minute! Who was it? And please don't tell me it was a stranger. I'll never believe it."

"It was the land agent."

"The land agent! That's a new one on me. Why would a clerk attempt a homicide?"

"He doesn't like me very much."

"You are a master of understatement." George clasped Sheridan's hand and squeezed his fingers. "I'm not strong enough to carry you. Can you stand? Can I lift you up?"

"I think so."

Even as George posed the questions, he was ripping off the sleeve of his shirt, pressing it to the head wound, ignoring the Captain as he hissed in pain. George needed help, and he called to the driver who was waiting by the carriage. The man hurried over to assist.

"Let's get you out of here," George said to the Captain. "We'll tuck you away somewhere safe, then you can fill me in on the gory details."

"I'll probably have to kill him."

"You won't have to bother over it. I'll be honored to deal with it for you."

"You're a good friend, George."

"Of course I am, and I didn't realize it could be so hazardous to visit a girl and propose marriage. It has to be a new low in nuptial planning." George chuckled, but miserably. "I should have warned you this was a bad idea."

The Captain grimaced and drifted off, but at least he was alive. He'd go through life with a ruined shoulder to match his ruined leg, but in light of the battles he'd waged, it wasn't surprising that he'd have a few scars.

He'd always been lucky, so he'd recover yet again. George would see to it, then he'd have to slay the land agent. He'd be delighted to do it, and there was no other choice really.

"He what?"

"He was shot—and almost killed—trotting up the lane to Riverglen. I just received a message from George Barnes."

At hearing Hunter's dire pronouncement, Neville staggered over to a chair and eased down. "Was he there to propose?"

"Yes—to Sophia Cantwell!"

"No, that can't be right."

Neville rubbed his temples, feeling a pounding headache form behind his eyes. "He was to marry Miss Newton. She's an heiress, and we talked about it. I convinced him it was for the best, and he agreed with me. It was all arranged."

"He didn't agree, you ridiculous fiend!"

"I'm his father! He wouldn't disobey me in this."

"If that's what you presume," Hunter caustically said, "then you don't know him at all. But then, you never knew any of us, did you?"

"He can't wed Sophia Cantwell. She's completely inappropriate."

"According to who?" Hunter asked.

"According to me!" Neville fumed. "Am I the head of this family or aren't I? Am I the patriarch or not?"

"You may be the patriarch, but you've never been interested in exerting any authority as a parent. Don't suppose you can apply some now, when we're adults and we're weary of you."

They were still at Swindon. Neville had been in his suite when Hunter had rushed in with the shocking news about Sheridan. Neville was trying to glean the particulars, but he was so stunned to learn of Sheridan's defiance regarding Sophia Cantwell that he could barely focus.

His birthday party was over, the last of the revelers gone. The accursed mansion was big, empty, and quiet. Like a mausoleum, only more depressing than that.

In the past, he'd never spent much time at Swindon. Originally, he'd thought he'd tarry after everyone had departed, perhaps through the Christmas holidays, but he couldn't abide the ambiance of the place. It was naught but a museum filled with priceless antiquities, and it was impossible to be comfortable.

If he was totally honest with himself, which he never was, he'd admit that he was anxious to return to London to speak with Sybil. He was wretched over their fight. What if he arrived in town and found out she'd been serious about cutting off his membership at the club? If he couldn't be with her every evening, how would he bear it?

"Sheridan may be eager to behave like a lunatic over Miss Cantwell," Neville said, his tone scolding, "but that's no reason for you to disrespect me."

"Neville, you're whining, and at the moment, your tender sensibilities are the least of my concerns. Stop assuming any of this is about you!"

Hunter whipped away and started for the door, and Neville said, "Where are you going?"

"I have to find Warwick, then we'll join George so we can ascertain Sheridan's condition for ourselves. We'll ride out at dawn."

Neville refused to believe the worst. "Surely it's not so calamitous that you must leave immediately."

"Pay attention, Neville. Sheridan was shot in the chest! What part of that sounds as if it's *not* a calamity?"

"Your brother is too tough to be laid low by a common villain."

"I will remain positive, but that is the sole guarantee I can provide."

Hunter continued on again, and Neville felt abandoned by his son. If Hunter and Warwick fled, their wives would flee too. He'd be stuck in the huge mansion to wander the vacant rooms like a ghost with no purpose.

He'd relished having all of them dote on him. He'd liked how cozy it had seemed, as if they could become a genuine family. Gad, he even missed Emily. The house would be so much merrier if her childish prattle was echoing down the halls.

"Hunter!" Neville called. "I didn't mean to quarrel."

"I don't think that's true. I think you enjoy it. I think you do it for sport."

"I'm sorry I bickered with Sheridan before he left. I can't imagine how this happened."

"Obviously, there was a person present at Riverglen who wasn't too keen on his swooping in and taking over. George Barnes apprises me it was the land agent who presumed Sheridan was there for Miss Newton, and the fellow had a prior understanding with her."

Neville frowned. "Sheridan was shot by the land agent? That is the oddest story you could have shared."

"My question is: Why would the bloody oaf have been watching for Sheridan? Why would he have thought Sheridan was about to propose to anybody?"

As Hunter voiced the query, Neville blanched with dismay. "I might have written to her mother to inform her that Sheridan was ready to betroth himself. I wanted to hurry the match along."

"You wrote to her without talking to Sheridan first?" Hunter's shoulders sagged with defeat. "What is wrong with you?"

"Sheridan and I decided that he would engage himself."

"He never intended to. He *loves* Sophia Cantwell, and he can't live without her. Despite your nagging, he'll have her or he'll have no one."

Neville winced. "Is this my fault?"

"Yes, you old fool. You set it in motion by butting your nose in where it doesn't belong."

"I was steering him in the right direction. Of you three boys, he's always been my favorite. He deserved an heiress."

Hunter snorted with derision. "He doesn't have to have a fat dowry. If he would like to own a country property—and he doesn't—he can buy it himself. He just needs to be happy."

"And you think he'll be happy with Miss Cantwell?"

"Yes, he will be." Neville must have looked extremely pathetic, for Hunter reined in some of his snide attitude, and he flashed a smile. "For the record, you've always claimed that *I* am your favorite. At this late date, you can't change your mind about which of us you like the most."

Hunter marched on, and Neville was slumped in his chair. He could have jumped up and run after his son, but he'd never chased after anyone in his life. He'd been raised to believe he was extraordinary, and that opinion was deeply ingrained. But recently, he'd begun to worry that his snobbery and detachment would bring about a very lonely old age.

To his great regret, he'd made so many uncharacteristic missteps. He'd fought with Sybil, had fought with Sheridan, had coerced him into shackling himself to a stranger. It was the sort of disaster he'd suffered in his own two marriages. Why would he demand such an untenable situation for one of his boys?

Hunter and Warwick had wed for love, and it was considered silly and unprecedented, but they were both delighted. Why shouldn't Sheridan have the same conclusion?

Neville had insulted and devastated Miss Cantwell. He'd disavowed his daughter, Emily. Sybil had asked his other daughter, Joanna, to attend his birthday party, but she and her husband had declined. Neville had shrugged off their snub, as if it didn't matter that another of his children loathed him.

Him! The man who was relentlessly charming and wallowed in the knowledge that everyone deemed him to be wonderful.

Well, it was clear he was the unlikable ass Miss Cantwell had brazenly accused him of being. How could he fix some of his mistakes? Over the years, he'd committed so many sins, and he barely noticed how much pain he was inflicting on those he should be cherishing.

He never apologized because he was too grand to be sorry. He rampaged through the world. He'd hurt and wounded, had scorned and maligned, with nary a ripple in his conscience over how his actions impacted others.

Would he be cruel and offensive forever? If that was his intent, how could he stand to live with himself? What if Sheridan died? Would Neville let him pass away, with the two of them quarreling? Why had they bickered anyway?

According to Hunter, Sheridan *loved* Miss Cantwell. If Sheridan wed her instead of Miss Newton, would the Earth stop spinning? No, and he couldn't be so persnickety about issues that were insignificant.

He pushed himself to his feet and hurried after Hunter. For goodness sake, his youngest son had been attacked by a homicidal maniac, and Neville had scarcely blinked. If Neville couldn't muster a bit of fury over such an outrage, what was the point of anything?

He found Hunter exiting his bedchamber, and his annoyance was obvious.

"What now, Neville?" he said. "Please don't aggravate me with any of your nonsense. Warwick and I are leaving in the morning, and I have a hundred details to handle before then."

"May I come with you?"

"No, you'd only slow us down."

Neville sighed. "I suppose you're correct, but when you reach Sheridan, would you deliver a message to him for me?"

"That depends on what it is."

"Tell him I would be thrilled if he wed Miss Cantwell."

Hunter hadn't expected the comment, and he pulled up short. "You'll give him your blessing?"

"Yes. I like her very much. She's feisty." Neville had to swallow three times so he could spit out the rest. "If he . . . he . . . is in mortal peril, would you fetch Miss Cantwell to his side? Would you locate a vicar to marry them before . . . well . . ."

Neville wouldn't tempt fate by uttering the prospect aloud, and Hunter said, "That's a beautiful sentiment. Thank you for suggesting it, but Sheridan is going to be fine, a little more battered than usual, but fine. George Barnes swore he would be."

"Will you deal with the land agent for me?"

"Yes, that's my plan."

"Keep it out of the newspapers. And how about if we meet at Stone Manor after you're finished? Bring Sheridan there, would you? I'll have the house opened up and ready for him, so he can recuperate and heal."

"You won't be here at Swindon?" Neville shook his head, and Hunter said, "It doesn't seem like home, does it? Suddenly, I'm longing for home."

"My feelings exactly."

"I will send a messenger as soon as I've assessed the situation," Hunter said. "Then I will convey Sheridan to you—even if he fusses about it!"

Hunter rushed off and flitted down the stairs. Neville tarried by the railing until he vanished from view, then he went to his suite. He had his own plans to make, his own trip to take, his own fences to mend, and he needed to get busy.

"Did you hear that?"

"No, Miles, I didn't hear a sound, and would you sit down? When you constantly jump up to peek out the window, I can't eat a bite."

Aurora glared at him, but it had no effect. He'd been greatly disturbed by her pending engagement. Captain Stone hadn't arrived though, so they were all watching for him. She wished he'd appear and cease his dithering. His delay had put them all on edge, most especially Miles.

He didn't look well. While he was generally tidy in his clothes and habits, for the past few days, he'd been slovenly and distracted, as if he was on the verge of some sort of breakdown. He was feverish and repeatedly mopping his brow.

"Have you implemented any arrangements for yourself?" she asked him, when she probably shouldn't have.

"What type of arrangements would that be?"

He was staring down the lane, as if he was waiting for Captain Stone, but no one was coming.

"There will be many changes," she said, "when Captain Stone moves in. He didn't like you very much, and I'm betting he won't retain you. Perhaps you should . . . oh, I don't know . . . head to London? Or maybe you could start applying for positions at other properties?"

He smirked and yanked his gaze from the window. "You're awfully certain that Captain Stone will follow through."

"It's what his father told Mother."

"He hasn't staggered in, has he? You shouldn't be quite so confident about your dashing swain. He must have pondered what it would be like to have you as his bride and he's reneging."

"Miles! What is wrong with you? I realize you're not yourself, but I can't abide insults like that. You should remember who you are and who *I* am."

"I am *family*, Aurora." He was lethally angry. "It's what your father always said. Will you pretend it's not so?"

"Father wanted us to wed, but Mother doesn't. You have to stop accusing me of orchestrating this debacle. I didn't persuade Mother to contact Lord Swindon. Her seeking this betrothal is as shocking to me as it is to you."

"Your mother isn't as smart as she thinks she is. We'll see if you're ever shackled to Sheridan Stone or not."

"I had thought to intercede on your behalf with Captain Stone, by asking him to let you remain at Riverglen, but you continue to harass me, so why would I help you?"

"Captain Stone may not wed you," he said, "so you'd best prepare yourself for that conclusion. If you wind up spurned, you'll be back at square one—with me as your fiancé—but you'll have to worm your way into my good graces. You and your mother have abused me most dreadfully!"

"Mother abused you. Not I! But in light of your foul temper, I'm not sorry for her decision."

He puffed himself up, his face growing so red that, for a moment, she was afraid of him. Would he march over and strike her? He was just able to refrain, and she recalled her mother's advice to stay in her bedchamber as much as she could.

She'd hidden herself away for several days, but she'd been bored, and she'd convinced herself to have breakfast in the dining room like a normal person. Yet clearly, Miles hadn't calmed down, and she had to keep away from him.

"You're indisposed, Miles. I wish I could cure what's ailing you."

"I've done what had to be done, Aurora, so you and your mother can just go to Hell!"

It was an appalling remark that stunned her and the servants who were tending them. He didn't notice their astonishment though. He simply stomped out without a backward glance, and she breathed a sigh of relief. The servants too.

She flashed a tepid smile, then said, "I'll finish eating in my room. Could someone bring me a tray? I'll have my door locked, so whoever carries it up, you'll have to knock extra loud."

She scooted away from the table and crept up the rear stairs, managing to get inside her bedchamber without encountering Miles.

It was obvious Millicent's antics had pushed him into a frenzy of rage that had escalated to an alarming level. They needed a man to deal with him, but there was just Aurora and her mother. Sophia was present too, but having her present was like having no one at all. Since she'd returned from her furtive trip, she moved through the house like a ghost.

The problem was worsening, and Miles was becoming more unhinged by the minute. Captain Stone couldn't arrive soon enough and, mimicking Miles, she went over to the window and watched the lane, hoping he'd be riding toward the manor.

Chapter Twenty-Two

"Hello, Miss Sophia."

"Hello, Harry."

"Mrs. Newton wanted me to speak with you."

"Yes, she told me. Won't you sit?"

They were in the front parlor at Riverglen. It was freezing outside, winter just around the corner, and it had been a cold walk from the village. He was chilled to the bone, but there was a cozy fire burning in the hearth. She gestured to it, and he walked over with her and seated himself on a chair. She nestled onto the sofa across from him.

"Would you like a refreshment?" she asked. "Shall I ring for a servant?"

"No, I'm fine. Thank you."

It seemed to be the extent of the conversation they could manage, and a dreary silence festered.

He was probably on another fool's errand, but after Mrs. Newton had sent her note, he'd decided to give matrimony one more try. Sophia had never been interested in him in an affectionate way. She was so merry and spirited, while he was stodgy and boring, but he suspected his dull traits would make him an excellent husband for her.

She was prone to mischief, so she landed herself in jams and constantly needed rescuing. As to himself, he never rocked a boat or caused a scene. His steady personality would be a great benefit to her. Plus, he was thirty and a bachelor, and he'd always lived with his dour, rather unpleasant widowed mother. He would relish the chance to attach himself to a pretty, cheerful bride.

He doubted he could persuade her though, but he was willing to debase himself a final time. What could it hurt? If she agreed to have him, he'd go home happy. If she refused him, he was moving to York shortly, so it was likely he'd never see her again. If he humiliated himself, there was no detriment to risking all.

In light of the topic he intended to address, small talk was ridiculous, so he mustered his courage and said, "Do you know why I've called on you?"

"Yes. You're about to propose."

"Did Mrs. Newton inform you that I have good news? I'm a man on the rise, and I have a very positive future unfolding."

"Yes, she mentioned it, and she ordered me to seriously consider your comments."

"Will you listen and seriously consider? I realize you've never thought I'd be much of a husband, but I'm hoping I can convince you that I have some valuable traits."

"You're only possessed of valuable traits, Harry. It's just that I never believed I'd wed. It's not *you* particularly. It's matrimony in general. My father filled my head with grandiose ideas, and I assumed I could orchestrate any life I envisioned. I'm twenty this year though, so I guess I should stop engaging in childhood fantasies."

He studied her, and she was reduced somehow, as if she'd been full to bursting and someone had stuck her with a pin. She looked worn down, wretchedly glum, and her usual verve and vigor had vanished. What could have happened to leave her so disconsolate?

"What's wrong, Sophia?" he asked. "You're so deflated. Is it my presence? Are you so opposed to what my question will be? If so, tell me straight out. You view me as a bit of a bungler, but I don't wish to be a complete fool in your eyes. If we are to part, after being acquainted for so long, I'd like to leave you with an optimistic opinion of me."

"You're so nice, and you've always been kind to me, but I've never been kind in return. Yet you've arrived, when I desperately need some help, and I'm having to force myself to be polite. I'm sorry I'm such a terrible person."

"No, I'm fond of you, and I'd like us to wed. May we have a frank discussion about it?"

"Yes, I suppose we should, but I imagine—on my end anyway—it will be much more frank than you were anticipating."

"What is it?" he said. "I'm aware that you deem me silly and stuffy, but I can be quite handy in a crisis. I won't faint. I promise."

She was so morose, and he braced for any awful disclosure. Whatever she was about to share, he would carefully assess her predicament and would furnish her with the advice she required. In the process, he might wind up with the result he sought, that being a wife to take to his new situation.

"May I begin by apologizing to you?" she said.

"I can't fathom what you might have done that would spur you to beg my pardon, but no matter what it is, your apology is accepted."

"It's just that Millicent prevailed on you to visit me, and she's urged me to lie or trick you, but I can't be horrid to you."

"Spit it out, Sophia. We'll muddle through."

She contemplated, choosing her words, then she said, "All right, here goes. I come with enormous baggage."

"I know that about you."

"I don't think you do." She vehemently shook her head. "I would have to bring Caroline's daughter with me. My relatives don't want her, and I can't abandon her."

"That's fine. It means I'll be a father a little sooner than I planned, but we'll figure it out."

"I have custody of an orphaned boy too. His mother worked for me when I was in France. She died from the same influenza that took Caroline, and he's been a tremendous assistant and companion to me."

"That's fine too. Is that it? If so, that wasn't such a heavy burden to unload onto my shoulders."

"No, there's something else. Something worse."

Tears flooded her eyes, and he leaned across the space separating them and patted her hand. "Don't cry, Sophia. It can't be that bad. Tell me what it is. Let's get it out on the table."

"It's not so much that I'm too sad to tell you. I'm simply ashamed to admit it."

The tears spilled over and dripped down her cheeks. She was so distraught that she didn't move to swipe them away, and he drew a kerchief from his coat and gave it to her.

At the gesture, she laughed miserably and muttered, "Of course you'd have a kerchief for me to use."

"I like to be prepared for any emergency, and you're a girl who will constantly suffer them."

She pulled herself together and said, "I'll just blurt it out. After you hear about it, if you're scandalized and would like to stomp out, I'll understand."

"What is it?" he asked again, but with a sinking heart, he could guess what she would reveal.

"I'm ruined, Harry."

She held his gaze in a brave manner that made him very proud of her. It was an appalling confession for any female, and he was surprised that she'd let herself be seduced. Then again, he wasn't surprised it had transpired. What man wouldn't attempt to overstep the permitted boundaries with her?

If he, Harry, had been more assertive, he might have behaved despicably too.

"Who was it?" he asked. "May I inquire?"

"Yes. It was Captain Sheridan Stone. His father is Lord Swindon. You met him a few weeks ago at the party where he was introduced to Aurora."

Harry couldn't tamp down a gasp of astonishment. "I'm flabbergasted."

"I hope you won't push me for details. I'd be too mortified to provide them."

"No, I wouldn't dream of it," he hastily said, even though he presumed he was entitled to numerous facts so he could adequately evaluate the situation.

She continued. "I must firmly declare that I wasn't lured into folly against my will. I was a gleeful participant, and I thought he would marry me afterward." Her cheeks heated, and she tsked with exasperation. "I realize that I shouldn't have believed he would pick me over Aurora, but I was so swept up that I convinced myself it would happen."

"It's an old story, Sophia, one as old as Time itself." Harry clucked his tongue with affront, being mortally offended on her behalf. "What is his opinion about this? Has he exhibited any remorse? Is he even the least bit sorry?"

"I never discussed it with him. His father harangued at me about it, and the exalted aristocrat informed me that he would never consent to my joining their family. He wrote to Millicent and notified her that Captain Stone would betroth himself, so she has to be rid of me. I can't be allowed to remain at Riverglen and wound his son's tender sensibilities."

"That's outrageous!" Harry harumphed, growing even more livid over how she'd been treated. "I'm stunned that Mrs. Newton would be his accomplice in hurting you. And what about Aurora? Captain Stone has such low morals. Why would she want him for a husband?"

"Aurora is not aware of my disgrace, and I'm not about to apprise her. If she's insane enough to shackle herself to Captain Stone, she'll have a very hard life with him, and I won't throw any wrenches into it."

"I see why Mrs. Newton contacted me. She needs me to whisk you away from Riverglen so you're not a *problem* when the newlyweds march to the altar."

"Yes, and Captain Stone is expected any minute. Millicent would like me to vanish before he arrives."

He smirked. "Your bad luck might become my good luck."

"I might be increasing!" She wailed the comment. "It's too early to tell, but it's definitely possible, and with that being the case, how could you wed me? I told Millicent I'd confer with you about matrimony, but I insisted you had to know the whole sordid tale."

"Well, that's a . . . a . . ." He cut off.

On the spur of the moment, he couldn't devise a suitable remark. There were a hundred issues that had to be pondered: How would he feel about having a ruined bride? How about if that bride bore another man's child? Could Harry raise it as his own? Was he that generous and forgiving?

He liked to imagine himself as a Christian, with charitable inclinations and a big heart. Was he?

If he married her, he'd immediately have two children who weren't his own *and* there might be a third on the way. Would that be so terrible?

He was an only child himself, with his father dying when he was a boy, so their home had been quiet. He'd frequently wished he'd had some rambunctious siblings to enliven the dreary place. If he wed her, he'd have a house full of children right away. It would be a huge change, but perhaps a nice change.

He scrutinized her, and she was the most woebegone creature he'd ever observed. Could he abandon her to Mrs. Newton's machinations? If he didn't offer for her, who would? They'd always been cordial. If he was truly her friend, shouldn't he help her?

It would be difficult for her to settle into being a wife, but with his steadying influence, she'd grow into it. He was certain she would.

Or was it simply that he was ready to tie the knot and wasn't keen to search for another candidate? It might be that. He'd been interested in Sophia for ages, and he couldn't bear to start interviewing other girls. It seemed an exhausting task.

Mrs. Newton would provide a small dowry too, and the money had left him greedy. Could he pass it up? It wasn't a fortune, but it was a solid amount he could put in the bank for a rainy day. They could reside in a larger house than he'd envisioned. Or they could buy some property with it.

Sophia was being honest, so he should be honest too. "Mrs. Newton has bribed me to relieve her of your undesirable presence."

"Dare I inquire if the sum is sufficient to make me worth the bother?"

"I'm counting on it." He chuckled, thinking it was precisely the type of perky statement he enjoyed hearing from her. "And you won't be a bother. Not much of a one anyway. We'll get on fine."

She turned and, for an eternity, she peered out the window. Was she looking for Sheridan Stone to gallop up the lane? Was she yearning for the dashing sailor to rush in with flowers and candy so they could live happily ever after? If so, she would be greatly disappointed.

Harry had met Captain Stone, and the man wasn't the sort for romantic gestures. In addition, his male relatives were renowned as cads. They shrewdly preyed on naïve maidens, as Sophia had learned to her detriment.

He inhaled a deep breath and jumped off the cliff where he'd been perched. "Will you marry me, Sophia? Let me take you away from here. How can you stay? If you don't agree to have me, what might Mrs. Newton do in order to be shed of you? You saw how hideously she treated Miss Caroline when she was in the same predicament, and she was Mrs. Newton's own daughter. If you tarry, you might be in some peril."

"Maybe." She pulled her gaze from the window, realizing no one was coming to rescue her.

Harry kept on with his persuasion. "I'm willing to be a father to Caroline's daughter and to your orphan. If you're in the family way, I'll be a father to that child too."

"Oh, Harry . . ." She sighed with dismay. "This is too much to ask of you."

"What other option have you, Sophia?"

"I don't know."

"I will offer all of this to you, but I will request one thing in return." He halted, then said, "Actually, it's two things. First, you have to be a good wife to me. I recognize that I'm not the husband you were hoping to have, but I will always honor and respect you. I should be able to receive the same consideration."

"Yes, you would deserve that."

"Second, you would have to forget about Captain Stone. He can't be a boulder sitting in the middle of our world. You would have to never speak of him, never waste away, dreaming of what might have been. You'd have to promise you can put him behind you, and if you can't swear that to me, I couldn't proceed."

"You're so incredibly kind."

He shrugged. "In this situation, I'm being very selfish for once. You will save me a ton of aggravation. I'm thirty, and I'm anxious to wed. I can afford it now, but if you don't want me, I'll have to hunt for someone else, and I'd rather not. I'll eagerly glom onto the money from Mrs. Newton too, and I can only deem it to be tainted by her conduct toward you. You shouldn't picture me as some sort of saint."

"You might not be a saint, but you're much too forgiving and helpful."

She peered outside again, as if enjoying a last glance down a road she might have traveled, but that route had closed. He was very still, waiting, waiting, then she spun to him and said, "Yes, Harry, I will marry you. I will try very hard to be a good wife. I've never had any domestic skills, so I can't guarantee any proficiency. But I'll *try*."

He snorted. "You'll be grand at it. I won't imagine any other ending."

"I swear to you that I will never mention Sheridan Stone. I will never pine away or wish I had chosen differently. If we discover I'm having a baby, the child will be yours, and I won't pretend otherwise."

He patted her hand again. "It will be all right, Sophia."

"I've been moping, but this will give me a reason to work and plan. I'm sure I'll feel better shortly." She smiled, but it was wobbly. "I guess we're moving away, yes? How shall we manage the details?"

"For a few weeks, I've been gradually shifting my affairs to York. I've rented a house, and I'm about settled in. I'm leaving in the morning; Mrs. Newton just caught me. Could you and the children go with me tomorrow? Could you be prepared that fast? You could accompany me, and you wouldn't have to ever come back to Riverglen."

"That sounds splendid. Yes, we can be prepared." She bit her bottom lip, looking nervous. "Where will we wed? What are you thinking?"

"I've joined a church, and I'm a full-fledged member, so we could have the vicar call the banns. We can hold the ceremony in a month."

She pondered silently, another eternity passing. He let her ponder. What must it be like to be her, to be so unique, but to not be appreciated by anyone? What must it be like to have her own kin pay him to take her away?

Well, Harry was delighted by her and always had been.

"Yes, we can call the banns," she said. "I would like that very much. I won't be able to dither and debate. I'll simply march forward."

He finally grinned. "I can't believe I convinced you."

"Neither can I."

"I should be off then," he said. "I have quite a lot to do before we depart."

"I have a thousand things to do too."

"I'll stop by at eight. We'll have space for several trunks and boxes. If we can't fit it all in, we can send for it later."

"I'll pack light," she said. "I won't have to send for any belongings."

There was a new resolve in her gaze, as if—with it decided—she would forge ahead with a steely determination. He hoped she would. It would keep her busy, would keep her mind off her troubles.

"I'll see you in the morning," he said. "At eight."

"I'll be ready."

"GOODBYE."

"Where are you going?"

They were in Millicent's boudoir, and she was draped across her fainting couch, but where else would she have been? She gaped at Sophia as if she were a stranger.

Sophia had popped in to announce her departure. She was dressed for traveling, in a woolen cap, mittens, and fur-lined cloak. It was cold outside, the temperature chilly, and they would be trapped in Harry's carriage all day.

She'd persuaded herself that she was thrilled by the abrupt turn of events. After all, who at Riverglen had ever wanted her? No one, that's who.

Harry had provided her with an escape. She wouldn't have to stand in the front parlor and watch Sheridan Stone stroll in the door. She wouldn't have to listen as he proposed to Aurora or sit in a pew at the church as he was binding himself.

She was free, and as she'd promised Harry, she would never contemplate Sheridan Stone ever again. He was the past, and Harry was the future.

"I'm off to York to wed Harry," Sophia said.

"Now?"

"Yes, now. He has a home rented for us, and I'll live there until the wedding."

"The wedding! When is it to be?"

"In a month."

"Am I invited?" Millicent asked.

Sophia scoffed. "If you'd like to be there, you're welcome to attend, but I can't imagine you bestirring yourself."

"This is happening so fast. Are you sure it's wise?"

"It's what you demanded of me, and I'm giving it to you—without argument. In case you're curious, there won't be any impropriety. Harry will stay at a men's boarding house until after the ceremony."

"Well . . . ah . . . ah . . ." For once, Sophia had rendered Millicent speechless.

Sophia started out. She felt frozen on the inside, her veins rubbed raw, but she'd ordered herself to keep in motion. If she paused and focused on her actions, she might begin screaming and never stop. No, that wasn't right. If she focused in, she might fall to the ground and weep forever.

She was so sad. She was so angry. She'd like to murder Sheridan Stone for his perfidy. Had he any notion of what his mischief had cost her? Had he spent one second worrying about what might become of her?

She could only conclude that—after she'd been evicted from his father's grand mansion—he'd never thought about her again.

"Sophia!" Millicent called, and Sophia sighed with aggravation.

She peered over her shoulder and snapped, "What?"

"I'm overwhelmed by your swift arrangements."

"You'll get over it. I'm bringing Emily and Pierre with me, so I haven't left you with any burdens. If you ever decide you might like to meet Emily, write to me. I'll have to debate whether I'd like her to know her grandmother or not. Since you've never been interested in her, I don't suppose we need you in her life."

Millicent tsked with offense. "That was unnecessary, and you've never previously been rude to me. What's come over you?"

Sophia didn't bother addressing the criticism. "My address is on the table in the dining room, but I seriously doubt you'd ever have to contact me."

"You are being incredibly ridiculous."

"Yes, but then, I always have been ridiculous, haven't I? Here at the last, why would I change my habits? Say goodbye to Aurora for me."

"You should handle it yourself. You can't sneak out without a word to her."

"She won't notice I'm gone. Tell her I hope she's happy with Captain Stone. She won't be, but tell her I'll pray for it anyway. And beware of Miles. He's really furious with you. You should probably lock your door."

With that, she continued on. Millicent shouted to her several times, but Sophia didn't halt, and Millicent would never chase after her. In that, things at Riverglen always remained the same. Briefly, she wondered how Captain Stone would deal with Millicent's eccentric ways.

As she realized she was pondering him, she shoved him into a vault in her mind and slammed it shut. He wouldn't be allowed to plague her. Not ever.

She went down the stairs to the foyer. She hadn't told any of the servants what was transpiring, but when she'd asked the butler to have some footmen carry her trunks out into the driveway, they'd figured it out. They'd hauled them down, the children too.

There were servants hovering, but none of them spoke to her. They appeared flummoxed by the entire situation.

The butler stepped forward. "Miss Sophia! I will be very indiscreet and state that I am concerned about you. You're so young, and you've had so little guidance in the past. Is Mrs. Newton aware of what's occurring?"

"Yes, she arranged it for me, but thank you for inquiring. It's lovely to hear that you're fretting."

He scowled, and it was clear he'd like to offer other comments, but there wasn't anything that would be appropriate. The dye was cast, her future rolling at her like a huge wave that was about to sweep her away.

He forced a smile. "I won't pester you further then. Mr. Roland is a fine man. A fine man! I'm certain it will work out for the best."

"I'm certain it will too."

She forced a smile in return, then walked out without glancing back.

"Are you sure about this?"

Pierre gazed up at Sophia. Emily was wandering in the driveway, picking up pebbles, studying them, then putting them in her mouth, but he was too distracted to fuss with her.

"Yes, I'm sure," Sophia said.

"But we don't even know Mr. Roland!"

"*I* know him. We've been acquainted for years. You'll like him."

She had no expression on her face. She looked frozen, as if—whatever Lord Swindon had done to her—she'd been altered into a marble statue that was incapable of feeling any emotion. He couldn't crash through the walls she'd erected.

"I thought . . ."

His voice trailed off. He shouldn't finish his sentence, but she frowned down at him and asked, "Thought what?"

"I thought Captain Stone would come for us, that he'd marry you. I was positive he would."

"Captain Stone is marrying Aurora. It's settled."

"He won't be glad to marry her. It is a grand mistake."

"Hush!" Sophia scolded. "We're leaving forever, and no matter what happens here later on, it's none of our affair."

"We're moving to this new city, to this place called York. Will we like it?"

"I've never been there, but it will be nice enough."

He wanted to shout at her, wanted to shake her, wanted to warn her that she was behaving like a lunatic, but he didn't tell her that. What did he know about adult problems? What did he know about how a poor woman kept herself safe?

A woman's lot was very bad, very difficult. His mother had taught him to be helpful to the women around him, to protect them and be gallant. Sophia had endured more than her share of tragedy, and he wished Captain Stone would arrive before they departed. Captain Stone was a fool and a dunce, and Pierre would like to punch him in the nose for breaking Sophia's heart.

A carriage rumbled out of the trees and started toward the manor. There were two men in the box. One of them waved and Sophia said, "There's Harry. Are we ready?"

Her knees gave out, and he leapt to steady her. She leaned on him until she'd mustered the fortitude to straighten and stand on her own. For just a moment, her mask slipped, and her true sentiments were revealed. She was sad, tormented, angry, and grieving. Then, as quickly as he'd witnessed her distress, she tucked it away.

He clasped her hand and squeezed her fingers. Her skin was like ice, and she was trembling slightly.

"You don't have to do this," he murmured. "We can find another road to travel. We can make another plan."

"I absolutely have to do it," she replied, "and it will be fine. You'll see."

She spun and merrily waved back at Mr. Roland, as if she'd been waiting for him all her life.

Chapter Twenty-Three

"It's Lord Swindon, Miss Jones. Will you see him?"

Sybil was seated at the dressing table in her boudoir. It was late on a Saturday afternoon, and she was about to leave for work. Her attire was always difficult to balance. She had chores to accomplish at the club, so she needed functional gowns and comfortable shoes, but she also spent most of her time in the gaming rooms, watching the place and socializing with the more important members.

For that task, she had to look like an heiress with a fortune.

She'd just bathed, so she was wearing a petticoat and chemise, a robe over the top. Her hair was pinned up, and she'd applied a few cosmetics. The extra color made her appear more glamorous, and at age forty, glamour was hard to manage.

She smirked at the housemaid who'd announced Neville's arrival. "He's such a haughty ass. If I ignore him, I don't suppose he'll go away."

Before the girl could respond, Neville bustled past her. "Sybil, darling, don't you dare kick me out. You're correct; I won't go. You'll have to muster the footmen to throw me out bodily."

Sybil rolled her eyes with disgust. Where he was concerned, she was such a milksop. She said to the housemaid, "Give him fifteen minutes to nag at me, then bring all the footmen. If he won't depart on his own, they can carry him out. I don't have a problem with that ending."

The girl had no desire to be caught in the middle of their petty spat, and she dashed away without a remark.

Once the door shut behind her, Sybil spun on her stool and glared up at him. Neville had never previously been inside her bedchamber. On several reckless occasions, she'd nearly invited him, but better sense had prevailed. His barging in was a surprising first.

"When I left Swindon," she said, "I could swear I was very clear that you should avoid me until after Christmas."

"I was certain you didn't mean it."

"I meant it, and when you act like an unrepentant fiend, I really don't like you."

He was hovered over by the door, as if unsure of his welcome. He should be unsure of it! But it was amusing to have him squirm and fidget. He was always suave and polished, and her ultimatum at Swindon must have had an effect. Though it was bizarre, he was feeling chastened and humbled.

She stood, thinking she'd step over to the liquor tray and pour them both a whiskey. As she moved to it, it spurred him to move too. He came over and wrapped his arms around her, hugging her tight.

"Forgive me," he murmured. "I'm a conceited prig. I'm ridiculous and annoying, and I admit it. Please don't be angry."

It was shocking to be embraced by him, to hear him begging her pardon, and without wondering if she should stop herself, she hugged him back.

"I guess I'm not angry," she sullenly replied. "Well, not *very* angry."

"Marry me," he suddenly said, and he trailed kisses across her cheek to her mouth.

Without a protest, she let him proceed. It was such a strange encounter, and they might have been walking toward a very high cliff. Would they jump off it into madness?

She was delighted to be kissed by him, but then, she spoiled the moment by quailing like an innocent virgin and drawing away.

"Hold on, hold on," she muttered.

She slid away and staggered to the liquor tray. She poured them a hefty drink, and she noted her hands were shaking. He took his glass from her, but he was determined to remain close. Their torsos were pressed together all the way down, and their proximity produced a perception of joy that was astounding.

"Marry me," he repeated. "If you tell me you won't, I can't imagine what will become of me."

"What brought this on?" She gulped her whiskey, anxious to slow her racing pulse. "When we last spoke, we quarreled viciously. In light of our hideous parting, why would you immediately contemplate matrimony?"

"After you fled Swindon, I couldn't bear to be there without you."

"You liar. Swindon Hall is a castle fit for a king, and you view yourself as royalty. It's the perfect spot for you."

"No, you're wrong. I was miserable without you, and when you weren't there to temper my worst impulses, I behaved stupidly over and over again. I've stirred a thousand different catastrophes."

"Name one thing you did that was imprudent."

"I sent Emily away. I persuaded myself that I don't want her, but I *do* want her. I truly do. Could we wed and raise her as our daughter? I was never a father to my boys, and I'd like to have a chance to parent one of my children."

"This spurt of nostalgia is so unlike you. I can't decide what to make of it, and I'm not convinced you're serious."

"You've considered raising Emily. I remember you mentioning it."

She *had* considered it—and quite furiously too. In fact, she could still birth her own child as well. She wasn't too old, but could she risk it with Neville?

He couldn't be trusted. He was a deceiver and cad, and no woman could rely on him. That had been the situation in his two marriages. His wives had believed he'd rein in his wicked tendencies for them, and they'd raged and pouted when he hadn't.

She knew him better than they had, so she would never expect stellar conduct. If he waltzed off to gamble and chase tarts, what was it to her? She'd simply take her children, along with a huge pot of his money, and vanish. He could stumble into his dotage alone, hoping his doxies would nurse him.

It was entirely possible that she liked him much more than she should. She also might like to be a wife, might like to experience domesticity. They reveled in the same bad habits, had the same dubious companions, wallowed in the same portion of the demimonde.

What if it turned out to be marvelous? Wouldn't that be lovely?

The biggest issue would be that they'd shock the toplofty world he inhabited, but that was his problem. Not hers. She didn't care what the snooty dolts of the aristocracy thought about her, but others would care. Currently, every mother in the land was dreaming of her daughter latching onto him now that he was an earl. If she yanked him off the Marriage Market, wouldn't she be saving many, many debutantes from disaster?

As she realized the extent of her musings, she scooted away from him again. She rounded the bed, using it as a barricade to keep him at bay.

"Yes, I've pondered raising Emily for Miss Cantwell," she told him. "I could contact her and ask them to live with me. It would solve Miss Cantwell's financial troubles, and I could give Emily the life she deserves. We wouldn't need you."

"You can't assume such a heavy responsibility by yourself," he said, "and you can't proceed without me. You have to help me with my other daughter too. With Joanna? I'd like to visit her and her husband, with you to act as an intermediary so I can befriend her."

"You don't really want that."

"I do, Sybil. I swear it to you."

She studied him, and she noticed that he seemed deflated, as if he was suffering genuine regrets. Was he?

"You're an old fool, Neville. Why would I shackle myself?"

"It's not so much that *you* should be eager. It's that I need you so you can prevent me from being so awful."

"What other mischief have you perpetrated? You claimed there were a thousand things."

"For starters, I found out that Sheridan had seduced Miss Cantwell."

"That bastard," Sybil crudely fumed. "I'd like to wring his neck."

"She expected him to marry her afterward, and Sheridan had declared he would, but I refused to allow it. I broke her heart and sent her home."

"What was Sheridan's reaction? Let me guess: He didn't care a whit. He's your son, so he presumes he can ruin a maiden with impunity. And he can."

"No, he's very angry too. I'm not sure he'll ever forgive me."

"Has he gone to fetch Miss Cantwell? Has he fixed what you wrecked?"

"You won't believe what happened. He disobeyed me—"

"Good. I'm thrilled to hear it."

"—and followed her to Riverglen, where she and Emily reside with her relatives, but when he arrived, there was a terrible incident."

Sybil frowned. "Miss Cantwell has had an accident? Is she ill? What?"

"No, Sheridan was gravely injured. I was positive he would propose to her cousin, Aurora Newton. He told me he would, so I wrote to her mother to inform her. Miss Newton had another suitor at the property who was very jealous, and he tried to murder Sheridan."

Sybil's jaw dropped. "Is he all right?"

"He will be, but the attack was my fault for writing that letter. I'm lucky he's alive. If the brigand's aim had been a bit straighter, I'd have orchestrated my son's death."

Sybil clucked her tongue. "You're being too melodramatic. As usual."

"Have I clarified why you can't leave me to my own devices? If you'd stayed at Swindon, you would have seen that Sheridan loved Miss Cantwell. You could have made me see it too. None of the rest would have transpired."

She chuckled, but miserably. "You're giving me too much credit for being smarter than you."

"You are smarter than me. I've always said so."

He set down his whiskey and walked over to where she was cowering behind the bed. To her stunned amusement, he clasped her hand and fell to one knee.

"Marry me, Sybil. You know you want to. You're as vain as I am. If you're my wife, think of how you can strut and preen as you stroll through the drawing rooms of High Society."

"If I was your countess, how would your snobbish friends ever survive it?"

"When have I ever worried about my friends' opinions?"

"How about always?"

He snorted at that. "You have to be my bride. You have to manage my life for me. You can't abandon me to flail like this. I grow more ridiculous by the day. Who can predict what disaster I'll stir next if you're not there to stop me?"

A knock sounded on the door, and her housemaid peered in. "It's been fifteen minutes, Miss Jones," the girl said. "Would you like me to escort Lord Swindon down to the foyer?"

Neville smirked and gazed up at Sybil, daring her to evict him.

She hovered, feeling perched on a tall fence. She could jump one way and continue to limp along in her rich, satisfying world. Or she could jump the other and take a chance on Neville Stone. She could be his countess, could lounge in his ostentatious mansions, with his wealthy, posh friends.

She could have a family filled with his strapping sons and his pretty daughters-in-law who were quickly beginning to have babies. She could assume custody of Emily and rear her in a stable manner. If she was fortunate, which she'd always been in the past, there might be a child of her own too.

And she'd have handsome, charming, unreliable Neville Stone as her husband. Why not try it? She'd never be bored. Of that fact, she had no doubt at all.

She glanced over at the housemaid and said, "Thank you, but Lord Swindon will be tarrying for a while."

"Very good, Miss."

The girl peeked at Neville, where he was still on his knees and holding Sybil's hand, then she tiptoed away. She hadn't been able to completely hide a flinch of surprise at what she'd witnessed, and Sybil could just imagine the rumors that would be swirling down in the kitchen.

Neville smirked again and stood. He reached in his coat and pulled out a gorgeous diamond ring. He slipped it onto her finger, and it fit perfectly. Diamonds were her favorite jewel; he knew that about her.

"Say yes, Sybil. I won't quit pestering you until you give me what I want."

Truer words were never spoken. He could be relentless.

"I will marry you, Neville," she said.

He blanched with shock. "Are you serious? I've convinced you?" His expression became very sly. "You're not teasing me, are you?"

"I'm not teasing, and I'll prove I can be a miracle-worker. I will wed you, obtain a guardianship over Emily, repair your relationships with your natural children, embrace the grandchildren who are coming, and maybe, just maybe, we'll have a child of our own someday."

"Could that occur?"

"Yes, so you may wind up in a bargain you never planned."

"I will never have enough of you, my dear. Not if I live to be a hundred."

He dipped in and kissed her, and they kept on for an eternity. She wasn't an innocent Miss, so it grew naughty very fast.

When he finally drew away, he was grinning, and he nodded to her bedchamber. "Let's have an early start to our wedding night. We can test your mattress to discover how comfortable it is."

"Are you joking? First of all, I'm needed at the club. Second of all, I won't lie down with you until you've repeated vows in front of a vicar. I may be smitten, but I'm not an idiot. I will *never* trust you."

"But you'll be mine forever?"

"Oh, yes, and with me as your wife, you're about to get exactly what you deserve."

~

"Who's there?"

Miles lurched awake and rose up on an elbow. He gaped around anxiously. What had roused him? Had it been a board creaking? Was a miscreant sneaking across the floor?

His heart was hammering so loudly that he couldn't hear a thing, and he collapsed onto the pillow. He was alone in the room! The slightest noises set off spirals of dread and alarm, and he had to control his careening nerves.

What had happened to Sheridan Stone?

The question was driving him insane.

He'd shot the man in the chest, and he was certain he'd been dead, dead, dead! But then, that carriage had approached, and Miles had raced to his office, keen to look innocent and appropriately concerned if Stone's body had been found.

He'd have voiced his dismay over the crime, would have summoned the magistrate, would have mustered the footmen to search the forest for evidence. He'd have appeared competent and involved, willing to help in a crisis, yet no one had stopped at the manor to report the incident.

After a sufficient interval had passed, Miles had crept back to the spot. He'd been prepared to bury Stone in the grave he'd dug in the woods, but Stone hadn't been there!

Miles had been in a panicked frenzy ever since. Stone's compatriot, George, must have located him, but was he deceased or not? Had George carried away a severely wounded man? Or had he dragged away a corpse? In either scenario, someone should have knocked at Riverglen, seeking information. What did it indicate?

If Sheridan Stone was still alive, then he could identify his assailant. If he'd perished, wouldn't there have been a notice in the newspapers? There hadn't been, and Miles checked every morning. Sheridan Stone was a prominent fellow. If he'd died, surely it would have been announced.

Homicide was a dirty business and much more disturbing than Miles had understood. He hadn't been able to conceal his distress. If the authorities ever launched an investigation, people would point at Miles and describe how cantankerous he'd been. His peculiar conduct might get him hanged in the end, for he had no doubt—if his transgression was exposed—he'd be executed.

No court in the land would show any mercy, despite how events had spurred him to murder. No judge would view his plight as an excuse.

Perhaps he ought to flee the country. He had a hoard of money that he'd stolen from Millicent. It was in a locked box under his bed. He could depart furtively, could trek to a nearby town, then ride the mail coach to London. He'd book passage to a far-off destination. He'd travel anonymously, and he'd vanish completely. Shouldn't he attempt it?

Yet it would mean abandoning Riverglen, so he would never receive what he felt was his absolute due. It was one more injustice dumped on the pile of wrongs that had consumed him since the day Sheridan Stone had waltzed in the door.

His wretched musings had him so aggravated that sleep would be impossible, but he tried to relax anyway. He shut his eyes and steadied his mind, when suddenly, a cold metal object was pressed to his cheek.

"Don't make a sound or you're dead," a man whispered.

Miles's eyes flew open and fear rushed through him. A black-clad stranger was hovered over him, a palm on his chest, a pistol holding him in place.

"Do you know who I am?" the man asked.

Miles's trembling almost pitched him onto the floor. "No, sir."

"I am Hunter Stone. I am Captain Sheridan Stone's brother."

Miles blanched with fright. "Oh, no . . ."

"Did you think we wouldn't come for you? Did you think you wouldn't have to pay?"

"What do you want?" Miles inquired. "Is it money? I can give you money. I have plenty of it."

"I don't want your money, Miles Bernard. I want *you*. Take a good look at my face. Take a good look so you never forget it."

Miles gulped with terror, and he would have screamed for help, but Stone stuck a kerchief down his throat, muzzling him, then he raised the gun and hit Miles alongside the head with the barrel. The blow was fierce and powerful, and he was totally discombobulated by it.

"Tie his hands and feet," Stone said to someone. "Let's get him out of here."

He raised the gun again and hit Miles even harder. After that, Miles didn't remember anything at all.

"I VOTE TO KILL him."

"I agree."

Miles roused slowly, male voices luring him to consciousness. He peered about, desperate to figure out where he was, but he had no idea.

He appeared to be in a deep thicket of woods, and dawn was breaking in the east. The temperature was frigid, and he was wearing only his nightshirt. His feet were bare, and he could see his breath when he exhaled, so he was freezing. Once he realized he was, he started to shiver uncontrollably.

He struggled to move his limbs, to shift himself into a more comfortable position, but to his horror, he was lashed to the trunk of a tree. He made a few paltry efforts to free himself, but the ropes were too tight, so he relented and sagged against his bindings. He would have called for assistance, but his mouth was gagged, so shouting was futile.

Three men stood in front of him. The one in the middle was the vicious fiend, Hunter Stone, who'd assaulted him in his bedchamber. The man on his right had to be his twin brother; they were that similar. The man on his left was older, perhaps forty or so, and he was trim and dapper, as if he could be a valet. He exuded a steely aura though that hinted he could be dangerous.

Miles visually searched for Sheridan Stone, but he didn't seem to be present. In his befuddled state, he couldn't decide if that was good news or bad. Was it better for Miles if he was deceased? Or if he was alive?

"Look who's awake," Hunter Stone said, and he loomed up in such a chilling manner that Miles cringed.

"Mmm . . . mmm . . ." The gag blocked his words, and Hunter Stone ripped it away.

"What was that?" Stone asked.

"Where are we? What's happening?"

"We're debating whether to kill you or not," Stone nonchalantly replied. "If the verdict is death, we intend to inflict the most painful ending ever delivered."

Miles quailed with alarm. "Kill me! We're in England, and we have laws about homicide. You can't just murder a fellow."

At hearing his comment, the three men hooted with laughter, and Hunter Stone whacked Miles with his fist.

"You have the gall," Stone said, "to claim it isn't allowed? You—who tried your best to slay my baby brother?"

"I can't fathom what you're talking about," Miles insisted. "I've never lifted a finger to harm another man in my life."

They hooted again, and Hunter Stone introduced his companions. "This is my brother, Warwick Stone. The other gentleman is George Barnes. He's a bodyguard who can be very violent when riled. They've both already voted to murder you."

"What about you, Mr. Stone?" Miles asked.

"It's Viscount Marston to you, you little prick."

"Sorry. I didn't know."

Marston whacked him again, forcefully enough that he saw stars, then Marston asked, "Do I have your attention now?"

"Yes, yes, you definitely have it. What is *your* opinion? I am innocent of any malfeasance, so I haven't the slightest clue as to why you're angry. I hope you'll inject some sanity into this discussion."

"You should be so lucky," Marston mumbled.

"If you'll take me home," Miles said, "we can pretend you never kidnapped me. I'll never tell a soul."

Marston snickered. "Nice try, Mr. Bernard, but I'm afraid I can't oblige you. Unfortunately for you, *I* voted to kill you too."

"For what reason?" Miles huffed. "I repeat: I've done nothing wrong!"

Marston feigned confusion. "Did you, or did you not, accost my brother, Sheridan, on the lane leading up to Riverglen and shoot him in the chest?"

"What a bizarre suggestion! I'm barely acquainted with him, so why would I attack him? If he says so, I demand you produce the deceitful cur immediately, and I shall call him a liar to his face."

As Miles uttered his challenge, Warwick Stone and George Barnes stepped to the side, and Miles was finally able to view what they'd hidden from him. Sheridan Stone was behind them, his hips leaned on a large boulder. His arm was in a sling, and he had a fading bruise on his forehead from where Miles had clocked him with his pistol, but other than that, he looked exceedingly hale.

Miles slumped with defeat. Of course Sheridan Stone was alive and well. Of course Miles hadn't succeeded. He was a complete incompetent. He couldn't marry the girl he'd been destined to marry. He couldn't seize the property that was supposed to be his. He couldn't slay his worst enemy.

If he hadn't been so thoroughly bewildered, he might have wept.

"Hello, Miles," Sheridan Stone said. "Fancy meeting you here."

"Captain Stone! You're looking awfully fit and . . . fit."

"I guess I am, considering how you shot me and left me for dead. You just told my brother that you'd like to speak to me, face to face, so you could call me a liar. Would you like to try?"

"No . . . ah . . . I don't have anything to tell you."

"Seriously? It seems to me you should have numerous comments to share. Are you sorry that you attempted to murder me? Will you apologize? Or are you simply wishing your aim had been a little better? If I had to pick, I'd bet you're wishing your aim had been better."

Miles glared at him, his hatred oozing out. There were many villains he could blame for his current predicament: Oscar, Millicent, Aurora, Sophia. But Sheridan Stone encapsulated every wound that had been inflicted. He loathed the man with an abiding passion, but he didn't suppose he was in any condition to admit it.

"I haven't been thinking about you at all," Miles claimed. "I'm especially not thinking about you at the moment. I'm freezing, and I'd like to go home. How can I convince you to allow it?"

"You can't." Captain Stone snickered with offense. "Do you know what really rankles me, Miles? You were angry because you thought I intended to propose to Aurora Newton."

"She was mine!" Tears surged to Miles's eyes. "Her father arranged it, and her mother is a lunatic who decided, at the very last minute, that my engagement shouldn't be honored. She gave Aurora to you instead! How was I to view such a duplicitous turn of events?"

"Here's a tidbit I expect will surprise you," Captain Stone said. "I was there to propose to Sophia Cantwell. She's who I'm marrying. Aurora Newton can jump off a cliff."

Lord Marston butted in with, "You see, Mr. Bernard, you shot him for no reason. If you'd behaved rationally, we wouldn't find ourselves in this situation."

Miles couldn't believe it. He could *not* believe it! Sheridan Stone had been coming for Sophia?

He started to laugh uproariously, his mirth growing until he sounded quite mad. Sophia had moved to York to wed Harry Roland, and evidently, Captain Stone had no idea! She was probably already married, and Miles realized, through the fog of his confused mental state, that he should be quiet about it.

He would have a final, petty revenge. If Sophia hadn't yet tied the knot with Harry Roland, Miles wanted them to have plenty of time to walk down the aisle. He detested Sophia and reviled Sheridan Stone. If he could wreck any chance for them to end up together, it would be a double retaliation he would always celebrate.

"I'm sure you and Sophia will be very happy," Miles spat out, and he laughed even harder.

"Must we continue to listen to him?" George Barnes asked. "I can't put up with much more."

"We don't have to keep listening," Lord Marston said, and he slapped Miles as a warning to control himself. "Pay attention now. What would you like to say to my brother?"

Miles glowered furiously at Captain Stone. "He tried to take everything from me, and I couldn't let him. If he was harmed, it was his own fault, and I have no sympathy."

Warwick Stone and George Barnes gasped, and Lord Marston said, "That is the most pitiful, self-serving drivel I have ever heard."

"It's the truth," Miles insisted. "He deserved what happened to him."

"Are you deaf?" Lord Marston asked. "He wasn't stealing your fiancée! He doesn't even like her. There was no need to shoot him."

There was logic in Lord Marston's argument, but Miles was just so aggrieved. He couldn't muster any remorse or regret. He'd simply like to have a magic clock that could wind back Time to the days when Sophia was in France.

Miles had been content then, but after Sophia had returned, his world had collapsed. At least it seemed that way. He was battered and befuddled though, so he wasn't entirely certain his assessment was correct, but it felt right. She was a menace, and he was delighted to deem her to be the guilty party.

And he'd gotten even, hadn't he? He hadn't breathed a word about her and Harry Roland.

Lord Marston glanced at Captain Stone and said, "What shall we do with him? What's your preference? You know the conclusion Warwick and I would like to implement."

George Barnes added, "It's not necessary for me to reiterate my opinion."

Captain Stone pushed himself to his feet, and he approached until he and Miles were toe to toe. He towered over Miles, staring down at him as if he were a snake in the grass.

"My brothers and Mr. Barnes are eager to murder you," Captain Stone said. "All three of them are adept at that sort of thing. Should I allow them to proceed?"

Miles peered up at Stone, thinking he looked like a calm, composed killer himself. His gaze was firm, his expression steely, his body taut as a wire. Even in his reduced condition, he could probably snap Miles in half like a twig.

So far, the encounter had played out like a dream, as if he'd eventually awaken, but it was very real. Could he save himself? Was it possible? He had to stop being petulant and start being repentant. Captain Stone would determine Miles's fate, so Miles had to sway him to mercy.

He vehemently shook his head. "No! You can't allow them to proceed!"

"Why shouldn't I? I'd like to murder you myself, but I'm not spry enough. You can congratulate yourself on that. You nearly killed me."

"Don't murder me! Please!" Miles begged. "I'll do whatever you ask. Just tell me what you want."

"I could untie you so we could fight—man to man—but again, I'm not spry enough. We could duel, but I won't furnish you with a second opportunity to shoot at me, so what would you advise?"

"I would advise that you permit me to go home, and we'll forget about this unfortunate incident."

"That isn't about to happen." Stone smirked, then he reached out with his good hand and grabbed Miles by the throat. He squeezed tight, cutting off Miles's air to the point where he wondered if he'd fall unconscious. Then Stone released him and shifted away. He limped to the boulder and eased his hips onto it.

Miles began to cry. "I thought you were there to take what was mine. Millicent Newton informed me it's what she'd arranged with your father. Was I to blithely step aside so you could have it all?"

"I understand your view of it," Captain Stone said. "It's why I haven't had you killed already."

George Barnes scoffed. "I'll likely kill you whether the Captain wishes it or not. I'm contrary that way."

Captain Stone held up a palm, halting any quarrel. "I've decided to give you a choice, Miles."

His brothers groaned, and George Barnes fumed, "Don't give the bloody oaf any choices."

"I feel sorry for him," Captain Stone told them, then he said to Miles, "You may choose to die right here, right now. It's been settled who will pull the trigger."

"I won the short straw," Viscount Marston said, and he grinned evilly. "I will be your executioner, and I won't make your death quick or painless."

The Captain continued. "My brother can proceed immediately. Or you can leave Riverglen and England forever."

"I'll . . . I'll . . . leave!" Miles hastily stammered.

"You should be aware of the terms first."

"I don't care what they are. I'll do it."

Captain Stone explained anyway. "Mr. Barnes will transport you to London, and you'll be conscripted onto a sailing ship for seven years. When your contract is complete—if you've survived—you will go ashore in America."

Miles blanched. It was a death sentence. He was a land agent, a glorified clerk. He'd never previously been on a ship, and he certainly didn't have the physical stamina for that type of grueling existence, but he would take his chances at sea.

"Yes, yes, that's fine," he said. "I'll be conscripted. I have no problem with that ending."

"You can't return to England," Captain Stone said. "Not ever. I'm positive you're scheming on how you would, but if I ever learn that you dared, I will have Hunter track you down. Then again, I'll be recovered in the future, and I won't need to have him kill you. I'll handle it myself."

"I'll never come back. I swear."

Yet the Captain had correctly assumed that Miles was plotting as to how he'd sneak back later on. How would Stone ever know? Who would tell him? It wasn't as if he'd be married to Sophia and would hear about Miles.

"I'm sick of him," Captain Stone said to Lord Marston. "Get him out of my sight."

"With pleasure," his brother replied.

Marston drew out a knife, and for a moment, Miles quailed with terror as he feared Marston was about to stab him and he'd be murdered after all. But the brute simply sliced through the bindings that had kept Miles lashed to the tree. As the ropes fell to his feet, his knees gave out, and he collapsed to the ground.

He huddled in the dirt, counting his lucky stars, as George Barnes marched over and spat, "Bastard."

He hit Miles very hard. Hit him again and again, and as Miles slid into oblivion, he figured it would be a good way to travel to London. He wouldn't have to worry about a single thing.

"Is it Miles? Is there finally some news?"

Millicent glanced over as Aurora rushed into her boudoir. She was seated at the table by the window, having breakfast.

"No, there's still no news," Aurora said, "but look at this!"

Aurora was carrying a box, and she brought it over and set it down. There had once been a lock on the front, but it had been pried away. Aurora lifted the lid to show her that it contained a substantial amount of money.

Millicent's jaw dropped. "What on earth . . . ?"

"The housemaids were cleaning Miles's room," Aurora said. "It was tucked under his bed, and he'd warned them to never touch it, but they thought I should peek into it, that it might provide a clue as to where he's gone."

"Did it?"

"No, but why would he have so much money under his bed? He had to have secreted it away for some reason. Was he stealing from us?"

"That boy never surprised me," Millicent told her. "I'm not missing him. Are you?"

Aurora scoffed with derision. "Definitely not. The last few weeks were absolutely hideous. I hadn't realized he was possessed of such a temper. On numerous occasions, I was downright afraid of him."

"So was I. It's why I had the maids sleep with me. I wasn't about to be alone at night. I'll be glad to have Captain Stone as your husband. If we have a strong man in residence, he'll deal with these kinds of problems for us. Not that I anticipate any such horror occurring again."

"Where do you imagine Miles went?" Aurora asked. "If you had to pick a spot, what would you select?"

"I have no idea where he might be."

"Should we be more concerned about him? Should we hire an investigator to search? Should we notify the magistrate? It seems dodgy that he vanished without a trace. What if he met with foul play?"

She and Aurora hadn't noticed his absence. Neither had the servants. It had come to light when a tenant farmer had been curious that he'd skipped a regular appointment, so Millicent wasn't exactly sure when he'd disappeared.

If he'd departed willingly, he hadn't taken any of his belongings. Not his clothes. Not his portmanteau. Not any of his coats, cloaks, or hats. The area was suffering a spate of very cold weather, so it wasn't likely he'd have left without wrapping up. What could have happened to him?

Millicent considered Aurora's question. Should they mount a search? What if they located him? Why would Millicent want him back?

Ultimately, she shrugged. "This is rural England, so the chance of him meeting with foul play is practically inconceivable. Whatever transpired, whether he orchestrated his own disappearance or whether there was a mishap, I really can't have him here in the future. Not after how he acted toward you and me. Do you wish he'd return?"

Aurora actually shuddered with dread. "No! I don't wish for it."

"Then we'll just wait on him. He may stumble in." She grinned. "Or he may not."

Aurora pulled out a chair and sat down. She grabbed a scone off Millicent's breakfast tray and nibbled at it.

"It's so quiet without Sophia," she said, "and I feel she and I were quarreling when we parted. Why didn't you make her delay so she could say goodbye to me?"

"Mr. Roland was in a hurry, and they had a long journey ahead of them, so she couldn't have tarried. We didn't know where you were, and there was no time to hunt for you."

"It's wrong that she crept off without a word to me."

Millicent smirked. "She didn't fly to the moon, and she's not dead. She's in York. You can visit her."

"I'll think about it, but first, may we discuss Sheridan Stone? Am I about to be married? He never arrived to propose, and he couldn't be bothered to contact us with an explanation as to why. What must he intend with regard to me? Am I still to be betrothed to him or what?"

"As far as I'm aware, that's the plan."

Millicent's mail had been delivered, and as Aurora was lamenting, she sifted through the stack. She found a letter from Neville Stone, and she yanked it out of the pile and waved it at Aurora. "It's from Lord Swindon. We must have conjured a reply simply by pondering him so avidly."

"What has he told you?" Aurora was giddy as a girl on Christmas morning.

Millicent yearned to share an exciting message, but when she realized what Lord Swindon had penned, she frowned and murmured, "Oh, dear."

"What is it? Is it bad news? From your dour expression, it must be."

"Apparently, there's been a mistake. Captain Stone has decided you wouldn't suit, but Lord Swindon was confused about his son's preference. He wrote to me, claiming the engagement would occur, but his son wasn't about to proceed."

Aurora gaped with astonishment. "Does that sound the least bit plausible to you?"

"No, it sounds ridiculous and furtive. I'm certain he's lying." Millicent snorted with disdain, then read to the end. "He is *very* sorry to have misled us."

"But . . . but . . . I've been waiting for Captain Stone for ages. What now?"

Millicent sighed. "We'll have to start over with finding you a beau."

"I'll have to debate if I should trust you about it. Your initial candidates—Miles and Sheridan Stone—weren't exactly stellar choices. I might like to run Riverglen on my own, without a husband to boss me. I'm positive I'd be more proficient at it than Miles ever was *and* I promise I will never steal money from you and hide it under my bed."

"I wouldn't mind if there was no man on the premises," Millicent said. "I agree that they can be very annoying. If you'd like to delay a betrothal, that's fine with me. The last two exhausted me, and we're happier alone. Let's keep it that way."

Aurora was in the main parlor and staring out the window at the crisp autumn day. The house was silent as a tomb, but then, it had never been a noisy place. Her mother never left her room, and her father had spent most of his time in London.

Caroline and Sophia had imbued the dreary abode with tons of giggles, and more and more, Aurora caught herself missing them. When they'd been growing up together, she'd been a horrid snot to them, and she regretted how she'd treated them. She'd viewed them as silly, impertinent, and very much below her grand self.

Yet Caroline was deceased, and Sophia had moved away. She'd taken Caroline's daughter with her. It was another regret for Aurora, that she hadn't befriended Emily. The toddler was a precocious darling, and Aurora had ignored her.

Would she ever mature into a better person? Shouldn't she make an attempt? Or would she be snooty and awful forever?

Besides her guilt for her prior behavior toward Caroline and Sophia, she was generally enjoying her life as it was currently structured. She liked being in charge very much.

She was learning how to read the estate ledger books, but it was a slow education. Money was unaccounted for, which was probably why they'd found some under Miles's bed. He'd been a competent thief, but the nerve of him! The gall!

After how her family had supported him for years! If he ever slithered back, there would be no spot for him at Riverglen.

She noticed activity out on the lane, and she focused in, trying to figure out what was transpiring. A cavalcade of horsemen and carriages was arriving, as if they were hosting a huge party and dozens of guests were pulling in all at once. The servants had noticed the parade too, and the butler retrieved her cloak and wool hat, so she could exit the house to welcome whoever it was.

There were several equestrians at the front, and they were leading four ornate coaches, complete with outriders in red livery with gold braid. The entire entourage was so posh that it might have been a royal visit.

The first coach rattled to a halt, and the door was quickly opened so the occupants could climb out. When Sheridan Stone emerged, she was incredibly bewildered. His father had been very clear that he wasn't interested in marrying her, and she couldn't imagine he'd changed his mind about that. Even if he had, *she* was no longer interested.

She had quite a bit of pride, and he'd wounded it. She would never agree to be his wife.

Another man jumped out behind him, and he hovered close, a hand on the Captain's back, as if he needed to be steadied as his feet hit the ground. To her surprise, his arm was in a sling, and he had a terrible bruise on his forehead, as if he'd suffered an accident.

"Greetings, Captain Stone," she said to him as he walked over to her. "I must admit that I'm stunned to see you at Riverglen."

"I've brought my father and brothers, plus an assortment of friends and servants. Is Sophia here? I must talk to her immediately."

"Sophia?" Aurora frowned. "I'm sorry, but no, she's not here."

He studied her curiously, as if she'd babbled in a language he didn't understand. "What can you mean by she's not *here*? Is she away on holiday? Has she taken a job somewhere? What's happened? Is she all right?"

"I guess that depends on what standard you're using. She's marrying our neighbor, Harry Roland, and they moved to York."

He gasped with dismay and sagged slightly as if his leg might give out. The other man leapt to brace him.

"She can't have!" the Captain said. "*I* have come to marry her myself."

"You want to marry Sophia?" Aurora was extremely confused.

"Yes. It's all I've ever wanted—since the moment I met her. Why would she do this to me?"

"Mother arranged it for her. Mr. Roland has obtained employment in York and was leaving. She went with him."

"No, that's not possible." He looked as if he might collapse.

Aurora could have been petty and cruel, as was her usual habit. She could have concealed desperate information he would love to receive, but she was working to be kinder, to improve herself.

"May I ease your shock just a tad?" she said. "I'm not sure the ceremony is over. They were planning to call the banns at their new church, but I don't know when the clock started running. I can't guess if she's a bride already, but if she's not and you hurry, you might be able to talk her out of it."

"Or I might be too late," he said.

"You can ride to York. You can try."

An older gentleman, who had to be his father, leaned out the window of the biggest, fanciest coach and asked the Captain, "Are we getting out or what?"

Captain Stone stomped over to him. "Sophia has gone to York—to wed someone else!"

Lord Swindon clasped a fist over his heart. "Oh, oh, that can't be true."

"They might not have held the service yet," Captain Stone said, "so I have to race there to stop her, but if I can't, I will never forgive you. I swear it."

He grabbed a horse from one of the equestrians, and his male companion had to help him climb into the saddle. Then he spurred the animal down the lane and vanished in the trees.

An outrider tipped his cap to her and said, "Our apologies for having bothered you, Miss."

The whole caravan continued on around the curved driveway and followed after Captain Stone. Evidently, they were headed to York to keep Sophia from marrying the wrong man.

Would they arrive in time?

The question was thrilling, and it made Aurora wish she could have tagged along to learn the answer.

Chapter Twenty-Four

"Pierre, can you quiet her please?"

"*Oui,* Sophia. Give her to me."

Sophia picked up Emily and handed her to Pierre. She'd been having a permanent temper tantrum, and he was the only one who could calm her down. Sophia couldn't blame her for being irritable. She was just two years old, but in that short interval, she'd suffered nothing but tragedy. Shouldn't she be allowed to protest her situation?

Sophia hated how it was impacting Harry though. He was such a nice man, and he'd assumed such heavy burdens in order to rescue her. Emily's constant fussing was very draining to him. He never lost his temper, but Sophia often caught him staring at Emily, probably wondering if he'd been mad to proceed.

Pierre balanced Emily on his hip and walked off with her. She was growing fast, so he could barely carry her. He murmured to her in French, and the language soothed her. Perhaps it had her remembering the period when her mother had still been alive, and people around her had spoken French too.

They were in the church, up by the altar and waiting for the Vicar to step out and start the ceremony. They didn't have any guests in attendance. They hadn't been in the city very long, so they had no friends.

Harry had his new boss and a few coworkers who'd been cordial, but he hadn't felt comfortable inviting them. Sophia had hired a nanny who was turning out to be lazy and unlikable, so she was sitting in the back with Sophia's housemaid. They were gossiping and clearly not interested in what was happening up front.

The empty pews underscored how alone Sophia was in the world. She had no father to escort her down the aisle, no mother to help her dress for the big day. She had no elderly aunties to grin and furnish nuptial advice. She had some scattered cousins, mostly in the Newton family, but they'd never cared about her.

She was on her own, as she'd always been. She had no tether to fetter her to the ground, no roots and no home. She had to hurry and bind herself to Harry before Emily overwhelmed him and he changed his mind. It was difficult to be optimistic, and she was certain she was making a huge mistake. She'd be miserable forever, so *he* would be miserable forever. After he'd been so gracious, she couldn't bear to be responsible for ruining his life.

She shouldn't have been bothered by the fact that it wasn't a love match, and she'd sworn to Harry that she'd never contemplate Sheridan Stone, but she kept recalling the affection she'd possessed for him. When she'd previously discovered how hotly amour could flare, it was so wrong to forge ahead, but it was too late to complain or renege.

She'd agreed to let Harry save her, and she was loyal and dependable. She'd given him her word, and she would follow through if it killed her—which it might.

"I'm sorry," she told him. "I know her prattling annoys you. She's been so grouchy since . . ." She cut off her sentence. She'd nearly said, *since we left Swindon,* but she'd promised to never discuss the dreaded spot. "She's been out of sorts since we left Riverglen."

"I've never spent time around a toddler. Are they always so peevish?"

"I think they are. It's what I've heard anyway, and she's just a baby who's endured too many disasters. It commenced with her losing her mother and rolled downhill from there. She'll settle down after she's more accustomed to our surroundings."

"I hope so," Harry said, but he didn't sound convinced.

He peeked over his shoulder to where Pierre was hovered in a corner, doing his best to silence her, but it was a thankless task. She had a story to tell him, and he couldn't persuade her to hush.

"Should we have him take her outside?" Harry asked.

"I guess we can."

"Will it distress you?"

"No, it's fine."

Emily and Pierre were her only family though, and if Sophia kicked them out, she'd have no kin to witness the important occasion.

Harry seemed to recognize her dismay, and he reached out and squeezed her hand. She struggled valiantly not to flinch. It was meant to be a supportive gesture, but the touch of his skin to hers was disturbing on so many levels. She'd learned about the physical acts that transpired in the bedroom, and in her rush to glom onto him, she hadn't paused to consider the true consequences of wedlock.

Once the service was over, she would have to share a bed with him. Her body would become his property, and he could do whatever he wanted with it. Could she remove her clothes and engage in the antics that Captain Stone had shown her?

She was nauseated over the entire notion, and it had her frantically wishing she'd pondered the ramifications a little more carefully. But hadn't that been her main problem in life? She never pondered.

Her courage flagged, and she almost blurted out that she couldn't proceed, but she was forestalled by a door opening off to the side of the altar. The Vicar strolled out in his vestments, clutching his prayerbook, and he came over to where they were standing.

"Mr. Roland? Miss Cantwell? Are we ready?"

"Yes, sir, we're ready," Harry said.

"It's always a splendid day for a wedding. Shall we start?"

"If you wouldn't mind," Harry politely replied.

He sensed Sophia's nerves, and he pulled her close, an arm across her back, as if he was bracing her so she didn't fall down. Or perhaps so she couldn't turn and run out of the building. She was trembling, her quaking quite noticeable.

"Don't fret," he whispered. "This will be over before you know it."

The Vicar glanced out at the empty pews. Did he feel, as she did, that it signaled a bad beginning? His expression was blank, concealing his opinion.

He straightened his spectacles, cleared his throat, then he recited the introductory words of the ceremony. "Dearly beloved, we are gathered here in the sight of God to join this man and this woman in holy matrimony."

She watched him with a sort of dreamy detachment, as if the event wasn't really happening, as if she wasn't about to be a wife. He droned on for a while, then the volume of Emily's fussing increased. Pierre tried to shush her, but to no avail, and the noise was very distracting.

The minister scowled at Emily, then at Sophia, his impatience obvious, and she asked, "Can you give me a minute? I'll talk to her."

She went over to where Pierre was holding Emily, and she leaned down and said, "Miss Emily, you are being very naughty. You must be quiet."

Emily babbled a string of complaints, in her toddler's mix of French and English, and Pierre translated. "She doesn't want to be here. She's cold and hungry, and she wants to go home."

Sophia sighed with irritation and offered a bribe. "If you'll pipe down, you may have cake once we're finished. Would you like that?"

"Oui! Oui!"

Emily often pretended she didn't understand scolding comments, but she was very spoiled, so it was her way of controlling a conversation. She understood *cake* well enough, and she clapped with excitement.

"To receive it," Sophia said, "you must sit in the front pew and behave yourself. Will you? Or there will be no cake later on."

Emily flashed a flirtatious grin at Pierre, and he said, "Yes, Miss Emily will behave. She promises."

Sophia carried her over, hoping—if she was in the middle of the action—she'd be more interested in what was occurring. She wouldn't sit down though, but remained on her feet, balanced against the bench. Pierre slid next to her, a palm on her tummy so she didn't trip and somersault to the floor.

Sophia trudged over to Harry, and to both him and the Vicar, she murmured, "My apologies. She's a handful."

The Vicar smiled a placating smile. "Yes, she definitely seems to be."

Sophia couldn't help it. She burst into tears. She was just so weary, and life was so hard. It was her wedding day! She should have been merry and glad, but instead, she was drained and beaten down.

On witnessing her morose state, Harry looked stricken, and he immediately produced a kerchief so she could dry her eyes.

"Don't cry, Sophia. The world won't end if Miss Emily chatters a bit."

She peered up at the Vicar, and his glower indicated he didn't concur with Harry's assessment.

Sophia couldn't blame him for being annoyed. Children were supposed to be seen, but not heard, especially in church. Other people had agreeable, well-mannered children who'd been taught how to act in social situations. How would she ever be a competent parent to Emily? If she ever had her own children, how would she parent them? She had no idea how.

Every task thrown into her road was particularly heavy, as if she were a hero in a Greek tragedy who'd been burdened by the gods to figure out how to get home in one piece.

"Miss Cantwell," the Vicar said, "are you sure you're in a condition to continue? I've had many odd moments transpire in my years of officiating at weddings, but I've never had a bride who was weeping. Are you certain you're willing? Would you like to pause so you can compose yourself? Or we could reschedule for a morning when you're not so distraught."

"I'm not distraught," she insisted. "I'm just tired." She returned Harry's kerchief, and she took several deep breaths to calm herself. She couldn't encourage any delay. If there was one, she—or Harry—might back out. What would she do then? "Please begin where you left off. Emily swears she won't interrupt, and I'd like to keep going."

Harry linked their fingers, and they gazed up at the irked minister. He bristled, then started in as she'd requested. She focused on his shoes rather than what was actually unfolding. Occasionally, he asked her questions she had to answer, but for the most part, she was so disconnected that she might have been seated on a star up in the sky.

The Vicar said, "If there's any person present who feels this couple should not be joined in holy matrimony, let him speak now or forever hold his peace."

There was the obligatory silence, where they waited for a protest that was never voiced, and it dawned on her that *she* could object. Why didn't she? The prospect was so riveting that she physically bit down on her tongue so she wouldn't spew a remark she didn't mean.

Suddenly, the church doors were flung open. It was chilly and blustery outside, the temperature frigid, and a gust of icy wind swept down the center aisle. It slithered under the hem of her gown, making her shiver, as if it was literally an ill-wind blowing in to warn her that she shouldn't proceed.

A boisterous crowd entered the vestibule. They were mingling, talking loudly, the ceremony being interrupted again.

The Vicar lost patience. He snapped his prayerbook closed and called, "Excuse me! There is a wedding in progress. I must ask that you exhibit the proper deference for such a sacred service. If you can't control yourselves, then you must depart until we're finished."

Sophia and Harry glanced back, wondering who the rude devils could be, when one of them stomped toward them. To her stunned amazement, it appeared to be Sheridan Stone. How could that be?

She blinked over and over, positive she was hallucinating. Was her misery so acute that she'd conjured him out of thin air? But no, it was really and truly him.

He was handsome as ever, dressed like the pirate he was: white shirt, tan trousers, knee-high black boots. They were scuffed and needed a good polishing though, as if he'd had a hard ride.

He was bundled against the weather, wearing a heavy wool coat, his nose and cheeks red from the cold, so he looked vibrant and dashing. Most peculiarly, his arm was in a sling, and he had an awful bruise on his forehead, and she was shocked by the wave of dismay that surged through her.

Had he suffered an accident? She was devastated to suppose he'd been harmed in even the slightest way.

Harry confirmed her suspicion that he wasn't an apparition by muttering, "What is *he* doing here? How dare he strut in! Hasn't he done enough?"

The Vicar frowned down at Captain Stone and said, "Will you state your business, sir?"

"Gladly," Captain Stone replied. "Have you reached the section where you ask if anyone objects to the match?"

"Well . . . ah . . . yes, I just posed that question," the Vicar told him.

"I most vehemently object." He wedged himself between her and Harry, pushing Harry away. "I'm sorry, Mr. Roland, but Sophia is mine, and she always has been. You can't have her."

Harry was quite gallant. He pulled himself up to his full height, but next to the Captain, it wasn't very impressive. He huffed and fumed and said, "You have the gall to show up? Now? When *I* am about to rectify your sins? Now? When I'm about to save her from disgrace and humiliation?"

It was impossible to castigate Sheridan Stone. He couldn't be cowed or berated. He was an egotistical maniac, and any chastisement bounced off him like dull arrows.

"I understand your pique," he said to Harry, "but in my own defense, I've been a tad busy, so I couldn't fetch her any sooner. And my exalted father"—he spat the word *father* as if it were an epithet—"didn't exactly help to spur matters along."

Emily was in the front pew and studying the people who were still milling in the vestibule. At his mentioning Lord Swindon, she shrieked with delight and called, "Papa! Papa!"

They all peered to the vestibule too, observing as the despicable roué sauntered in and promenaded down the aisle as if he owned it.

"Dear Emily!" he crooned, and he swooped in and picked her up, balancing her on his hip. "Where have you been?"

She patted his cheeks with her chubby little hands, prattling away in her patois, and it definitely sounded as if she was scolding him, demanding to know why he'd abandoned her to chaos.

"Did you miss me, my tiny pet?" Lord Swindon asked her.

"Yes! *Oui!*" she gleefully gushed, and she preened for the spectators, loving to be the center of attention.

A large mob flooded in behind the Earl: Sybil Jones, Captain Stone's brothers, their wives, the fiend George Barnes, and a score of servants who must have traveled with the Earl. What was happening? How had they found Sophia? Why would they have been searching?

She felt as if she should offer a comment, but she couldn't imagine what it would be. She was too astounded to speak. The Vicar had had enough though, and he glared at the Earl and said, "You, sir! You have delayed our ceremony. Would you like to explain your intentions?"

"I am Neville Stone, Earl of Swindon." At the announcement, the paltry collection of onlookers gasped and stood a bit straighter. "I have come to stop one wedding and to hold a completely different one."

"This is highly irregular," the Vicar huffed.

"Yes, isn't it?" the Earl blithely responded.

Harry stepped forward and bowed. "Lord Swindon, I mean no disrespect, but you're not welcome here, and your son's presence is very distressing to my fiancée. I must ask that you assemble your entourage and leave immediately."

Sophia was very proud of him, but Lord Swindon ignored his request. "I regret to inform you, Mr. Roland, that you won't be marrying anyone today. Not Miss Cantwell anyway. She's about to be my daughter-in-law."

"I am not!" Sophia mumbled. She couldn't tamp down the remark.

Hunter and Warwick Stone moved to Harry, one on each side, boxing him in with their bigger size, and Hunter Stone said, "Why don't we have a chat, Mr. Roland? I'll clarify some details, and we'll arrange everything to your satisfaction."

The brothers clasped Harry's arms and marched him away as if he were a criminal who was being carted off to jail. The initial few strides, he was too stunned to resist, then he struggled to yank away, but they were taller, stronger, and much more determined than he was.

"Sophia!" he called over his shoulder. "Don't listen to them! Don't let them bully you!" but that was all he could manage.

In seconds, they had him out of the church, and a deadly silence descended.

Then Miss Jones approached Sophia and said, "I can see we've embarrassed you, so I'm sorry for that, but you'll learn over the years that, when you're dealing with the men of the Stone family, you have to be prepared for any preposterous conduct."

"Too right, Miss Jones!" Sophia seethed.

"Sheridan would like to speak with you. In private. Won't you oblige us?" Miss Jones didn't wait for Sophia's reply. She glanced up at the Vicar and said, "Is there a room nearby where they can be alone?"

He sighed and gestured to the door off the altar. Sophia stared longingly at the spot where Harry had vanished, and it seemed as if a piece of her future had vanished with him. It was fading in the distance.

Lord Swindon said to Sophia, "You must confer with Sheridan, Miss Cantwell, but first, I must apologize to you."

Sophia scowled. "For what?"

"I was awful to you. To Emily too. I was arrogant and ridiculous, and I insulted you terribly, but I'm changing my ways. Sybil has insisted on it, and I can't bear to disappoint her. Can you forgive me for my horrid behavior?"

Everyone was on tenterhooks, eager to hear her answer. With all of them watching, how could she refuse?

"Yes . . . ah . . . of course I forgive you." She stammered the words, not positive she was sincere. She'd have to ponder later on in order to figure it out.

The Earl continued. "Sheridan tells me you can be silly and stubborn. Don't be stubborn about this."

"About what?" she asked, but Sheridan had been too patient.

He grabbed her arm and said, "Come with me."

He didn't give her a chance to argue. He simply dragged her away from the spectators and guided her to the room the Vicar had indicated. He shoved her in and closed the door. There was a key in the lock, and he spun it so no one could barge in after them.

It was a small chamber, where the Vicar donned his religious garments. There were cabinets and dressers crammed in every corner, and Sheridan Stone took up too much space. It was impossible to escape his magnetic pull.

He started the conversation, his grin cocky and infuriating. "How about if we begin by you thanking me?"

"Thanking you for what?" she inquired.

"I am saving you from a life of tedium by preventing you from shackling yourself to that dullard, Harry Roland."

"He's kind, and he was willing to rescue me from disgrace. Don't you dare denigrate him."

"What were you thinking? You went home for a few days, then you decided to wed a man you barely know. What is wrong with you?" He paused, then shook his head with disgust. "I can't believe I asked that question. It's obvious what's *wrong* with you: You are the most flighty, absurd creature the Good Lord ever put on this green earth."

"Your toplofty father sent me away! He insulted and harassed me, then he claimed you were entirely too grand to be my husband. After you promised you'd marry me! He kicked me out of his house, and you just stood there and let him!"

"I was an ass, wasn't I? But then, I must remind you that I am Neville Stone's son, and I was raised like an orphaned wolf pup. On occasion, I can be very stupid, especially where matters of the heart are concerned."

"Yes, you can be." She'd been prepared to chastise and malign him, but with his being a tad remorseful, some of the wind blew out of her sails. "Why are you here?"

"Weren't you listening to my father? We're having a wedding."

"Who is getting married?" she said like a dunce.

"Not you and Mr. Roland, that's for sure." She must have appeared bewildered because he scoffed. "It's you and me, Sophia! *We* are marrying."

"I'm not marrying you, you abusive fiend. I'd rather be boiled in hot oil than be your wife. Besides, isn't my cousin, Aurora, staring down the lane at Riverglen and wondering where you are?" Sophia pressed a hand to her brow and sarcastically wailed, "Poor, poor, Aurora. How will she survive without you?"

He clucked his tongue with annoyance. "Your cousin has been apprised that I'm not interested in her."

"A likely story. You're a typical male; you would never pass up her dowry. Tell me what you want and tell me quick. You've pushed me to my limit, and I can't abide being sequestered with you."

The comment was a bald-faced lie. Apparently, she had no pride or sense, but hadn't that always been the case with him? She was so glad to see him that she could scarcely keep from throwing herself into his arms and weeping with gratitude.

"You're so angry with me," he said. "Why are you?"

She sputtered with affront. "You have to ask? You don't know?"

"I recognize that my father and I treated you dreadfully, but I'm here now, and I'm waiting for *you* to explain yourself. How could you run off and wed a stranger? You had to have realized I would come for you."

"Why would I have realized that? Lord Swindon had my bags packed, and I was marched out to my carriage as if I was a scullery maid who'd pilfered the silver. And Harry Roland is not a stranger. I've been acquainted with him since I was a girl. He was kind enough to save me. Why wouldn't I have let him?"

"Save you from what?"

"From you! Have you forgotten that I spent the night in your bed? Do you recall what we did there? I might be increasing!"

"Are you?" he casually asked.

"No, but I wasn't certain until just recently." Her cheeks heated bright red. "Millicent received a letter from your father, announcing that you were on your way to propose to Aurora, and he ordered her to be rid of me before you arrived. You can't pretend you never planned to wed Aurora. You don't get to change horses in the middle of this stream."

"Oh, that letter." He waved it away, as if it were of no account. "My father is occasionally a very deluded man. He assumed he could coerce me into marrying your cousin. But he couldn't!"

"So you say," she spat.

"Yes, so I say." He pointed to his sling. "By any chance, have you noticed that I've suffered a significant injury?"

"Yes, I noticed, but why would I care? You and your father were very clear that *you* are none of my business. Why should I wonder about your condition?"

"We're leaving Neville out of this. He's an interfering busybody, and we're ignoring him."

"I'm fine with that."

"Let me clarify a few details for you, Cantwell. Perhaps if you're apprised as to what occurred these past weeks, you'll climb down off your high-horse."

Like a spoiled brat, she stuck her nose in the air. "I suppose anything is possible. Tell me your tale of woe, and we'll see if you can convince me to believe you."

"For your information, after you departed Swindon, my brother, Hunter, persuaded me to depart too. He recognized I wasn't keen to wed your cousin, even though my father was demanding it. I understood it was the best path for me."

"If you think I'll listen to you praising Aurora's stellar attributes, you are deranged."

"Would you stop interrupting? Hunter suggested I go home to our estate of Stone Manor and ponder my future until I reached some conclusions."

Sophia nodded, but a tad snottily. "That sounds like a solid plan. What did you decide?"

"I realized I couldn't live without you."

"You what?"

He scoffed with disgust. "You absurd ninny! I could never have picked your cousin. It's been you from the very start. How can you not grasp that fact?"

He dipped in and kissed her, and she lurched back, not in any mood for him to grow amorous. She was putty in his hands. She was a complete milksop. When he exhibited a little fondness, she couldn't behave herself or make good choices.

"What are you talking about?" she said, as she steadied her breathing and slowed her racing pulse.

"I'm *talking* about this: I saddled a horse and galloped to Riverglen to fetch you away, but as I rode up the lane, Miles Bernard was waiting to ambush me. He was laboring under the mistaken impression that I was there to propose to Miss Newton. He took great exception to the idea."

Sophia's eyes widened with fear. Miles had a terrible temper. "What happened?"

"He tried to murder me! He almost succeeded too. He shot me. Right in the chest. I was yanking the pistol away from him, but I stumbled on a rock, and it pitched me to the side, so his aim was off."

She was stunned by the news, and she staggered over to the room's lone chair and plopped down. A thousand questions flooded to the tip of her tongue, but when she opened her mouth, the one that emerged was, "Have you killed him to avenge yourself?"

"No. I should have, but I didn't. I pitied him. He thought I was there to seize what he viewed as his. How could I fault him for fighting to keep it?"

"Don't claim you're suddenly altruistic and you permitted him to waltz away unscathed."

He smirked. "No, I had him conscripted onto a sailing ship for seven years. He's left England. I gave him two options; it was either conscription or Hunter would have murdered him." He shrugged. "I wasn't sufficiently hale to accomplish it myself." He uttered the comment nonchalantly, as if homicide was a common incident in his family.

"He's gone for good?" she asked.

"Yes, for good. He selected a hard road though, so I can't predict whether he'll survive or not. If he does, he'll probably slither to England. He's just that duplicitous, so I'll kill him then. I'm not inclined to provide second chances."

"I can't believe any of this," she murmured.

"Believe it. It's true." He pointed to his sling again, as he grinned his devil's grin. "Do you feel sorry for me?"

"I might feel a bit sorry. Just a bit. Not a lot."

"I was coming to propose to you. Not your cousin. You! His antics delayed me, and I nearly died."

She blanched with dismay. "Don't tell me that."

"Why shouldn't I? I need you to understand why I didn't arrive any sooner. I finally recovered enough to travel to Riverglen again, merely to learn that you'd trotted off with a neighbor. Aurora told me you were likely already married, so I rushed here, expecting the worst."

She chuckled, but miserably. "You barely made it. A few minutes later and I'd have been Mrs. Harry Roland."

"Even if the vows had been spoken, I'd have carried you away. You're mine. No other man can have you. I'm afraid I have to insist."

She tsked with aggravation. "You're not interested in me. You're just irritated that someone jumped in line in front of you, and your ego can't abide it."

"Are you joking? Would I drag my father and brothers all the way to York on a lark?"

"You're eager to wed me." She stated it carefully, as if testing how the words sounded when voiced aloud. "How can I trust you're being honest?"

He strutted over to where she was still seated on the chair, and he dropped to a knee. There was only one reason a man placed himself in that position: to propose marriage.

"What are you doing?" she inquired, being slightly alarmed.

"You know what I'm doing. I'm about to ask you to marry me, so would you be quiet and allow me to finish?"

"Sheridan! You don't want this! You don't want me! I possess none of the attributes you seek in a wife, and I constantly set your temper to boiling. I've proved it over and over. A strange impulse has swept over you, but we have to tamp it down before you're ensnared in folly."

"I am already ensnared. By you! I was from the moment we met in France and you pranced by in those ridiculous trousers of yours."

She shook her hair in a vain manner. "I looked very fetching in those trousers."

"Yes, you did, and I've been totally besotted ever since."

She blew out a heavy breath. He ought to have to exert a bit more effort to wear her down, but she was brimming with gladness that he'd barged in. He seemed bent on proceeding, and he'd brought his whole family to York simply to show her how serious he was. Why dissuade him?

She yearned to be his bride with a hunger that was insatiable. If she wed him, she'd have the life her father had encouraged her to find. Sheridan would deliver fun and excitement to her staid existence. He was rich too, so she'd never have to struggle, would never have to worry.

And she would be marrying for love! Because yes, yes, yes, she loved him. Even when he'd been horrid, even when he'd let Lord Swindon evict her, she'd never stopped.

"I might be totally besotted too," she said.

"Of course you are. We're destined to be together. I've tried to separate myself from you, but Fate pulls me back. I have to quit fighting it."

She snorted with merriment. "You'll have to convince me that I should have you. You're so pretentiously sure I'll fall at your feet, but so far in our relationship, I haven't witnessed many traits that would indicate you'd be a good husband."

"Ha! I'll be the best husband who ever lived."

"You're definitely confident, but then, I've always known that about you. You're a bully, and you're arrogant and irksome. You're terribly spoiled, and you have to have your own way."

"You list those characteristics as if they're failings, and besides, *you* are arrogant and irksome too. You're spoiled and have to have your own way. In addition, you're reckless and deranged, and you wander into any dire situation without pondering the consequences. Yet despite all of that, I'm still willing to have you."

"If that's so, then I think you're a lunatic to want me, so we're both equally mad."

She stared into his handsome face. It would be foolish to forge ahead. They were like a bad carriage accident. They bickered and scrapped, argued and insulted, but they laughed too, and they teased and smiled.

With him by her side, she would never have to be frightened. She'd always be safe, and she'd never be bored.

Wasn't that one of her problems? She marched directly into hazardous predicaments because she was searching for something different, for something more. Now, here was Sheridan Stone, offering her a grand life—practically on a silver platter.

She simply couldn't refuse him.

"Will you marry me, Sophia?" he asked, and his gaze was warm and fond.

"Swear to me that you're certain. Swear to me that you're serious. If you changed your mind later on, I couldn't bear it."

"I'll never change my mind."

"You're a bachelor," she said. "Are you ready to be a husband? I'm so afraid you haven't thought this through."

"I'm a bachelor and cad, but you've made me realize I'm craving more for myself. I want you, Sophia. This is my cad's choice. Will you have me?"

"Oh, Sheridan," she breathed. "How could I not?"

Suddenly, he blurted out, "I love you and I always will."

It was a stunning confession, and he was such a masculine fellow. She was surprised that he'd uttered it.

"I love you too," she said, a sense of rightness settling in.

His cheeks heated. "I can't believe I told you that."

"It wasn't so hard to admit, was it?"

"It was pretty hard." His expression became a tad sly. "Are we agreed? We're getting married?"

"Yes, we are, but what about Harry? When he's been so kind to me, it would be awful to walk away from him. I'll appear fickle and disloyal."

"Don't fret over him. Hunter is giving him a huge pile of money as a consolation prize. He won't miss you."

"Money? Rather than me?" She batted her lashes. "I can't fathom why any man would trade me for money."

Actually, she suspected Harry would be ecstatic to be bought out of the debacle. He'd been overwhelmed by Emily, by the notion of being a parent to the petulant toddler. That very moment, he was probably counting his lucky stars.

Sheridan stood, and he lifted her to her feet. He fumbled in his coat, which was tricky with his arm in a sling, and he drew out a ring. He slid it onto her finger. It fit perfectly, as if it had been designed for this very purpose and none other.

"Will you marry me, Sophia Cantwell?" he said. "Will you be this cad's choice and make me happy all my days?"

"Yes, I'll marry you, Sheridan Stone. I'll be your cad's choice."

"Do you mean it? With me, it's forever."

"With me, it's forever too."

They laughed with joy, then he was kissing her and kissing her. They continued for an eternity, being so completely absorbed in each other that it took a minute for them to grasp that someone was knocking.

"Sheridan! What's happening in there?" his father demanded.

"I'm kissing my fiancée," Sheridan replied.

"Let me in."

Sheridan looked down at her and mouthed, *May I?*

She nodded. "Yes, let the arrogant oaf in."

Sheridan opened the door, with Sophia nestled to his side. Lord Swindon still had Emily balanced on his hip, with him not inclined to put her down. They went out to the altar, and no one had left. Everyone was frozen in their spots, observing events as if viewing a thrilling theatrical play.

Sheridan peered out at the assembled company, and he paused so the tension could build. "I proposed and . . . ? She said *yes.*"

People cheered and clapped, then his father stepped to her and said, "Miss Cantwell, you're about to be my daughter-in-law. May I call you Sophia?"

"Yes, I guess that would be all right."

"Will you join my family, dear?" he asked. "I've been hoping you would."

Sophia gazed up at Sheridan as she told Lord Swindon, "I love your son, and I would be honored to join your family."

"Marvelous!" The Earl beamed with delight.

He waved a servant forward and was handed a document. Then he gave it to the Vicar who was lurking and appearing very aggrieved.

"What's this?" the Vicar asked.

"It's a Special License that will allow them to wed immediately." He smiled at Sophia. "Are you available now, Sophia? It's your wedding day, and we can switch one groom for another. What would you think of that?"

Sheridan kissed her, with all of them watching, and she said, "I *think* that I can't wait to be Mrs. Sheridan Stone."

The crowd sighed with pleasure, then she and Sheridan spun to face the Vicar.

Epilogue

"I CAN'T BELIEVE YOU'RE going."

Sheridan gaped at Neville who had pulled out a kerchief and was dabbing at his eyes.

"Are you about to weep on me?" Sheridan asked.

"Yes," Neville said. "We're finally together as a family, but you're traipsing off."

"I've always been away at sea, so I've never spent much time in England. Don't pretend that hasn't been our history."

"Will you write?" Neville asked. "Promise you will."

"Sophia will write," Sheridan said to him. "I will instruct her to be a chatterbox. She'll be an excellent correspondent."

His father astounded him by giving him a tight hug. In his entire life, he couldn't remember Neville touching him in an affectionate way. It meant things had been altered so fast that Sheridan couldn't keep track.

"I'm so glad you married Sophia," Neville said. "Are you happy? You seem to be."

"I'm very happy so stop fretting. If you cry all over my coat, you'll wreck the fabric, and George will scold me."

They were at the docks, with Sheridan and Sophia about to board the ship that would deliver them to Gibraltar. He wouldn't captain it himself, which was very odd. He'd simply be a passenger, but with how matters had evolved, his days of privateering across the globe, of perpetrating mayhem on behalf of the Crown, were definitely over.

Instead, he would be a glorified clerk, a tedious functionary.

Hunter had convinced his acquaintance to offer the government position to Sheridan. There had been some difficult discussions as to whether he was ready to settle down and perform more ordinary tasks, but Hunter had lied and claimed Sheridan had matured since his stint in the navy, that he'd learned how to follow orders.

Ha! Time would tell if he'd succeed or not. His job would be to inspect vessels, to check cargoes and crews that sailed in and out of the busy port. At least he'd be peripherally connected to his prior career. He'd be surrounded by sailors and would live vicariously through them.

The weather would be warm and dry, and he predicted his injuries wouldn't ache so much. It would be worth a try to feel better. Usually, he was quite miserable, but then, the human body could only endure so much abuse before it protested its ill treatment.

"You'll miss my wedding," Neville said.

"Hunter, Warwick, and I are wagering over whether you'll make it to the altar or not. I bet a hundred pounds that Sybil will come to her senses and toss you over. Hunter bet a hundred that you will turn coward and run for the hills. Warwick refused to pick a side. He insists he's an optimist, and you might surprise us and be a good husband for once."

"I never have been so far."

"I know, so how about if you and I turn over some new leaves? It won't kill us."

He thought about how much could change in a year. His brothers were married. He was too. His father was about to be leg-shackled again, if Sybil could tolerate him long enough to tie the knot.

There were babies on the way, with Wilhelmina and Hannah both increasing. Sophia hadn't joined them yet, but to his stunned amazement, he was excited to have that situation become a reality. He'd always been competitive with his brothers, and he never liked them to beat him at any endeavor.

He studied the group that had arrived to see them off. Neville and Sybil were present of course. So were his brothers and their wives. But Aurora Newton was there too. With Harry Roland. According to Sophia, he and Aurora were courting, so the world was a very strange place indeed.

Harry had talked briefly with Sheridan, and he'd firmly stated that there were no hard feelings over what had occurred. He was genuinely fond of Sophia and wished her to be secure and content. A purse full of money had smoothed over Harry's pique about his failed wedding, and he claimed to be thrilled at how it had been resolved.

Emily bustled over, and she extended her hands to him. "Cap? Cap?"

He lifted her up and kissed her cheeks, loving how she giggled with delight.

"Don't you grow up on me while I'm gone," he told her. "And don't let any boys flirt too outrageously. You'll be an incredible tease when you're bigger, and you shouldn't start too early."

She babbled a string of her French-English gibberish, as if she'd completely understood his comment, as if they were having a serious conversation about boys.

She was staying behind in England—with Neville. Sophia had been leery about the decision, and they'd debated relentlessly. It was only after Sybil had requested custody for herself, rather than Neville, that they'd agreed to the arrangement.

Sybil had no illusions about Neville. She'd bluntly declared that, if he began acting like an ass, she was rich in her own right. She'd simply abandon him, with Emily, and they'd carry on in a grand manner without him around to muck things up. She was tough and practical, and she could cope with Emily's temper and quirks. If Neville didn't behave, she'd cut him loose without batting an eye.

Sheridan and Sophia couldn't argue with her logic or determination. Sybil knew exactly how to deal with Neville, so maybe there was hope for the old roué after all.

As to Sheridan, he was eager for the future to unfold. He was headed to Gibraltar, with Sophia as his bride, and he couldn't wait.

The tide was turning, and suddenly, whistles blew up on the deck. Orders were shouted, and sailors were running, preparing to cast off.

Sheridan glanced over at Sophia. She was huddled with Hannah, Wilhelmina, and Aurora. They were fast friends, and Sophia was crying, promising to write, promising to visit as soon as they could manage it.

"Sophia," he said, "we have to board. Don't dawdle."

The women blubbered weepy goodbyes, then she came over to him. Neville shocked Sheridan by opening his arms and giving her a tight hug too.

"Farewell, my darling girl," he said to her. "Take care of Sheridan for me. He's awfully bad at taking care of himself. Bring him home to me in one piece."

"He's mine now," Sophia said to Neville, "so he has to obey me. I'll be a veritable fortress that will keep him from ever being harmed."

Neville laughed at that. "Thank you."

Sheridan clasped hold of his brothers, hugging Hunter, then Warwick.

"Be happy," Hunter said, as Warwick added, "Be safe."

Sheridan could read their thoughts. They'd been dedicated bachelors, wicked cads who weren't cads anymore. Cupid's arrow had struck them, and they were better men for it. They had families. Children were about to arrive. Their father might become a normal parent.

Any spectacular conclusion seemed possible.

"Are you ready?" he said to Sophia.

She grinned up at him. "Yes, I'm ready."

They went over to the gangplank. George Barnes was there. Pierre too. They were accompanying them to Gibraltar. George couldn't envision a life where he wasn't guarding Sheridan's back, and as he'd explained—if he wasn't nearby—how would Sheridan ever pick out the perfect cravat?

Sheridan would assume the role of Pierre's father. Pierre had proved his worth by protecting Sophia during her troubles. Who wouldn't cherish him? Sheridan would furnish the cunning little thief with a stable existence, and with Sheridan guiding his steps, some of his rough edges would be smoothed away.

"Shall we go up, Captain?" George asked him.

"You two first," Sheridan said.

Pierre and George scampered up to the deck, then he and Sophia followed more slowly. They stood at the rail, smiling, waving down at their friends and relatives lingering below.

The crew was proficient, and they were quickly set to depart. Lines were cast off, the anchor raised, and they were pulled away from their mooring.

"Goodbye!" they called, as people on the wharf called the same.

Sheridan kept his gaze on his father and his brothers, and he remained where he was, his entire attention focused on them until he couldn't see them any longer. Then he spun away and faced the river, watching as they moved toward the sea and whatever lay ahead.

The End

About the Author

CHERYL HOLT IS A *New York Times*, *USA Today*, and Amazon "Top 100" bestselling author who has published over sixty novels.

She's also a lawyer and mom, and at age forty, with two babies at home, she started a new career as a commercial fiction writer. She'd hoped to be a suspense novelist, but couldn't sell any of her manuscripts, so she ended up taking a detour into romance where she was stunned to discover that she has a knack for writing some of the world's greatest love stories.

Her books have been released to wide acclaim, and she has won or been nominated for many national awards. She is considered to be one of the masters of the romance genre. For many years, she was hailed as "The Queen of Erotic Romance," and she's also revered as "The International Queen of Villains." She is particularly proud to have been named "Best Storyteller of the Year" by the trade magazine Romantic Times BOOK Reviews.

She lives and writes in Hollywood, California, and she loves to hear from fans. Visit her website at www.cherylholt.com.

Made in the USA
Coppell, TX
28 September 2021

63134098R00256